Links to the Past

This is a work of fiction. Any references to real people, living or dead, real events, businesses, organisations and localities are intended only to give the fiction a sense of reality and authenticity. All names, characters, places and incidents are either the product of the author's imagination or are used fictitiously, and their resemblance, if any, to real-life counterparts is entirely coincidental.

ISBN: 978-1-8046-7812-1

Perfect Bound

First published in 2023 by bookvault Publishing, Peterborough, United Kingdom

An environmentally friendly book printed and bound in England by bookvault, powered by printondemand-worldwide

Cover design by Creative Covers: www.ccovers.co.uk

Links to the Past

Dennis Jones

For Anne

Dennis Jones

Dennis Jones tragically died on 18 March 2022, unexpectedly and far, far too soon. He was a lovely man, who enriched the lives of all those who knew him. Unassuming and considerate, warm and open, he listened to and cared about people – rare qualities these days.

The middle of three brothers, he was born on 25 March 1950 in Balham, South London, and grew up in Tooting Bec.

He fell in love with Anne when, in 1967, they met in Pratts department store in Streatham. They were married in 1975 in Mitcham and set up home in Croydon.

Dennis and Anne raised, loved – and were extraordinarily proud of – their two children, Steve and Suzanne, and their two granddaughters, Ava and Chloe.

It was in 1999, while on a work trip to South Africa for his employer, Armstrong Ceilings, that Dennis achieved one of his ambitions – he visited the battle sites of Isandlwana and Rorke's Drift. Ever since seeing the film *Zulu*, Dennis had had an interest in these battles and their history, an enthusiasm that can be felt in this book.

As well as his passion for golf – he was a member of the Merrist Wood Golf Club, in Guildford, Surrey – Dennis had an interest in storytelling, and it was around the millennium that he started seriously thinking about *Links to the Past*. The story and characters developed and changed over the years until he began this version during lockdown in 2021. Thanks are due to all those who helped Dennis with their knowledge and support. You know who you are.

Dennis leaves behind a huge number of bereft people, all of whom feel so honoured and privileged to have known and loved him, and to have spent time in his company. He also leaves behind this book. We hope you enjoy it.

The Incident

A fortune.

That's what it was: a fortune. More specifically, *his* fortune. Colonel Sir Frederick Standish had never managed to count it all, despite setting out on many occasions to do just that. Each time, the sheer quantity defeated him. All he could say was: it was a fortune. True, the grand total had dropped by a tiny fraction when his one wooden chest had finally proved too small for all the neatly bagged notes, coin of the realm, and jewellery. Once he couldn't close the lid he had been forced, against the power of his avarice, to take a few notes and purchase another chest.

Colonel Standish had spent years living a comfortable life, especially by army standards. And all the time he had been accumulating his treasure. He told himself there was nothing wrong with bribery and corruption as long as the proceeds went to no one but himself. After all, he was a responsible man. Others, of course, couldn't be trusted and might misuse their wealth. Become corrupted by it. Not him.

He had been careful, obviously, but it was inevitable that some knew of his investments. He doubted, however, that any understood the true extent of his wealth. Some suspected, and naturally there were rumours, but he was certain nothing could be proved. After all, he was both clever and careful, and prided himself on ensuring his money stayed hidden and secured, away from his lodgings, in a safe place known only to himself. He had no use for banks, they gave others knowledge and allowed scrutiny.

Frederick Standish was aged eighteen when his noble and honourable father had purchased a commission for him. Early on in his army career – in 1853, in fact – a stray musket ball had hit him during training. Although it had left a scar, the wound hadn't been serious, just enough to convince him not take any unnecessary risks and to keep away from any future battles. He had been hurt once, and had no intention of putting himself in harm's way again. Using his high-born status, his father's name, and the connections he'd made, both at Whitehall and Horse Guards, he secured a position as officer at Woolwich – a safe administrative position in the commissariat. Here, he'd found his skills were more suited to his responsibilities and, with little effort, he could make things even more rewarding. Life became easier, much easier, and with a style of living very much commensurate to his ambitions. He married a suitable woman, from a suitable background, found a suitable house near Greenwich, became a member of the most suitable clubs in London, and settled very easily into his very suitable new life.

His role in the commissariat involved both the purchasing and distribution of supplies, everything to meet the needs of a modern army – an army hungry for men, hungry for food and hungry for all types of materiel. It did take long for him to realise that many companies desiring to win large contracts and orders were willing – no, wanted – to pay for his help. And he, of course, was a helpful man. His fortune grew.

Other opportunities presented themselves: letting the army pay twice for goods received and keeping the difference, or raising invoices for goods never seen or delivered. If the opportunities were there, what was he supposed to do? For example, it proved lucrative to have the army order and pay for supplies, which could then be diverted to others and sold again.

It was only fair that some of the proceeds should find their way back to him and into his wooden chests. He found he could authorise paying top price for inferior products, and if the difference was shared between the supplier and himself, then no one complained. If you were careful, had the right connections and knew what you were doing – and he prided himself he did – there were myriad ways of making money. And he knew and used them all.

His fortune grew.

But all this was not sufficient. His wealth was far in excess of what he needed; so, what, he asked himself, was he supposed to do, other than use that money to make even more. And once he accrued that, yet other ways of using his funds presented themselves to amass still more. He began loaning money to fellow officers, in the process becoming a small private bank. And if officers, with only minor encouragement from him, had a habit of living beyond their means and so had to secure further loans, well, that was not his fault. True, his interest charges may have been extortionate, but that was because these men had no other options. What was he supposed to do? Besides, he was always there for them when they needed him. He chose his marks – or friends, as he preferred to call them – very carefully. Usually, they were young officers he could manipulate. And he knew which of them had wealthy parents or families, so that when he called in his loan, plus interest, they would be able to pay rather than face the embarrassment of a scandal. And Standish always made sure they knew he would, without a second thought, embarrass them and their families; it was unfortunate that the occasional example had to me made, but that was the way it had to be. He always got his money. Yes, he'd heard rumours that at least one officer had taken his own life, but Standish didn't care. Why should he?

His fortune grew and another wooden chest had to be purchased.

He was soon involved in free-enterprise business deals, beyond his military responsibilities, which some might argue were not always legal. If he saw an opportunity outside the army, he took it. He was careful and clever and calculating, and everything he did made himself – and only himself – even richer.

His fortune grew and grew.

As the years passed and his lifestyle became ever more comfortable, fewer and fewer questioned his actions, especially as his status as an officer, gentleman and high-ranking member of society inevitably grew. Rumours and suspicions circulated, but no evidence to discredit him could ever be found. He was too clever for that. Besides, who would question a man of his standing? And all the while his fortune grew.

He enjoyed his time in the army, but eventually thoughts of retirement began to proliferate. He decided he would leave both his position and London to lead a new life as a landowner on a modest estate he had purchased, near the town of Basing, in Hampshire. Many were pleased to see him go and, looking forward to his departure, more than happy to assist and sanction any request to be rid of him. Standish himself looked forward to a new role as a squire. He would be spending his time between London and his estate, living the high-life that – after all his hard work – he knew he deserved.

As the day of his retirement approached, he made arrangements for the chests containing his wealth to accompany him on his journey to the country.

It was, after all, his fortune.

Part 1

1877–1879

Chapter 1

The canal barge pushed its way through the water, a gentle wake evidence of its slow speed. It was so far behind schedule that it was now travelling in the dark, and although the cold late-October rain had stopped, the small group of men aboard expected it to be no more than a brief pause. Lined along the slippery deck, the uniformed soldiers in the escort huddled under thin grey blankets, keeping warm as best they could. The bargee stood at the rear, one hand on the tiller, trying to see ahead to navigate. The two lanterns hanging on the bow barely gave enough light. Behind the bargee, and keeping quiet so as not to disturb the bargee's concentration, stood an army officer. He rubbed his gloved hands together, trying to keep his blood circulating. Like the bargee, he was watching the boat's progress intently. Another man, this one well-dressed, and warm in a thick coat with a fur collar and matching hat, sat slumbering upon the only stool on the deck. He rested against the bulwark; a heavy blanket wrapped around him.

The bargee half turned to the officer. "Bridge coming up, sir. Is this being where you wanted us to stop?"

The officer nodded but remained silent. This was the place. He glanced at the shivering soldiers. The bargee shrugged and turned back to the bow, looking for good place to moor. Towards the middle of the boat, one soldier looked up and shifted his huge bulk. He was a man so big that, it was whispered, if he put himself in the way of a runaway wagon, the wagon would come off worse. His nose was bent at a disconcerting angle; at one time it had been broken and not set correctly. He caught the officer's eyes, which glittered in the lantern-light, and the officer nodded. The big man stood, slid his hand inside his jacket and moved along the barge, absorbing the slight rocking movement of the vessel. The officer looked at the man on the stool. He remained asleep as the barge pulled to the side of the canal. As the boat touched and scraped against the bank, some soldiers stirred. Others, woken by the big man, were now watching and waiting. The bargee smiled and waved at a boy, his fourteen-year-old son, who jumped from the bow of the barge, rope in hand, onto the rough towpath. Rain dripped from the trees around him. He splashed through puddles until he found a suitable tree and started to wind the rope around it but stopped as a figure appeared beside him.

"We're here, sir," the bargee said with pride, and turned to face the officer, anticipating praise. Instead, he felt a cold blade slip into his stomach. "Now," he heard the officer say, then the word was repeated, shouted, as the knife was withdrawn. Thinking of his son, the bargee slipped to the wet deck – the one he had spent most of his life on – and, shivering as he bled out, slowly died. The officer stepped to the well-dressed man, who was waking, confused. The officer grinned. He would soon be rich, with enough to clear his debts and live as he wanted. First, though, many had to die. Including the boy.

Chapter 2

Captain Russell from the East Hants Light Infantry stood, arms behind him and one hand in the other, facing the bridge. Fine rain filled the air such that, when he looked for the corporal and two privates he'd sent to investigate, they appeared to be as insubstantial as wraiths.

Glancing behind him, Captain Russell could just about see the squad of a dozen soldiers he had hurriedly put together. That had been two hours ago, when the alarm had been raised. His men now lined the track leading to the bridge, and he was pleased to see they were watching, as ordered: crouched, rifles at the ready. Because the squad had been assembled so fast, they wore no greatcoats and were all cold and wet. They weren't complaining, though, Good.

A couple of heavy raindrops landed on his face. The weather was deteriorating, and he suspected the rain would return heavier and harder as the day wore on. A movement to one side of the track caught his attention. Under rain-weighted branches stood two men. The one with sergeant stripes supported the other, who had a blanket draped over his shoulders. Although clutching the blanket, Lieutenant Spencer Treloar was shivering. Russell could just make out the man's red uniform. It was dark and stained – wet not from the rain but from when the poor man had had to swim to make his escape. It was Treloar who had managed to bring the one other survivor to the camp and raise the alarm.

Trying to take in the terrain, Russell looked back down the

track. He could just make out a giant oak tree, standing like a guard at the nearby crossroads. For a second he wished it could talk, could tell him what had happened. A sudden break in the clouds and easing of the rain meant that, for a few moments, he could see the top of a wooden spire. He hadn't really noticed, what with the weather, but on their way here from Aldershot he and his men must have passed both the village church and the crossroads, with its great oak. Apart from his squad, there were no people he could see. He walked over to where his sergeant and Treloar stood.

"Does anyone know where the hell we are?" Captain Russell's voice was raised so that it was almost a shout.

Treloar adjusted the blanket round his neck and, as much as he could, stood to attention. He was having trouble stopping his teeth chattering. "Small farming village, sir. Think it's known locally as the Old Oak Crossroads, sir."

Russell looked at the thin shivering man and felt regret: he should have let the poor soldier change before bringing him back here. Lieutenant Spencer Treloar was tall, a couple of inches taller than Russell. His face was narrow but he had the appearance of a man younger than his 22 years. A beige cocked hat covered his head, borrowed as he had lost his own in his escape. Dishevelled black hair poked out from under the sodden headgear. Even the man's small moustache looked as if it had suffered from the night-time action. His dark brown eyes, however, missed little.

Russell pulled out his full hunter pocket watch, letting its silver chain, fixed to the inside of his jacket, hang free. With a click of the side clasp he opened the timepiece. "It's over two hours," he stated, "since you raised the alarm." He sighed.

"Whoever was here would have unloaded by now, and left."

He looked back towards the bridge. "Tell me again what happened."

Treloar shuffled his feet on the track, creating muddy puddles. "It happened so fast, sir. We were moving up the canal, intending to stop for the night near Aldershot. Captain Farrant, commanding the escort, intended to journey on to Basing in the morning. We were behind schedule, sir, but in no real hurry. The bargee steered the barge towards the bank, just there, before the bridge. As we touched the side, they appeared from nowhere, sir. We didn't have a chance, sir. They boarded, all unexpected. They took us by surprise."

"How many of you?"

"Sir?"

Russell sighed again. "On the boat, man."

"Captain Farrant, myself, six men for the escort, Colonel Standish and a Lieutenant Norton. He joined the barge at Weybridge for a lift to Aldershot, sir. Oh, the bargee and his son."

Russell nodded as he calculated. "Twelve in all, then. And Captain Farrant was in command of the escort. So you were overpowered by large force?"

"Yes, sir."

"What time was the attack? What were you carrying?"

"About eleven, sir." Furrows wrinkled Treloar's wet forehead, diverting rivulets of rain. "I am not sure of the cargo, sir. It was personal possessions of Colonel Sir Frederick Standish." Treloar paused, as if expecting a reaction from the captain. When nothing was forthcoming, he continued. "We were his escort, sir. Moving him from London to his new home in Basing. We have been travelling a few days."

"Why did he need an escort?"

The sergeant, a broad-shouldered non-commissioned soldier who had fifteen years' experience and often questioned his superior's actions also looked at Treloar. He had been wondering the same.

Treloar looked around before answering. Eventually he spoke, his voice lower. "Colonel Standish was retiring from his command in Woolwich, sir. I believe he had valuables aboard. His position secured him an escort. Sir."

Russell turned back to the bridge, still partially obscured by the rain. "So why move by canal? Why did he not take the train or use wagons?"

"I understand the canal passes through his land, near his new house in Basing, sir. I understand he thought it would save time and involve less handling of his possessions."

Russell continued looking at his ghost-like men, still crouching and facing the bridge. "So," he said, as much to himself as to Treloar, "who knew what you were carrying? And your timetable." He looked up and down the towpath. "I can't see a gang waiting just in case something came along. Can you, Lieutenant?"

Treloar did not answer.

Russell returned his attention to the man under the blanket. "What do you know about the second lieutenant that joined you?"

"Little, sir. I knew him from our company. He approached us when we stopped in Weybridge, introduced himself to the Colonel and Captain Farrant. They agreed he could travel with us as we were passing Aldershot."

"Do you think anyone here could have heard anything or be involved?

Treloar looked in the direction of the spire, its point hidden in lowering cloud, then shook his head. "I doubt it, sir. Apart from the church and the inn, what cottages there are here are occupied by people who work on the surrounding estates." As an afterthought he added, "It's a very poor community, sir."

"You seem to know the area well, Captain."

"My father owns a nearby estate, sir. It borders the village." He pointed to the right of the oak tree.

"Treloar? You're Sir John Treloar's son?"

Treloar nodded but before he could answer, the crunch of boots on the track drew their attention. The sergeant who had been silently standing to one side stood tall. "Stand ready!" he shouted. The two rows of men did as commanded and Russell withdrew his pistol. He aimed it at the figure approaching through the mist and rain, only lowering it once he recognised the corporal. The man, panting and trying to get his breath back, stopped in front of Russell and saluted. Rain dripped from the grey whiskers of his handlebar moustache.

"The barge, it's there, sir. But no one's alive. I went down to the canal, sir. I could see bodies in the water and on the barge."

"Where are your men?"

"Left them on the far side of the bridge, sir. Ah, sir, there is one other thing." He was still out of breath.

Russell waited.

"Speak up, corporal," the sergeant commanded.

"Yes, sir. There appear to be tracks, sir. Could be fresh. A single wagon, I think. Going in that direction." He pointed over the bridge.

Russell looked at the track, at the footprints made by his men. Were there fresh tracks on this side of the bridge as well? Could a wagon have come up here and got away, over the bridge?

"Treloar." Russell nodded at the bridge. "What's over there?"

Treloar glanced at the bridge then down at his feet. He pulled the blanket tighter about his shoulders.

Russell just stared, waiting for an answer.

"Lieutenant." The sergeant prodded him. "The captain asked you a question."

Treloar took a deep breath. "Sir. There's a small farm about a quarter of a mile away. After that, just scrub and forest tracks until you reach the next village. They could not get out that way, sir."

Russell turned to the still panting man. "Corporal, take four men to the farm. See if they know anything." The corporal nodded, took a deep breath and hurried away without complaint. Despite the patter of rain through the trees, Russell heard him, in the distance, shouting orders.

Wiping water from his face, Russell turned to the sergeant. "We will proceed to the far side of the bridge in two columns. Send a runner back to the camp with a message to wake Major Bradshaw. He won't be happy but we may have a serious situation here." Russell looked towards the bridge, then back at Treloar. "This could be something more sinister than just robbery".

Chapter 3

The wooden hut contained the barest essentials to make it an office. A desk, two uncomfortably hard chairs, six oil lamps placed around the room – all lit despite being it early afternoon – a wooden filing cabinet against which a union flag leant and on top of which were glasses and the obligatory half bottle of Irish whiskey. Outside, men could be heard shouting orders, while others were marching or working.

Captain Russell pursed his lips as he stood, waiting as the seated officer flicked through the correspondence and papers that spilled across his desk. Russell was used to this, waiting for his orders. He was a born soldier. His father, a junior officer, had distinguished himself in battle, gained promotion and had married a senior officer's daughter. Iain Russell had consequently been brought up in the army, learned his profession from an early age, and had also married a soldier's daughter. She had once told him he had a clear and intelligent mind. Certainly, he was aware his peers often felt uneasy around him, and it was obvious he sometimes made senior officers nervous. Many older officers he had discovered, especially those who had secured their commissions through wealth and status rather than competence, did not enjoy a junior officer questioning their actions, and certainly were unable to handle themselves verbally let alone physically.

The major plucked a sheet of paper, seemingly at random. "Rum deal, Russell, and that's no mistake."

"Sir." Russell was unsure what was being talking about.

"Rum deal." Major Bradshaw looked up, adjusting his spectacles. A cord joined each spectacle arm around the officer's neck. "The robbery on the canal, that 'incident', as it is being described. Rum deal, don't you agree?"

"Yes, sir." Russell frowned. Yes, he had been on duty that night and acted appropriately, but it had been over two weeks ago. It was nothing to do with him now, surely.

"No one wants responsibility, Russell. Civil authorities say it was a military barge; military men were killed so it's a military problem. They ignore the fact that two civilians are missing, and civilians could be involved. However," Bradshaw added disparagingly, "our efforts at finding out what happened do not seem to have got us very far."

"I took every action I thought necessary, and as fast as possible, after the alarm was raised, sir." Russell knew they still had not found the murderers of Standish, Captain Farrant – who had been in charge of the escort – and the other men. There was no evidence of the location of Standish's fortune, and neither could they find – either dead or alive – the bargee, his young son or Second Lieutenant Norton. They had all disappeared. The remainder of Colonel Standish's possessions were now in Basing but there were no chests containing his wealth. The 'incident' had been the talk of the camp.

The major raised his hand "Of course, Russell. Of course, your actions that night and immediately following the crime were exemplary." He picked some other papers from the mess on his table. "I have your report here," he turned a page. "After sending a messenger back to the camp, the patrols were sent in all directions." He looked up. "Is that correct?"

"Yes sir. A radius of five miles. They stopped anyone they

saw, searched and questioned them."

"But they found nothing."

"Correct, sir."

"And you questioned the ones that escaped? Lieutenant Treloar and the other man." The major turned to another page. "A Private Oxley. Known amongst the men as Ox, I believe. A large man I take it?"

Russell nodded. "Yes, sir. But they could not add anything new. However…"

"Go on, Captain."

"There were fresh tracks leading from the bridge to the farm, sir. There, we found a small wagon and small bag of gold coins under its seat. The farmer – Weller, his name – could not explain how they got there. He said he rented his wagon and horses the day before the robbery, late afternoon. It was returned and left in his courtyard early the following morning, the day of the robbery. We took the farmer and his sons – twins, sir, both about seventeen – into custody."

"Who did he rent it to?"

"It's in my report, sir. A soldier from our company. A Corporal Price. I've spoken to him, and he denies it. He also has an alibi on the day and evening of the robbery, which other soldiers confirm."

"Why did the farmer pick on Corporal Price?"

"Price told me he had been walking out with farmer's eldest daughter. It got too serious so he finished it. The daughter was upset, so naming Price was the famer's way of getting revenge."

"Do you think the farmer and his sons were lying?"

"I interviewed the farmer and his sons, sir. He is adamant about renting his wagon; insists he had nothing to do with the robbery. To be honest, sir, I just don't know."

The major nodded but said nothing.

Eventually, he shook his head. "Rum deal, Russell. A very rum deal." The major rose, paced to the cabinet, poured himself a whiskey, downed it in one gulp and returned to the desk.

Russell watched him, waiting for the right time to ask his question. Only once the major was standing over his desk, staring glumly at his paperwork, did Russell speak. "The farmer, sir, I take it he's still in custody and sticking to his story?"

"Of course. And his two sons."

Still standing, the major looked from Russell back to his scattered reports. "And that's my difficulty. We need more, Captain. We have no idea who this gang was, we cannot find any trace of what was stolen, we have the murders of a very senior retired officer, and Captain Farrant, as well as the enlisted men who were butchered. And if that were not enough, we have another junior officer, and two civilians, the bargee and his young son, also missing." He shook his head. "And there are even rumours that men from our company – here! – are involved, the whole incident has resulted in a total mystery and complete confusion."

"Perhaps that's what the thieves wanted," Russell muttered to himself as the thought struck him.

"What Captain? Did you say something?"

"Just thinking, sir".

The major's face tuned red as his anger flared. He snatched a handful of papers from his desk and raised them, as if to throw them at Russell. With the sudden movement his glasses fell from his nose and he left them swinging on their cord. He shouted,

"Well you might think about this, Captain Russell: think about what I get from this incident? Constant questions from my regimental superior. Because he, of course, gets questions from his superiors. And there are letters from politicians and other senior officers; and Mrs Standish wanting her husband's fortune; Sir John Treloar insisting his son is cleared, and everyone demanding I solve this crime and establish what happened. Find the culprits, they say; the possessions, the truth, the money, and I have nothing, nothing, Captain Russell, except for a wagon, one bag of coins, and a farmer and his sons, who deny everything."

Russell stood, silent and motionless. He had been in this army too long not to see when something was coming his way. How far he was going to be involved, he had no idea. But involved he was undoubtedly going to be.

The major dropped the papers onto the table, and sat down heavily. The chair creaked. "Please, Captain Russell, take a seat," he replaced his spectacles as he took a deep breath and waited for Russell to sit down.

Here it comes, thought Russell.

"You are an intelligent officer, Captain. That we all know. And you were the first on the scene. I want you to conduct a full investigation and establish what happened to Standish's money. You have complete authority to question anyone. But get me some answers that I can give to our superiors."

"What of my current duties, sir."

"This takes precedent, find that money, Russell, or find out what happened."

"How long do I have, sir?"

"How long do you need?"

"Well, the robbery was over two weeks ago. It's now early November. I would like to question Treloar and Oxley again, but there are also others who may be able to help."

"Who?" The major sounded amazed it could get even more complicated.

Russell counted them on his fingers. "Corporal Price. The barge owner's family. The farmer, Weller, and his two sons."

"How long will that take?" The major didn't wait for an answer. "Very well. I am giving you this problem. I want you to be thorough, but we must have some answers for our superiors as soon as possible."

"I could give a report in the New Year, sir."

"That long?"

"Certainly not before Christmas. If I am to be thorough, sir. I will have to question many people, including Lady Standish, as well as the family of Second Lieutenant Norton. And you will want me to b thorough, sir.""

The major stared at all the correspondence he'd received from those who wanted answers. His head moved slowly from side to side as he frowned, as though he could already hear complaints from his superiors.

Eventually, he looked up. "This is a rum deal," he said once again. "Very well, Captain. I will expect your report in January. Early in January. Very early in January. No later." He pointed his finger at Russell. "You are aware, you will also have to report to our superior. Perhaps the commander of the Camp, as this does not reflect well on the East Surrey Borders."

"Yes, sir."

"Get me some answers, Russell." He tried to keep the pleading from his voice. "Or we will both suffer."

"Sir."

Russel knew the buck had been well and truly passed to him. To save the reputation of the major, his own reputation had been put on the line.

That's the army for you, he thought.

Chapter 4

Russell gripped his pocket pipe between his teeth. The reassuring red glow of smouldering tobacco in the bowl at the end of the stem's smooth downward curve intensified as he inhaled. As he exhaled, aromatic smoke filled the air. Deep in thought, he walked for the third time along the same section of the canal path. He was thirty-five, and a proud and efficient officer, but he doubted he would ever gain higher promotion. Other than his wife and three children, his love was the army. He had always been conscientious in his duties, and his superiors appreciated his work, diligence, attention to detail and his organisational skills. He had seen a little action whilst serving in India as a young lieutenant, and although now back in England, he still kept himself fit. A van Dyke beard, narrow-pointed, was complemented by a thick moustache, of which he was inordinately proud. His thick hair rolled neatly away from a side parting and showed hints of grey. Hints that had not yet found their way to his moustache. He always made a special effort in his appearance. To him, the look of an officer, regardless of rank, was an important statement and a reflection of the quality of the army. In his time as a soldier he had occasionally witnessed injustice; as a result he despised brutality and abuse of power. From what he gathered, this 'incident' – as Major Bradshaw had called it – showed all three. It was why, when ordered to investigate further, he had offered no objection.

He at the bridge, where he'd tied up his horse. Lowering his gaze, he spotted a wooden stake. He had placed it by the path earlier, marking the spot where the bow of the barge had touched the bank. Nodding, he turned his back to it and stepped from the path into rough winter gorse, which stretched from the canal to the fields beyond. In places it was waist high. He fought his way through for a good few minutes, then once again looked back towards the bridge. From this angle he could see the brickwork under the arch. In places it appeared to be crumbling. Slowly, he pushed his way through the wild growth, walking back to the bridge and re-joining the towpath by the stake.

The trail he had left, of crushed and broken undergrowth was clear and gave thought to the same thing that had bothered him the morning of the robbery. Why had he not seen such disturbance? He pulled out the stake, threw it to one side and walked up the slope to the bridge. At the top, he looked along the empty canal in both directions, wondering whether Standish's money could be close. Seeing just open land and no buildings he dismissed the idea then focused his attention once again on the towpath where he had just walked. The last of the tobacco in the bowl glowed as he drew on his pipe and pondered. He had made one other visit back to the canal, one day after the robbery, with this same thought in mind. Treloar had stated that nearly a dozen men had attacked the barge. So where had they all hidden? And where had they all gone? Surely, they had not all been standing in a line on the towpath. Either they had been hiding in the rough undergrowth alongside the canal or they had been here on the bridge, crouched down. He tapped his pipe gently on the bridge wall, ashes spilling to the ground. His experiment of pushing his way through the undergrowth had proved that there would have been signs if they had been there, but there had been no such evidence on his previous visit. Alternatively, they could have been here on the bridge hiding. It was, however, still some distance from where the barge had moored. If the attackers had suddenly appeared and descended down the slope and along the towpath to the barge, surely the escort would have taken action. They may even have fired a few shots and brought some of their attackers down. But no, they had fought hand to hand. All those on the barge, except Treloar and Oxley, had been killed by knives in hand-to-hand fighting. What he had been told did not make any sense and, he wondered, if it didn't make sense, did it actually happen? He had interviewed Private Oxley, Ox to his comrades in arms, who was confined to barracks, and also the surviving officer, Lieutenant Treloar, who had been taken off duties and was living with his family at Treloar Manor Private Oxley had added nothing new; he had been asleep and remembered nothing. All Treloar added was that they had decided to stop here for the night before travelling on to Basing. But Russell was not convinced; both soldiers' answers sounded rehearsed, he was sure they were hiding something.

He had also interviewed the farmer, Weller, and his two sons. It was clear they were frightened, and their denial of any involvement had not changed from their first interview. They could add nothing and, even when interviewed separately, still told the same story: they knew nothing about the robbery. However, coins had been found in their wagon and so they would remain under arrest as suspects. In fact, the one thing they had added to was the confusion. They had implicated a soldier called Corporal Price who they said rented their small wagon and the horses and who, other than being in the same company and knowing Captain Farrant, Treloar and the others, appeared to have no other connection to the robbery.

Russell had spoken to Price but he had also added nothing new. As with Treloar and Oxley, Price had also been relieved of duties and, for the moment, confined to barracks. Could he in some way be involved, perhaps with the Wellers or with Treloar and the others? It was all still confusing.

He had hoped his visit to the bridge today would help, but it hadn't. And, of course, there was the other problem, over which he still pondered: where did they go with the money? Chests of coins, gold and notes would be heavy, so where did they hide them? They were not at the farm – that had been searched – but they had to be close by. Not for the first time he began to wonder if the villains would have had time to reach Treloar Manor.

Russell had visited the bargee's wife. That had been a difficult visit. Naturally, she was still upset at her missing husband and her eldest child. She had cried for almost the entire interview, with her two other children all the time clinging to her apron. It seemed the bargee and his wife were a devoted couple. Rather than on the barge, they lived in a small cottage beside the canal, more than five miles from Old Oak Crossroads. He therefore ruled out her house as a hiding spot. Neither could she shed any light on her husband's whereabouts. Russell had checked: the bargee was known to the army and trusted. In fact, the bargee's father had been involved with bringing equipment to the new Aldershot camp twenty years previously, when the camp was established and under construction. His son had helped. After the father's death, the son had continued running the barge business, and eventually enlisted the help of the next generation. Hence, when a trusted barge and bargee were requested for this assignment, he had been the ideal choice.

Russell had also spoken to Captain Farrant's wife, Mary Anne. He had been surprised at how young she was. Farrant was twenty seven and she was only just nineteen, blonde, and would have been attractive were it not for her red-blotched tearful eyes, which she continuously dabbed with a patterned silk handkerchief. Her husband, she said, told her very little about his work. If the army decided he was dead, she would make plans to return north, to her family. Russell excused himself as soon as he could, promising to do his best in finding her husband. Nothing new could be added by the poor woman, and he was only causing her distress.

Standing on the bridge, Russell withdrew a neatly folded sheet of paper from his inside pocket and looked at the list of names he had made after his meeting with the major. Those people he had already interviewed were crossed out and he had written to those further afield to whom he wanted to talk. Christmas was fast approaching and still he had nothing other than his suspicions that no hidden gang were involved. He looked back down the hill towards the village That was the next place to visit. He looked at his pipe, wondering if should tap more tobacco into the bowl before leaving. Deciding against, he tucked the pipe into his pocket, untied his horse, which had been happily feeding on whatever winter grass it could find on the bridge, and mounted it with ease. He rode down to the village.

Crossing the main road by the great oak, he stopped for a moment, admiring the tree. It sat in the middle of the road, tracks passing either side of it. He wondered how old it was. Certainly, it was old enough that the branches overshadowed the tracks on both sides. In fact, he calculated, at any place three or four yards from the trunk one would be in shade. The thing must be ancient, he realised, for the trunk was so thick that anyone leaning against it could not be seen from the other side. Looking up, because of its great height, he could not see through the tangle of branches to the top. He smiled. If this tree could see and talk it would have seen everything that happened that night and could reveal it all to him. He returned to the present with a sigh, and rode across the rough ground to the church. This, he decided, was the best place to start. The priest of this village would know everyone.

In front of the church stood a wooden rail with rusty metal hooks. He tied his horse to one and walked through a gate into the church grounds, where a path led through the cemetery to the main door. He was following the path when he spotted movement to the far side of the church grounds. A man was crouching, cutting and pruning trees. Russell walked over to him. A small collie dog was lying comfortably near its owner, its head nestled on its legs. It opened its eyes and looked up, curious, as Russell approached, but it did not move.

The gardener half turned, having also heard Russell's footsteps. He wore thick broadcloth trousers and a dark coat that trailed on the ground. A knitted scarf was wrapped warmly around his neck, yet upon his head sat a light straw hat, misshapen from years of wear. It was more in keeping with summer and out of place with the rest of his clothes. He smiled up at Russell, who estimated the man to be in his early forties.

"Can I help you?" The man smiled, welcoming.

"I hope so, sir. You are the reverend of this church?"

The man stood, pulled off his right glove and held out his hand. "Yes. I am Reverend McDonald. And you are Captain

Russell from the camp."

They shook hands. "That's correct. Have we met?"

"Briefly, the morning after the robbery. As soon as I heard what had happened, I thought it was my business to see if I could do anything, I came up to the bridge. You were all very busy and sadly there was nothing anyone could do. Terrible business. Terrible."

"Yes, it is. We are still trying to establish what happened, I was hoping you may be able to help."

"If I can. Shall we go inside? It's a little warmer."

The collie struggled to its paws as he saw his master and this stranger walking towards the church, and trotted alongside them. The reverend leaned down and patted its head.

As they made their way to his small vicarage, which stood at the far side of the church grounds, the reverend insisted on telling Russell about the church, pointing out the square bell tower. Russell made small talk: how the cemetery was well kept, including graves, a few old tombs, and pointed out a recently disturbed grave awaiting a marker, "My work is never done captain and many are too young". They moved on and the reverend gave a brief history of the building.

The small talk continued once they were inside the vicarage, as Reverend McDonald, his hat thrown to one side, made some tea. The collie found his spot on an old, worn blanket to one side of the fire that burned in the grate. McDonald poured the tea and placed some wooden logs onto the fire then poked them to draw some life into the flames.

"I hope you have come to tell me you have released Mr Weller and his sons," said McDonald. He picked up another piece of wood and threw it on to the fire.

"I am afraid not. They are still being detained; we believe they could be involved."

"Ridiculous, Captain Russell." The vicar shook his head and sat. He took a sip of tea. "Hmm, some whisky I think, to warm us up." He got to his feet again, walked to a cabinet, pulled a bottle from it and returned. He poured a small quantity into each cup. Russell did not object.

The reverend sat once again. "I have known the Wellers for years," he said. "The family have lived and worked that small farm since well before I came here. And I have been here over ten years."

"Be that as it may be. We found a bag of coins on his wagon. We believe they came from the barge."

"Someone put it there." McDonald shook his head. "Joshua Weller would not have been involved, and neither would his sons. Good gracious, they attend this church."

"Weller says he loaned the wagon to a soldier."

"Then he is the one who planted the bag of coins."

"But he denies it, sir."

"Then he is lying, Captain. Lying."

"Perhaps, Reverend. But I have no proof and he has an alibi, from a number of other soldiers. Someone is certainly lying."

"Well, I assure you, in Joshua Weller you have the wrong man."

"Could anybody else from this village be involved?"

The vicar laughed. "You cannot believe anybody from this…" McDonald raised his hand in a wide gesture, "this poor unhappy village could be involved with that robbery. Don't get me wrong Captain, they could all do with some money, but they all work on the local estates. Many of them on the estate for Sir

John Treloar. God help them, they have little time for anything else."

"You know Sir John?"

"Let us say we know each other in our official capacities."

"You don't like him?"

"Sir John is a bully and foul mouthed. He is rarely sober and always harsh, especially to those around him, including his wife, family, his estate manager – who I will tell you is a close friend of mine and has been for a number of years – and his own workers. He treats them all unfairly; harshly, as if they were his own little army. That, my good man, is Sir John."

"You speak openly, Reverend."

"I speak as I find, Captain." McDonald stood again, and this time he walked to his collie. Crouching, he stroked the dog's back, to which the dog raised its sleepy head and nestled it against the reverend's arm. McDonald looked up at Russell.

"Do you have a dog, Captain?"

"I am afraid not. I have no love for pets."

"Dogs can be like people. They respond to a leader or master, someone to follow. If that master is kind, sees they have enough to eat, their accommodation is habitable, clean and warm and their living pleasant, then they will respond accordingly, with a happy heart and do their master's bidding." He continued stroking the back of the dog. "If the master is not kind and does not care for them, is cruel, has no interest in how they live or what, or even *if*, they eat, they will still do their master's bidding, but with a heavy heart. They will be living an existence that is pitiful to watch." He stood up and returned to his chair. The dog returned to a comfortable sleep.

The reverend continued. "Sir John is that type of man. He

and I are no friends. He has even tried to get me removed because I try to help his workers in this village. Look around, Captain. You will not see a place in more need than this. These people have no time to plan robberies. All their time is spent staying alive."

"Can you tell me anything else about Sir John, his family – especially his son, Spencer – or the estate?"

McDonald shrugged. "Well, what do you want to know? Lady Treloar, I have time for, she is a good, charitable woman. How she lives with that man is beyond me." McDonald brought his hand up to his collar, as if it was too tight.

"I am sorry, Captain. I probably don't sound very charitable myself, considering my position, but there is so much that needs improving for these poor people."

Russell smiled but didn't reply, appreciating the reverend's embarrassment.

"You have to remember, Captain, what I know is what I hear from his estate manager and others." He thought for a moment. "Let's start again with his family. Sir John is married, his wife's name is Frances, and they have three children: Catherine is the eldest and Florence the youngest, and Spencer, who is also in the army. Spencer is the middle child and, when I have seen them together, Sir John treats his children appallingly. The girls are visibly frightened of him. Sir John brought the estate about four years ago. At that time, it was doing all right, not perfect, but it ticked along, needed some attention. He started well, spent some money, which I now understand he didn't really have, trying to be the local squire. Well, now Sir John has managed to take it to the edge of bankruptcy. Or so I am told."

"Sir John is losing money?"

"Sir John has always lost money. He gambles and he drinks heavily. Rarely see him here, He spends most of his time in London. Lost interest in the estate, unlike his son." He waited before continuing, turning look at his dog again. The reverend knew he had been indiscreet. Eventually he smiled at Russell. "Or so his manager, Mr Foster, tells me. In confidence, of course, Captain. I would not want this discussion to cause problems for Mr Foster. He is an old friend, after all."

Russell nodded, accepting McDonald's request for discretion.

McDonald returned the nod and continued. "Sir John has financial problems and can hardly pay the bills. I know he owes money to many merchants in the area, but he does not seem to care."

"You said his son was interested in the estate."

"Mr Foster tells me Spencer wanted to leave the army and help rebuild the estate. His regiment has been based near here so, whenever he could, he would spend time on the estate. He wanted to do some work with Mr Foster to improve things, but Sir John would not hear of it. Sir John insisted his son stay in the army. He fought in the Crimea, you know? Sir John."

"I did not know." Russell was more interested in Spencer and his involvement with the estate. "You said this Mr Foster and Spencer work together."

"Not exactly work. Sir John insists everything goes through him, although I'm sure Mr Foster confides in Spencer about the estate. From what Mr Foster tells me, I think Spencer had his own ideas about improving things. Foster told me Spencer had wanted to put what money he has into improving matters." He shook his head. "Mr Foster told me Spencer had persuaded his father to make a few improvements on the estate, but not enough unfortunately. Usually, he had to convince his father it would profit the estate, but Spencer was not allowed to have any day-to-day dealings. If his father knew his son was trying to interfere, he would be furious."

"This Mr Foster, could he have been involved in the robbery?"

"Foster?" boomed McDonald. "That is more ridiculous than accusing the Wellers." He leaned forward. "Mr Foster was manager of the estate with the previous owners. He is getting on. He came with the estate, Captain. The only reason he stays, and he is only paid a pittance by Sir John, is because he is too old to find a job elsewhere. He and his wife have a roof over their heads, which comes with working on the estate."

"And Spencer? Do you see him often?"

"Occasionally, usually early mornings around nine or ten, when he is out riding. He goes over the heath past the Weller's farm."

"Have you seen him recently?"

McDonald shook his head. "Not since the robbery. The last time I saw him was about a month before that. He was standing by the great oak, as if waiting for someone."

Russell looked at the vicar with interest. "You mean that large tree near the track to the bridge? How could you tell he was waiting for someone?"

"I could not. I said it looked like he was waiting for someone." He shuffled, a little embarrassed. "I am not in the business of spying on my parishioners you know," he said, and waited for Russell to nod before continuing. "I came out of the church and walked to the gate. I saw Spencer by the tree. He had dismounted his horse and looked like he was waiting. I have never seen him dismount before. He usually trots off up the track towards the bridge. I crossed to the inn as I had something to ask Sam Longhurst, the owner. When I came out and crossed back to the church, Spencer was still there, waiting."

"Did you see who he was waiting for?"

"No. I went back into the church. When I passed the gate again, which I guess would have been about an hour later, no more, Spencer was gone."

Russell said nothing as his thoughts tried to align themselves. Had he found a possible motive, and was it possible Spencer had been meeting someone who had something to do with the robbery? He thought back to his meeting with Spencer. The man had been hiding something, yes, he was sure of that, but how could he have known before the robbery what Colonel Standish was carrying?

Russell finished his tea, making general conversation about the parish until, finally, he thanked Reverend McDonald and made his exit. He patted the dog as he went.

Standing by his horse, he removed the sheet of paper from his pocket and looked at the list. The Waterloo Inn – part of the alibi given by Corporal Price – would be his next stop.

He withdrew his pipe from his pocket and from a small leather pouch, which he opened by loosening a thin cord, removed some tobacco, pressing it into the bowl of the pipe. Using a match he lit the tobacco and placed the bit of the stem between his teeth. Drawing the smoke into his lungs, he mounted his horse and rode away from the village. He still had many questions but was beginning to feel he may have a suspect, if not two. Perhaps he was finally getting somewhere.

Chapter 5

He found the ride from the village relaxing. The enjoyment of his smoke, the gentle movement of the horse and the solitude of the countryside gave him time to contemplate the meeting with Reverend McDonald and what he had found out about Spencer.

The Waterloo Inn he located with little trouble, situated as it was on the edge of the small town of North Endfield, north of Aldershot, a short distance from the canal. It stood close to the town's railway station. Russell estimated it was a good three miles from the village of Old Oak Crossroads, which made it too far for the money to have been brought here in the timescale of the robbery.

Approaching the inn, Russell was surprised at its size. It had two large windows either side of the main entrance and three large windows on the first floor. Benches were positioned under each of front windows. Four brick chimneys rose from the roof, one at each end of the building and a further two close together in the middle. A board leant against the wall next to the front door, advertising boxing. A sign above the front door had *The Waterloo* proudly painted in red, above a scene depicting a line of red-coated soldiers all pointing their muskets and bayonets at an unseen enemy.

Russell opened the door and took a pace back as the stench of stale beer, smoke and sweat assaulted his nostrils. He turned away, took a deep breath, and stepped into the tavern. It was large – Russell felt it could easily accommodate twenty, maybe more, thirsty soldiers – but somehow dark despite the windows.

The floorboards were black from mud and tobacco being trodden in, and the beams and ceiling were a similar colour thanks to the smoke from whatever tobacco had been saved from the floor. It took a few moments for Russell's eyes to adjust to the gloom. The bar ran along the wall furthest from the grimy windows and a man carrying a chair was limping towards him. While the man's dark beard was thick, an attempt had been made to part what little hair was on his head down the middle. He wore a striped shirt with no collar, a woollen jumper and a drink-stained apron. Seeing Russell's uniform, he sprang to attention. He waited for Russell to speak.

Russell smiled to himself. "At ease, soldier."

The man relaxed and placed the chair on the floor. "Can I help you, Captain?"

"I gather I am talking to an old soldier."

"Eighteen years with the Sussex regiment, sir, before I got this wound." He prodded his leg.

Russell held out his hand. "I am Captain Russell and I would like to ask a few questions Mr…"

"No problem, Captain. Name's George, George Lane." He pointed to a table and they both sat either side of it. Russell refused the offer of a drink.

"Do you own this place"?

"Would like to and hope to, but no, I don't own it. I manage it, though. For the moment at least."

"Do you know a soldier called Price? A Corporal Price, from the camp?"

"Henry Price? Yes, I know him. Why, sir? What's he done?"

"Is he a regular?"

"That he is, sir. Always in here, although… thinking about it,

I haven't seen him here in the last few days. He knew the owner of the place. Henry helped with the boxing and, if truth be known, sir," he leant forward, "took a piece of the action." He sat back. "All legal though. We have a covered ring at the back of the building."

Russell waited. He knew there was more. There always was in places like this.

Lane looked to the windows, then back to Russell. "He also helped with the bare-knuckle fights. Well, he would do, with that man of his, Ox."

"Ox?" asked Russell, remembering the survivor who came in with Treloar.

"Brute of a fellow. Fought all-comers and usually won."

Russell looked around, "Is the owner around, George? I would like to talk with him."

Lane shook his head. "Afraid not, Mr Parr was found dead in the canal not far from here."

"Dead? When?"

"Couple of weeks ago. Robbery we think. His head split open and he was dumped in the canal. Murdered, they said. A troop of soldiers riding along the towpath found him."

"Do you remember the date Mr Parr was killed?"

George thought for a moment. "The twenty seventh. I remember. Mr Parr didn't have a wife but his brother had an agent in here just few days later, before end of the month. He was assessing the place to sell it. Which, frankly, sir, I thought was a bit quick. The poor sod had only just died."

Coincidence? Russell wondered. Or was there some connection between Parr's death and the robbery?

"But he did know Corporal Price well?"

"I would say very well. Always talking together, they were. Price would encourage his mates to come to this place rather than one of the others. He was good for business, Mr Parr said. And Mr Parr needed the money. Always needed the money did Mr Parr."

"So, this place gets busy."

"It can be a madhouse." George Lane leaned forward and whispered. "I think, sir, his place could be a gold mine if run well. That's why I told the agent I was interested in renting or buying it. Old Mr Parr, though, was never happy. Always looking for more money, with this place and the one in London. Always in need of cash, never happy."

"Mr Parr had debts?"

"Not for me to say, sir, but he was always moaning about what everything cost him and what little he had for all the hard work he was doing." Lane huffed. "That's a joke. It was me and his girl, Maggie, in London, who did all the hard work. All he had to do was find the money to pay the bills. All right, this place cost him a fair bit, I think, when he built it. And he found it tough sometimes, usually when it came to paying the merchants. That's why he encouraged Henry Price to bring in the punters, fights and things I mean."

"Did Mr Parr live here or elsewhere?"

"He lived here. Had two rooms at the back, with a separate entrance. That's when he was not at his place in London."

"So, he owned just the two inns?"

"Yes, sir, and I think he had debts at his London place as well, or so he said when I asked for a little more money." Lane rubbed two fingers together and laughed. "Never got me anywhere."

"This place in London, what do you know about it?"

"It's an old coaching inn, sir, but not too much carriage trade anymore. He travelled between the two places regularly, that's why he took me on here. Been here about three years now; three years since I left the army to run this place when he was in London. He kept a tight rein on the money side, though. Let me see only what he wanted me to see." Lane's smile was one of resignation.

"This place in London, do you know where it is?"

"Sure, had to know if I needed to contact him. It's in Battersea, by the Thames, called, 'The Three Feathers'."

Russell made a note of the details and the address. "How long had he owned this place?"

"I joined him just after he opened it, so it's about three years now. He told me he bought the land and had the place built. Used to tell me he knew some influential people, officers I think, who invested with him."

"Did any officers ever visit the inn?"

"Oh, no, sir." Lane shook his head with firm commitment. "This was a soldiers' inn; officers went elsewhere for their entertainment."

"So, you never saw any officers here?"

Lane shook his head again. "No." He stopped; head cocked to one side. "Not in the inn drinking, anyway."

"But you have seen officers here, then?"

"Once. Mr Parr went mad at me. Nearly lost my job over it."

"Why? Who? And when was it?"

"About four months ago, perhaps a little more. It was early one morning, no one else here and I came downstairs." He twitched towards a door behind the bar. "I have a small room at the back." He pointed to the ceiling. "Well, upstairs. Anyway, I heard voices in Mr Parr's rooms. I came into the inn and the front doors were still locked so whoever it was must have come in thought his private door."

"Can I see it?"

Lane shrugged. "Don't see why not."

They stood and left through a door behind the bar. It led into a narrow corridor, doors off either side. Lane ignored these and walked to the end. He took out a key and unlocked the last door. They entered a well-furnished space that was obviously used as a living room. It had a round table in the middle, and a Welsh dresser against one wall. A few paintings, landscapes, hung on the walls but there were few other personal effects. Russell took in the surroundings whilst Lane moved around the table to another door, to one side of a window. "This is the door to the courtyard outside, and across the courtyard is the barn and the covered area where we hold the boxing." He limped to another door, on the opposite side of the room. Opening it, he turned to Russell. "This was Mr Parr's bedroom."

"This was where you saw the officer?"

"And Henry."

"Price was here as well?"

"Yes, sir. The three of them all sitting around that," he pointed to the circular table in the middle of the room.

Russell waited whilst he drew his thoughts together. "George," he asked slowly, "can you try to describe exactly what happened. It could be important?"

George stared at Russell and shifted his weight onto his good leg before speaking. "As I said, sir, I went from my rooms down into the inn but found the front doors still locked. I thought whoever Mr Parr was talking to had come here on business and, finding the front door locked, had gone round the back." He walked over to where Russell was standing. "So, I came through from the bar to these rooms. I knocked and walked in. Done it before dozens of times, but this time Mr Parr went crazy."

"Why?"

George shrugged. "Don't know. They were sitting around the table, talking as I walked in. I began to say good morning, and that's when Mr Parr jumped up and started shouting at me to get out and pushing me out of the room. Once out of the room I made for the bar and he followed me, still shouting saying about how dare I enter his rooms, how long had I been there and whatever I saw and heard was none of my business and I was to keep it to myself." George paused then continued as if apologising "But, honestly, I heard and saw nothing. There was nothing to see. They were just sitting and talking. Mr Parr, he threatened me with losing my job and God knows what else. The old sod apologised later. Said he over-reacted and I was to forget it. So, I did. Pressure of too many bills, he said."

Russell looked around the room and, without looking at George, asked, "What did you actually see when you walked into the room?"

"Told you, sir, nothing they were just sitting and talking. Three of them: Mr Parr, Henry Price and an officer."

"Did you not think it strange? All sitting around talking, I mean? And Parr's reaction."

"Well, I tried not to think about it, sir. Thought that was best. Mr Parr knew Price and obviously they knew the officer. It was nothing to do with me. I do as I am ordered."

That made sense, Russell thought. Lane would carry out the orders and not ask questions. A good soldier

"Did you recognise the officer?"

"Afraid not, sir. His uniform was covered as he was wearing a black cape, but I saw a flash of his red uniform and caught a quick sight of an officer's forage cap before he quickly removed it from the table."

"What about rank?"

"Afraid not. It was all too quick, Mr Parr was shouting and pushing me out of the room."

"Could you describe this officer?"

"Can't help you there either. It was the way they were sitting." Lane walked over to the table and stood behind the chair to Russell's right.

"Mr Parr was sitting here; he was closest to the door." Lane limped around the table until he was behind a chair facing Russell, who had his back to the door. "Henry Price was sitting here, so I saw his face as soon as I walked in." He carried on around the table to the third chair. This one to Russell's left.

"This was where the officer was sitting. As soon as I walked in, he looked away, so I could not see his face, but he was in uniform, that's how I know it was an officer. Then Mr Parr jumped up and pushed me out of the room."

"What happened afterwards?"

"I don't know, I kept out of the way in the bar. I heard the officer leave shortly afterwards. He obviously went out through the private door. I heard him ride across the cobblestones and away. We don't have windows in that side of the building, the front door was open so I heard him go. I didn't see him. Mr Parr and Price came into the bar." Lane seemed to shrink into himself. "I stayed behind the bar and kept quiet, I can tell you. Henry just smiled at me and said, 'hallo George,' and left through the front entrance. They had a few words out front, then Mr Parr came back in, passed me and scowled, and went back into his rooms. He stayed there for ages. I left him alone, but he came out later and that's when he apologised."

Russell nodded. He stepped further into the room and walked around the table, all the time looking about in the hope he would see something that would indicate what they had been talking about. There was nothing. He returned to the door. "Thank you, George, you have been very helpful."

George Lane smiled, rubbing his beard, a little embarrassed. "Don't see how. Anyway, sir, Captain Russell, can I ask you what this is about?"

"Sorry, George. I cannot say. But I would like you to keep what you have told me confidential. You can say I was asking questions but don't mention the story you just told me." He stared into Lane's face. "Will you do that for me? It's important with regard to what I have been asked to do."

Whoever was involved in the robbery and murder, Russell didn't want word getting back to them.

Worry crossed George Lane's weathered features. "Will this affect me buying this place?"

Russell smiled. "Not at all. You have been very helpful. If it would help, George, you can use my name as a reference. Us soldiers must help each other."

George smiled "Thank you, Captain Russell, I will. And don't you worry," he winked, "we hardly spoke."

They shook hands and Russell and Lane left through the private door. They walked around to the front of the inn where they shook hands once again.

Putting his foot into his stirrup, Russell lifted himself onto his horse. George disappeared around the side of the building and Russell looked up at the inn, stroking the mane of his steed, thinking. Had it all been planned here? Treloar being the officer George had seen? Mr Parr obviously knew Price, in fact, they knew each other very well. But when Russell had questioned Price, Mr Parr was never mentioned. But, again, there was no reason he should have been. And how had Treloar got involved with either of them? He was not from this area. And Parr was from London. It threw up more questions for which he did not have answers. However, he was even more convinced that it was a well-planned robbery involving people inside the military, and that the story of a gang was a diversion. Proving this theory, however, would be more difficult. Russell wondered if it would be worth a visit to the coaching inn in London, and decided, yes, it would. It was, however, not a priority. It could be left until after his planned trip in a couple of days to Cheltenham, to visit Second Lieutenant Norton's family.

He pulled on the reins to turn his horse and rode away from the Waterloo Inn and George Lane. He began to think of his next visit, to Basing and Lady Standish.

Chapter 6

The word that came to mind when Russell saw the drawing room was 'sumptuous'. The wing-backed armchairs and padded couch looked more than comfortable, and even though they were large, there was still plenty of room for a mahogany bow-fronted chest, a tall and full breakfront mahogany bookcase and a couple of side tables, which were neatly positioned around the room. A thick Axminster carpet held a pristine multi-coloured pattern. Russell had been waiting in the drawing room in Basing for ten minutes, standing in his spotless red uniform. His belt and buttons had been given an extra polish the night before, and – rather than forage cap – he held his helmet by his side. He had stayed overnight in a local inn to ensure he was fresh for this visit and, rather than ride a horse, he had arranged for a trap from the hotel, with a driver. He had calculated that, to get the best from this visit, it would pay to be well presented. Besides, he was entering the realm of the upper class.

When asked to wait in the drawing room for Lady Standish, he remained standing; it did not seem polite to make himself at home, although the two chairs that faced each other in front of a blazing fire did look inviting. And, although desperate to do so, he resisted making use of his pipe. He was amused that the maid who had opened the front door and led him through the house to the drawing room was also waiting silently, looking down to avoid eye contact, as if trying to identify something wrong with the thick carpet. She had obviously been told to wait with the soldier.

While he waited, Russell took a closer interest in the room. Paintings of various shapes and sizes hung on the walls. They made Russell think of a gallery. Small ornaments stood on mantelpieces, the side tables and on the bow-fronted cabinet. Ornate candlesticks, with fresh candles, and a selection of oil lamps could be seen atop much of the furniture and the fireplace. The bay window overlooked fields that gently rose until they reached a distant wood. Russell thought it a lovely view.

He was intrigued by a few of the modern photographic plate pictures. He knew of this new invention, had even seen other examples at the camp and marvelled how clear the results were. The pictures were crowded on top of two cupboards and a simple two-drawer mahogany writing desk, at the far end of the room. As far as he could see, they were all of horses – either of a single horse or various group of horses – none of people. Once he'd noticed this, he realised all the paintings and ornaments were similarly horse-themed.

Russell looked at the maid and smiled. She looked up, as she must have felt his eyes on her, and promptly looked straight back down again. With a creak loud enough to make both Russell and the maid jump, the door opened and a smartly dressed manservant stood to one side. Lady Alice Standish swept elegantly into the room. Behind her, the door was gently shut.

Ignoring both Russell and the maid, she glided to the window, moved the already opened curtain a fraction, and looked out across her estate. "I hate this weather," she said, "I hate the cold". She continued to stare out.

Russell evaluated Lady Standish. She was in her mid-fifties, in a full-length satin gown – black for mourning, but with the addition of a silver broach in the shape of a horse's head. It matched the silver of her hair, which was drawn back in a bun. An oval barrette, also silver, kept it in place. Finally, she released the curtain and seemed to float to the nearest couch, the one as close to the fire as possible. She sat and looked up at Russell.

"I hope you are here to tell me you have found my money, Captain Russell." Then, as an afterthought, she added, "And caught the men who murdered my husband."

"Unfortunately, Lady Standish, I cannot give you that news. We are still investigating and, if you will permit me, I would like to ask you a few questions, which may help our investigations."

Lady Standish did not reply, only stared at Russell with a look that made it clear she was unsure whether she even wanted to give him the time. "These investigations,' she said eventually, "appear to have gone on a long while, with little to show."

"You are correct, Lady Standish. It is a long process. Unfortunately, there was very little to work with, which is why I have been appointed to investigate further, with full powers and authority to question who and where I think necessary." He wanted to be polite but make it plain why he was in this room.

"I am not without influence myself, Captain Russell," she stared at him, calculating. "However, if I can help, then naturally I will."

Russell nodded. "Thank you."

Lady Standish glanced at her maid. "You can leave us. I will have some tea after the captain has left." Russell supressed his smile: he knew when he was not being invited to partake. The maid curtsied and almost ran from the room. Mrs Standish gestured to the wing-backed chair opposite. Russell nodded, sat and made himself comfortable, placing his helmet next to him and sitting upright. He made a fuss about finding his notebook and pencil, opened the book and, although he had no need to refer to his notes, gave the impression of reading something. He knew what he wanted to ask, but was keen to demonstrate to Lady Standish that he was very serious about his investigations and questions. Finally, he looked up, and closed the book. "I have reports that three or four large chests were stolen, each containing significant sums of money."

"So I understand."

"Did you ever see these chests, Lady Standish?"

"My husband handled our finances, not me."

"Can you tell me why Colonel Standish travelled with these chests, and why the money was not held in safety by a bank?"

"I told you, my husband's business was his business, Captain. I was not privy to why he did things. He did not like banks. I can only think he felt his money," she glanced at her pale hands, "our money, was safe in his keeping."

"But it was a considerably amount of money, Lady Standish." Russell had heard stories of how much was involved and where some of this wealth had originated.

"Yes, it was. My husband was a very clever man," she spoke as if reading Russell's mind. "He invested wisely, had many business interests that brought a good return. But I do not see the relevance of his investments to the theft."

"I am trying to understand why Sir John was not more protective and who else may have known about the chests."

"I would have thought an escort of half a dozen men would have been more than enough protection. That is if they had been doing their job properly rather than getting themselves killed and letting my money be stolen. As for who knew, I told you, my husband kept his own council."

Russell made a show of referring again to his notes. "Was any of the escort known to your husband, Lady Standish?"

"That Treloar boy was known to my husband. I don't think any of the others were. How would I know?"

"You know Spencer Treloar?"

"My husband knew the Treloars better than I. Frederick and Sir John were old army friends. We stayed at their house once, when Frederick first showed me this house. So, yes, I have met the family." She smoothed her dress around her legs. "I for one did not like him. Sir John, I mean. He always smelt of drink and was always looking for a loan from my husband." Her shrug showed her indifference. "But my husband liked his company, and they visited the same clubs in London."

"Would he have known a Corporal Price, from the camp?"

She stared at Russell before answering. "An enlisted man? I would doubt it very much."

Russell made a note. "I understand," he said, "your husband requested Spencer Treloar to be part of the escort."

"Possibly. I do not know." She looked to the window.

Russell sensed Lady Standish was getting tired of his questioning. He pressed on, nevertheless. "Can you tell me anything more else about your husband, Lady Standish?"

"Like what?"

"What else did Sir John enjoy doing? Whose company did he enjoy? What type of man was he?"

The tone in her answer was rough enough to plane wood. "You think that is relevant?"

"Lady Standish, your husband's barge was attacked late at night on a quiet part of the canal, near a small village. Whoever did it knew what they were after. It was not a random attack and, to be very honest, Lady Standish, we have very little chance of either finding who did this or retrieving any money without first finding who knew where he would be, and the exact reason for the attack."

"Surely you are not that stupid, man," she glared at him. "They wanted the money."

Russell nodded. "So, we have the why. Now we have to find who knew, so I really need your help, Lady Standish, if we are to stand any chance of being successful."

Lady Standish did not reply, she appeared lost in her own thoughts. She looked up at one of the pictures on the mantelpiece, stared at it for a few seconds before returning her gaze to Russell. "I would," she said, "like nothing more than to retrieve that money, Captain, believe me. But I am not sure I am the one who can help you."

"I don't understand, Lady Standish."

"You seem to be a thorough man, Captain Russell, are you also discreet?"

"I have been told so, Ma'am."

"Then what I have to say," she leant forward, looking him up and down, taking in his uniform, "must remain between ourselves."

"If it involves my investigation, I do not—"

Russell stopped mid-sentence as Lady Standish raised her hand. "It has nothing to do with your investigation, Captain. Not directly, or that I am aware of, at least."

"Then anything you tell me will remain confidential."

Russell placed his pencil in his book, closed the book and placed it on the table between them.

She waited and sat back before continuing. "Sir John and I had only one interest together, our love for horses. Outside that, we lived separate lives. It was, as some say, a marriage of convenience."

"Forgive me for asking, Lady Standish, but were you," he paused, aware of the delicacy of the matter, "fond of someone else?"

At that moment he thought she was going to erupt. He kept a questioning look on his face, one he hoped was non-judgemental and he was relieved to see her calm down.

"I have no time for men or their wants and needs, Captain. I never have. My love is and will always be my horses. No, I do not have a lover. As for my husband, I neither knew nor wanted to know about his business dealings. For that matter, I knew very little about his life. I do, however, know my husband found comfort elsewhere."

"Can you be more explicit?"

"If I must." She drew in a long breath. "During our marriage my husband spent a lot of time in London. Whenever he could, usually at his club or one of the many gaming clubs. Often in the company of others, including Sir John Treloar. He occasionally spoke about lending money to Sir John and told me on more than one occasion, almost boasted, in fact, how he had helped Sir John. Sir John's company amused my husband. And Frederick, well, he could afford to be generous." She paused and Russell had the feeling she was wondering whether to continue. He remained silent, knowing there was more and that he had no option other than to wait until she was ready to speak.

"He also kept rooms in London for entertaining. Personal entertaining, I mean. The sort of place he knew I would never enter." She stared at Russell to make sure he understood. Russell just nodded. "When I first found out I was disgusted, but I could not complain. I did not want him, but I did want what his wealth brought me, so I accepted it." She looked at a painting on the wall. It showed a black, muscular horse. "Over the years," her tone changed, becoming sadder, more matter of fact, "I came to live with it," she looked back at Russell. "That is why you see no tears, Captain. No outward signs of sorrow. I put up with everything because this is my life. This is the way I *should* live. I like this way. And now, Captain, now I finally have the house, and the land to enjoy my life, which I have wanted after all those years of living in London. I must have the money to continue this life, do you understand? You must find that money."

Her expression froze as she leaned forward. "My husband was stupid enough to lose the money and get himself killed. Because of that, I could lose everything. Well, I will not. I will not lose everything. Do you understand? I've already spoken to friends in London. My husband knew many people, influential people, and they were all shocked at this robbery. They can cause trouble, Captain, believe me. An escort failing in its duties, and getting a knight of the realm and fellow officer killed. Find me that money, Captain Russell." Her face relaxed. "I need that money. So, you must find it."

Russell waited. She had shown not an ounce of sorrow for her dead husband or any of the others, yet now she looked upset. All those he had spoken to so far in this investigation had given him insight or suspicions into those who had their own motives for wanting this money; she was just another of them.

He ignored her threat and quietly asked his next question.

"Do you know where this place in London is, where he kept these rooms?"

She nodded. "A public house near the river. Obviously, I never went there. It was not the sort of place with which we should have been associated. It was used by a different class of people. However, my husband said it suited his needs. Whatever they were," she added in disgust. "But I had to know where he stayed in London should I need him. I had the name of the owner if I needed to contact my husband. On a few occasions, over the years, I have had to send a servant to him with a message that he was needed urgently." She smiled but it was devoid of humour. "My servant is a trusted employee; he gave me the name of the woman Frederick was with."

She showed no emotion about her husband's betrayal. It was all matter of fact: if the facts helped retrieve the money for her, then she would divulge them. Russell remained silent, waiting for her to continue.

She picked up a small marble statue of a white horse from the side table. She cradled it in her hands and, without looking at Russell, she continued. "He's kept rooms for many years at a coaching inn in Battersea, called, "The Three Feathers". It's owned by a man called Parr. I think my husband and this man may have done some business together. There is a woman who works there, called Maggie. I'm told my husband was fond of her." She stared at Russell. "Shouldn't you be writing this down, Captain?" Trying hard to not smile, Russell shook his head. There was nothing he needed to write down.

Chapter 7

The train rattled through the countryside on its way to London and, as its movement jostled him, Captain Russell would occasionally raise his eyes from his newspaper to look out of the window. Peering through the smoke from the locomotive, he could see flooded fields. Another wet year. Sometimes it felt as if there was mud everywhere, as if the world were made of the glutinous stuff. Still, at least it wasn't holding up the mechanical beast pulling his carriage. Not for the first time marvelled at the speed: over 20 miles an hour! Amazing, he thought, but still admitted to himself that he did not like trains. He had travelled on them a few times, when he had to, yet still preferred the simplicity of a horse and carriage. Yes, in the latter the jolting would be more severe and the speed was only about five miles per hour, but it felt more natural. Where possible, of course, he preferred riding a horse; man and beats working together. However, it was certainly the case that trains made journeys much quicker. This trip to London would have taken a full day when he was a boy – not, of course, that he had been taken to London in his childhood.

He closed the pages of his paper and continued staring through the window, seeing nothing. His mind was on his previous week's meeting with Lady Standish. It had been a shorter encounter than he had expected, probably because they had found a mutual trust for each other. He appreciated her honesty even though it was clearly hard, even painful, for her, but she had made it very clear: recovery of the money was her prime concern. Before he left, he reassured her that her confidences would be respected. Her revelation about her husband knowing Parr had surprised Russell, but it made sense. Now he had a link from Standish to Parr and from Parr to Price, and also between Standish and Treloar. But was Treloar the officer seen at the Waterloo Inn? At the moment he had no evidence of a link between Treloar and Parr, but he hoped this journey would give him more answers. He was now convinced that the robbery was planned – well-planned, he had to admit – by more than one person and was probably conceived at the Waterloo Inn. It had been carried out very efficiently, most likely with the minimum of assailants despite the high number of victims. He was becoming convinced the whole incident had been devised to cause maximum confusion, and Parr somehow was part of that plot. However, if he had been one of the plotters, why was he later killed? Was that just an unfortunate act, something that was unplanned? Or something more sinister?

After meeting Lady Standish and returning to camp, Russell had prepared for his current venture, which he thought would take a few days, taking him almost to Christmas. He would then find time over the holiday to write his report. London was only the first part of this excursion; after completing his business in London he would take another train, west, to Cheltenham to talk to the family of the missing officer, Norton. The lieutenant had been given a lift on the barge, but had not been seen since the robbery. How had he fitted into the picture?

First, though, Russell would visit the Three Feathers in Battersea and hopefully find Maggie, to see if she could substantiate Lady Standish's story.

Whistle blaring, smoke pouring from the chimney of the

locomotive, the train slowly pulled into Waterloo Station, which was situated south of the River Thames. Russell shuddered backwards and forwards in his seat, his teeth grinding as metal screeched loudly against metal as the brakes were applied to slow the engine and its carriages. Finally, the mechanical beast stopped with a loud sigh and hiss of steam.

Russell smiled: he'd gone from the Waterloo Inn to Waterloo Station. He remembered reading the station had been named after the bridge, which itself was named after the Battle of Waterloo. During his training and service, he had read much of that famous battle and Napoleon's defeat.

He stepped from the train into the dust and smoke of the station and coughed, tasting the grit in the air. Hoping not too much soot would stick to his clothes, he marched up the platform, carrying his leather travelling valise. Once again, he was wearing his uniform, this time under a warm overcoat. It was his utter belief the sight of a uniform would help get him get the answers he wanted. As he walked, he noticed considerable construction work and it became clear that expansion of the station with new platforms was ongoing. It all contributed to the almost deafening sounds echoing around this cavern of a station.

It seemed all the new railway stations had been built on the edge of London, not in the middle, where everything was in walking distance. A cab was therefore required. He marched, back erect, to the main entrance and waited his turn to board a hansom cab. He handed the address of The Three Feathers to the driver.

It was late morning when the cab set off. Russell stared in disbelief at the traffic as they rode through the streets of

Southern London. On the few other occasions he had been in London he had been amazed at the vast numbers of people and horrified by the noises of different vehicles rattling over the cobbles. There were wagons, small traps, more hansom cabs and horse-drawn omnibuses, vehicles of all different shapes and sizes, all appearing to be criss-crossing before each other, but somehow avoiding collisions. He had been in battles that had felt less chaotic – and certainly felt safer. He sat back in his seat staring out over the rump of the horse, at people crossing the bridges to go north of the River Thames or heading south from the station to Lambeth. Many were travelling in the same direction as him, heading west alongside the river. Everywhere seemed busy and crowded and the narrow streets were crammed with houses, shops, inns and other businesses. The journey took almost an hour, with a few stops in Battersea for the cabby to ask for directions. They finally pulled up outside a narrow building, three storeys tall, with an ancient wooden sign over the main entrance. The faded picture showed three feathers set into a soldier's helmet, similar to the Prince of Wales emblem. Beside the inn, leading to the rear of the building was a large arch, almost as wide as the inn itself, certainly big enough for a coach and horses. Russell let himself out of the cab, still holding his valise, and told the cabby to wait. Compared with the army camp Russell had come from, deep in the country, it was not pleasant here. His nose wrinkled at the heavy smells assaulting him. He tried not to breathe too deeply. At the bottom of a narrow lane, lined with wood-framed houses, he could just see the sluggish river. Around him were locals rushing to fulfil whatever business they had. He could not tell from looking at them whether it was legal or not. He brushed some dirt off his scarlet overcoat, made his way to the main door to the inn, and pushed.

As with the Waterloo Inn, the public bar was dim. This one, however, was narrow, disappearing a long way back. Booths filled the walls like sentry boxes, and most of the tables dotted around the place were occupied. The room was noisy, as if everything was being echoed back from the rafters. The stench of stale ale, sweat and smoke also reminded him of his visit to the Waterloo, but here it was much stronger, more pungent. The bar itself took up half the right-hand wall, and Russell calculated that behind it was the coach entrance to the rear of the building. Groups of workman in dirty clothes were standing at the bar, drinking. Although a few glanced at him, no one paid him any particular attention. He guessed it wasn't unusual for a soldier to be seen here. Three people were working behind the bar – a man at the far end, wiping the counter and talking to one of the workmen, and two women, who were closer to Russell. The younger woman, who looked no more than fourteen or fifteen, was washing tankards in a bowl hidden under the counter, the other was drying them. She looked older but not much taller. Russell put her about five and a half feet and in her mid-twenties. She had a long face with hollow cheeks and narrow nose, as if her features had been stretched. Her hair was brushed back from her forehead and tied with a dark bow such that tangled tresses fell half way down her back. Some strands had escaped and hung to her shoulders. Russell thought she had a certain attractiveness but was too poor to be considered a beauty.

Removing his overcoat, draping it over his arm, he walked towards the two women.

"What can I get you?" asked the older woman, smiling. A worn apron covered her plain short-sleeved dress, and while both dress and apron looked as if they'd seen better days, they were – given her occupation – surprisingly clean. A St Christopher on a sliver chain hung around her neck and rested outside her dress.

Russell placed his valise on a stool and put his overcoat and forage cap on top, revealing his officer's uniform.

"Thank you, no. I drink very little and prefer my alcohol in coffee."

"Then you're in the wrong place, soldier." She turned to the younger girl. "Hear that, Lucy? The first soldier I've met who doesn't want a pint."

Lucy just smiled.

Russell remained expressionless. "I would like to have a few words with Maggie."

The older woman's smile faded, and she looked at Russell with suspicion. She placed the towel and glass she was holding on the bar, wiped her hands on her apron and placed her fists on her hips. "All right. I'm Maggie. What do you want?" In the gloom of the inn, Russell couldn't tell if her hair was red or auburn.

"I am from the army camp in Aldershot. I would like to talk to you about Mr Parr." Russell decided not to mention Standish until they were alone.

"You have come all this way to talk to me? Why? What's happened now?"

"Nothing to worry about, Maggie. You have done nothing wrong. You know Mr Parr was killed? We have a few questions about his business." Seeing her expression, he added: "It may help us find who did it."

Maggie turned to the younger girl. "You carry on here, Lucy, and stay at the bar." Looking over her shoulder she called out: "Tom, stay behind the bar. I'm going in the back with this soldier."

"You be good now," Tom laughed and the workman joined in.

"And you keep your words to yourself," replied Maggie swiftly, with an authoritative tone. She raised a wooden flap in the counter and came out to Russell. "Well go to the back, its quieter there."

Russell picked up his hat, coat and valise and followed Maggie through a side door into a kitchen. Two women were washing and preparing food. Both stopped what they were doing and looked at Maggie, blinking.

"You keep your mind on what you are doing," she said and they returned to their jobs, relief clear on both their faces. It was obvious who runs this inn, thought Russell, as he followed Maggie through another door into a smaller room, narrow, gloomy and filled with two beds such that the passage between the bedframes was the only route to the far end. A few clothes hung neatly from hooks over one bed. The other bed sat under a window that was so dirty Russell couldn't see through it. He wondered if, being on the ground floor, its grimy condition was partly for modesty and protection from nosy viewers. A thin and tattered curtain hung from a wooden rail. A cord looped across one corner of the room, tied between two misaligned hooks. Clothes were secured on the line with wooden pegs. Two small shelves holding a few pieces of crockery could be seen at the far end of the room. Also in the far corner was a small cupboard, situated above a table that could seat no more than two people, one of whom would have to sit with their back to the bed while the other had a delightful view of the unpainted wall. It was obvious to Russell that the room, sparse and undecorated, was used for sleeping and eating. Most definitely not for entertaining.

Getting his bearings, Russell figured that, if the window had been cleaned, the view would be of the courtyard beyond the arch. The area where carriages would arrive from the street. He shivered; the room felt damp and cold. There was no fire and for light there was only one candle, about three inches tall, sitting in hard wax in a saucer-shaped base. Russell wondered how anyone could sleep here. He wanted to put his overcoat back on but felt that would be rude.

"You said you like coffee?" Maggie asked, as if understanding his need for warmth.

"Thank you. Yes. That would be nice. It's a long journey from Aldershot to Waterloo Station."

Maggie's eyes widened and she looked at him, excited. "You went on a train?"

"Yes. This morning."

"Oh, I say." She shook her head in wonderment and squeezed past Russell unable to avoid the briefest of touches and eventually returned with two mugs of steaming coffee. Russell had moved down the narrow room, between the beds, to the table, leaving his valise, coat and cap on one of the threadbare bedspreads. He waited by the table as Maggie placed the mugs on the table. "Put in small drop of brandy," she said with a wink. Russell's mug was slightly chipped, hers was covered in scratches and also chipped. He took a sip and nodded a thank you. It was warming, at least.

"I've always wanted to go on a train,' she said, her face flushed. "But then I've always wanted to do lots of things." At that moment she looked younger, no more than a girl. "You know what I want to do most?"

"No, tell me." Russell acted pleasant, interested. He hoped it would help him get the answers he needed.

"Oh, I want to go to Brighton. To see the sea. I saw pictures in a magazine once, it looked amazing. I bet you've seen the seaside, haven't you. Oh, that's what I've always wanted to do. Can you imagine it? The seaside? All the water. And I've heard the air's clear. Is it? Oh, the very idea of the seaside." She sat at the table looked up at Russell. Her smile grew as she realised he had waited for her to sit first. "Sit down, sir. Please." She indicated Russell take the other chair, but couldn't stop her runaway thoughts. "You know," she said, still dreaming. "I sometimes go down to the Thames and watch the ships and barges going up and down the river. They have to go past the seaside, don't they, before going around the world."

Russell smiled at the simplicity of the question He imagined she was a different woman, here, in this room, from the one who ran the inn. "Yes, they do, Maggie."

"Have you travelled much, Mr …?"

"It's Captain Russell. And yes, I have. Not much, but I have been abroad."

Maggie's expression instantly turned to one of disgust, her nose wrinkled. "Don't want to go abroad." She shook her head, her tired hair limply brushing her shoulders and her back. She flicked loose strands behind her ears and away from her face, "Just want to go to the seaside." She looked around the room.

"Mr Parr said he would take me one day. Promised a lot of things he did. He was fond of me, but never did most of them." She sniffed dismissively. "And now he can't, can he?" She stood and took a small tin of sugar from the lower shelf. She pushed the tin and a tarnished spoon towards Russell.

"Did you know Mr Parr long, Maggie?" Russell scooped sugar into his mug.

"Most of my life, I suppose. I was going to be on the streets after me ma died. She worked for him; I was only a kid, younger than Lucy. Ma died and he took me in, said he would look after me. I've been here ever since. I can't remember how long, not sure how old I am, but I've always looked after him – an' this place when he's not here." Holding the mug between her palms and without taking a sip, she raised her eyes without raising her head. "An' doing those other things he wanted."

Russell did not reply but tasted the coffee. It was sweet and weak but the brandy was welcome. "What happens now he's gone?" he asked gently.

Maggie put her mug onto the table, kept her hands around it, and shrugged. "You tell me. I don't know. And no one's telling us anything. Mr Parr took care of us, and I looked after him. I've no family, unless you call Lucy family. He found her on the streets too, begging, a couple of years ago. He gave her to me to look after." She pointed to the beds under the grimy window. "We share this room."

She looked at Russell. "An agent, Mr Cummins, he's been here. Posh snob he was." She couldn't hide her disgust. "Didn't want to talk to us. Wouldn't say anything. Just wanted to make a list of everything. Said he was looking for a buyer on behalf of Mr Parr's brother, who would decide if they wanted us.

Otherwise, we'll be out on the streets again. And after everything I did for Mr Parr."

Russell assumed that would be same agent George at The Waterloo had mentioned.

Did you know anything about his inn in Aldershot?"

She shook her head. "Not really. He's owned it a few years now. Not as long as he has this place. I know it's called The Waterloo, and a man called George helps run it, but I've never been there, Mr Parr said he would show me one day, but never did."

Russell briefly wondered if she could be lying but dismissed that thought quickly. It was obvious she knew nothing about Parr's business in Aldershot, or the people there. She lived on promises here and this was the place she ran for Parr. Russell decided to come closer to home.

"You know a man called Colonel Sir Frederick Standish?"

Maggie lifted her mug and sipped her coffee. She stared at Russell over the cracked rim. "What's that got to do with anything?"

"I was told he kept rooms here. I assumed you knew him."

"He rents rooms here. Yes, I know Freddie, but haven't seen him in a while. Gone to the country, I think. What's he got to do with Mr Parr's death?"

So, Maggie knew nothing about Standish's death. Initially Russell was surprised, but then he thought about it. How could she know? With Parr dead, nobody would have told her and there was no visible connection between Parr's death and the robbery. Other, of course, than how close both incidents had been. Unless she was involved, there was no reason for her to know, and from her answer Russell surmised she was not involved.

"I am afraid, Maggie, he is also dead. He was murdered, during a robbery, shortly after Mr Parr's death. I was wondering if the two deaths were connected."

"Oh." Maggie's hand shot to her St Christopher and she almost spilled her coffee. She twisted the chain between her fingers. When she had regained her composure, she looked deep into her coffee, as if she were staring into a crystal ball, then eventually took another drink. She put her mug down before she replied, initially with affection. "Poor Freddie, he was fond of me also." Then she shook her head as if to rid herself of any feeling. "But he *was* getting on," she concluded.

"Did you know him well?"

She looked at Russell, calculating. "You know about me and Freddie?"

Russell nodded. "But I would like you to tell me."

She shrugged. "It was my job," she said simply, as if excusing her knowing Standish. "Mr Parr looked after me and told me I had to look after his special customers."

"And that involved Sir Frederick?"

"Freddie was his best customer when he stayed here, yes. I would move into the two rooms he kept here." She waited, as if expecting Russell to say something.

Russell just lifted his mug and took a drink before speaking. "Was he friends with Parr?"

"Not friends exactly, they came from… different backgrounds. It was more like Mr Parr worked for Freddie. But then Mr Parr liked it that way. As long as Freddie was paying for rooms, even if he was not staying there, it suited Mr Parr. Especially if he could rent his bedroom out again when Freddie was not sleeping here."

"Did they do any business together?"

"Sure, they did. I know Mr Parr borrowed money off Freddie. He complained about having to pay him back. Freddie was very rich, you know." She fingered the St Christopher again. "Freddie brought me this. It's the only time anyone has brought me anything." She looked up quickly, as if just having remembered something. "I think he helped Mr Parr build The Waterloo, or lent him the money to build it. As I said, paying him back made Mr Parr angry. He said if did not have to pay Freddie's interest charges, he could be making good money from his two places."

"He was still having to pay his loans back?"

"Oh, yes. Would be for years, he said." Russell thought about that as he took another sip of the cooling coffee.

"Maggie, did you meet any of Sir Frederick's friends?"

"Not really. When he was here, he did not have many visitors."

"Ever heard of a Sir John Treloar?"

"Oh, him. Yes, I've met him."

"When?"

"A few times. When they were both staying in London they came here together, for some fun. Treloar was usually drunk. Sometimes he had trouble walking. We would put him to bed in another room and leave him to sleep."

"This man has a son, Spencer Treloar. Did you ever meet him? Did he come here?"

"Don't recognise the name." She frowned. "Couple of times Mr Parr sent word to Sir John Treloar's house, in Chelsea I think. Usually after a very heavy drinking session and he could not be roused. A coachman would collect him but, now I think about it, a young man in uniform came with the coachman a couple of times." She shook her head. "I never spoke to him. He usually talked to Mr Parr."

"Did he?" Russell was interested. He wondered: could this man be Spencer?

Although they talked a little more about Parr and the inn, how there was less long-distance carriage trade now and how most money came from the regulars and men working in and around the river and docks, Maggie could offer little more information. When Russell had no more questions, he finished his cold coffee and stood. He smiled at Maggie. "Could I see Standish's rooms?"

Maggie shrugged again "Don't see why not."

Russell followed her out to the hall, up a narrow staircase to a number of rooms on the third floor, all leading off a dark and narrow corridor. Standish's rooms were at the far end. She unlocked the door using a key she chose from a number on a chain around her waist and explained the first room would be his bedroom. She swung the door open. The room was clean and furnished with a large double bed, a wardrobe, a chest, a floral chair, chaise longue and side tables either side of the bed. A wide floral-patterned washbasin and matching water jug sat in the middle of the chest. A large rug lay at the bottom of the bed and a few books were piled on one of the bedside tables. A single window overlooked the courtyard, a wooden chest lay under the windowsill. Old oil lamps were scattered around the room. Russell walked to the wardrobe and looked inside. There was nothing. He turned to Maggie. "Did Standish leave any clothes here?"

She nodded and walked to the chest, where she bent and, using another key from those on the chain around her waist, unlocked the chest. She lifted up the lid. "When he was not here, we packed his belongings. I told you, Mr Parr said I could let out this room to travellers for single nights."

Russell went through the items in the chest – more books, clothing including shirt collars, two pairs of shoes, a dress shirt, satin dressing gown – but found nothing that would help him. He closed the lid and Maggie locked the chest.

After another look around, they turned to an adjoining room. Maggie unlocked door to the second room and let Russell precede her into a sitting room.

"This is the largest room in the building," Maggie said. "It was only rented out to Freddie Standish. No one else was allowed to use or rent it." It was clearly used as a lounge. Russell took in a large Chesterfield, oil lamps, another armchair, which matched the one in the bedroom, and a table with four chairs neatly set around it. The room was clean. A small empty fireplace was set into the side wall, and two clean windows overlooked the street. When Russell looked, he could see his hansom cab waiting, the horse enjoying something from a nosebag.

"What's through there?" Russell asked, pointing to a door in the side wall.

Maggie shook her head. "Freddie used that room for storage. It was always locked, even when Freddie stayed here. We had strict orders never to go in there. Only Mr Parr could go in."

"Do you have a key?"

Maggie looked at the bunch on her chain "One of these may fit, but I never tried. This room, we just kept clean." She walked to the door. "Suppose with both Mr Parr and Freddie gone, it doesn't matter much now." The first key she tried didn't work, nor did the second. The third, however, clicked open the lock. The door opened on to a narrow room, about six feet wide, nearly eighteen feet long. It was dusty and dark, low-ceilinged, with no windows and no other access other than the doorway in which they stood. At the far end stood a wardrobe. Russell walked to it and opened the door, the hinges squealed in complaint and the smell emitted was of damp. Inside hung a few clothes, including an overcoat and an old military uniform. A single oil lamp stood on the floor next to the wardrobe. When he looked, Russell noticed scratch marks, scraped lines that made their way across the wooden joists. He got down onto his knees for a closer look. He could see three rectangular areas where there was little dust and where the wooden joists were a subtly different colour. Russell looked at the differences and nodded. Three chests had sat next to each other with small spaces between them.

He looked back to the door where Maggie was standing quietly. She was in the entrance watching him. Something on the doorframe caught eyes. It was damaged: paint chips and flakes of bare wood were still hanging loose or on the floor.

"Three chests were stored here," Russell looked at Maggie. "And had been here for some time." He pointed to the lack of dust, then pointed to the doorframe. "That's the damaged they did when they were removed. I think recently."

Fright filled Maggie's features as she brushed loose hair behind her ears again. "Well, I don't know where they went. Honest. I've never been in here before. Didn't even show Mr Cummins this room, because Freddie rented it. He wanted to see it, but I told him it was rented." A coy smile slowly bent her lips. "I told 'im I didn't have a key." She raised her eyebrows.

Russell returned her smile and stood. He brushed his hands down his trousers to clear the dust from his uniform. "I'm not saying you did, Maggie. I think I know what happened to the chests. I just wish I knew where they are now." Russell looked back at the marks. He was positive this was where Standish kept his money. And Parr, who was trusted, would have known about them.

He walked back to the window. The Thames wasn't far, so the chests had probably been loaded onto a barge somewhere close by. Treloar and Oxley had not mentioned stopping to collect anything, and probably wouldn't confirm it if they were asked.

He smiled again at Maggie. "You have been very helpful, Maggie. More than you can imagine. Is there nothing else that you remember that was different or strange?"

Maggie shook her head but did not answer and did not move. Russell had the impression she wanted to say something. Her features were filled with concern. "Captain Russell, sir, can I ask you something?"

"Of course."

"You seem a nice man, not like many I have to be with." She looked around the room. "What do you think I should do? With Mr Parr gone."

"What do you mean, Maggie?"

She paused, looked about her again. Finally, her gaze returned to Russell, and she shrugged. "Don't really know." She walked over to the settee and sat on the edge. Russell followed and sat beside her.

"I'm really worried. With Mr Parr gone, I don't know what's going to happen. I've got nowhere else to go. If I have to leave, I've Lucy to look out for." She looked at Russell, wiped her eyes. "I suppose I would have to find another job." She looked at the floor, as if seeing through it to the bar below. "I know how to run an inn. Mr Parr trusted me and left me to run this place when he was away." She hesitated and pushed her finger into the fabric of the settee. Without looking up she continued. "This may sound daft, but I think..., I mean..., I've thought about going to the seaside and getting a job. Me and Lucy, I mean, start afresh. I've always thought it would be nice to work in a teashop, but if not, well, they have inns, don't they?" She looked up, and Russell could see her relief at his smile.

"Yes, they do." He smiled at her, amazed at both her resilience and the childish naivety of her dreams. "Not much happening now though, being winter, but I read that every year more people are visiting the seaside towns in the summer. I think you would be ideal at the seaside, Maggie. You and Lucy."

She returned his smile. "Do you really think so? I could do it, don't you think? I could take one of those ships down to Brighton, me and Lucy."

Russell laughed, then stopped as he saw her face change, get older, and she stared back at him. He would not be the one to tell her that the Thames did not go to Brighton. He took her hand, in comfort and apology. Her skin felt course and rough. "It would be better if you took the train. It goes all the way to Brighton. Do you have any money?"

Maggie studied him for a moment, then smiled again as she realised, he was not laughing at her. "A little. Not much. Mr Parr don't pay much. Says we get lodging for free. I've saved tips given to me, but that's not much. Taken a few years it has. I've kept it hidden, even from Mr Parr." She thought for a moment. "And I could sell this." With the hand that wasn't in Russell's, she held up the St Christopher. "I don't care. It was just a gift. Would that be enough?"

"Maybe. You will need to find lodgings whilst you look for a job, but anything will help for a while. Could you get any more?"

Maggie took her hand from Russell's, and looked down at the settee. Russell wondered if she was finally realising her thoughts were only dreams. The reality of her situation was in front of her: in London, in Battersea, in this old inn, in that room.

She shook her head. "I can't leave," she said simply. "What about this place? Mr Parr looked after me. Didn't always treat me well, but expected me to help run it for him, I'd be letting him down."

Russell stood and, placing his hands on her arms, encouraged up to her feet. "Mr Parr's not coming back Maggie. They are selling this place. You and Lucy could be out on the street next week, or even tomorrow. You have to look after yourself. You're sure you can't get any more money, perhaps borrow some?"

"Maybe." Her voice was filled with suspicion. It was clear to Russell that Maggie had learned at a very early age not to trust men, any men, but she was wondering whether he would be different.

Russell continued holding her arms, as gently as possible, and spoke softly, as an uncle would offer advice to a favourite niece. "Look, Maggie, you're thinking you don't know me, and wondering whether I can be trusted, I understand that after what you have told me, but you have helped me by answering my questions. If I can, I want to help you. I think you need it. No tricks, no false promises, no lies, no hidden motives, I just want to help." He repeated his question. "Can you find some more money?"

Maggie stared at him, indecision written across her features. "Captain Russell, what's a motive?"

Russell burst out laughing. "Maggie you're priceless."

Maggie waited, her forehead furrowed as she calculated. "Come with me," she said eventually, and left the room. Russell followed and waited while Maggie locked the door before hurrying back down one flight of stairs. He followed her back along the corridor; she turned left along a short hallway, halting before a heavy wooden door. The paint on it was old and cracked. She took a large black key from the bunch on her chain and unlocked the door. She motioned Russell to follow her inside, then closed the door behind them and locked it.

Shelves lined the walls and boxes covered most of the floor. A bureau and single chair stood on a threadbare rug. Russell could also see an oil lamp and a cabinet.

Maggie walked to the bureau and moved the chair from it. "This was Mr Parr's private office," she said, kneeling. She moved the rug, took a thin key from her chain and used it to prise up a section of floor, about a foot by six inches. She pulled up an adjoining piece of about the same size and slipped her hand and then, by stretching, her whole arm into the hole. She pulled out a black cash box. It had gold edging around the lid and was about the size of a church bible. She lifted it onto the bureau and opened it. It needed no key. She stepped back to show Russell its contents.

Russell stepped closer to the bureau. The tin held an old leather wallet, which was stuffed with notes. There was also a bulging brown leather pouch. "There's at least 200 guineas here. Mr Parr called it his 'Lucky Pot'. He always said if he was in trouble, he had this to fall back on. Mr Parr planned for everything."

Apart, Russell thought, from his own death.

Maggie looked up at Russell. "Only Mr Parr and me knew it were here, no one else. Now he's gone, should I…, I mean, what should I do with it? I thought, … I thought I should show that agent, Mr Cummins. He knew nothing about it and, anyway, he would not help me, so why should I help him. I didn't like him. I didn't trust him."

Russell stared at the cash.

Maggie spoke softly. 'You, I think I can trust.'

"You're sure only you and Mr Parr knew of this money? No one else? Not Lucy, those women in the kitchen? That man downstairs, Tom? Anyone else? You're sure?"

She nodded. "Only me. He told me that. That he trusted only me. He knew I wouldn't steal it. He said that if he ever sent message, I was to retrieve it, take it to him or send it to him straightaway."

Russell didn't hesitate. "Take it. Take it now. Pack your bags and leave. Mr Parr's got no use for it. Call it payment for all those years you looked after him."

Maggie's face went blank then, gradually, a smile appeared. "I hoped you would say that. I needed to hear it from someone." She leaned and kissed Russell on the cheek.

Embarrassed, Russell turned to move away but Maggie took hold of his arm. "You asked if anything else happened that I thought strange. Well, there was one other thing, Captain. I don't know if it will help, but some time ago Mr Parr told me to be especially nice to Freddie, to keep telling Freddie that Mr Parr was his friend, and he could trust him and should take his advice." She laughed. "That was a joke. Freddie was Mr Parr's friend only whilst he could use him."

"Do you know why Mr Parr should have wanted this?"

"No. He would not say anything else. Just told me what to do. He wanted Freddie to believe that anything Mr Parr told him was to Freddie's benefit." She looked back at the contents of the tin. "Then, just before his last visit to Aldershot, Mr Parr was excited and told me he was making plans, that he had some good partners in a new venture, which would soon be completed. Then, one day, not long ago, he sent me and Lucy away for the day. Gave Tom the day off and actually closed the inn. Didn't say why, just said don't come back till very late. Never done that before. And that's all he would say. Does any of this help you?"

"Thank you, Maggie. Yes, it does help. I think that was when those chests were moved. What I have seen and what you have told me answers a lot of questions. Unfortunately, it does not get me any closer to solving my problem." He touched her arm. "But what about you? Are you leaving?"

"I don't know. I will have to think it over."

"Why?" Russell was amazed. "What's stopping you from leaving now?"

She looked surprised. "You mean leave, *now*?"

"Why not? What's to keep you here? With that money," he pointed to the tin, "you could rent a tea shop, perhaps even try to buy one, let alone work in one."

Her eyes widened with understanding. "I could, couldn't I. Mr Parr, he taught me to read and write and I can count. He said I was good with figures. Nobody runs this place like me. I could do it for me and Lucy, couldn't I?"

"You could. And now is the time to look. It's winter, so you could have a place ready for the summer."

"But where would we stay, how would we get there?"

"I have a hansom waiting outside. Leave now with me. I'll take you and Lucy to the station; help you buy your tickets. Once in Brighton you could find a small hotel or inn until you find something permanent, perhaps with rooms over the shop."

Maggie stood there, her mouth open, staring and thinking. Eventually, she smiled at Russell and made for the door only stopping and turning when Russell called her name. He pointed to the tin and the hole in the floor, Maggie's hand flew to her mouth 'Oh, Lord," she cried, then glanced at Russell, embarrassed. Quickly, and with Russell's help, she replaced the floor, rug and chair. Picking up the tin and pouch, she made for the door.

"Let me hold the money. Maggie."

She stopped and stared at Russell, eyes narrowed, suspicion written deeply into her features.

He smiled and nodded, aiming for reassurance. "You're right, Maggie. Don't trust anyone. But I want to help, and you don't want everyone seeing you with all that money, do you?"

She looked from Russell to the tin and back again, several times. Finally, she nodded passed over the tin and pouch. She watched closely as Russell put them into pocket. "You will look after it all for me? Please."

She unlocked the door and relocked it after they'd left the

room, and then, once in the corridor, she screamed Lucy's name. Russell winced and Lucy came running up the stairs from the bar. Maggie held her face tightly. "Quick, get all your things and come with me. Put your coat and scarf on. It's cold, we're leaving."

Lucy looked first at Maggie then at Russell, confused. "Are we going with him?"

"No, we are going on our own. He is helping us. We're getting away, you and me, together. Now. Come on, quick." They ran downstairs to their room.

While they were busy, Russell retrieved his overcoat, hat and valise, into which he placed Maggie's money. Walking back into the bar, putting his cap and overcoat back on, his thoughts span. Doing the buttons up, he wondered whether he had the right to give such advice to Maggie. Was he right in helping her to run off to Brighton, or to anywhere else? To steal the money? But she had asked him, and where else could she go? She was on her own now. Despite her childish dreams, she was tough, he was sure of that. And with Parr's money she and Lucy could live a better life. He just wanted to help her. He thought of his own family, and hoped someone would do the same if he wasn't around. He could not change what had happened: Parr was dead, and Maggie and the girl had a chance to make their lives better. A decision had been made to suit the situation. Russell had always believed that stealing was wrong, but here were these poor girls about to be sold with the building, or worse. What was the greater sin? His thoughts were interrupted by Maggie and Lucy reappearing, each carrying their few belongings in a bundle wrapped in a woollen blanket, knotted with string. He recognised the well-worn linen from their beds.

Maggie smiled excitedly at Russell who smiled back, trying not to show his doubts. He walked with them to the door. A shout came from behind the bar. They turned to see Tom, still holding a bar towel, running to them. "Maggie where are you going?"

"We're leaving, Tom."

"You can't. You run this place. Who's going to look after it?"

Maggie unclipped the chain of keys from around her waist and handed them him. "You're looking after it now, Tom. Till it's sold."

Tom stared in amazement at the three of them. "Where are you going?"

Maggie smiled. "To the seaside." She turned and strode out of the inn, quickly followed by Lucy, who almost ran, scared she might be forgotten. Russell looked at poor Tom, standing open-mouthed, confused. He shrugged, wished Tom good luck, then turned and followed the two women out into the cold, bleak, busy city.

Chapter 8

The rain hammered on the carriage window as if demanding to be let in. Despite the deluge, the train wasn't slowed on its journey back to London from Cheltenham. However, as Russell thought about the past few days, he concluded the atmosphere inside the carriage was as miserable as that outside. His visit to Cheltenham had been both the furthest and possibly least productive of all his trips. After his visit to London, he had felt confident in his ideas, but now he had to put all the pieces together to see if they solved his problem. He believed he knew what had happened, and how and why, but was irritated that he was no closer to finding the money. And without finding Standish's fortune little could actually be proved.

Russell had spent some time with Lieutenant Norton's father. The man was sincerely distraught about the disappearance of his son and even more concerned at the implication of his involvement in the robbery. He willingly answered all Russell's questions, confirming he had not seen or heard from his son in the weeks since the robbery. He was eager to assist Russell to correct the implication of his son's involvement in any crime. All his family, he said, including his two other sons, would answer any questions Russell asked: he wanted his son's name cleared, which Russell had to admit was difficult as the lieutenant could not be found, alive or dead. All the family had seemed very cooperative and even put him up for couple of nights, but they could add little to what he already knew. Norton had been returning to the camp after a visit to his family, had stopped off at Weybridge to deliver some letters regarding farming business for his father, and then, for some unknown reason, decided to continue the journey to the camp along the canal. The Nortons could add nothing more. To Russell, they looked like good people, not rich but not poor. They appeared to have a good farm, not long in their ownership, and which the father and his eldest son worked hard to run, along with the help of the youngest child and a few other workers. Russell got the impression that the father knew his business very well and, over time, would do well. None of them appeared to have any connection with any of those involved with the robbery, and Russell could only accept the reasons already given for why Norton, a junior officer in the same company as Spencer Treloar, Captain Farrant and the escort was on the barge. Russell stared through the rain-splattered train window, not seeing the grey flooded countryside, as the train continued through downpour.

To raise his spirits, he thought back to a few days ago, after he had left the 'Three Feathers' and his plans had changed. The memory made him smile. His original intention had been to continue on to an inn in Praed Street, near Paddington Station and from there to catch the train the following morning to Cheltenham. Instead, the three of them – Maggie who could not stop grinning, Lucy and himself – had been squashed together in his hansom, each holding their own luggage on their laps, a large blanket spread over their legs for warmth. Lucy had been bubbling with excitement, traveling in a hansom for the first time, and annoying her fellow passengers as she leaned over both, moving from one side to the other side desperate to see everything and miss nothing. At first, the cabbie had objected to taking three, even though Lucy was a child, but Russell's guarantee of a large tip convinced him.

Receiving his instruction, the cabbie travelled towards Lambeth where they made one stop at a shop that sold luggage. After some haggling by Maggie, which impressed Russell, she purchased a large suitcase with straps and with leather reinforcements on the corners, to take both her and Lucy's bundles. She also bought a lady's drawstring pouch, to hold the contents of the tin box. The box itself was going to be 'lost' at the first opportunity. She completed the purchase whilst Russell went to a confectioner he had noticed along the street. He bought a small selection of toffees and pear drops in a cone, hoping these would keep Lucy still for the remainder of the journey.

They crossed Westminster Bridge amongst busy traffic, the horse trotting effortlessly, following the many, many other cabs, and they made their way through the busy London thoroughfares to Victoria Street and the railway station there. Russell, now with Lucy sitting munching away on her treats, was enjoying the journey. Feeling like jovial uncle – a role he was not used to, despite having three children – he asked the cabbie to pass Buckingham Palace, which Lucy stared in amazement as if seeing a magic castle.

"Just the Queen and her children live in that big house? How do they find each other?"

"Idiot," answered Maggie, wondering that herself, but upon hearing Russell's laugh and seeing his grin, realised that Lucy's comment contained something humorous and she did not want to be associated with it, whatever it was.

They wound their way through the busy afternoon traffic, stopping occasionally as their route was blocked by wagons, either stopping at the side of the road or travelling slowly due to their precarious loads. They manoeuvred their way around omnibuses when they stopped to disgorge and collect passengers.

They rode up Victoria Street, passing the station which they all stared at, marvelling at all the people heading for their trains.

"That will be you and me tomorrow, Lucy," said Maggie, smiling happily. Lucy's hand once more rummaged in the paper cone, only for the young girl to let out an 'oh' of disappointment when she looked down into the cone and realised the sweets were all gone. The cab pulled to the edge of the pavement outside an inn, a short distance beyond the station. Russell had asked the cabbie if he could recommend somewhere both clean and safe, where they could stay the night and get a good meal.

He knew just the place, the cabbie claimed, adding that it was friendly and quiet, despite its proximity to the station, and had clean sheets. On arrival the cabbie insisted he would speak to the owner first, just to check it was not full. He returned with a big broad smile.

"All sorted, sir". He eased the blanket off their knees, allowing a cold blast to chill their legs. "Two rooms at the back, nice and quiet."

The cabbie licked his lips: for him this had been a good fare. First Waterloo to Battersea, where he had to wait, adding to the fare, then back to Victoria with a stop, and a good tip promised. Then he had also just got some commission from the innkeeper for bringing him new customers. And, he thought, it was only mid-afternoon; he may be able to pick up another fare at the station. Yes, a good day's work.

Russell settled up with the cabbie, giving the man what he

thought was fair including a tip. The cabbie continued holding out his hand, looking from the coins in his palm to Russell and back again. After Russell dropped a few extra coins into the man's hand, the cabbie touched the front of his head in gesture of thanks, climbed aboard his cab disappeared towards the station.

The rooms were, as promised, next to each other and clean, although not as quiet as Russell had expected. Despite being at the back of the inn they could still hear the traffic. When he pointed this out to Maggie, she laughed. "You call this noisy? It's wonderful. It's London." Lucy was running around the room opening and closing drawers and wardrobe doors as if she'd never seen them before.

That evening, they met for dinner in the bar, sitting at a reserved corner table where they enjoyed a meal of meat, potatoes and cabbage, with jug of ale. They were still dressed in the same clothes, and Maggie asked if she looked acceptable, as they had little else to wear. She had tied up her hair with a white ribbon instead of the black one she had worn all day. Russell assured her that she looked fine, and she smiled. He was enjoying the atmosphere and whilst some ten or so years older than Maggie was feeling some fatherly affection for her. He understood how Standish and Parr had become fond of her; she was a strong lady who had not got her share of the breaks in life.

Maggie enjoyed two tankards of ale and Russell allowed himself a small glass, celebrating their freedom. Lucy was also allowed a small glass and received a clip around the head when Maggie caught her trying to pour another. Whilst Lucy enjoyed both her and Russell's apple pies, Russell having decided he had eaten enough, Russell and Maggie talked quietly. Russell had come up with a plan for when the two women arrived in Brighton, to explain why they were there and why they had such a large quantity of cash.

"Keep it simple, Maggie," Russell advised. "Don't make it complicated. Simple, effective and difficult to question." It occurred to Russell that what he was saying was just like the robbery: simple, effective and difficult to question.

"Captain Russell," Maggie broke into his thoughts as she finished her own pie. "Can I go over our story again? I want to be sure I've got it."

Russell nodded, a glazed expression on his face; he was still thinking how well planned that robbery had been.

"I was left a small sum of money, when my old employer – I was his housekeeper – moved to live in Italy or France for his health. I'm not sure where, and he didn't leave a forwarding address. With my cousin, Lucy, who lived with me after her parents died, we decided to move here, with my money, to start again. Perhaps even start a small business, if possible, a tea shop maybe, or something similar." Maggie smiled. "And I have your details, Captain, should anyone be in need of a reference."

"Once you have a bank account, ask if the manager can help you find suitable premises to invest in. If he thinks you may add to his banking business it will help get him on your side, and he will ask fewer questions."

Maggie's smile grew. "I cannot believe how things have changed, Captain Russell." She was sitting upright, already enjoying her new status.

Russell returned the smile. "As long as you keep up the pretence, it will go well." The word 'pretence' snagged in Russell's mind, and again his thoughts returned to the robbery.

His expression showed he was now some distance from their conversation, as if he had spotted someone he had not seen for some time entering the bar. That's what it all was, he thought, the escape of Treloar and Oxley: pretence.

"I will write you Captain, tell you how we are doing."

"No." Returning his attention to Maggie, his reply was firm. Maggie looked disappointed and hurt, as if he'd gone to slap her. Even Lucy stopped eating, and stared at Russell.

"I'm sorry, Maggie, I spoke harshly. I would have loved that really." He was trying hard to express his sincerity. "But I visited the Waterloo before coming to you. They will know me and I was seen leaving with you. If anybody tries to find you, to find the money you took, and I am ever asked about your exact whereabouts," he shook his head, "I can't know."

Maggie listened, hearing her Captain Russell ending a friendship that hadn't even got started. She had begun to look on him as a guide, a mentor, perhaps even more and now he was cutting her loose. Another typical man. Russell saw the hurt in her eyes and leaned across the table, taking her hand.

"Maggie," he spoke quietly so only the two women could hear. Lucy was looking at the two entwined hands of her new friends. "I promised you no tricks, no lies, and to be honest. As much as I am beginning to want to help more, I can't. You know that. For your own safety. We have to distance ourselves forever. This has to be just you and Lucy."

As he spoke Russell was also feeling the hurt, but he was a realist. He had a job, a wife, children, a career. "If I'm ever asked, I can lie about knowing you went to Brighton. I can say I left you at a different station, but would be impossible if someone knew I were communicating and knew your address. If someone found letters from you." His smile covered his sorrow. He really did want to know how Maggie and Lucy got on, but at the moment it was too much of a risk. Maybe in a few years. When he and his wife were retired, possibly, they could travel to Brighton and visit some tea rooms.

"There is the possibility, after all, I might come looking for you." He blushed.

Maggie squeezed his hand in assurance and understanding before taking it away, aware Lucy was still looking. "And no," she thought for a moment, searching for the right word, "mo… tives." She laughed.

Russell also burst out laughing. It was to be a short friendship, and would end soon, but he wished he could hug her. "No. No other motives."

Lucy looked at them both as they laughed, wondering what they were talking about.

The following morning they met for a breakfast of ham, bread and coffee. Russell said nothing as Maggie and Lucy hid some of the bread and ham for their journey.

Russell settled the bill for both rooms while Maggie and Lucy collected their possessions. They walked together to Victoria Station, where Russell helped the two women buy tickets to Brighton. Maggie was still grinning as they walked along the platform. "We look like proper travellers with my bag and suitcase," she said, swinging the case as if showing off.

He saw them onto the train and managed to find a carriage with only one other couple, and they were old enough to be their grandparents. He put their bags on the racks, left the carriage and stood on the platform until Maggie opened the window.

"Now, you have your purse," he spoke quietly so the couple

could not hear. "Keep it safe and don't trust anybody. Put the money into a bank as soon as you arrive."

Maggie nodded. Russell's hand was on the edge of the open window and Maggie placed her hand on his. "Thank you, Captain Russell. It's so frightening, I would not have dared done all this without your help."

"You take care, and good luck. If anyone asks about the money, you tell them what we agreed, right?"

She nodded: they had gone over this story again and again in Maggie and Lucy's room last night, as the flames from two gas lamps cast flickering shadows. Lucy had dozed off during the conversations, but they had already explained to her why they were concocting this story, that it was important she understood, that it was to ensure they had a good new life.

Somewhere in the station, louder than the calls and clatter of departing and arriving travellers, a train sounded its whistle and Russell looked over his shoulder. The air felt full of smoke and soot.

"And you have my name and address, should anyone want a reference."

"I have, and will always keep it," Maggie smiled. "Even if it is never used, I have something of you, a sort of thank you."

Russell didn't answer, surprised at the gesture, and the new-found fondness he felt for Maggie.

She turned his hand over and placed a small, folded piece of paper into his palm. He could feel something through the paper and he closed his hand, gripping whatever it was.

"Now, don't open it until we are out of sight, and don't you worry about us." She turned to Lucy, who was looking out the window opposite. "I think our luck has just changed." She leaned forward as much as she could and kissed Russell tenderly on the lips, then pulled away, almost falling back in the carriage.

"It's nice to think some good has come out of all of this," Russell said.

Maggie whispered, "Even if it meant stealing Parr's money." She laughed as a loud whistle from their engine made Lucy jump.

Russell stared at Maggie, her head still out of the window. Their eyes fixed on each other's as the train – with a couple of false starts and shunts and clunking and clanking – slowly began pulling away. Still holding his own valise, he followed the carriage, keeping up with its slow speed, both he and Maggie looking at each other as if there was more to say. He thought he probably looked ridiculous but, like a rejected lover, was unable to stop what he was doing. Tears were now rolling down Maggie's cheeks as the train increased its speed, and he halted, unable to keep pace with the carriage. He waved as he saw her mouth the words: 'thank you'.

Russell stood on the platform until the Brighton train was out of sight. All the noises and motion and hustle and bustle around him were nothing and he felt an overwhelming feeling of loss, as if he'd experienced a bereavement. His eyes went to his hand, feeling the folded paper there. Putting his valise down, he carefully unfolded the paper.

His hands shook as he found the silver St Christopher. It was the one item Maggie had received as a gift, a link to her past life, a life she was leaving. He remembered that, despite her once desperate need for cash, she had decided not to sell it. His throat tightened, as did his fingers around the silver disc and chain. He recalled what he had said to Maggie about something good coming out of Parr's death, and he wondered what good was coming from the robbery and Parr's involvement; nothing.

The stolen money's origins were suspect, its uses had been for a select few, and its existence had been the cause of further harm, due to simple greed.

He found himself despising those he believed benefited from the wealth: its original owner, whose avarice had amassed it, those desperate for its recovery, and those he believed had stolen it. He wished he had never got involved with this investigation. Angry, like a man with a score to settle, he marched from the station, hailed another hansom cab, yelling as if it was all the cabbie's fault, and rode in tight-lipped silence to Paddington Station to catch the train to Cheltenham. This cabbie didn't receive such a generous tip.

* * *

A strong gust of wind hammered the rain harder against the window and shook the carriage. The noise and movement, like a slap, brought his thoughts to the present and his current journey from Cheltenham back to London. During his time in Cheltenham he had mostly managed to block thoughts of Maggie. It had been difficult, but he knew the reality of his world. Besides, the contentment he felt knowing Maggie was strong and making a new life helped. And, of course, hidden by his clothing, around his neck hung a silver St Christopher.

Taking his pad and pencil from his valise, he referred to his notes and began writing. First, who was involved? That, he thought, was very clear: Treloar, Parr and Price. They all knew each other and planned everything. Parr and Treloar had both known of Standish's wealth. Price could have been brought in by Parr.

The thought of Parr resurrected the thought of Maggie and Standish. Was that relationship an important part of the crime? He thought not. He looked up at the passenger sitting opposite him, who was reading *A Tale of Two Cities*, by Charles Dickens. Russell had read and enjoyed the book, a story about individuals and forms of resurrection. Maggie, he thought, had been resurrected to a new life and he wasn't going to make that life any more difficult by involving her. He would not mention her or her relationship with Standish in his report. Let sleeping dogs lie.

Russell returned to his notes just as he felt the train slow. It shuddered to a halt in a station and he watched as passengers came and went. A porter manhandled a large case onto a trolley followed by a well-dressed man and lady. No one left his carriage. He heard a loud piercing whistle from the train as it started moving again, slowly building up speed.

The next question, of course, was 'why'. He started writing again. Treloar's family was in great debt, needing money for the estate and, obviously, for Treloar's own future. Parr was in debt to Standish and perhaps others, so the demise of Standish as well as obtaining a cut of his fortune would solve his problems. As for Price, this would be an opportunity for him to get his hands on easy money.

Price was a man who obviously liked a little extra. George at the inn had told him Price got a cut from his deals with Parr, plus he obviously got a cut from managing that boxer, Ox. His cut from this escapade would be more than he could have imagined. Now came the 'how'. Russell knew this was all assumption but was convinced he had it right, so he carried on writing. Sir John's Treloar's friendship with Standish was a factor in the choice of his son Spencer's selection for the escort. In turn, Spencer had proposed Farrant, as a senior officer from his company, to command the escort – another move to shift any blame, he supposed. He also guessed guess that it was Treloar who selected the escort, probably with the help of Price, an escort that included the man Oxley, known as Ox.

He pondered whether his dislike for Price was equal to his dislike for Treloar. They were either end of the social scale, but both greedy violent human beings.

The man opposite had put down his book and was staring out the window. Russell looked in the same direction as the other passenger, viewing the scenery through the smoke from the locomotive's chimney. After a while, he returned to his notes.

Parr was the only one outside the military who travelled between London and Aldershot. Therefore, Russell concluded, Parr would be used to move the chests from the area. But why had he died? Unless it had been an event that they had not planned? But Parr's death was too much of a coincidence. Everything else was too well planned. Somehow Parr's death had to fit in. But how? Russell did not know. Lieutenant Norton's involvement was also a mystery. The 'when' was the easy question; as was the 'where' – the location was the isolated canal. The ideal place. Somehow, the villains had overpowered those on the barge, including Norton and Farrant. Probably Price had a few others on the towpath, but Russell was unsure of that.

It appeared from the number of survivors that the fewer involved in the robbery the better. Once the crew had been overpowered, the chests had been transferred to the wagon Price had hired, despite his denials, and which he probably drove. They moved the chests to their new hiding place and that was that. Treloar and the other so-called survivor returned to the camp, and Price returned the wagon, planting some of the coins.

Another gust of wind lashed rain against the window and the carriage rocked as it clattered over points. The movement stopped Russell writing and he stared through the glass. Instead of seeing the waterlogged landscape, he was thinking about the bodies of Standish and Farrant, which had been found on the barge, unlike those of the other men. And then there were the questions of where the bargee, his son and Lieutenant Norton went, and why Parr had died. Perhaps he would never know, and, of course, he still had to find the chests. And that was the final problem. This question, no matter how hard he tried, seemed unanswerable. He had suspicions: the chests had to be close to the canal because of the timing and the weight. They were not at the farm – that had been searched thoroughly – the village he discounted after his talk with the reverend, so that left somewhere out in the fields, they could be anywhere. And how do you dig a hole that will take three or more chests? And that's without the possibility of a farm worker stumbling upon the cache.

They had planned too well to allow that to happen. His best guess was it was hidden somewhere on the Treloar estate. But it was all supposition, with no real evidence or proof and, without much higher authority, he could not start searching on Treloar land. He decided that's how he would present it, needing more time to question the Treloar family. He felt confident he could find the chests if he were given more time and increased authority. He closed his notebook and wondered how his suggestions would go down with his superiors. He was, after all, proposing a deliberate conspiracy by men from the camp, including an officer, to murder and steal for personal gain. The repercussions could be far-reaching, but that was for someone else to decide. He closed his eyes. The carriage rattled and shook again.

He would press on to find the truth. Of that, he was sure.

Chapter 9

The office smelt musty, like old curtains. Although only early afternoon, the light outside was fading and so oil lamps had been lit. They were placed around the room and down the middle of the small conference table. Those lamps on the filing cabinets around the edge of the room just about illuminated the walls, on which were hung maps, mainly of the camp, and a few paintings of military campaigns. Large regimental flags, their poles crossed, hung on one wall; on the opposite wall were crossed Union flags. Taking up the entire length of one wall were rows and rows of pigeonholes, most filled with letters and files and rolls of writing paper tied with black calico ribbon. All the furniture was made from dark wood, which looked black in the lamp light.

Christmas had come and gone, and a new year started. Outside, a covering of new snow lay atop the previous day's dusting. Another icy evening threatened. Inside the office, a fire kept the room warm, its coals occasionally replenished by soldiers. However, although it had been a roaring fire when the meeting had started, now just a red glow remained.

General Briggs, commander of the East section of the camp, sat in silence at the head of the highly polished conference table; two other officers also sat at the table. They were all staring at Captain Russell, who was standing to attention by his chair. Briggs thought Russell's report was one of the best he had ever encountered, which didn't help his mood. Needing to contemplate the report's conclusions without its author standing over him, he asked Russell to wait outside.

"General," Russell said, "if I could reiterate my belief that I should continue the investigation. I am sure with your authority we can find the culprits and bring this incident to a satisfactory conclusion."

The general placed his hand on the report, his tone dismissive and angry. "Thank you, Captain. You have made that abundantly clear. Now, if you would please leave us." Russell saluted, turned and marched out the office.

Once the door had shut, General Briggs returned his attention to the open report before him. To one side of it was his fountain pen, a glass inkwell and a sheet of paper on which he had neatly written a number of questions. Whilst Russell had given his long and comprehensive report to the officers in the room, each question – as it was answered thoroughly and decisively by Russell – had been crossed through. And with each strike of the pen the general's anger had grown.

The two other officers in the room sat on opposite sides of the table and waited. Occasionally they glanced at each other, but they remained silent. Both held lit cigars.

Colonel Jefferis, a small man in his late forties, round of faced and round of body, was the aide of the general. His appealing feature to Briggs was that he always agreed with his commanding officer, a fact that had contributed to Jefferis achieving his current position. A cord attached to Jefferis' uniform led to a monocle. Jefferis took the monocle from his eye and started to polish it using a clean handkerchief. He kept his attention on the glass lens, not wanting to make eye contact with the general. He had seen Briggs in this mood before. He glanced at the third member of the party, Colonel Hendrie, and envied the man's confidence and the fact he was taller and younger than most of the same rank. He had also seen more action in his career. When he thought the monocle looked spotless, and he could not decently spend more time on the cleaning, he replaced it in his right eye.

Colonel Hendrie, immaculately dressed, was broad shouldered but still thinner than the general's aide. Even sitting he gave the impression of being a tall man. He may have been younger than Jefferis but his hair was thinning, the remaining strands being silver. Unlike Jefferis, he was watching the general; he was not so intimidated. He was Colonel of the Battalion of which the East Hants Light Infantry was part, so he was both Major Bradshaw's and Russell's superior officer, and he represented the company from which the escort for Sir Frederick Standish had been chosen. Bradshaw should also have been present at this meeting, but aware Russell had found neither the gang nor the money and only had suppositions, he was certain more questions would be asked which he could not answer and so had decided to find some other business which required his attention.

The general looked out of the clean, clear window into the courtyard. He could see Russell pacing up and down, making new footprints in the fresh snow, clearly occupied with his own thoughts and unaware he was being watched. The general was acutely aware Russell was now awaiting their decision as to what to do next. Russell had made it very clear, had repeated himself, he wanted to continue investigating and even widen his brief. He had also stated his own opinion as to whom he thought was involved – hence General Briggs' anger. What Russell was suggesting was monstrous. Briggs personally knew John Treloar well. They had had fought together during the Crimea War. The effects of the accusations would be catastrophic, not only to those Russell was implicating but also to others, who were closer, as well as to the battalion and the general's command. It could even be damaging to the general personally; without answers or a favourable conclusion this whole dreadful, bloody business could end his career. No, this had to be handled with great care and the minimum of fuss, especially if what Russell was suggesting was true – that it was an inside and well-planned robbery involving respected officers linked to this very camp, officers with good and respected military and family backgrounds. And enlisted men were also implicated.

General Briggs let out a loud sigh. He knew all the officers had heard rumours about Standish, his dealings and the origins of his wealth. In fact, if the general was honest, he knew most were more than rumours, they were fact. Yes, Briggs thought, Standish had always been discreet, had never brought shame or embarrassment to his office. The general knew of others who had lined their pockets in much the same way, although not so profitably (for he had heard Standish's wealth was substantial) so, because of Standish's discretion, he, like others, had chosen to look the other way. After all, to bring attention to the problem would mean more embarrassment. Also, other than hearsay, there really was no real proof, not *real* proof, and Standish's wealth did not affect Briggs directly. So he, General Briggs, was not going to be the one to question the origins of Standish's money. No, *he* would concentrate on the real problem. And the real problem was what to do next.

Russell had no firm evidence, not really, only suspicions. He had caught no villains, had only suspects. Most importantly, he had not found any money. The general felt his anger burn hotter.

There was a tap on the door. Jefferis called, "Come In," and a young soldier, no older than sixteen, opened the door. He wore an apron that was dirty from coal dust. "Can I check the fire sir?" He stepped into the room.

"Get out!" roared the general, his face taut.

Jefferis swung round to face his superior, his monocle dropping from his eye. Swiftly, the soldier backed out, closing the door behind him.

The general picked up the sheet of paper on which he had written his questions, and slowly screwed it up. The ruddiness in his face slowly faded as he calmed. He stared at each of the two officers in turn.

"Well, gentlemen," he said. "You've read and heard Russell's report, what are we going to do?"

Jefferis spoke first, believing the screwed ball of paper indicated his superior's thoughts. "Well, I think Captain Russell's findings are outrageous," he said smugly. "And so, we should ignore his findings."

"Don't be bloody ridiculous, Edward," snapped his superior officer, louder than necessary. "Captain Russell has written and just presented one of the best reports I have ever heard. Detailed, precise and, in places, it makes sense. In other circumstances, I would be recommending Russell for promotion." His eyes focused on Colonel Hendrie. "Perhaps replacing that sheep of an officer called Bradshaw."

Hendrie didn't reply.

"But these circumstances are very particular." The general returned his gaze to his aide, and held up the crumpled paper. "We can't just ignore this."

"I agree, sir." Hendrie spoke quietly, as if someone else was in the room and he did not want them to hear. "It could be – shall we say – embarrassing, for… well, everyone."

"Exactly, William. *You*, at least, see the real problem."

Jefferis looked at his fellow officer, not understanding the 'real problem'. He could feel his skin burning with embarrassment at having been slapped down in front of this colleague. He resolved to remain quiet until spoken to.

The general continued, sounding exasperated. "Edward, the main problem we have is: what do we do to bring this unhappy incident to a swift conclusion? We can't change anything. What's happened has happened, and," he pointed to Russell through the window, "letting him continue investigating, even though perhaps he should, will only keep the wound open. Allowing him to unearth more embarrassment could be damaging to everyone here."

Colonel Jefferis glanced at both men, his monocle tightly clenched in his eye. He understood the word embarrassment.

Briggs glared at the two men. "The very idea that enlisted men conspired with officers for gain, through this 'incident'. Good God, it's inconceivable. We have to think of the camp, the company, regiment, battalion and, gentlemen," he nodded, "ourselves."

Edward Jefferis sat straighter; he was beginning to realise how serious this was.

"Again, I agree, sir." William Hendrie's voice was still quiet. "Until now, I did not realise how much Russell was hell bent on getting to the truth, regardless of what that may be, or who it harms. Allowing him to keep looking could lead to even more complications."

"Exactly, William, exactly." Once again, the general looked out of the window.

The aide looked also followed his gaze, but his angle of view restricted him from seeing Russell. "I agree also."

"I do have one suggestion, sir," Hendrie said. Even though his voice was a little louder, Jefferis still leaned forward to hear, not wanting to miss a possible solution.

The general stared at Hendrie. "Speak up, William. Speak up. Any suggestion would be welcome if it helps matters. Agreed, Edward?"

Jefferis nodded; it felt prudent to flatter the general's ego more than necessary.

William Hendrie hesitated, the suggestion he was about to air had been made to him very recently, although he had been surprised at both the suggestion and its contributor. "It could fit quite well, sir,' he continued, still not raising his voice. 'Sir, all the men involved are, and always will be, under suspicion in their own units, that suspicion will be a constant itch in any company, a nagging wasp sting, irritating and harming morale. Therefore, I would suggest we give serious consideration in taking action to move them, reassigning them."

There was a nod of agreement from the general, which was quickly followed by his aide.

"You mean," said the general, "transfer them out of their company? I was thinking this myself. We should move them to another company, in another battalion, away from Aldershot."

"And, ah, out of the country, sir. *Out of the country.*" He repeated the words slowly, to make sure they understood his meaning.

"Out of the country?" Jefferis couldn't hide his surprise.

Hendrie turned to Jefferis and sighed. This, he realised, would need explanation. "Yes, Edward, away from any further questions or suspicion."

General Briggs tapped the table to regain William's attention. "You mean all the suspects? Treloar and the private?"

Hendrie turned to the general. "If no proof can be found against them, and it would appear at the moment none can, there is just suspicion. If I may suggest, sir, it should also include Corporal Price. And, although I had not considered him originally, I now feel perhaps we should include Captain Russell. All those involved for everybody's… benefit, sir."

The general's eyebrows rose in surprise. "Russell? Why Russell?"

"He wants justice, sir." Hendrie spoke with some despondency, having now thought about it and seeing it as the only solution. "He has shown this with his report." Hendrie pointed to his copy of the report, open in front of him. "He is one of those rare breeds that will not let this go, men have been killed – Colonel Standish, Captain Farrant, other ranks, civilians, and very probably Lieutenant Norton and – and he is convinced that Treloar and the others are involved. He practically accused Treloar outright, sir. He is determined to make sure that some action is taken." Hendrie pointed his half-smoked cigar towards the window. "He is no fool, sir. He can argue his case confidently, as you just said. And he has just shown that presenting his report to three very senior officers did not unnerve him. He even got us to allow him to speak freely about other officers, including Spencer Treloar, his father Sir John Treloar, and even the Treloar family's financial situation. Treloar's father is a friend of yours I understand, sir."

The general glared at William Hendrie as if he himself had just been implicated. He thought of slapping the colonel down, although what he had said about friendship with Sir John Treloar was true. He did not know the son, but neither did he want to.

"Don't you think Russell will object to a posting overseas?" asked Jefferis.

"Very possibly. But he is a liability." Hendrie took a deep breath before continuing. "He is thirty-five. Despite your opinion, sir, we dare not consider a further promotion if he is still in our battalion, but giving him more authority could be a reward in another battalion.

The general said nothing, just stood and walked to the window. Outside, soldiers marched in the snow, stamping on the crisp powder as they went about their business. Russell was still in the open courtyard, snow settling on his shoulders but seemingly oblivious to the cold and waiting to be called back. He gently stroked the head of a dark grey horse that was unsaddled but covered by a thick blanket and tethered to a rail. The army always looked after its animals. It was clear Russell was deep in thought, but what, wondered the general, was he thinking? Briggs frowned: this was an awful mess.

Breaking the silence, Jefferis spoke quietly. "It makes sense, sir."

General Briggs ignored the comment, strode to his desk, opened a drawer and reached for a sterling silver cigarette case. It had ornate engravings on both sides and was one of the few things Briggs considered beautiful. Opening the clip, he took out a cigarette, tapping both ends on the lid. He placed it between his lips and, taking a match from a box on his desk, lit the cigarette. Satisfied, he returned to the conference table, but remained standing. "Having done what you suggest, William, and removed all those possibly involved, we still do not have anyone who can take the blame. We have to give answers, gentlemen. We have to have someone to blame."

Jefferis coughed. "If I may make a suggestion, sir." The aide had his voice back. "We do have the farmer and his sons."

The general glared at his aide again, annoyed at having to state the obvious once more, "Russell does not believe they were involved."

"No, sir. Edward is right." Hendrie said, excited as he contemplated the suggestion. He counted the points on his fingers. "One: we have the farmer and his sons who owned the farm where a wagon was found. Two: we found gold coins, believed to be from the robbery, in that wagon. Neither the farmer nor his sons could explain their presence. And three: they do admit loaning out this same wagon. These were the facts as written in Russell's report. So the evidence is there. They *could* have been involved, and they *could* have been part of a gang, or at least part of the plot. One other thing, sir." His mouth tightened. "They are civilians. They are not military, and so there would be no blemishes on us. Shift the blame and we lose the shame."

The room went silent, as they all contemplated this idea. A solution may have been found. Briggs felt as if a lost key had been discovered, allowing an escape. Edward Jefferis' smile grew slowly. "As civilians, can we punish them?"

"This is a military matter, Edward. If they are guilty, as I now believe they are, they will be punished. I promise you that. However, our first move is to reassign the men involved." The general re-took his seat, his now mind clear, and took control as senior officer. He turned to his aide. "Check immediately for any troop or other ships that are leaving. Ideally as far away as possible. South Africa, or maybe India. We will re-assign, them." He turned to Hendrie. "That will be your responsibility, William. They are from your company and you have my authority, but I want it done quickly and without fuss. I want that corporal and private away from the camp in the next couple of days at the latest. We can billet them anywhere – at the docks, anywhere until the ship sails. Treloar also. And Russell, if he so chooses, can leave when required."

"Sir, we have guards on the two enlisted men and will ensure no one talks to them," said Hendrie.

"Good."

Hendrie raised his hand. "Sir, what can we say to Russell?"

"Leave him to me. This has become a matter of honour, gentlemen, to protect the battalion, and its reputation." The general turned again to his aide. "As for Russell, there may be another solution to stop him asking any more questions. "Edward, I want you to leave as soon as possible for Whitehall. Give them a briefing on our actions and decisions. There is no need to dwell on Russell's report, just the sensitivity of the situation. Outline Russell's beliefs, take a copy of his report, but do not, *under any circumstances*, leave it with anybody. I want our own people aware of the consequences, as much as we are, and involved as much as we are, so they can bring those asking questions to heel."

Jefferis nodded in acknowledgement. "And how do you intend dealing with Russell, sir?"

Once again, General Briggs looked out the window at

Russell, whose expression he found unreadable and so irritating. He was pleased they now had a course of action. It was clear, like any battle plan should be. Now they would move, and move fast, take the initiative, bring their forces into place to achieve the objective before the enemy could regroup.

"Quite simple, he will do as he is ordered," the general finally smiled. "I will say as little as possible, and give away as little as possible, and thank him for his efforts. I will ask him to await my decision. In a day or two, I will advise him, perhaps with some reward, that other facts we cannot divulge have led us to different conclusions, and that will be the end of the matter. As far as he is concerned anyway."

He pointed to his aide. "Once I have heard from you, Edward, that we have Horse Guards and Whitehall's support and we have established where these men are being sent, then Russell and Treloar will receive their new orders and postings. And that," he slammed his palm on the table top, "will be the end of the matter."

"What about Lady Standish?' Jefferis asked, remembering her visit and her insults he had to endure. "She will not stop pursuing her money."

"Forget the money, Edward." Briggs snapped. "We can find money for Lady Standish to shut her up." He drew smoke into his lungs before he spoke, now contented. "Don't forget how Standish may have come by that money. We have all heard the rumours. We can put pressure on her to keep quiet. She is not the only one with influence. We can bring this incident to a conclusion for the Battalion, gentlemen, for the Battalion and," he spoke as if this addition was the most important fact, "ourselves."

He turned to Jefferis, who was already closing his copy of the file that held the report. "Edward, you are to stay in London, to be responsible for arranging the trial. William," he turned to Hendrie, "please make arrangement for the farmer and his sons to be transferred to London under constant guard. They will leave as soon as our people are out of the way. They are to be kept in isolation until their departure and transferred to Edward in London."

"I understand the farmer's wife has tried to visit," said Jefferis.

"No visitors!" the general ordered.

Jefferis nodded and stood, holding his file under his arm. He smiled. "I think this is an excellent solution, sir. These men will spend a few years in warmer climates and when they return all will be forgotten."

The general's stare froze Edward Jefferis, making him wonder what he had said wrong.

Slowly, in a firm and clear tone, the senior officer spoke. "It will all be forgotten, colonel. A lot faster than a few years. This, gentleman, finishes here and now, I do not want any further mention or to hear of any accusations, rumour or discussion, either in the camp or in the mess, from any officer. Is that understood?"

Both officers said nothing, just nodded.

"You will keep me fully briefed on everything. These decisions have been made and agreed by all of us. By us all, gentlemen. Is that understood? Again, nods were given from both officers. "We are all responsible and jointly accept the consequences should any of this become public. Is that clear?"

They both nodded, this time as one.

"We take this action for the good of us all, to safeguard the reputation of us all."

The general stared at each of his officers until he was sure they had understood what he was saying. Finally, he nodded, then decisively stubbed the cigarette out in a small silver ashtray on the table. He watched a slow ring of smoke rise. Once it had faded, he looked at the report on his desk. Picking up the papers he shuffled them into a neat pile and placed them into a leather folder. This, he handed it to his aide. In his mind he was clear about the necessary actions. "Thank you, gentlemen. Please carry out your orders, and ask Captain Russell to come back in. And, Edward…" Jefferis stopped and turned, a frightened look on his face as he wondered what he had said or forgotten. The general smiled, enjoying with sadistic pleasure the effect his voice could have on his aide. "…can you ask someone to build that fire up? It's getting cold in here."

Chapter 10

Less than a week after the meeting at which had Russell presented his report, he received two sealed envelopes. Hand delivered. He was at home, given leave of absence, to await further instructions. Each stiff envelope was sealed with red wax, and one had URGENT written in bold scarlet letters. Both were clearly addressed, in the same handwriting, to him: company, battalion, address; although both wrongly called him Brevet Major Russell. He opened the URGENT envelope first, unfolding the parchment inside, and reading its contents. He sat with a thump on a nearby chair. With a broad grin, he handed the letter to his wife to read, knowing she would be pleased. Martha read the order and gave a small cry of delight. Whilst she re-read the missive, he unsealed the second, read this communication and passed it across. This message, he knew, would be met with less appreciation. Martha's expression changed in an instant, from joy to disappointment. Her hand flew to her mouth and tears formed in her eyes. She held the letter out towards her husband and asked him whether this was what he wanted.

The first and urgent message, was a long letter of appreciation from the general for his excellent investigation and report. It was signed by all the officers at the meeting. It acknowledged that his approach to the task and his attention to detail were exemplary and easily equal to those expected from a senior officer. Consequently, in recognising Russell's potential, it was therefore confirmed, with immediate effect, he would be promoted to Brevet Major. The term Brevet was an honorary promotion to a higher rank, conferred for outstanding service, but without the corresponding pay or privileges.

The letter then continued by declaring that the investigation would no longer proceed, and his services were no longer needed. There were no reasons given. The second message held even more of a surprise. He was to be transferred from the East Hants Light Infantry to the Second Battalion of the 24th Regiment of Foot, the South Wales Borders, sailing to South Africa early in February 1878, with the position of a supernumerary. He was to report to the battalion commander at Chatham in 10 days, whereupon he would be given further instructions.

His comrades were just as shocked as Martha at his posting overseas. They believed he had asked for the transfer. They were also unhappy as, for them, things always went smoothly when Russell took charge. This state of unhappiness was especially felt by Major Bradshaw who not only did not want to lose Russell, but was jealous Russell was receiving promotion. It was a rum deal, Bradshaw fumed, as it had been he who gave Russell the task of investigating, the task that had got Russell his promotion. But when Bradshaw sent a complaint up the chain of command, it was quickly and efficiently silenced. The orders for his posting abroad, it seemed, came from the very top. When Russell himself queried the orders, he was told: "You've obviously upset or impressed someone". In addition, when Russell made enquires, to his chagrin he discovered that Treloar, Price and Oxley would also be joining the same battalion in South Africa.

Upon trying to contact the general, Russell was directed to

Colonel Hendrie, his old battalion commander, and the only person who agreed to meet him. The meeting was the briefest he had ever experienced. On arrival he was not offered a seat and ordered to remain standing whilst Hendrie sat at his desk, head down, and read from a sheet of paper. "There will be no further discussion on the incident and under no circumstances are you to ask any more questions. Decisions have been made; orders given."

Hendrie glanced up at Russell to ensure he had heard, then continued reading. "Your excellent work has been appreciated, although you were unable to confirm the identity of the assailants or retrieve the stolen goods." Hendrie looked up again. Russell thought he looked like a lawyer questioning a suspect, praising him to get attention, but maintaining his grip with accusation. Hendrie looked back at the paper he held and continued reading, his tone emotionless. "Unfortunately, Russell, you have received attention and notoriety within the camp and battalion." This time when he looked up his face was blank. "I hear you're called," he referred to his sheet of paper, about to strike another blow, "The Gang Chaser." Russell had also heard this new-found title, accepting it as a form of jest from his fellow soldiers. In the circumstances he had not taken it seriously, preferring to ignore it.

The colonel continued. "It has been found that your position within this battalion is untenable, and a transfer with your new promotion to another command was seen as more appropriate. However, because of your excellent service, if you have no wish to transfer to a new command, the general has generously offered you the opportunity to resign, or take early retirement, maintaining your new rank. You have until your ship leaves to make your decision."

The colonel placed the sheet of paper to one side, face down, folded his arms and leant back in his chair. "Do you understand, Brevet Major Russell? Either you leave for South Africa or you leave the military."

Russell, having not moved an inch, nodded. "Yes, sir."

"Good." The Colonel unfolded his arms and picked up another file on his desk. He didn't look up when he next spoke. "You are dismissed. And congratulations on your promotion."

Russell was about to reply with a thank you, then realised the colonel was engrossed in his reading. Russell couldn't tell if it was genuine or for effect. Either way, he left without saluting.

Martha's response, when he had told of the meeting had been to laugh. "How generous of the general," she said.

She said it again when, with just three days to go before the ship sailed, they were spending breakfast discussing the problem yet again: does he travel abroad or leave the army? A fifteen-year-old girl in a black dress with a crisp white apron and small white cap stood silently by the door of the dining room, hands behind her back. Jean and she came in six days a week to help Martha prepare, clear table and wash up after breakfast and evening meals, and generally help around the house. She could help but remind Russell of Lucy, and when he looked at Jean, he wondered how Maggie and Lucy were doing. He had told Martha of the two women, how he had helped them, and the gift Maggie had given him, and then hearing of his possible transfer she had said, "If you go, let's hope the patron saint of travellers stays with you."

Russell knew his new promotion would not see much of a change in his financial affairs and hired help was an additional cost, but he believed in doing things right and if Martha needed help around the house and with their three children, then so be it.

"Can we some more hot coffee please, Jean?" Martha held her cup up, and Jean disappeared to the kitchen.

"I must have been closer than I thought," he mused to his wife, "perhaps close to something personal and very sensitive."

"'But what, dear?"

"I wish I knew." He shook his head, frowning. "But the lengths they have gone to, just to silence me. I've been blocked out. They're afraid of what else I might find. That could be their only reason for this posting. But," he sighed, "I sail soon, so I very much doubt I'll ever find out." He stared at his cooling porridge, suddenly lacking an appetite. "I really must have been close to something."

"We'll have today, though."

"Hmm."

"Today?"

"Hmm. Oh, sorry?"

Martha put her hands over his. "I think, my husband, Major Russell," she said proudly, "should go for another ride, you always say it helps you to get your thoughts in order. You have done all you can, even written it all down in your journal so you won't forget."

"Brevet Major," he corrected her with a smile, sharing her joy at his promotion, even though he knew it was part of the scheme to silence him. Martha said something, but he was only half listening as Jean returned with pot of fresh tea. His wife finished by saying, "And when you return from your ride, dear husband, with your thoughts clear, then we can spend the rest of the day together.'

It was an attractive proposition, so Russell rode out after breakfast. The snow that had fallen days before and on the day of the meeting with the general had not returned, and only diminishing patches remained, in spots sheltered from the sun. His frustrations gradually eased thanks to the combination of a clear sky, crisp air, and the strength and motion of a fine horse. He cantered along tracks and when that got him no closer to an answer of whether to continue his career or not, he galloped over fields. Finally, he slowed to a walk, patted the steaming flanks of his steed, and looked around. He felt he should have been surprised when he found himself trotting towards the village of Old Oak Crossroads, but he was not. Whilst on leave, he had made this same journey two or three times before. It may have been a village so small it was not included on any map, so inconsequential that even the local signposts couldn't agree on its name, but to him was an obvious destination.

Looking around, he saw a group of men working on two cottages that backed onto the fields of an estate. Two men were sitting next to a window frame and an ornate wooden scrolled gable, both of which were leaning against a newly built cottage, ready for fitting. The window frame still had to receive its glass, and the men had stopped for a drink. They watched him approach. Both nodded in acknowledgement as Russell halted his horse.

"Looks like warm work," Russell said to them. "Even this early in the morning."

"That it is, sir," said one of the men, taking a deep swig from a bottle.

"Would you like a drink?" the other asked, wiping the neck

and holding out his own bottle.

"Thank you, no," Russell acknowledged the kindness of the offer. "Are you from the estate?" He nodded in the direction of the main house.

"Aye," replied the man holding the bottle. "Couple of new cottages, nearly finished, sir. More rents for the estate."

'Well, take care," smiled Russell, impressed with the man's generosity. It made him feel even better, there was goodness to be found. Pushing his heels into the horse, he sat taller as he carried on towards the village. It was only a few minutes ride from these two cottages to the centre of Old Oak Crossroads village. Russell passed a few other dwellings, approaching the centre of the village along a road that was little more than a track. To Russell, everything seemed in a bad state of repair. He had visited the place and the scene of the crime a few times since the robbery, and each time the sight of the village had depressed him. He recalled his conversation with the reverend, and had to agree that anyone looking for a poor community need look no further. Half-timbered wattle-and-daub cottages, which comprised the centre of the village, stood side by side, some leaning against each other as if for support, all in a sorry state – their wattle showing through. All required new rendering and were in need of significant repair. There was little indication that paint, whitewash or limewash had been applied for some time. Most of the ridges on the thatched roofs needed attention, and holes from birds and vermin were obvious.

The human occupants of these cottages, he knew, worked on the surrounding farms and estates. All were on low wages and rarely left the village except for work. True, some of the children left to join the army, where life was just as hard but there wasn't the relentless drudgery of village life. At least the army gave you regular meals.

An inn, originally converted from a large house, in slightly better condition than its neighbours, stood on the corner of the village, by the main road. It had been around for a hundred years or so, opened for the navvies digging out the Basingstoke canal, and it was now the only place for the locals to find a hint of relaxation and relief. A small church had been erected later by the estate owners, for the estate's workers and their sins. These two buildings sat opposite each other across a muddy patch of ground on which four children played.

The main road, with ruts and craters from coach traffic, took travellers from the coast in the west to Guildford in the east, and then on to London. The inn would have disappeared years ago but, being just 20 miles from Guildford, was one of the resting places for coach travellers. Few, though, stayed too long.

A smaller track led away from the great oak and the village to the canal and bridge, then continued on to the farmland that Russell now knew had been work for many years by the Wellers. They were one of the very few farming families in the area not part of a larger estate. However, father and sons Weller were now under arrest in London. Beyond their farm was heathland and narrow paths passable only by horse. Russell felt dispirited, even watching the four youngsters chasing each other on what the villagers called their 'green', despite its rough, undulating surface and muddy puddles. Altogether this village was an insignificant little place; its residents lived, worked and died finding what pleasures they could on what little they could afford. Poverty was part of its inhabitants' existence: they survived, just – as did many rural communities. It was the location of this small hamlet, however, that had made it ideal for those whose violent actions had now made the place notorious.

His thoughts returned to his repeated visits to the village. Although he had been instructed – well, unambiguously ordered – by Hendrie to cease investigating, he couldn't. His conscience wouldn't let him. He needed to expose the villains. It was, he believed, his duty. Despite trying to convince himself that arriving in the village was a coincidence, he knew it was not. And he hoped, although knowing there was only a slight possibility, that he might just meet Treloar. After all, Reverend McDonald had mentioned that he often saw Treloar in the mornings, out riding and heading for the heathlands over the bridge. And during his enquires Russell had spoken to Sam Longhurst, the owner of the inn, who also confirmed occasionally seeing Treloar riding through the village towards the canal and heathlands. Longhurst had added that, over past year, he had occasionally seen Treloar returning accompanied by a female rider. Men from his own unit also confirmed Treloar's interests included riding, and officers said he rode as often as he could. Russell therefore wondered if he could catch Treloar on his return and question him again. So far, his visits to the village had been unsuccessful.

Today, hoping to put Treloar at some ease should they actually meet, Russell wore what he thought of as civilian clothing: dark trousers, a morning coat, dark with a wide lapel, over a waistcoat that held his precious pocket watch. His shirt was white and he wore a dark tie. The only concession he gave to his military background was the company's forage cap.

Now, sitting on his horse by the great old oak, Russell was beginning to think the whole exercise of 'accidently' meeting

Treloar was a waste of time. However, he was here, as he had been previous days, at roughly the right time Treloar might return. Russell was convinced Treloar was out there somewhere, possibly on the heathlands, so he continued across the main road and up to the bridge. Once on the bridge he stopped, looking over the wall to the canal below, where it had all begun. The canal was quiet, calm, no barges, no people, just a thin layer of mist over its still surface. Dismounting, Russell slowly led the horse down to the towpath. He secured the reins to a tree and left her to feed on the meagre winter grass while he found a place to sit. He found a good spot near the bridge: the fallen trunk of one tree on which he could sit and lean back against another. Staring at the crumbling brickwork under the arch, he removed his pipe and, holding the shank, filled it with tobacco from a leather pouch. His thoughts began wandering. What was he going to do? This question kept troubling him, for he was not only becoming ever-more convinced of his accusations but also convinced that Treloar was the villain, along with Price and Parr. But how could he prove his theory? He had tried, but ranks hadn't just been closed against him, they had been slammed shut, locked and the key thrown away. And now he was being posted to Africa as part of another battalion and in some unknown role. He looked at his curved pipe and held a lighted match over the bowl, sucking on the mouthpiece. He always enjoyed his smoke. It was a moment to relax, to help put things in perspective. Once again, as with so many times before, he knew what needed to be done but was powerless to do it. He considered his options. Sail as ordered: if he did, he could keep an eye on Treloar and the others. Perhaps one of them would make a mistake and he would be there to catch them out, and so prove his case. But then what if they were reassigned once they reached Africa? Alternatively, he had been told he could leave or retire. But who would listen to him then? Lady Standish had initially shown some interest when he had spoken to her regarding her husband's death and loss of the money chests. He had deliberately used her to stir up concerns, hoping the army would be forced to take action, but now it seemed she did not want to pursue the matter. She was convinced – or had been convinced – the culprits were in custody and had advised him that compensation had been found for her. And Lady Standish, thought Russell, was the only person Lady Standish cared about. And what of the so-called culprits? Russell felt the crushing weight of guilt – the farmer and his sons were not only under arrest but it looked as though they would be tried and probably hanged. And all because of that the real culprits, the villains.

He thought of the journal he had started writing. It had been Martha's suggestion. "Put it all down on paper," she had advised. "Then, whatever happens, it's recorded." As usual from Martha, it was a good idea. All his thoughts, evidence, suspicions were now in writing rather than just in his mind and in the 'lost' report he had presented. Somehow this seemed to make everything more factual. But now that journal was finished. "To hell with their secrecy," he thought as he leaned back against the tree, drawing deeply on his pipe, then opening his mouth and releasing the thick smoke. He had no wish to travel abroad and leave Martha and their children. He would retire. Yes, that would be the best solution for all concerned. Martha's uncle ran a private school near Hastings and more than once had offered him a position teaching history, a favoured subject of his. This time he would take the offer, he would forget the army and the robbery.

With his mind made up, he relaxed and, as the morning sun grew warmer, dispersing the mist hanging above the still waters of the canal, his thoughts began to drift. He contemplated how he could make history lessons interesting; recounting the exploits of others, how it felt to be in a line of men facing the enemy. He could tell of the noise, the cannons blasting away, the shells landing, men screaming, and for a moment he became excited at the thought of sharing these exploits – not out of pride, but knowing what boys would want to hear. Maybe he could help prepare future generations for the defence of the realm. In his reverie he could smell the gunpowder, hear the hooves on hard ground and the neighing of the cavalry horses. He awoke with a start, realising they were real hooves and real horses. Sitting up sharply, he saw two riders crossing the bridge. His movement startled the riders, and one – a woman riding side-saddle – glanced towards him and immediately looked away. It was so quick he did not see her face but he could tell she was young. Her blonde hair was tied up and held in place with a net that was attached to her black brocade top hat with a red silk band. She said something to her male partner. He wore a dark morning jacket, the back of which had a long parting so that it split over the horse's rump, and the collar of a white shirt sat above that of his jacket: civilian clothes. He looked towards where she indicated – at Russell – then both horses broke into a canter over the bridge, down the hill, and on towards the village.

Russell leapt to his feet. It was Treloar returning from his ride. But who was the woman companion? And why had they wanted to get away so fast? A sister perhaps, someone who may know the secrets, may have some answers?

Russell rushed to his own mount and almost leapt into the saddle, adrenaline coursing through him. Showing his horsemanship, he forced his steed up the steep bank onto the track and took off after Treloar and the woman. Could she say where the chests were hidden? Question after question spurred him on as he spurred on his horse. He could see, in the distance, Treloar and the woman had reached the giant oak. They pulled their panting horses to a stop. Russell saw the woman exchange a few words with Treloar, before wheeling her horse around and galloping full pelt through the village, passing the church. Clumps of loose mud churned up from the hollows on the green flew into the air from the speed of the hooves. Treloar remained at the bottom of the road, looking up at Russell, who was now leaning forward in the saddle as he galloped down the hill. Russell had no intention of stopping; he wanted to know who the woman was and why she was in such a hurry to leave. He expertly twisted the reins to pass Treloar who, anticipating the move, swung his own horse in front of Russell's, which whinnied and complained and fought, until eventually Russell got her under something like control. With some effort Russell pulled his horse in a complete circle, until he faced Treloar and, in the distance, the flying mud of the departing woman.

Russell was enraged. "Get out of my way, Treloar. I want to speak to that woman."

"Leave her alone. She cannot help you."

"I will be the judge of that." Russell managed to calm his startled horse. "Now, out of my way."

He lined his horse up again to pass Treloar, then stopped suddenly. A pistol had found its way into Treloar's hand.

"I said," Treloar pointed the gun at Russell, "leave her alone."

"Don't be a fool, put that away."

"She has nothing to say to you. She cannot tell you anything. Leave her."

"Who is she?"

Treloar's response was to look from the pistol to Russell's chest.

"But you have plenty to tell me," said Russell. "And unless you tell me I will have to ask her."

"Captain Russell, please," Russell noted Treloar had not heard of his promotion. "If you move, I will shoot you."

Russell stared, rage and anger building up within him. If this was not clear evidence, he was right, then what was? "Then shoot," Russell screamed as he encouraged his horse past Treloar, as close as possible. "Why should one additional murder bother you?"

As he spurred his horse first into a trot, then a cantor and finally a gallop, he waited for the sound of the gun, braced himself for the pain of the bullet's impact. He waited, and waited and… nothing happened. No shot. No pain. No nothing. When he looked ahead, he saw there was not even any woman. She was gone.

Russell rode up to where he had spoken to the builders, but they were also gone. He stood tall in his stirrups and looked, finding the men at the bottom of the garden, working in a small stable. A workman came out of the cottage; Russell asked if he had seen a rider go by but he said he hadn't. Russell figured she must have turned between one of the cottages, finding one of the numerous tracks, and ridden over the fields towards the

Treloar's manor house. She would be hidden behind the slight slope of the field. He turned his horse back towards the old oak. He didn't expect Treloar to still be there, and indeed he wasn't. Russell stopped just beyond the tree, on the track to the bridge, and, wheeling his horse around, looked in all directions. A movement on the bridge caught his eye. Treloar was standing on the bridge, holding his horse, looking down into the canal. Encouraging his own steed, Russell trotted up the hill, stopping just before Treloar. "Who was she? Your sister? Have you told her where the stolen money is? Have you, you bastard? You deserve to be shot and if I had the…' He couldn't bring himself to say any more.

Treloar did not look up.

Russell felt his anger burst through. He couldn't control himself. "You should have shot me, Treloar, when you had your chance, because from now on I will be watching you. Every move you make, every penny you spend, I will watch because I am coming with you to Africa. Do you hear me, Treloar? I'll be watching you and the others. And when I have the evidence, and I *will* get it, I will see you pay. That's a promise." He swung his horse round until it was facing back down the track. Twisting in his saddle he looked back at Treloar. "You won't be able to spend a penny of what you stole. I will make sure of that. And you won't be able to hide in Lord Chelmsford's army either. I will find the truth if it's the last thing I do." Still Treloar did not move. He continued looking down into the canal. Russell saw he was still holding the pistol in his hand. "I'm giving you another chance to kill me, Treloar, as you did the others." He rode away, slowly, down the hill. Only once did he look back, and when he did, for a brief moment he felt pity.

Treloar was standing with his pistol limply held at his side. A sad, lonely figure with drooped shoulders. Although he could not be sure, Russell thought Treloar may have been crying. His compassion quickly passed though, once he thought of those Treloar had murdered and how one day the truth would be told.

Then he realised this brief encounter had somehow brought about a change of plan.

He wasn't going to retire.

He was going to Africa.

Chapter 11

Russell, Treloar, Price and Oxley sailed to South Africa on the HMS Himalaya, together with their newly assigned battalion, the 2nd Battalion of the 24th Foot.

The journey took four weeks and was uncomfortable. Space on board the ship was so cramped that men slept on the top deck or below, in hammocks. After drill and kit inspection there was little to do except socialise and play cards. Word had got around regarding Russell and Treloar's connection, and it became obvious to the other soldiers that Brevet Major Russell and Lieutenant Treloar did not socialise or converse together. They had as little contact with each other as possible. All four men were integrated within the 2nd Battalion, with the officers as supernumeries – an extra person without specific responsibilities. On arrival in South Africa, Russell worked as an administrator with Colonel Richard Glyn who commanded the 24th Foot. Glyn liked Russell.

Treloar, with suspicions trailing him, did not fare so well. On the voyage he tried to keep himself to himself, reading and writing back home, in whatever solitary space he could find. When not writing, he exercised to the point of exhaustion: press ups, push ups, and sprinting around the deck regardless of the weather. He enjoyed the brisk air, strong sea winds and occasional rain as it blew across the decks, drenching him. The officers in the battalion, having heard the rumours, mostly avoided him, unwilling to be associated with such an officer. A few were a little more generous in nature. One was Lieutenant

Pope, of G Company; another was a young Second Lieutenant, Robert Butler, on his first assignment. Not knowing anyone else in the battalion, and seeing Treloar's demanding exercising routine, Butler joined him every day, wanting to keep himself fit. This he did despite being cautioned about his association with Treloar by other officers. Butler, despite being only 18, showed he had his own mind and continued with the new-found friendship.

On arrival at Cape Town, Treloar was placed with the Army Service Corps, in their transport corps. As he had always enjoyed horse riding at home, his first act was the purchase of a good horse – a sturdy black Friesian. He spent the next few months doing routine work for the transport corps, spending his free time exercising and riding alone through the green countryside, enjoying the hot dry days. He thought the scenery more beautiful than Aldershot, offering rides along the wild coastline, overlooking sparkling blue waters, or inland, past the tribal mud huts, over lush green hills. Usually he went early morning or evenings, avoiding the burning sun. All such a contrast to England.

As Christmas 1878 approached, Treloar heard more talk of war with the Zulu nation. Armies were being prepared, wagons, mules and oxen obtained, and large quantities of supplies secured. Volunteers from the Cape Colony enlisted and were trained, and then all moved to the Buffalo River on the border with Zululand and the British-governed Colony of Natal. Finally, the invasion order was given and both the 1st and 2nd Battalions, with volunteers from the Natal Native Contingent, were marched into Zululand.

Treloar's role during the invasion was well away from any

possible fighting; his duties continued with transport for the 2nd Battalion, ensuring the constant flow of supplies to Rorke's Drift – a Swedish mission station that had been requisitioned and had only two small buildings – a house for the missionary and a barn turned into a chapel – on the Natal side of the Buffalo River. The chapel was used for stores and as a temporary hospital. The location of Rorke's Drift – on a well-worn track to Helpmekaar, the nearest town inside the Colony of Natal and one of the few crossing points across the Buffalo River – meant it was ideally situated to be a command post for the invasion.

Treloar had awoken at Rorke's Drift around 6 am on the morning of Wednesday, 22 January 1879. It had rained during the night and, leaving his tent, he shivered. It was still dark, and the air felt filled with cold mist. The ground was muddy and it stuck to his boots, as if trying to halt his progress. He had risen early to ensure a column of 30 now-empty wagons were despatched back to Helpmekaar, and as he stepped through the clinging mud, he hoped the weather would improve and it would become a hot sunny day. The hired civilian driver was already on the lead empty wagon, with oxen harnessed and ready to go. Treloar, gave a "Good Morning", and received a polite nod in return. He checked his clipboard with the lists of supplies required and handed it to the driver, who adjusted his broad hat, turned to check the drivers of the other wagons were ready, and released the wooden brake handle. As if he were casting a fishing line, the driver gave two flips of his long whip over the heads of the oxen. Upon the cracks of the whip the oxen began to move slowly, eventually reaching three miles an hours over flat terrain.

Treloar turned back to the camp. The sky was beginning to

lighten and, in the morning mist, he could see men were already walking, going about their business, moving between the only two buildings and amongst the numerous tents. A fire was burning at the area where breakfast – bread or biscuits – was being prepared. The smell of coffee drew Treloar and, picking up a tin mug of hot fresh coffee on the way, he visited the storehouse where he surveyed the piled-high supplies of mealie sacks and tins of biscuit. There was space for more, he reassured himself. Leaving the storehouse, he walked along a rough track, through the camp, to the river. The mist felt thicker here, almost fog. Men waded in the thick swampy water, pulling and tying ropes attached to punts, as they attempted to build a bridge into Zululand. On higher ground, above the river, he found John Chard, a Lieutenant in the Engineers, whose role at the Drift was to oversee the bridge building and to keep the routes to Helpmekaar in good repair.

"Spencer, good morning," Chard said, seeing Treloar approach. "I was just thinking of riding to the main camp. It's at a place called Isandlwana, on the track towards the Zulu capital. Not too far. Would you care to join me?"

Treloar thought for a moment. "I have no more supplies arriving until this afternoon. Yes, it'll give my horse some exercise."

"Good," said the broad-shouldered lieutenant. He had a moustache so bushy it entirely covered his top lip. "I suggest we leave it until the mist has fully cleared. Oh, and bring your pistol," he grinned. "We will be in enemy territory, you know."

As it was around 10 miles from Rorke's Drift to Isandlwana they rode easily so as not to tire the horses.

"What's all this I hear about you, Spencer, and stolen

money", Chard asked flatly, without any hint of accusation.

"It's a subject not up for discussion," Treloar answered, as he always did, in a forceful and brisk manner. It ended that conversation, as it had when others had had the temerity to enquire.

Chard looked across at Treloar, who silently and resolutely stared straight ahead.

Chard shrugged, and tried another subject. "I heard that only the First Battalion is left at Isandlwana, under Brevet Colonel Pulleine. Lord Chelmsford and Colonel Glyn, so I was told, left at three this morning, with the Second Battalion, in the direction of the Zulu capital. I think his lordship will find his battle soon."

"He split the army?" exclaimed Treloar.

Chard answered carefully, unused to a junior officer questioning his superiors. "His lordship obviously had a few concerns, but there are still over fifteen hundred men left, Treloar. More than enough. Anyway, the enemy will be near to their capital. They couldn't come this far without our scouts knowing."

Isandlwana could be seen in outline even as they left Rorke's Drift. There were good-natured arguments in the camp over whether it was a mountain or a hill. It stood almost four thousand feet high and it looked as if one of the hills in the north had detached itself and moved to clearer ground for some peace and quiet. Some liked the shape of the mountain, and a few officers actually took time to sketch it because it was so out of the ordinary. There was no pointed peak, instead it had an unusual flat-topped rocky formation, which to Treloar resembled a sphinx or a crouching lion surveying the land all around. It had little colour, or beauty, and the highest part was just hard rock, unclimbable. It could be seen from miles away, from any direction.

Treloar and Chard rode east, following the now rutted, muddy track. Dozens of wagons had passed that way and the ground was crushed from the heavy army boots of hundreds of men coming from the Drift. The track took them over a wide slope, below what Treloar thought of as the head of the lion, which rose again, joining Isandlwana to a lower Stony Kopje or row of lower hills. This track brought Treloar and Chard to the far side of Isandlwana, where they got their first view of the camp, situated to their left, on ground that sloped down to the plains, and in the shadow of the great hill. To their right, the track headed away, towards the south, below the Stony Kopje. This was the route taken by Chelmsford that morning.

On arrival at the camp, they found the men were under arms and had marched out a thousand plus yards to face a possible, but as yet unseen, enemy. They were informed that a large number of Zulus had been sighted coming from the northeast, between two and three miles away. Chard looked at Treloar, concern for the work at the river was written on his face. "If they swing northeast," Chard said, "they could sweep past and make a dash for the Drift." He glanced around at the men preparing for battle. "I'll rest my horse, then head back."

They agreed Treloar would wait at Isandlwana and return later that day, with updated news. Chard visited the mess for to refill his water bottle while his mount rested, then rode back to Rorke's Drift. Treloar made his way towards the centre of the camp looking for the headquarters tent to ask for fresh orders, weaving through men running seemingly in all directions. He stopped a soldier, a fellow officer, to ascertain in which tent was the headquarters and asked about the latest news, what was happening. He was surprised to hear Lieutenant Pope's was the only Company from the 2nd Battalion still there. In fact, this company was now positioned facing Conical Kopje, the cone-shaped hill about three miles away to the east. After resting his own horse, Treloar made a decision and wasted no further time. He rode out to find his friend, Pope.

As he approached Pope's company headquarters, a rider from the Natal Native Horse Company passed him, travelling so fast the rider's hat, secured as it was by a cord, flew behind, as if trying futilely to catch up with its owner. The man was desperately kicking the haunches of his horse, and yelled at Treloar, "They're coming," before continuing his frantic gallop towards the camp. Sweat flew from the horse. In the distance Treloar heard rifle fire. He knew the rider was a scout and guessed that the Impi, the Zulu army, had been discovered.

Treloar forced his own horse into a gallop, and found Pope and his men on the plains, stretched out in two lines. Pope smiled with calm surprise upon seeing his visitor. "What are you doing here, Spencer?" Pope was another officer who favoured a monocle, which was now tight in his eye.

"Thought I could help. Looks like you may have a skirmish on your hands." Treloar indicated the two rows of men, their red uniforms and white helmets already dusty. The soldiers were standing, all looking in the same direction, with their Martin-Henry rifles at the ready and pointing towards the easterly horizon. No enemy could yet be seen. Treloar turned to look into the distance, squinting as he scanned left to right. He could see a far distance but the scenery appeared barren, with rocks and boulders everywhere and a few patches of greenery dotted around. Light-brown grass stuck up like bristles on a shaving brush. While the terrain was not flat, it could easily be mistaken as so, and dongas – hollows – and dry river beds were hidden, lost in the vastness of the vista. Conical Kopje stood a mile or so away. More mountains and hills could be seen in the distance.

Treloar surveyed the ground beyond Conical Kopje, straining his eyes. Riders were heading towards them. He squinted again, this time in confusion at what he was seeing. It appeared to be a great wave, as if a black tide, a mile wide, was rushing towards them. He realised what it was a faction of a second before Lieutenant Pope shouted, "Oh my God, Spencer. Look at them". Treloar stared at the seemingly infinite number of Zulus running towards them. They were chasing the riders, who were still a couple of miles away. Treloar glanced down at Pope to reply, but his attention was drawn to a soldier, taller than the others, standing in the rear line – a big man with a nose that had been broken and badly set. The man's focus was on Treloar and his expression was one that pleaded for help. Treloar looked back at the approaching wave. *Ox, you are on your own now,* he thought.

Unexpectedly, Pope laughed. "Look at them," he repeated, but this time the word was filled with pity rather than awe at their numbers. "Poor things, they don't stand a chance." He looked around at his men and their rifles. "Spears against the firepower of the British Army." The Martini-Henry rifle was a breach loading single-shot weapon, capable of firing 12 rounds per minute, with a range of 400 yards. Its power over the spear and outdated muskets of the Zulu army, Pope clearly believed, would not just stop the advancing enemy, it would give his

Company an easy victory. The men of the 24th were all seasoned soldiers, and they all had, strapped to their sides, a brown leather pouch that carried four packs of ammunition, ten rounds in each pack.

Pope shouted his orders and his men readied themselves for battle. Pope was certain they had sufficient ammunition, especially as his men were – considering the vast number of enemy bearing down on them – unable to miss a human target. Once the firing began though, it soon became obvious that the enemy's sheer numbers, more than 20,000, put them at an incredible advantage over just 1600 soldiers.

The Zulus pushed forward with such determination that, despite constant firing and terrible casualties, they kept on coming. They just didn't stop. They were encouraged by their leaders, hiding behind rocks and in the dongas. Pope's company, at the extreme right, was using ammunition at an alarming rate just to keep the Zulus at bay. Rifles became hot with constant firing, and new ammunition to replace the spent cartridges being ejected from the rifles was slow in coming. The enemy did not appear to have any intention of retreating from the awful consequences of their attacks.

"Spencer!" Pope yelled, walking behind the lines of his sweating men, directing fire, shouting above the noise of battle. "Ride back to the camp. Hurry the supply of ammunition. And give Pulleine a report on our situation. They're moving to the right, and we are stretched too far. I may have to fall back towards the main camp."

Astride his mount, Treloar nodded, and set off as fast as he could. Horse and rider working well together as they covered the ground at great speed. All the time, over the noise of his steed's galloping hooves, Treloar could hear the sound of gunfire and the screams of dying men. He found Brevet Colonel Pulleine, in command of the 1st Battalion, in the open, at the centre of the camp. He was giving orders to those around him while scanning the horizon. Those given the orders hurried off to fulfil their duties. Treloar all but leapt from the saddle, keeping hold of the reins in case his horse should scare and bolt due to the screams, Zulu chanting, gun and cannon fire.

Pulleine listened as Treloar, trying to stand to attention while still holding the reins of his horse, repeated what Lieutenant Pope had said, shouting over the cacophony of battle. After explaining the situation, Treloar waited impatiently to be dismissed, tapping his foot, almost shaking. He was desperate to do as Pope asked and find more ammunition, yet he knew he should not even be at the camp, let alone in the battle.

As Treloar waited, Pulleine looked into the distance, clearly wishing he could see Lord Chelmsford and his troops returning. Colonel Pulleine rubbed his sweating hands together, only stopping when an explosion from one of the two cannons – firing in support of his troops – brought him back to the danger.

"Thank you, Lieutenant, we have sent messages to his Lordship, but the situation changes as we speak. We should send a message back to Helpmekaar with news of our situation. Tell them the Zulus may cross the border and could be heading to outflank his lordship's return. If you would take the message—?'

"Can I suggest, sir," Treloar interrupted, his still voice raised, "I change horses with Second Lieutenant Butler and he goes instead?" Treloar pointed to the young officer nearby. Butler's father and family were known to Pulleine. As a new officer, having only just received his commission, Butler had begged to join Pulleine in Africa and Pulleine had happily agreed. He now wished he had not been so accommodating.

"He's a good rider and lighter than me, Sir. Using my horse, he would make good time and I have to secure more ammunition for Lieutenant Pope's company."

A cannon fired again and Treloar glanced towards the noise as his horse reared and tried to pull from his grip. Beyond his horse he was surprised to see Russell, pushing his way forward to get next to Pulleine so he could hear better. Both Treloar and Russell were astounded to see each other; Treloar should have been at Rorke's Drift and Russell, being on Colonel Glyn's staff, should have left with him and Lord Chelmsford that morning. Treloar was not to know that Glyn had thought Russell would be better used in helping Pulleine and bringing the 1st Battalion to Chelmsford when needed. Treloar saw Russell shake his head; he knew Russell was confused at hearing him refuse the opportunity to escape.

"I think that would be a good idea, Lieutenant." Pulleine turned to the younger man. "Lieutenant Butler, change mounts with the lieutenant here. Ride back to Helpmekaar and report." He held up his hand. "Wait, though. I have something for you to take. Stay here while I fetch it." He strode to his tent.

The young officer dismounted his smaller horse and exchanged reins with Treloar and was about to speak when Russell stepped between them. "This does not make sense, Treloar. Why wouldn't you want to escape? Why give up that opportunity?"

"Perhaps all is not as it seems." Treloar shook his head.

Russell recognised the look on Treloar's face. It was the same one he'd seen during their confrontation at the bridge back in Hampshire. It was filled with desolation and regret.

Russell raised his voice to make himself heard above the noise of battle. "What do you mean? Why are you staying? Guilt, remorse? I don't believe it."

Treloar said nothing.

Lieutenant Butler heard the exchange as he put his foot in the stirrups of Treloar's horse, and lifted himself into the saddle. He was aware of some of the rumours about these two officers.

Pulleine reappeared from his tent, holding a brown rucksack, as Butler – now sitting comfortably on Treloar's horse – spoke. "Mr Treloar, this does not seem right." Treloar smiled, holding Butler's horse, stroking its neck and mane, comforting it as the sounds of cannon and rifle fire mingled with the ever-closer screams of dying men.

Treloar answered as if arranging a meeting at a later date. "Just carry out your orders, Robert." He offered a confident smile, which turned into a grin as if in mock rebuke. "And look after my bloody horse till we meet again."

Pulleine handed the rucksack to the young officer. "If necessary, pass these to my family. Now, you have your orders. Go, Lieutenant." He turned back to his officers, not waiting to see Butler depart.

Taking one last glance around the camp, Butler turned the horse from the battle, settled himself and spurred the animal away, riding along the crest of the hill towards the slope and track back towards Rorke's Drift, and away from the battle.

Over an hour had elapsed since the battle had commenced, and staff officers were standing in groups surveying the battlefield, which messengers were running and riding to and from. The two cannons kept up their barrage, killing and injuring dozens of the enemy with every discharge, supporting the lines of red-coated men who were slowly retreating. They were moving in good order, returning to the centre of the main camp, now only quarter of a mile away.

Pulleine turned to Treloar. "Thank you, Lieutenant." Treloar realised Pulleine had not used his name; he had no idea who he was. "I suggest you report back to Lieutenant Pope." Pulleine lifted a set of binoculars hanging round his neck to his eyes and started calling to his staff officers for messengers, giving new orders. Only one man was not listening, Russell, who was staring at Treloar as he swung into the saddle of Butler's smaller horse. Without looking back, Treloar rode towards the ammunition wagon.

The necessity of fresh ammunition was becoming acute, and hot, dusty, impatient men waited by the wagon jostling and pushing to collect their fresh supplies. Their eyes scanned the battle whilst they waited, watching the approaching enemy who were now covering the plains in a giant crescent formation. They were getting inexorably closer, forcing the lines of soldiers back. Treloar tied his horse to the ammunition wagon and, with the help of another officer found an empty sack and began filling it with packets of cartridges, forcing as many as they could into the bag. The other officer was sweating profusely. All the cartridges were taken from hastily opened wooden ammunition boxes that, once emptied, were swiftly cast aside, falling with dozens of others that lay empty, broken and in disarray around the wagon. The sweating officer heaved another full box of ammunition into place and, taking a large wooden-handled screwdriver, started to undo the large screws holding down the lid of the crate. "Your sack will not take anymore," he shouted to Treloar. "Get it to the men. Quick."

Treloar twisted the end of the sack closed and, mounting his horse, holding the sack across his saddle, began riding as fast as he dared back to where he'd left Pope. Treloar tried to calculate; it must be at least 20 minutes since he had left Pope and in that time the battle had changed. Natives from the Natal units were running across the plains towards Treloar, away from the battle on his far left, their focus to reach the slope of the hill they hoped would lead to their escape. Men who had been facing the main thrust of the Zulu attack were now retreating towards the rows of white bell tents, every backward step bringing them closer to the centre of the camp. Several soldiers in the camp itself were running from the tents, heading in his direction.

As Treloar galloped under the shadow of the hill, the Zulus appeared to be covering the entirety of the open plain. Thousands of them; so many Treloar realised they were unstoppable. As he looked, more were coming around the hills on his left, ready to attack the companies that were facing them. It meant the line of soldiers protecting the camp was now stretched, getting thinner and thinner, like a rubber band about to break. The spacing between men, in places now dangerously large, left gaps that the enemy was trying to exploit.

All the companies had fallen back under the weight of enemy numbers, their firing not stopping the oncoming onslaught. From the rapid fire Treloar could hear, it was obvious ammunition was being used at a terrifying rate. Trying to get every last fraction of speed out of this new horse, Treloar looked ahead. Riders from Lieutenant-Colonel Anthony Dunford's Natal Native Troop were returning from the Conical Kopje. This troop were expert riders and galloped towards the furthest point of the defensive line, near the track to Rorke's Drift, firing behind them as they rode, trying to stop the Zulus advancing and encircling the army.

The Zulus were exercising their battle plan expertly, sending men out left and right, spreading their forces wide to then curve inwards and meet behind the enemy. Encircling and crushing the British. It was no use, Treloar realised, trying to find Pope or his men; they were no longer where he had left them. They were retreating. He still had the sack of ammunition, but no one to deliver it too. He pulled on the reins, slowing the horse, and, whilst deciding his next move, saw eight full wagons positioned just off the track from Rorke's Drift. Each filled with boxes and sacks of supplies. They were the last of the wagons sent by him the previous evening from the Drift. Obviously arriving late at the camp, they had been left by the road to follow Lord Chelmsford's army wherever it would go.

The wagons had a small group of men around them. Treloar recognised them as the drivers, and guessed they were wondering what to do. The oxen that had pulled the wagons were nowhere to be seen. Treloar turned his horse in the direction of the wagons and spotted a figure in a brown infantry patrol jacket and buff-coloured cord riding breeches. On his head sat a wide-brimmed hat with a red puggaree around the crown. He was one of the Natal Native company and appeared to be injured. Treloar watched as the man hobbled as fast as he could, struggling, using his rifle as a crutch, as he tried to follow the other natives escaping the battlefield. Treloar dug in his heels and pushed the horse towards the soldier.

"Quick. Can you climb up behind me?"

"Leave me," the soldier cried. "I twisted my ankle falling down a donga."

"God damn you, man," Treloar shouted, taking his left foot from its stirrup. "Get up behind me."

The soldier dropped his rifle and, despite the injury, managed to pull himself up behind Treloar.

"Hang on to this." Treloar passed the sack of supplies behind him for the soldier to hold, then heaved on the reins with both hands and, again using his heels on the horse's rump, spurred it back towards the wagons. Despite its extra load, it managed to break into a hurried trot. The man put one arm around Treloar's waist, his other clutched the sack as if it were a bag of jewels.

Treloar recognised, in the distance, a sergeant, one of the men sent with the wagons. He had given the man his orders at Rorke's Drift the day before. Now, the sergeant was hastily gathering around him what men he could. They were firing at the enemy. Treloar kept kicking the horse until it reached the wagons. He half turned and grabbed the sack from the Natal officer and dropped it in front of the sergeant, then slipped neatly off the horse, leaving the soldier still mounted. "Wait here and stay in the saddle," commanded Treloar, "but keep a tight rein, he's jumpy, and tired." With each explosion of cannon fire amid the thunder of the battle the poor horse twitched its ears and threw its head back, its eyes wide.

"Sergeant!" Treloar had to shout to make himself heard. "Hand out this ammunition."

"Sir," the sergeant replied and emptied the contents of the sack onto the ground. "Thank God," he muttered when he realised what the sack contained.

Taking command, Treloar turned to the other men. "Empty

these wagons quickly, use the boxes and sacks for barricades. We need to give those men pulling back support and cover."

Soldiers from the 24th, coloured labourers and brown-clad volunteers from Natal, all now just terrified men, either escaping from the camp or pulling back from the front line, saw the activity around the wagons. They realised what was happening, sprinted to the wagons and joined in, heaving the boxes and heavy sacks that were being flung from the wagons, piling them on top of one another: makeshift protection from an enemy that, despite so many of them falling under the hail of bullets, was still advancing. The gunfire was now close and deafening. When he glanced up, Treloar could see evidence of the power of the British weapons: hundreds, possibly thousands, of Zulu bodies lying across the plain. Amongst them were interspersed the occasional red coats of those poor bastards caught out in the open.

Looking around, Treloar saw Lieutenant-Colonel Dunford's Natal volunteer force, who had been enlisted into Chelmsford's army as part of the invasion force, now finding what cover they could behind the larger rocks. They were firing at the Zulu hoards, trying to keep the road to Rorke's Drift open and also halt the enemy's pincer movement.

Across the main field of battle resistance was patchy. More from other Natal companies were now running up the steep slopes of the hill behind Treloar, with no thought of stopping to help, their only aim was escape. These Natal companies, which had been distributed between six British companies of the 24th Foot, were now breaking ranks, running, weakening the line. The strength, ferocity and sheer numbers of the Zulu had finally broken these men. It was clear that modern rifles just could not stop such an overwhelming enemy. Terrified, the men were fleeing and their departure left openings which the Zulus immediately exploited. They swarmed into the gaps in vast uncontrollable numbers, coming at the companies of soldiers from behind. The Zulus were going to wash their spears in blood, no matter what. Their land had been invaded.

Ahead of Treloar, soldiers were continuing to retreat whilst others were standing firm and, as the Zulus reached them, simply being slaughtered. The once-solid lines of red-coated soldiers were becoming isolated or had disintegrated altogether.

Assessing the situation from on top of the wagon, Treloar began shouting. "Sergeant, put some men up onto these wagons. Fire over the heads of those in front," he pointed. "Give them cover."

Treloar looked at the injured Natal officer still on the horse. The man's rifle was gone, but he held the reins tightly in one hand. In the other hand he held his revolver. Treloar saw him wince as he twisted his foot in the stirrup so he could survey the scene unfolding around him. They caught each other's eyes, and Treloar felt they were reading each other's thoughts about the inevitable outcome. Treloar turned again to look at the battlefield. The Zulus had stopped moving forward, if only temporarily, taking what cover they could, due to the ferocity of the new firepower from the men around the wagon, now with replenished ammunition. The soldiers stood, shoulder touching shoulder, firing as one. Elsewhere, companies who had tried holding the line in the open and had found themselves cut off or outrun, were forming small groups, making the best defence they could. He watched as those furthest away began fighting hand to hand, having used all their ammunition. They swung their rifles like clubs, stabbed with their bayonets or finally just used their fists as their final defence before the inevitability of a painful death.

The enemy line was pushing to encircle the soldiers, but was being delayed by Dunford's men holding their defensive positions. As the Zulu army continued moving slowly forwards, it probed for weak spots in order to get in amongst the soldiers.

To his left, at the camp, all order appeared to have gone. Zulus and soldiers were now fighting amongst the tents. The final rout had started. Men were fleeing the camp, climbing the nearest slope, heading for the track between the hills. Some men on horses were kicking their mounts, encouraging them up the steep slope and faring better than those running on foot, all desperately trying to put as much distance as possible between them and the unstoppable Zulus. All who stayed in the camp were either dead or soon would be.

Some Zulus chased the British and Natal soldiers fleeing the camp, stabbing them with their spears as they overtook them. Most Zulus, however, stayed, ransacking the tents and seeking out those still in the camp. These warriors were now closer than when Treloar had first seen them, when he was with Pope and his men. They were a fearsome sight, barefoot, almost naked except for a loin cloth and some bird plumes and feathers. Most terrifying of all were their weapons, a long spear, razor sharp, held in the same hand as their decorated cowhide shield. Treloar saw the assegai, or stabbing spear, being used to deadly effect as the Zulus got amongst the soldiers.

To his right Treloar could see pockets of men fighting. They fought, and they fell. Some made it to Dunford's troop or to those of his men who had remained on the battlefield and were putting up a spirited but doomed defence to prevent from the enemy from encircling them.

Looking to his own defences, Treloar could see that at the rate they were using ammunition it would not last. The air was heavy not only with the stench of cordite and blood and burning, but also with the howls of the wounded and the screams of those being slaughtered. Finally there were the shouted chants of the enemy, who – seeing so many fleeing – were even more encouraged.

Treloar leapt off the wagon, grabbed the horse's bridle, and shouted at Natal officer. "Get away while you can."

The man leaned down, so Treloar could hear, and spoke English, but with a strong Dutch accent. "I cannot do that, it is your horse."

Treloar ignored him and pulled the horse away from the wagon. "You're injured and no use here," Treloar yelled. "My place is here. I have nowhere else to go. Quick, you must leave now. Ride!"

The soldier spoke but the gunfire and screaming made it difficult to hear and Treloar had to lean up to listen what the officer was saying. "I said, who do I thank for saving my life? What is your name?"

"Treloar. Spencer Treloar. And good luck to you, you're not safe yet!"

The Dutch Natal officer held out his hand. "Christian Janssen," he said. Treloar shook the man's hand briefly then quickly turned to his men, shouting orders for them to get closer together and, for the first time that day, he pulled his Adams revolver from its holster.

Christian Janssen turned the horse towards the track

between Isandlwana and Stoney Kopje. Some men had already reached it and were running over the slope as fast as they could, finding the track back to the Drift. Janssen gritted his teeth and, with his good foot, kicked his new mount. Pain shot up his injured limb but the horse responded as if it knew it was also in danger. The steed speed up the slope, joining the throng of other escapees, some riding but most running. Janssen forced his horse over the peak of the slope, pausing for a fraction before starting the descent. Wincing, he managed to look behind him and saw the carnage. The camp and its surroundings were now filled with celebrating Zulu warriors, chanting, ululating. The flicker of flames showed where fires had been started in the camp. Some warriors who still had not had enough of the slaughter had turned and were now moving towards Treloar and the other smaller groups of men making their last stands. Dunford's troop were firing, but the Zulus had broken the outer circle of the defenders and, in places, the fighting was hand to hand, with the Zulus stabbing and slashing and impaling the Natal fighters. Although many hundreds of Zulu bodies could be seen over the valley, the number still fighting was huge. They were unstoppable.

Having lived in South Africa most of his life, Janssen knew the Zulu and, unlike the British, had never underestimated them. Even so, he was amazed the whole battle had come to a climax so fast and with such devastation. The British had had a modern army, with so many men and superior weapons and firepower, yet they had been hacked apart by a tribal nation with spears. Then, as his horse followed the track, his view behind was blocked by the side of the hill. He continued the descent, following the other escapees. Every step of the horse blasted pain up Janssen's injured leg. His head went up as he heard new sounds in front: chanting, then loud rattling. He knew that sound. Had heard it before. It was spears banging against shields. He raised his pistol. Moving slowly along the track he began to hear screams and cries for help. The Zulus had come around the hill, crossed the track to the Drift, and had waited. They were now mercilessly attacking those fleeing, those who were already exhausted and desperate to escape, slaughtering them before they realised what was happening. Zulus were waiting on the hill forcing them all away from the track, slicing through the men in their way. Any soldier wearing red was their first target.

A Zulu ran at him, trying to spear his horse. Janssen shot the man, who spun and fell, landing on other bloodied bodies. Janssen yanked on the reins, turning his horse to the left, pushing his way through the panicking survivors, all trying to take the only route open to them – down into a rocky ravine. They were forcing their way through bracken and bush, ignoring their ripping clothes. Hard branches and sharp thorns pierced skin, drawing blood. It was not really a path at all. Some of the men were shouting, calling for help. No one stopped; it truly was every man for himself. All around Janssen were the cries and screams of men being speared, as the enemy pushed them further from the main track. Janssen was a good horseman, and even with one damaged leg he kept his balance as his mount fought for footing down the slope. To come off would be certain death. He fired his revolver at any Zulu who came near, and even when he had used all his rounds he continued to point and fire in the desperate hope that they would turn away. The fugitives continued making their painful way through the rough bush, forcing a path for their escape.

Janssen felt the slope suddenly become much steeper, and he heard rushing water. The Buffalo River cascaded to his left, thrashing its way downstream as if it was also escaping. Where the ground looked easier, he tried to turn but was committed, his horse now sliding and slipping towards a steeper slope. It stumbled and Janssen was thrust forward. Unable to gain his balance, he yanked his feet out of the stirrups, yelling with the agony, not wanting to be entangled if the horse stumbled further. The horse made a strange and terrified noise, tried to correct its fall, but could not get any footing. It tripped, fell forward, and Janssen was thrown out of his saddle and over the horse's head.

Suddenly horse and rider were both falling. Janssen's first thought was of the poor horse that had done so well, then he landed on rocks and felt something inside him crack. A searing pain exploded in his chest a fraction of a second before he rolled into water. Surfacing, he gasped for breath, which sent white-hot agony through him. He trod water for a moment before realising his whinnying and panicking horse was splashing next to him. He grabbed at the animal, once, twice, then found a stirrup and held on. The horse pulled him to the edge of a bank, its instinct for self-preservation saving them. Only once he was lying on the bank, painfully catching his breath, still holding the stirrup did he wonder: which bank?

Hauling himself upright and looking left and right, it registered he was the only man this side of the river. Glancing back, he saw others arriving on the far bank from the slopes above, immediately followed by Zulu warriors. A few men reached the water, the others didn't die quickly. No one was paying any attention to him, so he held on tight to the horse's bridle, took a deep breath and managed to haul himself to his one undamaged leg. Every instinct told him he had to get back onto the horse and flee. Using what strength remained and not suppressing his screams of pain, he pulled himself clumsily into the saddle. Once settled, he squeezed his eyes shut and took several deep breaths until the agony had subsided. Upon opening his eyes, he looked across the river. Some soldiers on horseback had pushed their way forward but very few. Most men were being butchered. Janssen kicked his horse and immediately cried out. His gasp of pain was almost as loud as the horse's whinny of complaint. But the animal moved forward, limping, across the suddenly open lands, towards Rorke's Drift. Janssen constantly glanced behind him and, as far as he could see, no one followed him. Finding the track, he made his way to Rorke's Drift.

Word had already reached the Drift of the massacre, and Janssen could see preparations were already being made to defend the small garrison. The two thatched buildings, built of stone, and a stone cattle kraal, were all built on a ledge between the Oskarberg hills and the track passing the station, and now these building were being linked with a barricade of grain sacks and boxes taken from the storehouse, which had once been the chapel.

Lieutenant John Chard helped Janssen down from his exhausted horse and called a private over to assist the new arrival. After Janssen had given a short description of what he'd seen and an explanation of his escape, Chard left, shouting orders to build the defences higher, using everything from the stores, everything from heavy sacks of grain to metal biscuit tins. ‘Everything,’ he said. ‘Strip the place clean.’ The private, from B Company, stationed to defend the camp at Rorke’s Drift, helped Janssen to Surgeon Reynolds in the Missionary’s house. This was now to be the hospital, and was hastily being prepared for casualties. Reynolds diagnosed a cracked a rib. Bandages were quickly and tightly wrapped around Janssen’s chest. He was given a rifle, which he used as a crutch as he made his way to a corner against the storehouse, facing the Oskarberg hills. He watched the men, sweating and panting, clearing the building of the grain sacks, wood and tin boxes, all being placed one on top of one another. The barricade was as tall as he was when standing, and stretched from the storehouse to the hospital and beyond. When he looked, he could also see upturned wagons resting on their sides, also piled with grain sacks and biscuit tins. The whole camp was being encircled with a barricade. He found a good spot, giving enough protection and allowing a reasonable view of the flat land in front of the hills. He made himself as comfortable as he could, believing this was the direction from which they would come. Lieutenant Gonville Bromhead, the other senior officer at the Drift, sought him out and, because he was a Natal volunteer and wounded, offered him the opportunity to leave for Helpmekaar. Janssen thanked him saying he had his own reasons to stay – a debt to pay an officer called Treloar.

“I knew Treloar,” Bromhead said. “This was his post; he should also be here.”

Janssen’s voice was quiet and respectful. “I am afraid he won’t make it, Lieutenant. So I will take his place.” He continued peering over the rampart in anticipation of the enemy’s arrival. His rifle and spare ammunition lay on top of the barricade.

The Zulus came around the Oskarberg hills around five in the afternoon. Janssen and the other watching men shouted of their arrival, forcing the defenders to race to grab their rifles and take up their allotted positions at the barricades, Janssen fired as soon as he got a clear shot and brought one down. He would later say it was one of the first, if not *the* first, shot in the battle. Janssen, with men mostly from B Company of the 2nd battalion, fought bravely at Rorke's Drift. The battle was as just as ferocious and terrifying as the battle at Isandlwana. It lasted through the late afternoon and into the night. Buildings were set alight, but this gave the men enough light to see and fight the enemy. This time there could be no retreat. The besieged stood behind the full sacks and the biscuit tins and kept up a constant barrage.

Around four thousand Zulus attacked around one hundred and fifty defenders, with those Zulus who had not fought at Isandlwana even more desperate to see British blood. The warriors believed that, with each attack, the lines of red-coated men would break, but the defenders held out for twelve hours. They simply had nowhere else to go.

And as the sun made its appearance on the second day, the Zulus, tired and hungry, vanished.

The survivors at the Drift waited, alert, not believing that their small band had managed to hold their ground against much, much greater numbers. In fact, they would not believe they were safe until their commander, Lord Chelmsford, arrived with the remains of his army, around eight in the morning, the same day.

Janssen, being a survivor of both battles, was one of those brought forward to tell his story to Chelmsford. He included the bravery of Lieutenant Treloar.

His own features powder-blackened, Janssen could see Lord Chelmsford was ashen-faced and dejected, his head held low as he listened, not wanting to believe the tragedy that had befallen his army. They had lost everything, including their pride.

He asked Janssen a few questions, then thanked him for his bravery and dismissed him. Chelmsford's mind was reeling from the disaster, and to cap it all Janssen had said Treloar deserved a medal. At the time, Chelmsford had nodded, but he had lost half his army and was looking for scapegoats not heroes. The heroes would be here, Rorke's Drift, where they had fought and survived.

Still using a gun as a crutch, Janssen limped back to his corner; others walked like the undead around the burnt ruins of their camp. Empty cartridge shells lay everywhere. The air was still heavy with the reek of gun smoke, with swirling soot from the remnants of the still smouldering buildings, and with the stench of sweat and death. The bodies of hundreds of Zulus lay where they had fallen, food now for hungry flies. The survivors slept from exhaustion, keeling over where they had fought, too tired to move. Those who had just arrived with Chelmsford were detailed to check and move the bodies, whilst others were to rebuild the barricades; they expected the Zulus to return. Christian Janssen had been awake for over twenty-four hours and had not eaten for as long. His ankle ached, his chest throbbed with the pain of a cracked rib, and his hands were burnt and blistered from firing his rifle, non-stop, for hours. He'd ripped pieces from his shirt, wrapping them around both the barrel of the gun and his hands in order to give him some relief. Survival and hate had eclipsed thoughts of pain and injuries; he'd just kept loading and firing, loading and firing. Now came disbelief, which was followed by relief, and immediately following that came exhaustion.

Collapsed in his corner he was almost asleep when a soldier came up to him. The man spoke without introduction. "Are you sure Lieutenant Treloar is dead?"

Just about managing to open his eyes, Christian Janssen saw a fellow whose face, like everyone else's, was powder-black, whose open-necked ripped red tunic was stained with blood. His trousers were covered with dirt from the fighting. He wore no hat.

Janssen shielded his eyes as he looked up at the man. He could see the man had been badly injured; a dirty, bloodied cloth was wrapped around his head, so just his right eye and mouth showed. The outside of the cloth was dark and stained; the wound beneath had clearly bled copiously.

Janssen could barely talk. His lips were dry, cracked and bleeding, and it seemed almost too much effort to form words. "Believe me," he croaked, "I am certain. No one could have got out of that, on foot and alive."

"Damn the man. Damn him."

Janssen heard the man swearing as he walked away. He was about to take issue at the blasphemy against the soldier who had saved his life, but was so tired – so, so tired. He fell into something that was thankfully more unconsciousness than sleep.

Part 2

1977. The Links

Chapter 12
The Fete

Fifties and sixties pop blared across Oak Cross village green from the PA system. Banners announcing the annual event fluttered and flapped, the wind straining the rope ties.

REVEREND MCDONALD'S CHARITY FESTIVAL

Grey speakers, suspended on tall poles in each corner of the triangular village green, were connected by cables and wires which ran across the grass like snakes. Stalls of different shapes, sizes and colours – from holiday tents to hand-built frames covered with clear tarpaulin sheets – lined the three sides of the village green. They acted as barricades against the roads behind them. Multi-coloured bunting, which rippled and twisted in the wind, hung between the stalls. Over on land adjoining the church and its associated hall, a team of volunteers was preparing for the evening fireworks. They paused when the music faded and a male voice spoke.

"Ladies and Gentlemen, in 15 minutes children from Oak Cross Junior School will be in the marquee, in the centre of the green, giving a performance of country dancing." The announcer took a breath. "And in memory of Reverend McDonald, the children will be wearing Victorian dress." Some rustling could be heard, before: "Also, don't forget the fireworks tonight, starting at 8 pm."

The music returned to its previous volume, only now it was The Beatles wanting to hold your hand. In fact, holding hands was exactly what Gary and Anne Stevens were doing while they strolled around the fete. Married seven months, and only recently moved to Oak Cross, they sauntered from stall to stall, comfortably warm in their anoraks against the late summer weather. The wind could politely be called invigorating, but it was not bad enough to put a damper on the day's activities.

Many others were also strolling on the green, and all were smiling. This fete, as with other Oak Cross events, was well attended and supported; people liked living in and around this peaceful village and participating in its activities. Oak Cross, once known as Oak Tree Crossroads Village, and before that – amongst other names – Old Oak Crossroads, was also where Anne had met Gary. That had been two years ago in the Old Oak Inn. She had been at her friend's wedding party; the friend was Gary's cousin.

Anne, who had lived in nearby Farnborough, loved Oak Cross so when, during their engagement, an old cottage in the village came onto the market they had investigated and put in an offer. The place needed modernising but the occupant – a lovely old lady finding life difficult due to her arthritis, and about to relocate to a local residential home – took a liking to the young couple and accepted their offer. She proclaimed: "Lived here all my life and I want this house to go to the right couple."

Anne, a ward nurse in Aldershot Hospital, had been overjoyed. Gary, a sales rep whose patch covered Southern England, was more apprehensive. He could see the amount of work involved, renovating and decorating, and that was before account was taken of the overgrown garden. The cottage had once been two cottages, which shared a drive leading to a – now long gone – stable. The dwellings had been called High Swallow and Low Swallow, and once converted into a single home had taken the name High Swallow.

Anne and Gary meandered around the village green, relaxed and enjoying the atmosphere. They stopped at the various stalls that always grace such fetes: tombola, hook-a-duck, hoopla. Each time, Anne dived into Gary's anorak pocket for coins. "You haven't forgotten," Gary said in a low mumble, "I was made redundant last week, and we are meant to be cutting back." He was still embarrassed about losing his job. It had been absolutely no fault of his, the management had explained, but rather the economic situation. It was a situation that, Gary thought, was going to affect many more in the coming years. Anne took another fifty pence coin from him for yet another stall. Holding the coin up, she smiled at him. "Don't moan. You got a good redundancy package. This is for the village charity." She winked at him. "You skinflint."

"We'll be the ones needing charity if you keep this up," he replied, just as light-heartedly. His grin grew as she punched him in the arm and he feigned pain. In retaliation, at the next stall, Anne found and spent a pound buying raffle tickets to win a hamper. Gary then plunged his hands in his pockets, refusing to part with any more money as they arrived at the coconut shy. "Those coconuts look like they wouldn't move if you threw a hand grenade at them." Anne chuckled, playfully punching him again, then wrapped her arms around him. "Let's have a look at stalls inside the hall, then get a coffee," she said, guiding him in the direction of the Church Hall.

"Who was Reverend McDonald anyway?" Gary asked, looking at one of the banners hanging above the entrance to the Church Hall car park. Anne, he knew, had researched the village history when they moved in. It fascinated her and made her happy.

"Reverend Angus McDonald, born 1832, died 1899," said Anne in a plummy, school mistress's tone as they crossed the road. Gary's pleasure in her knowledge of the village she intended to be their long-term home equalled her own. "He was," she continued, "an important name in these parts. In the latter half of the 1800s he came to this church, one of the oldest in the parish. He helped change and improve the area, which was going through hard times, using church money, donations, contributions, finding benefactors to improve the lives of those in and around the village." She spoke as if reading from a textbook. "He got funds to start the first school in the area, and supported shops and trade. He found land for the park and recreation ground. He was a real forward thinker."

Gary nodded, only half digesting the information.

The inside of the hall was a warmer and calmer version of outside, but with craft and cake stalls. Like many halls, it had a musty smell. Anne walked off to investigate all the stalls while Gary, not so interested in baking and sewing, stayed at the first stall. It displayed a sign with a painting of a large oak tree followed by: OAK CROSS HISTORY SOCIETY.

A man in his mid-fifties, with long greying hair tied behind his head, and wearing a pair of silver-framed dark glasses, was staffing the stall. Gary thought, with the round lenses, the man looked like John Lennon, only older. His attire was supposed to be Victorian: black waistcoat, collarless white shirt and red handkerchief tied around his neck. He lounged in a deckchair behind a wooden trestle table at the back of the stall, and was smoking a small Henri Winterman's. On the table were pamphlets, plain notepads and pencils, all engraved with the society's name. Gary nodded, respectfully, making eye contact as John Lennon mark II struggled to stand, stamping out his cigarillo.

Gary studied the display boards hanging on frames around three sides of the stall, all with photographs, diagrams and descriptions. He recognised many of the photos from a wall in the Old Oak, the inn owned by his cousins Fred and Ethel.

"Live in Oak Cross?" asked John Lennon II, inquisitive yet friendly.

"Moved here from London, seven months ago, when I got married. But my Grandmother came from here, lived over at the Inn before she moved to London for work." Gary pointed towards where he thought the inn was.

"Really?" John II said. "Name's Bob Hodges, and we hold our meetings there, in the inn, once a month if you're interested." Gary smiled, ignoring the offer; Bob continued: "Fred gave us copies of many of these photographs."

"I recognise some," replied Gary, still looking at the photographs, but without adding that he'd never really bothered with them before.

"So, you already know the village history?"

"Not really," Gary shook his head. "I visited as a kid in the fifties and early sixties. Usually at Christmas, for a few days. Not the most exciting visits. But I married a local girl and we brought High Swallow Cottage."

"Miss Turner's cottage? Yes, I know it. Both her and her Grandmother were well-established residents." Bob moved to one of the boards at the back of the stall, that's Mrs Turner's grandmother, Ma Turner as she was known in the village."

Gary stared at a sepia picture of an aging, smartly-dressed

woman – long gown, shawl and short hair – who was looking to the right of the camera. His interest perked up when he saw his house in the background.

"Ma Turner," Bob continued, "lived here when the village was very isolated. Its occupants were very poor and they lived in run-down housing. Poverty-stricken you might say." He glanced around, then leaned forward and sniggered, as if about to reveal a secret. "What today I would call a dump." He tapped the picture. "She was one of those Revered McDonald coerced into helping improve things." He leaned back. "It's why we celebrate the Reverend today. He improved life for those that lived here. Everyone's lives." It was a repeat of what Gary had just heard from Anne.

"So," Gary asked, "was there really an old oak tree?"

Bob stared for a moment and Gary realised Bob thought he was joking. Gary kept his expression inquisitive until Bob realised he was serious. "There certainly was." Bob pointed to another sepia picture. "This one's of the giant tree." The photograph had been taken from a distance so that the whole tree could be seen. Its wide trunk and size definable by a man wearing a top hat and a long frock coat, buttoned up to his chin, standing under the branches. He appeared tiny against the massive oak. "It stood in front of, what is now called Standish Lane, which goes up to the canal. It was chopped down about 1912 to allow for the main road to be widened."

"Progress," Gary remarked dryly.

Bob nodded. "Indeed, big event back then. All the villagers attended when it finally came down." He smiled, taking his glasses and polishing them with a not-so-clean handkerchief. "The entrance gate to the church grounds and cemetery," he said, "and the columns supporting the church archway, came from that oak tree. They were all installed, obviously, before the war memorial was added."

Gary remembered seeing his grandmother's maiden name, Lewis, listed on the memorial, and realised again how little he knew of the village.

He felt a hand slide into his and turned to see Anne standing beside him. "Ready?" she said. "I've seen enough and want a coffee."

Gary was pleased she hadn't brought anything. "Just hearing about the village." He indicated the stall.

"It's a lovely place," Anne said to Bob. "The village, the countryside, and the canal. We enjoy walking along the canal." She glanced at her husband and, in that moment, Gary knew she was reminiscing about those peaceful walks along the towpath when they had first started dating, when they were just chatting, getting to know each other better.

"Ah," Bob exclaimed, visibly excited, "the canal. Now that's another story, it's exactly 100 years ago this year—"

"I am sorry, love to hear." Gary spoke quickly, before Bob got started. "But we must go." He squeezed Anne's hand as a signal, having heard enough,

"Oh, no problem," replied Bob, although clearly wanting to talk more. "But get the local paper this Friday." He leaned forward and sniggered again, as if divulging yet another secret. "They are printing a story about the village this week. Tells how Standish Lane got its name. Not a very nice story, and it doesn't put village in a good light. Their reporter called me in case I could add anything." He shook his head despondently. "I couldn't help her. All in the past and long forgotten by most folks. Most people here have no idea who Standish was, but the story may be of interest to you."

"Thank you. I'm sure it will," Gary said pleasantly, then began shuffling away. He pulled Anne's hand before she asked anything else.

"Hey, here." Bob smiled, trying to hang onto his audience. He looked at his table and took a couple of leaflets from a pile. "This will tell you a little more, about how the area has changed and the improvements. Normally I charge fifty pence each for these pamphlets, for our funds. But as you are now new residents..."

Anne returned his smile, took the pamphlets and passed them to Gary. "No," she said, "we can't do that. Can we, Gary?"

Gary shook his head in defeat and, grinning at Anne, handed over another pound.

Once out of earshot, Anne asked: "What was that all about?"

"Haven't got the foggiest." Gary pushed the leaflets indifferently into his anorak pocket before adding, with a smile: "But I bet you can't wait for Friday."

Chapter 13
Friday

Gary had forgotten all about the village fete of the previous Saturday, until the local paper, *The South Counties Herald*, dropped through the letterbox early Friday morning. The paper sat open beside his plate as he ate breakfast in the kitchen. Today he planned to do some jobs in the garden and had put on old cords and a worn denim shirt – what he thought of as his work clothes. However, despite his plans for the garden and the radio being tuned to Noel Edmonds, his interest was currently captured by an article on the forthcoming 100th anniversary of the "1877 Canal Murders". Anne, in her dressing gown, was taking cosmetics out of a makeup bag.

"That story, the one the fete chap mentioned, it's in the paper," Gary said as Anne rummaged through her bag.

"Can't find my mirror," she muttered to herself before tipping the contents of the bag onto a chair.

Gary continued regardless, "It seems there was a robbery and several brutal murders 100 years ago on the canal."

"Got it," cried Anne seeing her mirror on the worktop.

Gary chewed his toast without taking his eyes off the paper; a lump of marmalade dropped unnoticed onto his work cords. "Money, jewels, bank notes, all in large wooden chests." He looked up as Anne sat opposite him, taking a bite of her own toast before finishing her mug of barely warm coffee.

Gary continued reading. "Would you believe it? They hanged a farmer and his sons, all believed innocent. The wife lost the farm. She hanged herself, and their daughters were sent to live elsewhere."

"Hmm, why did they hang them?" Anne set her mirror on her table.

Gary looked at her and realised she had not been listening. "There was a robbery here, a hundred years ago, by the canal bridge, the money hidden and never found, and all those possibly involved or investigating, were sent to Africa and died."

"What, of disease? How horrible." Anne started to apply her make up.

"No, not disease," Gary replied, a little irritated. "All wiped out in battle." He wanted to discuss this more, but gave up when he saw the look on Anne's face.

"Make us another cup of coffee please." She looked at Gary and smiled. "And you've got marmalade on your trousers."

Gary looked down and lifted the escaped dollop back onto his plate with his fingers before licking them. He laid the paper down, picked up another slice of toast and stood. Eating his toast, he retrieved a tin of instant coffee from the cupboard. He tried again to enlighten Anne as to why he was interested, even though it was obvious her attention was still elsewhere. "Somewhere in this village," he said, "is a vast hidden fortune." With her research into the village, he was surprised at her lack of interest.

Anne didn't reply immediately, instead she adjusted her round mirror. When she did speak, she sounded distracted. "What's your plan today?"

Gary looked through the French windows – old enough to be on their list of things to change – into the garden. He thought it looked like a jungle: tall grass, which waved in the wind, surrounded a bulky pile of bracken, branches and brambles. It filled the middle of the garden and successfully blocked the view to the end. "I guess I'll finish clearing that lot to make room for our vegetable garden." He pointed with his piece of toast to the area where the stable once stood. "Perhaps take some of that to the tip."

"You'll need the car, then," said Anne.

"Well, the horse and cart went when they pulled the stable down."

Anne stopped applying make-up, and gave him a scornful sideways look. "Very funny."

He thought again how attractive she was. Her smile could light up a dreary winter's day. His life always improved when he saw it. She was slightly shorter than he was, and wore her light-brown hair short, barely brushing her shoulders.

She finished applying her eyeshadow around her hazel eyes, which he always thought were deep and inviting. "If you run me to work," she said, "you can have the car and you can pick me up later. I'm doing a couple of extra hours, finishing about seven."

Gary nodded, and placed the mug of coffee in front of her. She leaned up to give him a kiss. "Ah, hate that moustache," she said.

Gary grinned. He thought his Mexican moustache, which Anne had never liked, complemented his coarse dark hair and made him look like a member of The Yardbirds. While his hair covered his ears and collar, it was not as long as the current fashion. He kept it neat: he thought it important when meeting customers. He stood a fraction under six feet, with a longish face and a dimple in his chin. For the past seven years, due to being long-sighted, he had worn glasses.

"What are you doing for lunch?" Anne switched make-up brushes.

"After all my hard work this week," he said with a grin, "I thought I would treat myself and get something at the inn."

Anne nodded and smiled, and studied her work in the mirror. "Now," she said, "I must get dressed."

Later, having dropped Anne at work and returned home, Gary made himself a fresh mug of instant coffee and looked out into the garden. He then returned to the newspaper and spent another half hour re-reading the story of the robbery. His thoughts kept returning to the article as he spent the rest of the morning digging and hacking at more dead and overgrown plants. The central mound of rubbish grew ever higher. It was hot work despite the chill; autumn was on its way. Just before midday he was ready for a break. After a quick wash and a change of clothing, he set off on the short distance to the Old Oak Inn.

A row of woodpigeons, looking as if they were on parade, sat on telegraph wires as the clouds above parted, allowing the sun through to finally bring the day some warmth.

With only a few customers the inn was quiet, although Gary was sure more villagers would be arriving within the next half hour. An open fire sat at the far end of the room, with logs crackling and sparks flying around the grate. A wicker basket with dry logs sat beside it. The bar ran from the fireplace to the entrance, beside which hung a gallery of old photographs. He recognised some of the pictures – they had been used in the newspaper article and he had seen a few at the fete. Above the bar were shelves, supported from the ceiling, upon which waited clean beer glasses ready to be grabbed and filled. Gary approached the bar and glanced to his right, towards the photo gallery, then to his left. At the far end of the bar, on a stool with his feet dangling, sat his Uncle Tom. He was in his eighties, with a few wispy white hairs still retained on his head. The fire warmed him. A thin cigarette protruded from his mouth and he was staring thoughtfully into a pint of bitter. A flat cap sat on the bar next to his drink. He helped in the pub, collecting glasses. Gary had often seen regulars buy him a drink, hence it appeared he always had a glass close to hand.

"Hallo, Uncle Tom," called Gary.

The old man looked up. "Gary!" The welcome was accompanied by a happy grin. "Come to buy your old uncle a drink?"

Gary's cousin Fred, owner of the inn, a broad-shouldered man in his sixties with a receding hairline and warm smile approached from behind the bar. Unlike Tom, in his grubby work overalls, Fred was smartly dressed and even wearing a tie. Like Gary, he also had a distinctive dimple in his chin. "I'm sure," Fred said with a wink, "Gary has better ways of spending his money than buying an old curmudgeon like you a drink." Gary grinned at his cousin as he ordered a pint of lager for himself, offered to buy Fred a drink, and finally turned to the older man. "What's yours, Uncle Tom?"

Gary stared at his cousin and his uncle, both from different generations of his wider family. He could see a similarity with his own late grandmother. She was the middle child of three; Tom was her the youngest brother. The older brother, also now deceased, was Alfred – grandfather to Fred.

A widower, Tom lived with Fred and his wife Ethel at the inn, maintaining its garden, tending its impressive flowerbeds and mending lawnmowers and almost anything else mechanical for the villagers. When not doing all that, his favourite job was collecting glasses in the inn.

"That's very good of you," Tom nodded his gratitude. "I'll have my usual whisky."

"You'll have a beer, Uncle. Half pint at that, and be thankful." It was Fred's age and affection for his oldest relative, Gary knew, that allowed him to speak that way.

"No, it's okay," said Gary. "Make it a whisky."

The old man grinned mockingly at Fred, who returned the expression as he flicked the lager tap. "Keeping busy working on your new house?" He handed Gary his lager then picked up a tumbler and turned to the Scotch whisky optic.

"Oh, that's right," Tom licked his lips as he watched Fred. "You're in Carrie Piggott-Turner's house."

"I thought her name was just Turner," said Gary, confused.

"Her father and mother died when she was young; she lived with her nan, Ma Turner, who brought her up, and she reverted back to just Turner," said Tom, his forehead furrowing at the effort of remembering. "When Carrie was very young, your nan, Gary, used to babysit her. Now, Ma Turner, she was what you would call a real aristocratic lady."

"That's some time ago, Tom. I only vaguely remember nan." Fred handed Tom his drink then wiped the counter with a bar towel that advertised a strong bitter that Fred both sold and enjoyed. "Excuse him, Gary, lives in his own world." Fred took a sip of his own drink.

"How's Anne and the job-hunting," asked Fred, showing his

credentials as a good host with a good memory.

"Anne's fine; job hunting's on hold." Gary said enjoying the company. Fred and Tom had been adults when he was a child so they had never been close. Now the age gap seemed much less. Gary asked about lunch, Fred recommended the shepherd's pie and Gary ordered it.

"Make yourself comfy over at a table. Tom will bring it over; he can earn his keep."

Gary moved to a table by the window, overlooking the village green, and sat on a high-backed wooden bench. A padded cushion prevented the hard seat from becoming uncomfortable. More customers entered the inn, and Gary drank slowly, enjoying his pint of lager while people-watching. It occurred to him how pleasant his life was despite the loss of his job and the hard physical labour in the garden.

Tom brought over his meal with another pint. "That's from Fred." Gary looked over to Fred, raised his glass, and acknowledged with a nod. Tom had somehow renewed his own pint, and still had some whisky left. He took a seat opposite Gary, screwed up his flat cap, and pushed it into the front pocket of his overalls. Obviously, he intended to stay. He opened a small square tin, which showed its age through its dents, and took out a Rizla cigarette paper. He held the paper in one hand and expertly filled it with tobacco also taken from the tin. Gary watched, fascinated, as he had done as a child. Tom rolled the paper with fingers stained yellow-brown then licked its edge, sealing the cigarette. He looked up, smiling broadly at Gary as he put it into his mouth, lighting it with a battered silver lighter. Gary caught the aroma of petrol as the ignition sparked a flame. Tom drew on the cigarette, then spoke as he exhaled, smoke filling the air. "Always liked you, Gary; never gave me any lip."

"You scared me as a kid," Gary replied whist eating. "Nan said you were a rogue."

Tom laughed out loud. "God love her." He thought for a moment then laughed again. "We had some fun round here. We were close you know. Being older, she looked after me." Now he went quiet, filled with his own thoughts. His eyes followed his smoke, although what they were actually seeing Gary couldn't guess. When Tom spoke again his voice was softer. "Lived here all my life, Gary. Except for the First World War. I made it back, unlike many others." He wiped an eye. "I'm the last of my family line. Seen some changes, I can tell you."

Gary smiled as he ate, sure other generations had heard this. To raise his mood Gary asked: "It's a lovely place to live, how old are you Uncle Tom?"

He answered proudly. "I'm 88 this year, born 1889." He winked. "Or so I'm told. Can tell you some stories about things that happened here."

"I read one this morning," said Gary scooping his fork through the mash of his shepherd's pie. "The canal robbery. Wonder where they hid the money?" Tom's expression changed as if he'd been slapped. He stared at Gary, open mouthed, the cigarette stuck to the wetness of his bottom lip, ash hanging in mid-air. "Read what, where?"

"The local paper, a robbery 100 years ago on the canal. I—"

Tom was up and at the bar in an instant. "Fred, Fred. Where's the local paper? You hiding it?"

"Now calm down," said Fred. "I'll find it, who told you?" Tom pointed to Gary who stared – feeling guilty but unsure why – at Fred. Gary's filled fork remained held in mid-air.

"It's okay," Fred said, holding up his hand. "Tom, sit down I'll get it for you." Tom, red with anger, returned to the table and sat in silence, his cigarette drooping from his lips, burning slowly.

Gary had demolished half his shepherd's pie by the time Fred brought over the newspaper. He handed it to Tom. "It's all right," he said apologetically to Gary. "Uncle Tom knows this story."

Ignoring them both, Tom opened the pages flicking though them until he'd found the article about the robbery. Gary noticed Fred shake his head and return to his position behind the bar. Tom read, gripping the paper as if scared it would be stolen from him. Gary ate his meal quietly, occasionally hearing a huff from across the table. Finally, Tom closed the paper, with a rustle. Gary thought he appeared calmer.

"Old story," sighed Tom, "read it before, nothing new, still wrong."

Tom looked at Gary, who said uneasily, "You obviously know this story."

"Know it? Know it?" His tone rose to a shout. "I know the *real* story, son. Because my father," he pointed at Gary, "your great grandfather, was the man who planned it."

Chapter 14
Friday

Tom had the look of a man who had revealed a confidence but was now wondering if it was a mistake. Gary placed his fork on the plate, which Tom promptly laid the paper over as if it were more important that Gary read rather than eat. "It says," Tom continued, "they were all killed. Read it, read it."

"I have read it," said Gary perplexed. "They all died."

Tom's head shook his head, ash floating onto the table from his dying cigarette butt. "But they didn't. He wasn't even at that battle. He fought at Rorke's Drift."

Gary looked around, uncomfortable, hoping Fred would return. He pushed the paper back, but Tom leaned in. "I never knew him. He left us before I was born, but he planned it, used others, but it was his plan."

"This happened a century ago." Gary raised his eyebrows, and added an insincere laugh. "You're winding me up."

"Doesn't make it untrue." Clearly taking offence, Tom sat back and stubbed out the remains of his cigarette in a brewery ashtray. He crossed his arms and shook his head again, his anger obvious. "Same as everyone else. You don't believe it." He stood, upset.

"No wait, Uncle Tom." Gary leant forward and placed a hand on Tom's arm. "Please explain."

Tom glared, his aging face taut, unforgiving, but he sat back down.

"I thought it was just a joke," said Gary

Tom pulled out his tobacco tin to make a fresh cigarette. "Everyone thinks I'm a joke. Dismisses me. But my mother told me: after Rorke's Drift, he deserted. His name was Henry Price. Once a Corporal." He finished his whisky, his face screwing up as the liquid hit the back of his throat.

"How can you prove it?" Gary asked, his disbelief wavering.

"Why should I tell you?" Tom replied, sulking like a child. "Shown others, inside and out of this family, but no one listens." He pointed towards Fred. "Telling others embarrasses him. I showed a pretty girly a few weeks ago. She was looking at the pictures on the pub wall, she was." He shrugged. "She thought me daft, I could tell, and she left before I could tell her more and prove what I was saying."

"I don't think you're daft, Uncle Tom." Gary's interest was piqued. It reminded him of watching a trailer for a new film. He pushed his almost empty plate to one side. "Neither Nan nor Mum ever mentioned this story." Then, as further persuasion, with added bribery, he said: "Let's have another drink, whisky?"

Tom grinned. "Get the drinks, son, and I'll show you something." Despite his age he stood and almost ran through the side door next to the fire.

Gary took the plate and tray to the bar. "Another whisky and a pint please, Fred." Then, thinking: "No. Make it a half, I've still some gardening to do."

"He's not bothering you?" Fred asked as he flicked the lager pump tap.

"No, he's okay," replied Gary, then added, sheepishly, "Tells me we're descended from a thief."

Fred snorted. "And a murderer. The story of Henry Price;

heard it all before, although my grandfather said it was all rubbish."

"You've heard it before?" Gary asked, surprised. A story like this, he thought, would surely have been passed down, like some sort of genetic inheritance.

"Most of the older family have, and just ignored it. They think Tom's time in Flanders shook him up a bit. Also the death of his son." Fred paused, turning to the same whisky optic as before.

"The real story," Fred spoke slowly, "is Tom's father was neither reliable nor a good provider. He came here in the 1890s, looking for work, with his mistress, Susan, and their two kids, Harry and Nell – who'll be my grandad and your nan. Sam Longhurst, the original inn owner, gave them both jobs. Tom's father worked in the bar and did casual work, while Susan cleaned and worked in the kitchen. Tom's father also did other labouring jobs in the village to get by, and then, one day, not long after arriving, he disappeared. Abandoned Tom's mum with no warning. She was pregnant again, this time with Tom. That's probably why he went." Fred placed the whisky tumbler on the counter. "If not for Sam Longhurst, and the generosity of the locals, Susan would have been in a right mess. Did you know, Tom was born right here, in this inn?" Fred looked up as if trying to locate which room. "Tom's mother continued helping to run the pub, and when Tom was aged about 14 my grandad also worked here." Fred looked up as a man approached the bar, carrying an empty glass. "Another pint, sir?" Fred asked, a professional smile stuck on. The man nodded and Fred furnished him with a fresh pint. Gary waited, trying to take it all in. After wiping the counter, Fred returned to Gary.

"Sam, the inn owner, was a widower himself and 10 years older than Susan; when it became obvious Tom's father was not coming back, Susan and Sam lived together as man and wife. When Sam died, he left the inn to our family. It seems Susan told her three children that their father had brought the family to this village looking for enough money to make them all rich. Tom's the only one who's always believed it." Fred shrugged.

"The proceeds of the canal robbery?"

"If you believe it."

Gary thought. "Henry Price is what Tom called him."

"Lewis was your grandmother's maiden name, right?"

Gary nodded, handing a £5 note to Fred, who turned to the till behind him. The till pinged as Fred pressed its button and the draw shot open. He collected the change and handed it across the bar. "From what I was told," Fred said, "life was difficult for Susan after this Henry left. A single mother with three children and one of them a newborn." Fred glanced over to Gary's empty table and grinned. "Tom's probably gone to get two family photos his mother gave him. They show his father's face, badly injured. Granddad said it was a knife fight. The man was a wastrel, Gary. Tom believes otherwise, sad really. Still, we can't complain. His father's disappearance did us some good." He looked around the inn. "It got us this place. If you want my advice, do as others have done and disappear now, I'll sort it with Tom. He can get embarrassing."

"No, it's okay. Nothing else to do." Gary decided to ignore the garden. Fred just shrugged again.

On his return to the table, Gary held out the whisky while Tom placed his proof, three photographs, onto the table before taking his drink. Gary picked up the three-by-four inch sepia photographs. Despite their age and size, the definition was good.

Tom smiled. "Recognise that? That's the bridge where it happened.'

Gary looked at the picture. The place did look familiar, the bridge, the canal the towpath, but before he could dredge the location from his memory, Tom was off again, handing over the other two pictures.

"That's my dad, nearly a century ago."

Gary dropped the first photo on the table and looked at the new pictures thrust before him. The first showed a man and a woman with two children. The man was broad shouldered, his short hair was parted in the middle and he sported a very bushy moustache that drooped either side of his mouth, framing a dimple in his chin. He wore waistcoat and jacket, with a white scarf around his neck tucked into his jacket. The picture was clearly taken in a studio with a parkland background of trees and hills. No one was smiling.

Tom pointed at the picture. "That's my father, with my mother." Tom tapped the glass to indicate each of the children. "And that's Fred's grandad, Harry, and Nell, your grandmother." He glanced again at Gary. "Never realised, but with your moustache, you have his looks."

Gary scowled, ignoring Tom, and looked at the second picture.

"See the ear and the scar?" said Tom. The picture was clearly taken at the same time and place but showed only the man and children. The photograph was taken from much closer and the man had turned and was looking at his eldest boy, so that it showed his left profile. His daughter sat in his lap. The top of the man's ear was missing, and a deep scar ran from his ear to his chin. Tom's finger appeared above the picture, tracing at the wound. "He got that during the battle of Rorke's Drift. The fighting really shook him up, so mother said, as it did all the other men who fought there. One-hundred men against four thousand Zulu's, enough to scare anybody. Have you seen the film *Zulu*?"

Gary stared at the pictures confused. That scar: knife fight or battle? Knife fight seemed most obvious but…

Tom interrupted his thoughts. "According to mother, when he recovered from those wounds he deserted. Killed a man in Durban, same height and build, and swapped identities. He made sure he could not be identified." Tom raised his hand to his ear and face, Gary raised his eyebrows realising the implication. "Mum said he hid out, doing casual work, then worked his passage home on a freighter to Bristol." In the fire, a red-hot log fell, glowing, onto the grate. Fred walked to the fire and, with metal prongs, lifted the log back into the inferno. Gary noticed Fred glance at their table and, seeing the photographs, smile and return to the bar. Gary blushed as if caught lying.

Tom was still talking, "Back in Bristol he took up with mother. She got pregnant with Harry, Fred's grandad. They started travelling around, working, had Nell, your Nan, on their way, but mother said he was always heading in one direction. To get back here."

Gary held up the picture and then, confused, he turned and stared through the small glass panels of the leaded window onto the peaceful village green, with the church in the distance. The fire crackled, customers talked, and glasses clinked but Gary heard none of it. He was pondering what he had seen and the story he'd never been told before. Someone near the bar dropped their pint glass. It shattered on the stone floor, and everyone jumped and turned at the noise; everyone except Gary, who continued looking through the window oblivious to his surroundings.

Finally, he returned his attention back to the picture. Was this man in the picture a thief, he wondered, a murderer and his also his great-grandfather? He looked up at Tom who had a newly lit cigarette between his lips. Tom tipped his head sideways like a puppy expecting a treat. "You believe me, don't you?"

"So you're saying he did all that, went through all that, and then came back here?"

Tom nodded.

"But…, you're saying he believed or knew the money from the robbery was still here. That it hadn't been found? Is that likely?"

Tom's nods became more excited.

"And he disappeared, and it's still never been found?"

"Never." Tom shook his head, grinning.

"Have you looked for the money yourself?"

"Did as a kid, with your grandmother, before she got fed up. Old Reverend McDonald told us off when we were kids, said looking and talking about it was bad. God would be unhappy."

Gary handed the photographs back to his uncle. "To tell you the truth, I don't know whether to believe it. It's a story I only read today." He thought for a moment. "It should be easy to check with the paper if it's a mistake. If a man called Price was at Rorke's Drift and survived."

Tom pushed the two photographs back to Gary. "Go ahead, they're yours."

Gary responded, embarrassed. "I can't keep them, Uncle. I mean, they're yours "

"And what will I do with them? You're family, Gary. I don't have anybody. Fred won't appreciate them when I'm gone."

Gary glanced at his watch and was surprised to see that over an hour had passed since his arrival. The inn was now much busier, and people were looking for free tables.

"Prove I am not an old fool, Gary." Tom pleaded, faltering.

Gary, still a little embarrassed, picked up the photographs. "Let me check, but I really must go."

As Gary was leaving, he looked back and saw Tom, a sad, lonely figure making his way back to the bar. Gary heard Fred call, "Was he all right?" with genuine family concern.

"He's okay." Gary held up the photographs. "I said I would check some of the details, about the battle. If that's okay with you."

Fred nodded, "Fine with me, if it keeps him happy. Not sure what's to check, but kind of you." Before Fred turned back to his customers, he added: "You'll be the one has to tell him it's all rubbish."

Gary hadn't thought of that. He walked out of the pub just as the sun disappeared behind clouds. The day had changed, it was not as bright, and it put a damper on his enthusiasm to help his uncle. So, what was he going to do? He knew the garden still needed seeing to, but in his heart he also knew he was going to find the local newspaper offices.

Chapter 15
Friday Afternoon: I

Gary found the offices of the *South Counties Herald* down a side street in the town centre. Formerly a double-fronted shop, the once welcoming bright green facade was now weathered, worn and almost colourless. Behind the grimy windows could just be seen a display of pictures and articles that had appeared over the years. Many of the photographs were faded and a lot of the articles curled at the edges.

A bell tinkled as Gary pushed open the door. On the way to the offices, Gary had decided it was best to start with the person who wrote today's article.

A glass-fronted haberdashery counter – empty of stock and a remnant from the building's retail days of the 1950s – formed the desk of a middle-aged receptionist who was busy typing. A closed door behind her displayed the sign 'Offices'. She stopped her work and looked up. "Yes?" she inquired with a smile,

Gary held up the paper, reading the name on the article, "Could I see Kate Richie?"

"I'll call her." She picked up her phone and dialled an extension. "Kate, someone here wants to see you." The woman covered the mouthpiece. "What's it's in connection with?" she asked, still smiling.

"Her article," said Gary, "in this week's paper."

The woman advised Kate of the reply, paused and put the phone back in its cradle. Returning to her typing and without looking up she said: "She's coming down."

Gary looked around the poorly lit room with its walls of faded green paint, and wondered when it was last decorated. A table and chairs looked newer than the counter, but not by much. Fixed to two walls were glass cabinets containing even more photographs, mainly sepia but some in pristine black and white and a few in colour. One of the colour photos showed three young women in swimsuits, each holding an A4 card showing their first, second and third positions in a beauty contest. The photo was dated five years ago. He was studying the photograph, trying to decide if he agreed with the judges' choices, when he heard a voice behind him. "You wanted to see me."

Gary turned to see Number 2 from the photograph. She stood slightly taller than Gary, in her late twenties, he guessed, and very attractive; her thick black hair was styled just like Jaclyn Smith's from *Charlie's Angels*. He pointed back at the picture. "You?"

Kate looked around him at the photograph. "My twin sister." She pointed to the name, Louise Richie, at the bottom of the photograph. "We both have the looks, but I have the brains."

Gary smiled at the joke, then held up the newspaper. "I'm Gary Stevens, can I ask you about this article?"

"Oh, God." Kate's voice was weary, and she raised her eyebrows. "Please tell me you're not from Mr Jackson. He has been told the paper authorised the article."

"No, I am not from anybody," said Gary, quickly, yet wondering who Mr Jackson was. "I just wanted to clarify something in the article."

"Shall we sit down?" Her interest appeared renewed. "You have something to ask or add?"

"Ask. You did write the article?" he said as they sat on two hard-plastic chairs at a table near the counter.

"Not exactly. The original article was written for the fiftieth anniversary of the robbery. I came across it shortly after I joined the paper. I brought it up to date. Why do you ask?"

"Who wrote the original story?"

"A young journalist called Douglas Jackson. He started at this paper and eventually became well known working for the nationals. He's now retired." She shook her head and her hair swayed. "He read the article and keeps phoning, complaining we should have contacted him first. Damn cheek if you ask me. The paper owns the article. I got them to reprint it. I thought you were from him. But why the interest?"

He opened the paper. "It says here that all those connected with the robbery were killed in the Zulu battle of Isan…dlw…ana." He figured he was pronouncing it wrong, but ploughed on anyway. "Is that correct? I mean you're sure they were all there?"

Kate, leaned back, her face showing scepticism. "Yes, sure they were. Now though, you've got me intrigued. I mean, history books tell us almost all died and only a few got away." She nodded at the paper. "And any that did get away were not believed to be involved with that robbery."

"You're sure? I mean, all those implicated or involved in the theft were in that battle."

She turned her head to one side, pondering, her mind clearly elsewhere. Gary guessed she was trying to remember the original article, along with figuring out what he knew and what she did not.

"You think a suspect survived?" she asked, her thoughts

clearly returning to the present.

Gary folded the paper, placing it on the table. "Not sure. There's a possibility a suspect may not have been at that battle." He opened his wallet and took out one of the photographs Tom had given him. He held it out and Kate took it, her initial inquisitive expression changing to a flash of recognition. She looked away as if to hide her surprise.

"What's the matter? Do you know this man?"

"No, no," she said quickly. "It's just an old picture. Can I ask where you got this?"

"I would like to know if the article is correct first."

Kate handed the photograph back. "Give me a few minutes. I have the original article upstairs, let me check." Without a further word she left through the door behind the counter. Gary waited, spending the time looking at more photographs on the wall.

On her return, her beaming face gave him his answer. "Well," she said joyfully, sitting back at the table, holding a box file. "You were right. Douglas Jackson identified a Corporal Price, not in the escort accompanying the money, but implicated by Captain Russell's investigations." She hesitated, getting her thoughts together. "Corporal Price was *not* at that battle, Isandlwana," she said. "He fought at Rorke's Drift, and was later killed. I saw no special relevance in complicating my version of the story so included him with the other victims." She took the photo again. "Is he the one in the picture? If so, how did he get back?" Kate's eyes interrogated Gary, as if she were doing a quiz and Gary had the answers tattooed on his forehead. When he didn't respond, she tried another tack. "What's your link with the photo? I may know someone who would be interested in what you know."

Gary considered his answer. If the story was true, perhaps Tom should make the decision. Also, it affected others, such as Fred, who didn't want any more embarrassment. Gary retrieved the photograph.

Kate must have seen his uncertainty. "I'm not talking about the newspaper articles that have been published," she added. "I mean it's old news. But I know someone else who also knows this story. He could be interested in talking to you, perhaps even buying the pictures. If they're for sale. I'll contact him if you wish."

"I'll have to talk to someone first."

Kate was now excited, jumping up and bounding to the counter like a youngster. She called to the woman still typing behind the counter. "Maureen. Give me a pad and pen." She held out her hand, exhilaration showing in her face. Gary thought her demand to Maureen rude and wondered why, if the story was 'old news', she was so excited. Kate turned back to him. "I will talk to David, my friend." She passed the pad and pen to Gary. "Give me your phone number and address."

Gary wrote his details and passed them back.

Kate stared at his address, "I borrowed some pictures from the inn near you, for the article. Did the photograph come from there? I didn't see it."

"Do you have more on Corporal Price's death?"

Kate shook her head. "Jackson's the only person who may have more information."

"Where does he live?" Gary figured Jackson could be a helpful link.

"He's retired and lives in Farnham." Kate looked at her notes and added with scorn, "And he certainly knows how to use a bloody telephone."

"Farnham's not far. Do you have his address? Perhaps he could fill in some of the spaces."

Kate thought, then answered excited. "Yes. After today he might be more receptive. Especially if you contacted him rather than me." She spoke as if agreement had already been made to meet her friend and, checking her file, she wrote Jackson's phone number and address on the pad, ripped out the page and handed it over.

"I will call my friend, we can speak again tomorrow." After shaking hands she left thorough the door to the offices. Gary walked to the counter, "Maureen, sorry to bother you again, could I please use a phone?" Maureen smiled, pointing to a phone fixed to the wall. Gary dialled the number he'd been given. It was answered by a woman.

"Hello. My name's Gary Stevens. I would like to see Mr Jackson today if possible, regarding an article in the local paper. I understand he wrote the original." The line went quiet as he heard the woman talking to someone, followed by a male voice shouting in the background, then the woman returned and he was asked when he could get there. "I'm at the local paper and just leaving. I could be with you in half an hour." A pause, then he was told that would be acceptable. "Thank you, see you soon."

He replaced the phone, thanked Maureen and left. All thoughts of returning to any more gardening had vanished.

Chapter 16
Friday Afternoon: II

He almost missed the lane. It was on a bend off the A31, hidden by a high hedge. The house, a quarter mile down the lane was large: Gary's mother would have enviously described it as "posh detached double-fronted". A silver Volvo was parked on the horseshoe drive. Before Gary could press the doorbell, the front door was opened by a woman wearing slacks, blouse and bright blue cardigan. Her hair, although a faded brown, was thick and hung over her shoulders, down her back. Gary found it difficult to guess her age: she could have been in her late sixties, but her face looked younger.

"Welcome," she said, indicating Gary should enter. "You must be Gary."

Gary recognised her voice from the telephone call. He stepped into the hall and his mouth dropped open. A seven-foot-wide open staircase with scrolled wooden pine rails rose from the centre of the hall. Above, an open landing circled the ground floor. Gary marvelled at the beautiful place. It was pleasantly warm, cosy. Five doors led off the hall: two to the left, three to the right.

The woman was explaining that her husband, Douglas Jackson, was not a well person, when one of the doors burst open and a man burst into the hall with such speed they both jumped. He was easily six-foot tall, sturdily built with sideburns and tufts of white hair on his otherwise balding head. He was unshaven and wore black-rimmed glasses and an old-fashioned red tartan dressing gown. It was tied around his middle with a multi-coloured cord. Beneath it, and despite it being afternoon, he wore pyjamas – the bottoms of which could be seen under the gown. Slippers without socks completed his look. To Gary, he appeared to be in his seventies and, despite being described as not being fit, strode briskly towards them, making Gary take a step back.

"From the paper, are you?" He halted and stood next to his wife, who had to crane her head upwards to look at him. "You've got some explaining to do, considering you've not been returning my calls." His voice was harsh and with a strong Scottish accent.

Gary looked at the woman, then back to the man, realising the mistake. Gary having called from the newspaper office, the old man thought he represented the paper. "I think there's a misunderstanding Mr Jackson, I'm—"

"Too bloody right there has," Jackson said, determined to make his point. "You use my story and because it's fifty years old and you think I won't notice?" He jabbed his finger at Gary. "I wrote it and I don't even get a mention. Well, let me tell you that—"

"Please let me explain." Gary held up his hands, but the man was on a roll.

"Why? So, you can spout some prepared excuse. Perhaps you thought I was dead? Well, I'm not dead yet. You should have contacted me before plagiarising my feature. It was almost word for word, and under some Kate person's by-line. That's my story and you did not even have the courtesy—"

"If you shut up for a second, I will explain." Gary had heard enough, and although he was blushing, his voice was resolute and delivery forceful. "I am *not* from the paper, either to give an apology or excuses. I merely telephoned *from* their office. I'm a reader, like you." Gary saw the change on Jackson's face. His mouth opened, as if to speak, then closed. He glanced at his wife. Gary was now in the driving seat. "I went to the paper for help and information." He lifted his copy of the paper. "The *South Counties Herald* couldn't help and told me you wrote the original story."

"You said you were from the paper." Jackson tried to regain some territory.

"No," asserted Gary, "*you* said, I was from the paper. If you hadn't been like a bull in a China shop, I would have explained. I was *phoning* from the paper, from their foyer."

All three stood in silence. Jackson fiddled with the cord of his dressing gown and looked at his wife for support. He saw none. She was smiling, about to laugh. "I think that told you," she paused, letting the rebuke hit home. "You're a daft bugger sometimes, Jackson." She used his surname easily, as one would a Christian name.

Douglas Jackson mumbled something unheard, then louder. "Well, if you're not a journalist, what do you want?"

"Do you remember your original article?"

Jackson sighed, raising his eyes. "Are you serious? That's why I've been making all the fuss and calls to your… to their offices."

Gary continued. "If you remember details, would you answer a few questions?"

Jackson's wife spoke. "You've already got over-excited, Jackson, making a fool of yourself, why not just listen to Gary's questions?"

Jackson stared with suspicion. "Are you a journalist?"

"No. I have nothing to do with newspapers. I only came across the story this morning, but if it's inconvenient... your wife said you were not well."

Jackson replied flippantly. "I had a heart attack eight months ago and used to smoke too much, now paying for it." He turned to his wife. "Sorry, should have introduced my wife, Eleanor, she's also my conscience. My name is Jackson." He held out his hand. "Let's start again, with some tea."

Gary shook the offered hand, then watched Jackson stride back to the room he came from.

Eleanor leaned into Gary. "Tea or coffee?"

Gary smiled "Coffee please, one sugar.

"Stand your ground," Eleanor said quietly. "He's a tough, blunt old bear. Be straight with him, he respects that; you'll get your answers."

Jackson was already in his study, seated on a bow back swivel chair, at an oak pedestal desk that had a creased black-leather top. Gary marvelled at the size of the desk; he could play table tennis on it. Jackson was coughing as Gary entered, then placed the palms of his hands firmly on the leather top. Behind Jackson were patio doors, letting in light and leading out to the garden. Two chairs faced the desk. The room felt as warm as the hall, was well-furnished and filled with books and box files and filing cabinets. Papers were strewn across a table against a side wall, and framed pictures and awards hung wherever wall space was available. Gary recognised some of the people with Jackson in the photographs as politicians or celebrities. Several filing cabinets stood in a row either side of a fireplace which, as far as Gary could tell, had not seen flames for years. A television sat in one corner with an old plug-in aerial. A record player stood next to it.

"Come in, come in," Jackson called. His attitude had changed and his voice had lost its harshness. "Make yourself comfy," he pointed to the chairs opposite, "Gary, wasn't it? Don't see many visitors these days." And bluntly: "What do you want to know?"

Gary put his newspaper on the desk and pointed at it. Another copy of the same edition was also open on his desk; there was room for both. "Was your original article changed?"

Jackson passed a copy back to Gary, like a school master handing back homework, "That's a surprising question," Jackson said after a pause. "What makes you think it's changed?" Gary pointed to the article again. "It says all those involved with the robbery were killed during the battle in South Africa. Is that correct? I believe your article identified one survivor."

"There's plenty of documentary evidence about who died and who survived. I researched quite thoroughly before writing the story. What makes you think any survived?"

Gary shifted in his seat, feeling a little uncomfortable.

"I clearly don't know the story as well as you, Mr Jackson," Gary felt unable to address this man by his surname only. "I heard, perhaps, someone died later."

Jackson leaned forward while swivelling his chair slowly, side to side. "I know this story inside out, as if I'd written it yesterday." He tapped his copy of the paper, and declared, "It's written almost word for word, a few changes, the bit about finding some human remains, that's more recent. In my article, one of those under suspicion did survive and, as you say, died later." He stopped swivelling, leaning forward as far as he could. "Now, unless you read my original article, and I don't think you did, you must have new information. What is it?"

Gary stared at the paper. "Do you think one of them made it back to England?"

"Do you?" Jackson quickly retorted.

Perplexed, Gary said nothing. All these events happened a hundred years ago, he thought, yet here he was working on the tale, feeling uncomfortable, out of his depth. Perhaps Fred was right, accept what everyone else believed. One old man had told him a story, now he was with another old man. Time to leave, he thought, and get back to the garden. He stood. "I'm sorry, Mr Jackson, I think I have been wasting your time, I saw something and ...," He paused, shrugging his shoulders. "Sorry I bothered you." He held out his hand.

"Corporal Price survived," Jackson declared. "But you knew that. I never believed he was killed in Durban. Too much of a villain."

Gary kept his hand stretched out, but Jackson ignored the gesture, clasping his own hands together. "How," he said, as if speaking to himself, "would you know that, if you only read the story today." Jackson shook his head. "You started to say you saw something." He noticed a change in Gary's expression. "You have some evidence or you wouldn't be here. So, please stay." Jackson smiled. "Sit down, you have my attention."

Gary dropped his hand to his side, uncertain what to do next. "You're good," Gary said, impressed. He returned the smile and sat back down. The photographs felt like they were burning in his wallet, and he realised if anybody could help, it would be Jackson. But he did not want to make a fool of himself.

Jackson recognised doubt in Gary, so he made his next move.

"Three years ago, excavating for a new housing estate by the canal, they found three skeletons. From their age, appearance and dress, I identified them as those who disappeared after the robbery: the bargee, his son and a soldier. Jackson stood and adjusted his dressing gown cord for modesty as he walked to one of the filing cabinets. He pulled out a selection of A4 buff folders and an A5 leather journal, spreading them across his desk. Gary read the bold black lettering of one of the folders, even though it was upside down: CORPORAL HENRY PRICE.

"My original article, my first big story to be published, upset a local wealthy family. They were descendants of the Treloar family, they said my article implied a Treloar masterminded the robbery, and threatened to sue for libel unless I was sacked. I lost my job at the paper. That implication was cleaned up in this article."

"It was the best thing that could have happened to him." They both looked to the door. Eleanor had entered the room holding a silver tray of crockery and was placing it on the coffee table in front of the sofa. "Jackson went to London," she continued, "got a job on a national, found himself in Spain, reporting on the Civil War in thirty-seven. Was very good at his job and never looked back."

"Maybe, but I have never forgotten what that family did." Jackson couldn't hide his bitterness. "Nor forgiven," he added, spreading his hands across the files. "These are my reminders, research, collected over years, including newer details like those skeletons."

Eleanor Jackson chipped in as she poured the drinks. "It's been his secondary occupation for years: trying to solve the puzzle, researching books, articles, anything to do with the Zulu wars or Old Oak Crossroads, where the crime took place." She didn't know he lived there, Gary realised.

"That money never left the locality," Jackson broadcast, getting Gary's attention. "I am convinced." He held up the old A5 journal, leather-bound with a black cord tied around the discoloured cover. Gary thought it looked like an old family bible.

"I am convinced," Jackson added, "just as Captain Russell was convinced."

Chapter 17
Friday Afternoon: III

"This..." Jackson said, placing the journal on his desk, as a curator would a priceless artefact, "…is Brevet-Major Iain Russell's journal." He tapped the book. "A record of his own investigation. He wrote everything down before he was posted to Africa."

Realising how little he knew of the full story, Gary stayed silent.

"I was shown it fifty years ago, and it was the basis of my original article. Isn't that right, dear?" Before Eleanor could answer, Jackson continued. "Russell believed the Treloars stole, hid and were going to use that money for their own gain."

Gary pulled out his two photographs and laid them side by side on the desk, as if trumping the artefact. "I was told this is Corporal Price, taken in the 1880s."

Jackson stared at the photos, then lifted both pictures. He handed one to his wife. Jackson's face a picture of elation. Grinning, he returned to his folders, opened the HENRY PRICE file, and withdrew a selection of photographs and writings, all individually contained in plastic covers. The first photograph he selected showed a group of uniformed men relaxing, stretched out in rows on the ground. A small dog was also in the picture.

"This is a copy of a famous photograph of the defenders from Rorke's Drift, taken a couple of days after the battle in 1879. In the early 1940s I contacted another surviving defender who identified that man," he pointed to a figure, "as Price." He passed Gary a second picture, to which was paper-clipped a newspaper cutting. "This was a story written for the papers in Durban and London, later in 1879. It describes an incident during the battle. The photograph was taken a month after the battle." Jackson's delight was evident; he was almost skipping. "Obviously, it is some years before your picture was taken. They are all the same man: Corporal Price, who was believed killed, only later, well after the battle."

Gary, holding a picture in each hand, flicked his gaze from one to the other.

"Look closer, Gary," Jackson commanded, "use your eyes." He passed Gary an enlargement. "This is same photo blown up. Look at his ear, and the side of his face." Jackson leant over his desk. "It's seriously swollen and, see, a scar. His injuries, and his death were both reported. Read the article."

Gary started reading.

> Whilst the Zulus, despite heavy losses, continued their assaults into the night, all were gallantly repulsed by our brave soldiers who used the light from the burning hospital to their advantage. Lieutenant Chard led Private Price and Private Hitch, shown in our photograph, in a valiant charge in the dark to secure the much-needed water barrel left near the hospital. A Zulu was shot by Private Price. Another Zulu attacked, slicing Price's cheek and ear. Hitch killed that Zulu with his bayonet. Price, ignoring his wound, with determined conduct, bayoneted another Zulu and both men continued engaging in hand-to-hand fighting with more Zulus, making a strong defence, whilst Lieutenant Chard with others pulled the much-needed water barrel back to the high redoubt made of biscuit tins. Lieutenant Chard and Private Hitch subsequently were

> awarded Victoria Crosses for their bravery. Price was also recognised for bravery but this was withdrawn when he was killed during a brawl in Durban.

Gary raised his eyes. "This says private. I thought he was a corporal."

Jackson stared at him. "Didn't you know? He was demoted on arrival in Africa. But look at your photograph, it's even clearer than mine. Go on, look."

Eleanor handed Gary his picture. "With your moustache Gary, you look like him," she said.

"Someone else told me that," muttered Gary, comparing the pictures.

"That's Price." Jackson pointed, jubilantly. He began pacing up and down behind his desk, not knowing what to do with his new energy. "This confirms what I always thought: Price lived." Jackson spoke as if he had won big on the premium bonds. "When they found what they thought was his body, the face was badly disfigured and unrecognisable. Only his papers and his uniform confirmed his identity." He turned suddenly. "Did he return to this area?"

Gary nodded, and Jackson thumped the desk. "I knew it."

"Like a dog returns to its own vomit," whispered Eleanor to herself, the two men heard her words and stared at her. She put her hand to her mouth. "Sorry, just quoting, Proverbs 26:11."

"Where did you get your picture?" Jackson asked, still unable to contain his excitement.

"It belongs to my uncle." Gary answered, feeling sheepish. "He says he's Price's son."

"So, you're related," Jackson said. "No wonder you look alike. When did Price return?"

"Late 1880s, but disappeared again soon after, leaving his family."

"Really?" said Jackson as Gary took his coffee from Eleanor. "Can you tell me any more?"

Gary re-told the story that Tom had told him. Jackson sat with his cup and saucer held tightly, both he and his wife listening intently. When Gary finished, Jackson sat back and collected his thoughts. "So," he said, "Price returned to Old Oak Crossroads because he knew the chests were still there. Let's assume the Treloars paid him off; so why did he leave his family?" Jackson turned away from Eleanor and Gary, lost in his own thoughts, murmuring to himself. "Price knew where the skeletons were buried." His eyes widened, as if he had seen a vison, and he gave a coy smile.

"Eleanor, the only other link we have is those bodies." He walked to the filing cabinets. "When they found the bodies, the story was in the local paper. I guessed immediately whose bodies they were and helped the authorities fill in the backgrounds. Naturally the developers wanted it kept low key, having homes built where bodies have been found is not a good selling point. It wasn't too difficult. First, the bodies themselves: two adults and a child. The child must have been the son of the bargee. Second, the uniform of one of the men. It had disintegrated but the belt buckle and badge were identifiable as the East Hants Light Infantry, so it wasn't Colonel Standish or Captain Farrant, besides their remains had already been identified on the barge. It was Norton." Jackson dropped back into his chair. "I identified the descendants of the victims. The bargee's family line had died off, but Norton's family, we knew from Russell's journal, had lived in Cheltenham, and they still do: a thriving farming family. I contacted them and a woman and her husband attended the funeral of Second Lieutenant Norton. The woman was a great, great-niece and surprisingly knew the story of his disappearance. How, though, after all this time? She wouldn't say. In fact, I got the impression there was more she wasn't saying. So I keep in touch. Now, I think the time may have come to re-visit her with our new evidence." He glanced at Gary. "Don't you think?"

Gary nodded. It made sense.

Jackson continued. "Perhaps now she may fill in some gaps, as a few more years have elapsed and we have more evidence. Today's Friday, I will ring her over the weekend and arrange for you to see her on Monday."

Gary heard what had been said without realising its implication. Then his eyes widened.

"Me? Now wait a minute. I can't possibly go." Gary felt as if he'd been booked into two appointments for the same time.

"Well, I certainly cannot undertake that kind of journey in my condition. My wife cannot leave me. So that leaves you." His logic seemed unanswerable.

"But I don't know enough or what to do."

"Well, you haven't done too badly so far."

"But I have other commitments." It sounded very feeble even as he said it.

"Like what? What's more important than this?" Jackson demanded.

"We have just moved into a new home, I should be working on the house. It's out of the question. My wife will need our car, so I won't have a car or the money to hire one and drop everything to go to Gloucester. I was made redundant," he added, "I'm now out of work."

"Well, now you have a job whilst we check this. You and me, working together."

Eleanor spoke. "Jackson, I think you are being unreasonable. Gary can't drop everything and go gallivanting off."

Gary stared at her, appreciating the support.

Jackson was not impressed; his face revealed his determination. "Help me. Give me a little of your time to try to solve this riddle. I could write another article, you could share my fee fifty-fifty, as little as that would be. But we could also nail the Treloars."

The room went silent, and Gary had a few seconds to ponder what 'nailing the Treloars' meant before Jackson went on the attack again.

"Look, we work as a team. You do some footwork; I continue the research; as for expenses, they are down to me. How much will you need to hire a car? Let's start with a couple of hundred." Opening a desk drawer, Jackson pulled out a cheque book.

Gary stopped him. "Please wait. I am interested, but…"

"Then take it. Look son, I don't know how much longer I have. I've been chasing this for as long as I can remember." By now he was almost pleading. "Something about this story stirred you, just as it did me fifty years ago. I need you, Gary. If it takes dishing out a few pounds to dig a little deeper, so be it. I want this story and I want those Treloars."

Gary kept quiet, which indicated to Jackson he was wavering, so he pushed ahead. "Don't forget, you also have an interested party, your uncle."

Gary looked at the newspaper on the desk. Faltering, he picked up the old journal, gazing at it as if it gave him his answer. The story was intriguing, and it would be nice to prove Tom right. His look towards Jackson was reticent, but he answered: "Maybe a short quick trip would be okay."

"Excellent. Here's the cheque." Jackson spoke quickly in case Gary changed his mind. "You fill in the details."

Gary looked at his watch. "Is that the time? It's almost six. I have to meet my wife."

"I'll phone the Nortons tomorrow. You come for lunch on Sunday." He smiled. "Both of you. I will get some reading for you and prepare list of questions." Jackson picked up a pen and started writing. "See you Sunday," he said without looking up.

Gary stood, looking at Jackson, who was now in a world of his own, scribbling away.

"We should leave," said Eleanor, placing her arm on Gary's shoulder.

Jackson lifted his head, a sympathetic smile on his face. "Pleased you came, Gary. Thank you."

In the hall, a little shell-shocked, Gary asked, "How did he get the journal? He certainly knows the story."

Eleanor's smile was similar to the one that Gary had admired when he arrived. "Major Russell was my great grandfather. His journal was in our family. When I showed Jackson, we hadn't realised the Treloar family still had influence. Spencer Treloar had two sisters, one married into a wealthy family of merchants in this area. Their descendants still live locally. After Jackson's firing, we both left for London and we married, he never forgave the Treloars for abusing their influence. Major Russell believed Spencer Treloar planned the robbery, but it went wrong, and if Jackson can find the truth…" She gave Gary a rueful smile. "It's the misuse of power he hates. But now my husband has a little of that power."

Gary left, thinking how the day had changed. Now he had to meet Anne and explain why he was off to Cheltenham Spa on Monday.

Chapter 18
Saturday

Gary encountered what he thought of as a 'cold front' upon being late to meet Anne. The subsequent drive home that Friday evening was done in an atmosphere so frosty the heater had no chance. And then, upon hearing he was going to Cheltenham on Monday, and with an overnight stay, the blizzard began. It was a tempest of an argument.

Saturday morning, after an awkward breakfast, Gary drove Anne to her work at the hospital, then returned to his gardening. He toiled without stopping, hacking shrubs and clearing branches. He picked up a hired estate car, much larger than their little runaround, and used it to load the cut vegetation for trips to the tip. On his return from his second trip, he was surprised to see a silver sports saloon, a Mercedes-Benz, parked in front of his drive, preventing him from pulling in. Glancing at the licence plate, he noted it was this year's registration. He also noted two people sitting inside the vehicle, which was so highly polished its glints made Gary squint. As he parked the hire car by the kerb, Gary tried to figure out who he knew with such an expensive vehicle. And who would be so thoughtless as to obstruct his driveway. He couldn't think of anyone; he was glad to say he didn't move in such circles. Certainly, his brother didn't own such a car or would park so thoughtlessly. His answer came when the doors of the Merc opened and out stepped Kate Richie, from the newspaper, and a man – the driver – who he did not recognise.

"Hi, Gary," said Kate with a pleasant smile. "We passed you as you drove away, all loaded up. We guessed where you were going, and figured you'd be back soon."

Gary returned her smile, but was unable to hide both his surprise and irritation at their choice of parking place. "Kate. Didn't expect to see you again." His annoyance faded as he regarded her. She looked beautiful, snuggled inside in a coney fur coat that gave every impression of being warm and cosy. Her black hair tumbled over her collar. He rubbed his dirty hands down his filthy gardening clothes as Kate's friend walked to her side. Gary looked at him, appraising.

"This my friend, David Reynolds, who I told you about," said Kate. "He's interested in your photos."

David Reynolds smiled and held out his hand. "Call me Dave," Gary held up his dirt-covered hands as if surrendering. Dave dropped his hand to his side, but his smile didn't waver. He was well-built and reminded Gary of a rugby player – strong and toned. His dark hair looked as if it had recently been cut short and neat. His tan sports jacket was tight against his barrel chest and offset his dark trousers and rollneck jumper. Gary guessed the man was not short of money. He looked to be in his early thirties, slightly older than Kate. Gary couldn't help but speculate about their relationship.

Still smiling, Reynolds spoke, his voice surprisingly light. "Kate's told me what you showed her. You know, coming from this area, I've always been interested in this story. I'm very keen on seeing and hearing any information you have. Especially the photographs."

"I'm sorry," Gary shook his head. "I don't have the pictures."

Reynolds nodded, as if he'd been expecting that answer. "I'm prepared to pay," he chuckled. "As long as it's worth it." Gary noticed Reynolds' expression hadn't changed at all, as if his smile was stuck on. It never reached his eyes.

Gary shook his head. "Can't do that, sorry. I'm working with someone else."

Kate and Reynolds exchanged glances, Kate's expression sliding from friendly to disappointed.

"Jackson?" asked Kate, her expression making it clear she did not want to believe this. "Douglas Jackson?"

Gary nodded. "I met him after my visit to you. He was very interested. He's been researching the robbery for years."

"Doesn't stop you talking to me." Reynolds' smile now had a hard, icy quality about it. "I said I would pay."

"And as I said," Gary stared at him, "Jackson has them at the moment. I'm sorry I can't help." He stepped towards the gate to his front path.

"Look, Gary," Reynold's voice became low, secretive, "can you get the pictures back?" Reynolds pulled out his wallet. "After all, they are your pictures." He opened the wallet; it bulged with notes. "Just between us, Gary, show me and tell me what you know." His expression had become a smug grin, and Gary wondered if he would also add a wink.

Gary glanced at the wallet, before replying. "Sorry, Dave, wouldn't be fair. I made an agreement with Mr Jackson. I'm a man of my word." He moved to go through his gate, but Reynolds stepped closer.

"Kate assured me you would be interested." Reynolds glanced at the reporter, as if for confirmation. "I don't like being messed about."

Kate stepped forward and placed a hand on Reynold's arm.

"Dave, please," she implored.

Gary and Reynolds faced each other, neither giving ground. Gary guessed Reynolds usually got his own way and, from the look of him, would easily win if things turned nasty. Gary hated bullies, had done ever since school. Although never bullied himself or looking for trouble, he had once aligned himself with a fellow pupil who was being picked on. It was after a sports lesson and they were back in the changing room, dressing after having showered. This rotund pupil had the unfortunate surname of Ditch, wore old thick-lensed glasses held together with a plaster, and was always a target. Both Gary and Ditch had stood firm as the cowards, outnumbering them, used wet towels as whips. Both received a number of hits, resulting in red wheals on their bare skin. Ignoring their wounds, and led by Gary, they had retaliated, managing to land a few lashes, making the attackers realise it wasn't as easy as they thought. And, one by one, the bullies had moved on, found another victim. Now, Gary waited for Reynolds to make his next move.

David Reynolds glared into Gary's eyes. Gary could feel the heat from the man's frustration, but he stared back, unblinking. Reynolds raised his arm, but only swept his hand down the back of his neck. He made a sound that could have been a swallowed curse, and turned to his car.

"I'm disappointed, Gary," Kate sounded resentful. "I thought we had an understanding."

Gary looked at Kate and her pursed full lips. "I am also sorry, Kate. But Mr Douglas has been working on this for some time, ever since he wrote the original article."

Kate looked away, shuffling as if embarrassed. Gary glanced up to see Reynolds stepping forward, jabbing his finger at

Gary's chest. "What's it got to do with you anyway?" His smile was now a snarl as he turned and stalked back to the car.

Kate watched him leave, then turned back to Gary. "I know those pictures…" Gary could see her restraining herself from saying any more. She took a deep breath and started again. "You don't understand." She shook her head: disappointment and frustration clear in her features.

Frowning with surprise at her response, Gary watched her follow Reynolds back to the car, where he saw her slap the dashboard in anger as they drove away. He scratched his head as he entered his house, mystified at what had just happened. If, as Kate said, the paper was not interested in the story anymore, then why was she acting like this? And who was David Reynolds? And why had 'Dave, please' become unnecessarily aggressive? Gary reflected on what had happened whilst he made a coffee, then shrugged and put the matters out of his mind. They were of no importance. He needed to concentrate instead on filling the car with another load for the tip.

Later, not only was he ready for Anne as she came out the hospital, but he had arrived fifteen minutes early. It wouldn't have done to be even a second late. He held out the flowers he'd bought, pink and yellow. Anne smiled, seeing the effort, and when the two of them returned home she proclaimed how impressed she was with the garden. By the time they reached the Old Oak Inn for dinner that evening, the thaw had started.

"I told you so," Tom declared, unable to control his enthusiasm, while Fred shook his head in disbelief. Uncle Tom, however, was euphoric, downing his remaining half pint in one gulp.

Gary and Anne, having ordered dinner, were giving an

update to both Fred and Tom, including the proposed trip to Cheltenham. Tom, being shorter than Gary, stretched an arm awkwardly and uncomfortably around Gary's shoulders, squeezing as hard as a clamp and grinning like a Cheshire cat, while Fred kept shaking his head.

"I think we should keep this to ourselves for the moment," suggested Anne. "At least until there's more evidence." Fred changed from shaking his head in disbelief to nodding in agreement. Gary could sense he was still unsure of the truth.

"They all should have listened," gloated Tom, giving Gary an extra squeeze. Gary groaned and flinched, yielding to his uncle's affection. Anne put her hand to her mouth and giggled.

"Thank you, son, for believing me," said Tom, taking his arm away and staring at his empty glass. "Fred, this deserves a free celebration drink."

"Let's wait and see shall we, uncle," said Gary, trying to play down his news.

"We can still celebrate what you've found," Tom protested, lightly banging the glass on the counter.

Fred, playing the perfect host, kept Tom away while Gary and Anne ate their meal, drank their celebratory drinks and discussed Anne's day at work. Later, felling mellow, Gary and Anne strolled back home, arm in arm.

Once home, and having removed their coats and hung them on a wooden hallstand, Gary turned Anne to face him. "I am sorry for being—"

Anne placed a single finger to his lips.

"I've had flowers, a lovely meal, and I'm looking forward to a lunch planned for tomorrow. Uncle Tom, Fred, and probably even this Jackson fellow, think you're a thoughtful, caring man.

But I already knew that. It's one of the reasons I married you." Gary embraced and kissed Anne, who responded willingly: winter had passed and spring had returned.

Chapter 19
Monday

The light traffic on his drive to Cheltenham allowed Gary to contemplate the past few days. Reflections only interrupted by the obligatory roadworks. He recalled Kate's visit, and her angrily banging the dashboard. And realised that, enjoying the Jacksons' company yesterday, he had forgotten to mention Kate and Reynolds' visit. He made a mental note to tell Jackson when he returned.

After checking into the Cheltenham hotel recommended and booked by Jackson, he drove out to the Norton's farm.

As far as Gary understood, over the weekend, Jackson had had a telephone conversation with Janet Norton-Leigh, the descendant of Lieutenant Norton, one of the skeletons recently unearthed. According to Jackson, she had listened as he told her about the possible new link and his wish to talk again. She had hinted she may have something new and agreed to a meeting. He had explained about his health, and she had accepted meeting his representative, after 3 pm on Monday.

Finding the estate entrance was easy, identified as it was by two large signs, "NORTON ESTATES, HOME FARM", inset into twelve-foot-high stone walls which ran either side of a tarmac driveway. The entrance was wide enough to fit a tractor and trailer – sideways. Gary checked his watch; it was just before three. Good. He passed a large bungalow with its own separate red-brick drive leading off the main road. To Gary, the size and style of the bungalow wouldn't look out of place in

California; it looked like those he'd seen in *Columbo*.

At the end of the driveway stood the three offices of the farming estate. One had been converted and modernised from an old grey-sheeted corrugated barn. The other two were identical two-storey purpose-built offices, their grey-brick walls facing down the drive. Between the old and new buildings was a large car park. He parked in a space marked for visitors.

To Gary, the farming estate appeared prosperous: people were hurrying between the offices, nothing looked old or repaired, and a brand-new Land Rover pulled out as he drove in. Gary saw, on its polished doors, the words "Norton Estates" in black lettering against a background of a green tractor. He remembered Jackson had said the family farmed in the UK and abroad.

Gary followed a sign towards reception, which was in one of the newer buildings, where a phone call was made and a woman in her early fifties arrived in another new company-logoed Land Rover. She was a fraction taller than Gary, well-dressed as if about to attend a board meeting, and introduced herself as Janet Norton-Leigh, wife of the General Manager and co-owner of the estate. She drove them back to the bungalow in the Land Rover, pointing out as she drove the workings of the farm and recent capital investments. Once at the bungalow, she led Gary through to the lounge, where a woman who reminded Gary of Hattie Jacques followed them into the room. She pushed a trolley laden with pots of tea and coffee, cups, and plates of home-made pastries. She positioned the trolley by a table which sat in front of a crackling open fire and left, leaving Gary and Janet to talk and to enjoy the pastries. Above the fire, a portrait of a hirsute man stared benignly down at them.

Janet began. "So, you're working with Mr Jackson, still trying to solve the mystery?" she said with a smile. "Tea or coffee?"

"Coffee, please."

"Sugar?" Janet asked as she poured.

"Please, just one, and yes, we are. Working with Mr Jackson that is. He thinks you can help."

She let out a small laugh. "Mr Jackson is very persistent. I've had more than one letter from him over past couple of years. And many phone calls." She handed Gary a full coffee cup, sat down opposite and offered him a pastry, which he refused.

With care, Gary placed the cup on the coffee table. "You have a lovely place here," he said, pulling a notebook and Jackson's notes from his briefcase.

She looked around. "We have, thank you. Some luck and a lot of hard work. The family's been here almost 120 years." She gave a brief history of the estate, finishing with: "It's called Home Farm, because the original farmhouse stood where the car park is." She was obviously very proud of the history.

"Jackson," Gary had slipped easily into using his surname as a first name, "told me you met three years ago, at the funeral of Lieutenant Colin Norton. Jackson was surprised that you were aware of the circumstances of your great uncle's death."

"He was the younger brother of my Great Grandfather, Thomas Norton. Thomas inherited the farm from their father Richard. Colin's death is part of our family history."

"Why? After all, it was years ago, and Colin was a young man, no wife or family of his own." Gary posed the questions, pen in hand, his notebook page blank.

"Richard always believed that both his sons," she emphasised the word *both*, "Thomas and Colin, helped build this business. You see, Colin's death helped in a financial way." When Gary's eyes widened, she laughed, stood and removed a plain white envelope from the mantelpiece.

"No, Gary. I'm sorry, you won't find any money buried here, it's not that easy." She returned to her chair and sat down before continuing, still holding the envelope. "Let me explain. Colin's death was tragic. His father hoped he had a career ahead of him in the army," she paused, as they both took a drink. "I never knew the full story, only that Colin disappeared, and was later cleared of involvement in the robbery. Mr Jackson told me the full story, about the stolen money going missing and never being found. And about the other murders, of Colonel Standish, Captain Farrant and the others. Also, Jackson said his wife was related to Captain Russell, the officer who investigated the theft. It was him, that officer, who came here to meet Richard." She still held the envelope as if it was a final demand.

"After hearing Mr Jackson's tale of the robbery, I thought of telling him our story, but some secrets are not ours to tell. You see, there was a trust fund agreement made years ago. Our silence was part of that agreement, and the family respected our part of the bargain. We never asked the reason for secrecy or gave it any thought until I heard the full story of the robbery."

Gary decided to ask the obvious. "What can you tell me, now?"

She looked up at the portrait above the fireplace before continuing. "After what Mr Jackson told me, I have decided to talk about this trust." She took a moment, getting her thoughts together. "As I understand it, a little less than a year after Colin's death, Richard received a letter from a company in London advising him that a trust had been established to help financially compensate him for his loss."

She pointed at the portrait and Gary found himself staring at a straight-backed, dark-suited gentleman, a striped bowtie setting off a white shirt with a winged collar. His grey moustache and beard were both thick and bushy. Behind him, the background was dark, almost black.

"That's him. Richard, our founder. I understand a more honest man you couldn't find." She sounded unnecessarily apologetic as she gazed on the portrait, and Gary saw admiration in her eyes, as if she was looking at a Rembrandt.

Janet looked back at Gary and smiled. "The implication was that the trust fund came from a special regimental fund, with a secrecy clause attached. This company advised that Colin's early death, not linked to military action, was much regretted in army circles. It prevented Colin from serving his queen and country. Consequently, every year, on the anniversary of Colin's death and until advised otherwise, Richard would receive from the fund, a dividend of approximately £500 per annum. Equivalent to about £10,000 today." She stopped and rose from her chair, holding up the coffee pot to ask if he wanted more to drink. She was, Gary assumed, giving herself time, formulating the words as if dictating. He shook his head. He was impatient for her to continue but knew better than to force things. Give her time, he told himself. He watched as she poured herself more tea before she continued.

"Richard ran a good farm. He was not wealthy, but had foresight, with hopes and plans for the future. And now he had the capital to enact his plans."

Gary placed the notebook down, next to his coffee cup, and listened attentively to Janet's family history. It interested him as much as his own had done. "How?" he asked.

"Richard brought land, and kept buying more. Knowing he was to receive that money annually meant he could speculate, and he speculated well. The money arrived on time every year and it helped him expand the farm. By the time he died, he had built a sizable farm and business. His son, Thomas, continued speculating after his father's death, and also used the profits from the farm to expand further. This included investing overseas, until he had established a substantial company."

"So, this trust fund, is it still operating?" asked Gary.

"It certainly helped get things started, but no, the trust closed before the First World War. It lasted for about twenty to twenty-five years. It was finished well before I was born."

"I can understand why the family remembers Colin." Gary rubbed his chin, pondering before asking the next question. "But why tell me, and Jackson, now? Why not three years ago, when they found Colin's remains?"

She swept her hair back with one hand, and looked up at the portrait again. "I have thought about that a lot. People can get trapped in history, and history trapped in them. Colin's dividend was always considered a generous gesture, no one ever questioned its origins," she raised her hand, as if in justification. "Don't get me wrong, I still can't believe there is a connection, but with hindsight, and after hearing the full story of the missing money, the trust does sound unusual. Its origins, the secrecy." Gary noticed that her tone was questioning, and that she hesitated, as if trying to excuse an action she thought long-forgotten, one she believed and hoped did not need justification.

"The family," she continued, "all those years ago, accepted

and used that money. It was given and taken in good faith." She focused on Gary. "Colin's financial input, and Richard and Thomas using that capital left an inheritance, which was passed down through the generations, linking us all together. We have a lot to thank that trust for. That sad episode in our family's history helped build a considerable business. That legacy brought a lot of work to a lot of people."

"I can see that." Gary understood her justification.

"We have kept all documentation relating to the company's history, going back to Richard's time." Janet's face was now serious, unsmiling. Gary could imagine her giving evidence in court. "Since meeting Mr Jackson, I've also had questions. And I've found the original documentation." She held up the envelope. "These are details of that company, Cooke Hamilton, who sent the original letter. They still exist, but their name changed in the 1920s to Hamilton Associates. I thought maybe these details might help." She stretched out her hand for Gary to take the envelope.

He took it and, without checking its contents, slid it into his briefcase.

They talked a little more, Janet refilled their cups and they enjoyed the pastries, and, while driving Gary back to the car park, Janet invited him for dinner that evening. He accepted.

At the appointed time, a company driver collected Gary from the hotel in yet another Land Rover. Two estate managers joined Gary, Janet and her husband for dinner. The food was good, the conversation relaxed and, towards the end of the evening, the discussion segued to the subject of Gary's visit and he retold the story as he knew it. Janet chipped in occasionally with her family's connection. The hosts and managers, after enjoying a few bottles of wine, speculated where the money could be. Gary left them to their conjectures at around ten thirty and the same car and driver took him back to his hotel. Lying on the bed Gary read a few of Jackson's files, getting a better understanding of the crime, until the soporific effects of the wine caught up with him and he slipped into sleep, his reading material scattered around him. He slept well, dreaming of farms, Zulus and money chests.

Waking around seven, he showered, dressed, then found the hotel restaurant, where he ordered a full English breakfast. It was something he always enjoyed, especially when served piping hot. In his experience, some hotels never seemed to find the right temperature. Checking out, he headed home, looking forward to seeing Anne. Only a single day away but he missed her so much it hurt. Also, and surprising to him, he was looking forward to discussing his findings with Jackson.

The day was bright, but the air cold and bracing. Inside his cocoon of an estate car, with the heating on and the sun shining through the windows, he felt good. The roads were clear, which put him in a good mood and he sang along to the music from Radio 2, as loud as he wanted.

His mood changed the moment he arrived home.

Chapter 20
Tuesday

Gary arrived home on Tuesday in a joyful mood, singing as he entered the kitchen, and casually flinging his coat onto the nearest kitchen chair. He was delighted to find Anne at home, he went to kiss her and… froze, his legs seizing, his happiness transforming in an instant to worry, his heart feeling as if it were being clenched in an ever-tightening fist. He couldn't speak, could only watch Anne approach him, wiping her red, raw eyes with a handkerchief, her cheeks still wet. She threw her arms around him, announcing the news in breathless sobs. Uncle Tom was dead.

He slumped onto a chair, shocked, winded, not believing what he was hearing. It felt as if the fist squeezing his heart had also crushed the air from his lungs. He knew he was wheezing but could do nothing about it. His flesh felt suddenly clammy, drained of blood; his body was heavy, yet he was lightheaded, everything spinning. Uncle Tom was dead. The only words he could manage were: "How? Why?"

Anne composed herself, still wiping her eyes. "Fred rang… early this morning. It… it happened yesterday. Tom… he was rushed to hospital, but… I'm so sorry, he… he didn't recover." She shook her head. "I said we would go to the inn as soon as you were home."

Gary's thoughts whirled. He wanted to spring to his feet, but he had no strength. "Tom?" was all he could say. He closed his eyes, concentrated on taking deep breaths, while images of

Uncle Tom floated before him. Gary slowly stood. He felt as if he was moving like an old man. Like Uncle Tom. How could Tom be dead? He'd only seen Tom on Saturday. Anne put out a hand and helped him. She picked up their coats and they walked as fast as they could to the inn, hand in hand, supporting each other.

Fred was waiting for them. He began pouring a lager as soon as he saw Gary, and passed it across the bar. He waited for Gary to take a gulp before he spoke. "Police *think* it was an accident," he said, then poured a white wine for Anne. "Tom left yesterday, late morning, for his usual daily walk along the canal." He chuckled, but it was sadness Gary heard rather than humour. Fred pointed to the door, his voice cracking. "I can still see him, wrapped in his old brown duffle coat, wearing that tatty flat cap, cigarette hanging from his mouth. He made his usual wave goodbye. He always takes…" Fred swallowed hard, his emotions and affection for his uncle exposed and raw, "took," he corrected himself and winced, "the same walk every day. He always chatted with any anglers as he strolled along the canal path," he paused, smiling at the memory, before turning back to Gary. "Two regulars walking their dog found him in the canal, by the bridge. According to the police, he must have hit the back of his head on the edge of the bridge, where the arch curves." He turned to Anne. "You know that canal path. It's narrow going under the bridge, and it's low, you have to duck down to get under the arch." Anne nodded. "But the police wonder how, if he was walking under, did he hit the back of his head and not the top or front?"

"I'm sorry, Fred," Gary said, his voice breaking. "I don't know what to say. He was so cheerful the other day."

"Have the police said anything else?" Anne took over the questions, seeing their effect on Gary.

Fred shook his head. "Chris and Joyce, they're the regulars that found him, came in last night. They told me they heard a splash and their dog, Enzo, shot off barking. Chris said they found Tom unconscious in the water. Chris jumped into the canal, but Tom's coat weighed him down. It was water sodden; you know, like a heavy sack. Well, Chris pushed whist his Joyce pulled and they managed to get Tom onto the bank. Joyce ran back here to phone for an ambulance."

Fred looked to the door as another couple entered. He smiled, nodding hello, in the most professional way he could muster, as the pair crossed to a free table by the fire.

"They think someone else was there," Fred said.

Gary's head shot up, his eyes wide.

"They found Enzo barking at a track through the trees. The one to the small car park. They say they heard a car driving away. The police also want to speak to you Gary. I have the name and number of the detective sergeant in charge." He retrieved a card from a board behind the till and handed it to Anne.

"Don't know what I can tell them," said Gary, baffled, his glass clenched in his hand. Fred, fiddling and cleaning the beer handles, shrugged. "Just routine they said, talking to people who saw him last, establishing what state of mind he was in. I mentioned the photographs."

Gary glanced at the table by the fire, where he had last sat with Uncle Tom. It was now occupied by the couple who had just arrived. They were drinking and laughing at something, oblivious to Tom's death. The fire crackled, just as it had a few days ago. Life, it seemed, went on.

"I need to go," Gary suddenly said to Anne, and made for the door.

They returned to the house in silence, hand in hand, walking slowly. It was mid-afternoon and overcast; streaks of blue tried to poke through the heavy clouds but were quickly covered by a thick grey blanket. A couple of villagers passed them with a cheery 'good afternoon'. Anne responded, but Gary was lost in his own thoughts. He broke the silence as they neared their house. "It seems strange don't you think," he turned to face Anne, "that after talking to me about the canal story, he dies."

Anne replied with power in her voice. "I knew you were thinking that. Come on, it'll be an accident." She spoke sternly but sympathetically, looking at Gary, knowing he was thinking the worst.

"But how did he hit his head? If it was hit from behind? And what about the car driving away?"

"Perhaps he tripped, the car could be anybody. Other walkers, dog walkers. We don't know what happened, accidents happen all the time. Believe me, I see enough of them. We just don't know, perhaps he had a heart attack."

Gary nodded. As always, Anne was making sense. Was he trying to read too much into a terrible accident? Looking for reasons?

Arriving at their house, he opened one of the two heavy wooden gates to the drive. For a cottage this old, the drive was originally intended for a horse and trap, so it was easily wide enough for a car. Even so, they generally left their car on the road.

Anne stopped at the gate. "Gary, we'll find out soon enough.

I know how important it is to help Uncle Tom, but please," she nodded for emphasis, "don't make more of it than there is, until we know more."

Together, they continued up the drive, onto the path that led to the back garden. The gate swung shut with a heavy clunk.

Once indoors, Gary made two phone calls: the first to Jackson, whose excitement at the thought of Gary's return visit became disappointment as Gary mentioned the family crisis; the second call was to the police station. He agreed to attend there at five the following afternoon.

He was as good as his word, and just before five o'clock he entered the ugly police station. It was concrete, modern and boxy. He gave his name and was shown into an interview room where he was told to await Detective Sergeant Ian Wright. From his plastic chair, which was bolted to the floor, Gary could see through the window to a large roundabout. He watched a seemingly endless stream of vehicles as car after car inched its way to the double white lines before waiting for the right moment to pull into the circling traffic.

Detective Sergeant Wright entered the room. "Sorry to keep you waiting," he said, and introduced himself. Looking at his thin frame and pinched face, Gary thought the policeman could do with a few decent meals. Wright was in his late thirties, and looked uncomfortable in his suit. It was navy blue and he'd chosen a light grey shirt and blue tie to match it. The shirt looked un-ironed. His brown hair was centre parted in a mop-top style, as if he wanted to be a popstar. Patiently, he sat and listened to Gary's story, making notes.

When Gary had finished, he looked over the single sheet of scrawl. 'And that's all you can tell me?" he said.

"Afraid so. I didn't see Uncle Tom again after leaving the inn on Saturday night."

Looking at his notes, DS Wright scratched his head with his pencil. A car's horn outside made both men turn to look. The policeman was the first to return to the reason they were there. "So, let's get this right. You and Mr Jackson are looking into a crime committed a hundred years ago. You have no clear evidence. Your uncle gave you a photograph of a suspect, a relative who may or may not have been involved, and may have died in some fight or battle in Africa?"

"Correct," answered Gary confidently, as if it sounded like an everyday event.

"You have just returned from Cheltenham. Could this stolen money be hidden there?"

"Wouldn't have thought so. It's too far away. Besides, the family I saw, their connection is with another victim of the robbery."

Wright looked at his notes again, "And Mr Douglas Jackson will confirm this story?"

"Yes, Mr Jackson is – or was, I should say – a journalist. He's retired and he's asked me to work with him."

"I've heard of him and his work, that's why it makes some sense. Although I've never heard about this canal robbery." He raised his eyebrows. "Bit before my time. However, I can't see any relevance to your uncle's death." Wright took another look at his notes, nodded, then stood up. "Thanks for coming in. We have your address if we need to speak again."

Gary took the opportunity to raise the question he'd been dying to ask since the interview began. "Have you any further information?"

The detective sergeant paused, looked down at his file, and shook his head. "I'm not at liberty to say.' He leaned forward, 'but I can tell you we believe someone else may have been by the canal. Perhaps he or she saw your uncle."

"Do you know how Tom died?"

Detective Sergeant Wright picked up the file and shuffled through a few sheets. "I rang your cousin earlier and, as I told him, so far we have only received a preliminary autopsy report." He read from a typed A4 sheet. "It was an internal brain bleed from the blow to the rear, right-hand side, of his head. It caused an extradural haemorrhage, resulting in immediate unconsciousness. The haemorrhage killed him, the question I can't answer is why the back of the head." He demonstrated by holding the back of his head with his palm, then moved it to the front. "The front," tapping his forehead, "I can understand. Maybe walking into the sharp edge of that bridge's arch, but the back implies he fell or was pushed backwards, perhaps talking to someone."

He replaced the A4 paper into his file. "When interviewed, the couple who pulled him out said they were sure their dog was barking at someone, and they heard a car drive away, but they didn't see it." He lifted his file, as if a waiting for a solution to fall out. "We are continuing our investigations for the moment." Wright held out his hand. "Thanks for coming in," he said, "I am sorry for your loss."

It was nearly seven when Gary arrived back in Oak Cross, and on a whim decided to visit the inn. He wanted to tell Fred he had visited the police. Inside it was warm and the air was filled with happy chatter. All tables were taken, so Gary sat on a bar stool, watching Fred serve meals and collect glasses from the tables. Fred saw him and held up a hand holding three empty glasses in a wave. Once he'd returned behind the bar, and put the dirty glasses in a tray for washing, Fred poured Gary a half-pint of lager. He refused Gary's offered money. Gary shook his head: "This is becoming a habit, Fred. You must let me pay."

Fred waved the thought away. "Next time," he said.

Fred listened as Gary told of his visit to the police, before saying: "The sergeant phoned me earlier with the preliminary details of the post-mortem." Fred sniffed. "Still wondering if it was an accident or Tom was pushed."

"But why would someone push him?" Gary slowly turned a square beer mat on its edges. "I keep wondering, was it something Tom knew?"

"You think there was something in Tom's story?"

Gary stopped turning the mat. "We can identify the person in the battle was linked to the robbery, and the person in the photo resembles the man in the battle: both have the same facial injuries." Gary swallowed a gulp of lager. "Jackson has been researching for years and he believes it's the same person. I still have to tell him about my trip and another possible link to the nineteen-hundreds, a business once called Cooke Hamilton, now called Hamilton Associates."

"Yes. In London."

Gary, in the middle of taking another mouthful of lager, coughed, then spluttered. He put his hand to his mouth at Fred's comment. "You know them?" Gary asked, thunderstruck.

"Solicitors. They act for the family in ownership of the inn. Their company name is on the transfer deeds."

"Do you have the deeds? Can I see the correspondence?"

"Don't see why not if you think it will help." Fred turned to the girl along the bar, pouring a drink for a customer, and asked her to keep an eye on things, then disappeared. He returned in a matter of moments, carrying an old box file under his arm. He placed the faded brown box on the bar and looked around the inn.

"Tell you what Gary," said Fred, "I miss old Tom collecting glasses." He turned again to the girl and asked her to collect some empties, he opened the file and handed over a couple of documents to Gary.

"These are the original deeds for the Old Oak, when Grandad and his mother took ownership, after Sam Longhurst died. Cooke Hamilton were the agents, no idea why. Probably recommended or something. We retain Hamilton Associates for changes to the business, wills, disputes, and so on. Both names, Cooke Hamilton and Hamilton Associates, are on the old and new correspondence. Look."

Gary looked at the printed names in bold script. He recognised both names, having seen them recently in Cheltenham. Both names had been given to him by Janet Norton-Leigh. These solicitors, he thought, had dealt with more than just ownership of the Old Oak.

Chapter 21
Wednesday

Wednesday morning. Anne left to go to work; Gary left to go to the Jacksons. Anne's plans included arranging a holiday; Gary's to inform Jackson of a new link in the case, and of Tom's tragic death.

Gary was still attempting to process his feelings about Tom's death as well as trying to understand how such a tragedy had occurred, and so the first thing he did when he arrived at Jackson's was sniff back some tears. He knew it was going to be difficult to control his grief today, but that he had be strong. He sat in the car, gathering himself, before getting out. Before his finger touched the doorbell, Jackson had flung open the door and Gary was faced with a man unable to hide his own excitement. Jackson was almost giggling at his own eagerness to hear the news from Cheltenham. He grabbed and shook Gary's outstretched hand while, like a child at Christmas, bouncing from one foot to the other. His appearance, Gary thought, was improved from their first meeting. Jackson wore an open-necked blue shirt and grey trousers. He had shaved and looked brighter but, once in his study, Jackson suddenly doubled over, caught by an eruption of husky coughing. Gary waited, unsure what to do, until Eleanor joined them with a tray of tea and coffee and also a saucer filled with six pills of different sizes and colours. She helped Jackson into his worn, leather chair.

Having recovered, and wiped his mouth, Jackson stared at the saucer on his desk but made no move to touch what it held.

Instead, he pushed the saucer to one side. "So," he asked Gary, is voice husky but strong, "what was the family crisis? I nearly came to you, but realised I don't know your address. Something we will correct today." Eleanor stared at Jackson and pointed and the saucer. "Tablets," she ordered. "You have a hospital appointment later. You know you can only have a short while with Gary. And don't forget you're seeing Doctor Marshall tomorrow morning for..." she glanced at Gary and her expression grew more concerned. Gary was still standing, facing the desk, head down, both hands clutching the top of a chair as if to steady himself. She raised a hand to stop Jackson speaking.

"What's happened, Gary?" She waited, sitting on the arm of a high-backed armchair. Jackson stretched out an arm, indicating for Gary to sit.

Gary shifted some papers from a chair onto the desk before sitting down. He took a deep breath, and slowly, with a voice cracking with emotion, told them about Uncle Tom.

Jackson and Eleanor listened without speaking, but Gary knew his voice faltered in places. Once finished, he stared at the carpet, composing himself, fighting to stop his tears. He lifted his head only when Jackson spoke.

"I am so sorry about your uncle." Jackson's voice was quiet, just above a whisper. Eleanor stood, moved to Gary, leaned down and gave him a hug. "I don't know what to say, I am so sorry," she said.

Gary waited, embarrassed, until she moved away. "I have spoken to the police," he said, "and I mentioned you. So you may get a call about Cheltenham and the robbery."

"Do you want to leave this for another day? I am quite happy to, if you want to?" Jackson's reluctance was clear, so Gary's shook his head. Jackson smiled and received an indignant look from Eleanor.

"Before I forget again," Gary frowned, "I had two visitors at the weekend. I meant to tell you on Sunday, but completely forgot. I was enjoying myself." Eleanor smiled at the compliment. "They were asking about the photographs and what I knew."

Jackson's head turned slightly, indicating his interest.

"It was Kate Richie from the paper, with a man, a David Reynolds."

Jackson slapped the desk, giving out a roar of laughter, which turned into another coughing fit. He drank some water from a glass on his desk, then spoke, his voice rough and grating. "Did he now? Do you know who he is?"

Gary shook his head.

Jackson, his coughing easing, walked to a table and shuffled through a pile of papers until he found a newspaper cutting. He showed it to Gary who, recognising the face, nodded. "That's him." Jackson returned to his desk holding another white-labelled file.

"He's a descendant of the Treloar family, through Treloar's eldest sister, the one who married into a local very wealthy family. The family still live locally and are still wealthy. They have a large house near Crondall. He is also a local councillor, one with ambitions."

Eleanor broke her silence. "But why, Jackson? Its old family history now, why would he even know or want to get involved?"

Jackson shrugged. "Family pride. He's a very successful businessman, and young. And, as I said, he has aspirations in politics." His tone changed to one of sarcasm, and he broke into a broad smile. "Can't have a family skeleton revealed for all to view. Don't you see my dear? This Treloar would do anything to supress his secret past. Well," he declared as if sealing his judgement, "he won't get my vote."

Eleanor moved to the desk, moving the saucer of tablets in front of Jackson, who looked towards her, disgruntled, then she turned to Gary. "If you are upset, Gary, we should leave this meeting for another time."

Jackson, holding the glass of water and taking the first of his tablets, coughed, spilling some water. He turning to his wife, shot her an expression of vexation, before continuing, slowly, to take each tablet.

Once again, Gary shook his head. "No." The word came out hard and blunt. "After Tom's death, I feel this is important." He glanced around the room, and realised there had been changes since his last visit. He had been more concerned with Uncle Tom and the rest of his news to notice the differences when he'd arrived. Two blackboards on A-frames had appeared. Pictures were stuck to one of them, including photographs of Price and copies of Gary's photos. A map of the Oak Cross area was stuck to the other. A well-worn wooden trestle table had been set up and held a selection of buff document files, all carrying white self-adhesive labels with writing on. There were also books, articles and newspaper cuttings in neat piles. The settee had been removed from the room and replaced by two high-backed wing chairs.

Eleanor saw him looking. "It's become his incident, or planning, room. Like he used to have when planning and writing his articles and books. I've not seen him like this since they found the three bodies. He was a fitter man then, of course."

Gary looked at her, and nodded his head towards Jackson. "Is he all right?" He kept his voice low.

Jackson taking his last tablet turned, frowning, and glared at them. "All right? Of course, I'm all right. And I'm still here." His voice was loud and indignant.

Ignoring the castigation, Eleanor walked to Jackson's desk. "We couldn't miss you," she said, lifting the empty saucer.

Jackson huffed, and poured another glass of water from a jug as Eleanor left the room. He focused on Gary, unable to hide his mounting excitement. "Come on, then. Let's hear about your Cheltenham trip."

Gary related the story he'd been told by Janet Norton-Leigh, about the origins of her family's wealth. He handed her envelope to Jackson, who removed the contents and held up his hand for silence whilst he read the A4 sheet of paper. Eventually he made a rolling gesture with his hand, signalling Gary to continue. Listening in silence, Jackson made a few notes and, when Gary had finished, he leaned back and opened his mouth to speak. Now it was Gary's turn to raise a hand.

"That's not all," Gary said, "I happened to mention the name Hamiltons to my cousin Fred, who owns the inn."

Jackson sat upright, his face a picture of concentration. His were hands crossed, his fingers tightly entwined. Gary took the deeds and correspondence from his briefcase. "Evidently my family has also had dealings with them."

Jackson took the deeds and letters as if handling something precious, unfolding them carefully, reading and absorbing every word.

Still reading, his eyes shining, he spoke excitedly, his voice getting louder and deeper, causing his Adam's apple to bob up and down. "Gary, Gary. Well done son." Unable to contain his exuberance, and holding up Janet's A4 sheet in one hand and the deeds in another, he stood, placed the documents onto his desk and lifted his notepad. "This name, the name of the attorney or solicitors. I've heard it before, or something like it. I need to check my cards."

Gary, baffled, asked, "Cards?"

Walking to the table, Jackson replied without looking behind him. "I built a database, names, locations, incidents, for reference."

"Don't you mean *we* built one?" Eleanor said as she re-entered the room.

"Yes, yes," he replied petulantly, without looking up. "All right, *we, we* built a database."

Gary smiled and took the opportunity to make a request. "I've been wondering. Having read Russell's journal, and some of the other information you gave me, it seems to me that Russell appears to be very biased against Treloar." He turned towards Eleanor as if to apologise. "Almost fanatical." Knowing her relationship to Russell, Gary was relieved to see her smile and nod.

Jackson stopped looking through his cards and listened intently as Gary continued. "I would like to read more on Treloar." Gary chose his words carefully, appreciating Jackson's firm belief in the guilt of the prime suspect. "Price and Treloar were from opposite ends of the social ladder," he looked from Eleanor to Jackson. "Treloar came from an influential titled family. It occurred to me, if I had secured a vast, life-changing sum of money," his raised his eyebrows, "why allow myself to go to Africa or anywhere else? Anything could happen. I mean, other than battle. Treloar could have died of an illness, disease or," grinning, "been eaten by wild animals. No, if I'd planned this as well as it appears he did, I would have fought to stay where I was." Gary took a breath. "He didn't. Why?"

His questions got the expected reaction. "You think Treloar was innocent?" barked Jackson, his indignation clear. "The evidence shows he is as guilty as hell; you've read Russell's Journal, seen the evidence."

"Yes, I've read Russell's journal, in this room." Gary's voice was resolute; he was annoyed at the censure, but undaunted in expressing his opinion. "And the other articles you gave me, but have read nothing about Treloar, the main suspect." He stopped and stared at Jackson before defending his request. "You spoke of reports and memoirs about Treloar in Africa, perhaps I should get some insight into Treloar himself. I know so little."

Jackson smiled and nodded at Eleanor while pointing at Gary. "Told you he was a good-un, saw that minute we met."

"Is that why you shouted at him when he first came here?" asked Eleanor sarcastically.

Jackson cleared his throat with a "hmmm," ignoring the comment. "You two drink your coffee. I will sort things out." He returned to his box of cards.

Gary and Eleanor drank their hot drinks, relaxing, facing each other in the two wing chairs. Gary was surprised that, after such a short time, and the tone of what had been said, how comfortable he felt in the company of the Jacksons. Eleanor asked about Anne, her job, their future plans; her questions unobtrusive and showing genuine interest. Enjoying the conversation, Gary's mind briefly shifted away from poor old Uncle Tom. Occasionally Eleanor glanced at Jackson when he coughed while collating the information, muttering to himself. He was clearly in his own world.

Jackson, returned to his desk and placed a new collection of papers on its surface. He beamed at Gary, who rose to join him. "Eleanor," Jackson didn't look at her but his voice was loud, almost a shout. "I think I've found a soulmate. It's also got you thinking, son, eh?" He pointed at Gary. "That's good. Now," he waved his hand at the papers, "you go and read so I can work before this bloody appointment." Gary heard Eleanor cough loudly. Jackson ignored the rebuke, lifting a card box. "I will do more research on this company, and we can meet tomorrow, for lunch I think." Jackson smiled and looked at Eleanor. "Now, leave, please. Let me get back to work, before being dragged off to see some old sawbones."

Gary filled his briefcase with his reading and followed Eleanor into the hall. When he looked back, Jackson was at his desk, working through his cards. Gary hesitated once they were at the open front door, holding it, stopping it being opened further. "Eleanor," he couldn't hide his concern, "is Jackson fit enough to be doing this? I mean, shouldn't he be resting more?"

A warm smile of gratitude spread across Eleanor's face, and a shiny spot formed in her eye. "Perhaps you're right," she said in a low croak. "He is ill, seriously ill." She faltered for a moment, and Gary saw her try to swallow. "We all know that. Including him. He's taking numerous antibiotics and fighting *now*. He's always been a fighter. Nothing or nobody stands in his way when he thinks he's right. But he's fading. That call to the local paper was half-hearted. Their article was a clone of his own. Once he would have been in their offices creating all kinds of havoc." She was clearly remembering such occasions, and Gary smiled; his understanding was that Kate had re-written most of the article. Eleanor grasped his right hand in her small hands.

"Your visit with those photos reawakened him. He's found new strength and I thank you." She gave Gary's hand a gentle squeeze, then shook her head. "Whether you solve this mystery or not, you have given me a link to the past that Jackson and I shared. It's a glimpse of the old Jackson, the one I love, the one I married." A single tear slid down her cheek, and she wiped it away with the back of one hand. "But thank you for your concern." She leant in and kissed his cheek.

A loud and brusque cry for Eleanor made them both instinctively turn towards the study, before turning back to each other and laughing.

"Lunch tomorrow is at midday," Eleanor said, turning back towards the study.

Gary let himself out of the house, shutting the door behind him.

Chapter 22
Thursday

Outside, it was a wet autumn day. The sky was an endless grey, as if it were a thick grubby blanket, and heavy rain veiled the view of the garden where Gary had been working. Raindrops hit the glass panels of the patio doors, forming rivulets that descended, fast at first, then slower as they joined other streams, like cars merging lanes. Gary and Anne didn't care. They were enjoying a late breakfast.

Today, before starting a week's holiday, Anne was on a late shift and Gary was not due at Jackson's until midday. They loved these catch-ups, and this time there was only one topic.

"So, now we have some links," Gary continued, enthusiastically waving a slice of toast in the air. "This firm, Hamilton Associates, seems to be connected." He brought the toast to his mouth and bit off a corner. "So, we must keep researching," he added as he chewed.

"I hear you," grinned Anne, indulging his preference for investigating instead of gardening. She smiled. "So, as I understand it, I married a descendant of a vicious murderer."

"And thief; don't forget thief," Gary added with a chuckle.

"If it gets worse, can I get an annulment?"

"Only if we part before I find the money, so it's not part of the settlement."

Anne raised her hand in a mock punch. "Do I assume you're visiting your new best friend again, rather than working here?" She grinned as she said it, already knowing the answer.

"Look at the weather." Gary indicated the view through the patio doors. "But don't worry." His face split into a wide grin. "Over the weekend I will start digging and levelling." He pointed with his knife to an A4 sheet taped to the fridge door. It was a plan made by Anne, her ideas for the garden. "It'll be to the side of the vegetable patch. For the new greenhouse. You won't recognise it." The vegetable patch, now sitting where a stable had once stood, had been well dug over and was ready for whatever Anne wanted planted.

"I will keep you to that," she replied, returning Gary's grin. "And I will be here, helping and checking."

Reaching across the table, and taking her hand, Gary spoke, his voice suddenly serious. "I know it sounds crazy, but this is important. I have to do this with Jackson." There was more than a hint of pleading in his voice. "It's my family history. A bit strange admittedly, finding I am related to that foul man, Price. Since him though, we have had a great family, loving, caring, like families should be. I have to find out what happened, not just for me but also for Tom and Jackson." He paused to compose his words. "Those two men have known this story longer than I have. One is now dead, the other old and terribly ill. I must help where I can."

Anne, her cheeks glowing, beamed, "I know that now, but I'm not sure you will find answers. And I'm not going to stop you. After all, what a story we'd have to tell our children." She tilted her head suggestively. "You still want children?" She already knew his answer.

Gary gripped her hand and offered her a sly grin in reply. "Of course I want children," he hesitated, "but can I finish my toast first?" He took another bite as Anne pulled her hand away and could prevent herself from laughing.

Breakfast cleared, they settled in the lounge with the radio on in the background, and while Karen Carpenter sang of saying goodbye to love they both read material from Jackson. Gary made himself comfortable at one end of the settee, with his legs stretched out; Anne lay the full length of the settee and rested her head on his thighs to read. She read the *South Counties Herald* again, and the article that, for them, started it all. She followed it with a re-read of Russell's journal. Gary studied accounts of Treloar in Africa. He read the first account, identifying Treloar at Rorke's Drift, but found the second more interesting. It was contained in autobiography of a First World War general. As he read, he glanced up at a jagged plaster joint in the ceiling. His thoughts, though, were elsewhere. His forehead creased as he questioned the character of Lieutenant Spencer Treloar.

Eventually, he looked at his wife, engrossed in her own reading. She must have felt his eyes on her, for she tilted her head back to look at him, her brown eyes bright, her smile – Gary thought yet again – was beautiful, and not for the first time he appreciated how lucky he was. Anne spoke, interrupting his thoughts. "Russell does not mince his words, does he? Treloar and your ancestor both sound nasty bits of work." She twisted, making herself more comfortable, and Gary leaned down awkwardly. He lifted her face to his and she rose, willing, until they kissed. He dropped the document that had previously held his attention just as the phone in the hall rang. They broke apart and Anne laughed. "Typical," she said. Gary twisted away from to answer it. When he returned, he stood at the door, admiring his wife as she stretched out invitingly on the settee. "It was Fred," he said. "They are releasing the body of Uncle Tom on

Friday and Fred and Ethel are arranging the funeral at the local church. It'll be next Wednesday. They're contacting the family. Also, he reckons a number of locals have asked if they could go, so he's expecting a good attendance."

"Gary," her stern tone interrupted his thoughts. "You are having lunch with your new best friend, and I need to rest. And don't forget I'm working late." With a rueful expression, she returned to her reading.

Gary sighed. "You hold my thoughts till later," he said as a huge swell of love for her filled his chest.

"Will do," was all she said, although disappointment at his leaving was written clearly in her expression.

Gary blew her a kiss as he disappeared upstairs to change into less comfortable clothes.

The rain was easing, the sky a lighter grey – now more off-white than the heavy charcoal of before – as Gary drove to Jackson's. He spent the journey contemplating what he had read, questioning it, and he decided to read the next article soon before giving his thoughts to Jackson.

On arrival, Gary noted that Jackson, when he opened the door, was in good spirits. He was shaved, dressed in a clean white shirt beneath a double-breasted sports jacket, and matching black trousers. His welcome showed his excitement; Gary guessed Jackson had good news.

Eleanor joined them in the hall as they walked towards the study, but re-directed them to a conservatory that, despite its spacious size and floor-to-ceiling drizzle-covered windows, was surprisingly warm. Gary looked for a heater but couldn't see one. Eleanor insisted they have lunch and forbade any further discussion about the robbery while they were eating. This instruction received a loud groan from Jackson who ostentatiously failed to hide his annoyance. They sat overlooking a manicured lawn and well-tended flower beds; Gary guessed these would have been filled with colour in the summer. He wished he'd been here then. The drumming of the rain on the glass roof intensified, making Gary look up. He could just make out a large kestrel circling overhead, its wide wingspan helping it float elegantly over the garden, as if looking for somewhere to land. Then, as if realising it was being watched, it instantly corrected its course and flew away.

During lunch of homemade carbonara, Gary noticed Jackson picked at his food, eating little, occasionally coughing. Eleanor, without looking at him placed another saucer of tablets in front of him, he swallowed them all without complaint. The talk was friendly; Eleanor asked Gary about his previous job. Gary in return asked about their lives together. Jackson and Eleanor had no children, and had travelled extensively. It sounded to Gary as though there wasn't a country they hadn't visited. He was surprised to find he was a little jealous.

After a while Jackson began showing his impatience, shifting in his seat and tapping a buff file Eleanor had let him bring to the table. After finishing dessert, homemade apple pie and custard, they left the conservatory for the study and, despite Jackson's displeasure, Eleanor still banned any talk on the main subject until they had finished their coffees. Gary admired the control she had over this old journalist, and remembered reading how determined Russell had been during his investigation. Gary wondered if Russell's genes had been passed down to Eleanor.

Eleanor topped up the coffee cups, then, as if signalling a

relaxing of her commandment, she said: "The police visited last night. We met a nice officer called Sergeant Wright, didn't we dear?"

Jackson, recognising his cue, jumped in. "I confirmed your story, Gary. He seemed quite happy about your movements. I spent most of the time showing him the evidence of our investigations, and I mentioned Reynolds, so he will probably be questioned too." Then, with the speed of the kestrel changing direction, he changed the subject. "Now, down to work." He glanced at Eleanor, as if anticipating some interruption. When one didn't materialise, he continued. "Cooke Hamilton did change its name." He touched a buff file, with the word HAMILTON highlighted. "It's a small family firm that operates from offices in Victoria, London. As far as I can tell, it has no clear connection with the robbery or military. The family come from near Guildford."

"You seem to have found out a lot in such a short time." Gary was impressed.

Jackson snorted, scratching the side of his head, irritated at being interrupted. "A lot of it is work from over the years, adding a bit here, finding a bit there, looking for links. Plus," he smiled, and added with some conceit, "I have been around a long time. I know who to ask and where to look." He brought the subject back to his agenda. "Now, Cooke Hamilton Associates, originated in the early nineteenth century. Back then, they were, what were called 'Attorneys' or 'Men of Business'. That could mean a number of things." He shuffled his papers as if about to start a lecture. "Travelling between towns was time consuming, sending letters was difficult and slow, so it made sense to appoint a person – one who was trusted, who acted or deputised for you – to carry out business on your behalf with a form of legal authority. The term still exists today," Jackson grinned like a teacher passing on his wisdom to his favourite student, "with the term Power of Attorney. It's developed over the years into the legal profession we have today. Cooke Hamilton represented a client, a family," he paused, "like the Treloars, or perhaps a regiment, as your new friend Janet, in Cheltenham, mentioned." He took a card from his index box and placed it neatly on top of the file, moving it so that top left-hand corners of both card and file lined up exactly.

"I recognised the name, Hamiltons," Jackson continued, looking at the aligned card and file, "when you first mentioned it, but I couldn't place it. So I checked my cards." He tapped the index card in front of him. "The firm was not involved, but a Simon Hamilton, a lawyer, tried defending the farming family, the Wellers. He couldn't do much, we know they were hanged, but his name is mentioned in the records. I also looked at my other research on the Treloar family." He opened another file, placing it neatly on top of the first. Gary could see it was labelled SIR JOHN TRELOAR FAMILY. "Russell tells us a lot about Sir John. I can only think his debts, drinking and the death of his son hit him hard. He died the end of 1879, the same year as his son." Jackson paused to take several gulps of water.

Like fascinated pupils, Eleanor and Gary waited and listened intently as Jackson continued. "With Sir John's death, the creditors closed in on Lady Treloar. We can guess what happened next. It appears, with no money and few friends willing to help, she sold the estate to clear her debts." Jackson smiled and added, "Cooke Hamilton represented her."

Gary thought for a moment. "What happened to Lady

Treloar and her other children"? he asked.

"I found that out years ago. Lady Treloar was ostracised. With debts, bankruptcy, her son disgraced, she was, as they say, persona non grata. She retired from her social circle, distanced herself from her so-called friends and lived, almost a recluse, in a cottage in Old Oak Crossroads – now Oak Cross – until she died. Both her daughters distanced themselves from her, making new lives of their own. Her eldest daughter married into the family from which Reynolds is descended. The younger sister went to live in Sussex. Just outside Brighton from what I could establish. She lived comfortably in a new circle. Now," he tapped the neatly aligned files to make his point, "I believe it was one of these sisters Russell saw riding with Treloar on the bridge." He closed the Treloar family file.

"But that still does not give any indication who had or hid the money. If anything, it shows they had nothing." Gary was confused.

"Perhaps," Jackson said slowly, again holding the floor, "but combining our information, we have the Wellers' attorney, the Treloar house, the Cheltenham connection and now Oak Cross." He counted off the points on his fingers, then brought his hands together in a clap. "I am beginning to think Treloar and Price planned this together, possibly with Treloar's sisters, so we have to get someone in the know to fill in the spaces. And to do that we have to visit this firm in London." He looked at his wife and Gary, his expression that of a cat who had discovered a saucer of cream. Gary and Eleanor looked at each other, wondering what was coming. "We have," concluded Jackson, "an appointment, at eleven tomorrow, at Hamilton's offices."

Startled, Eleanor said, "They're in London. You're not fit

enough to travel so far."

With a wave of his hand, he dismissed her concern. "Nonsense. It's not that far. We can go by train or, better still, by car. Gary can drive, and park close so I won't have to walk any distance. I'll just ask the questions." He spoke as if the decision had been made.

Gary looked at the man with admiration, impressed with how determined he was, then a thought occurred to him. "If it's a firm of solicitors, surely they will want to protect their client? Confidentiality?"

"Gary, Gary, think," Jackson tapped the side of his head. "What client?" His eyes were bright, reflecting his confidence. "No, we are researching an incident from a hundred years ago. If things was wound up then perhaps there is no longer a client, just records, perhaps a paper trail telling the truth. If we can only see those records, and if we can find someone who will talk about something that no longer has relevance to anyone else. Then who knows…"

Jackson had a plan, and no one would change that.

Chapter 23
Friday

Hamilton Associates resided in Pimlico, near Victoria, London, and – despite Eleanor insisting they leave home half an hour before Jackson thought they needed to – the delaying tactics of south London traffic meant Gary and Jackson and Eleanor arrived with barely 10 minutes to spare. Gary had visited London a great many times, he and Anne taking in shows, galleries and museums, and it seemed to him that, in the capital, it was always rush hour. Gary often insisted they drop into the National Gallery to find some quietude.

The offices of the solicitors were located in a three-storey Victorian terrace, originally built as a row of family homes. While other properties had also been converted to commercial use, a number of these ever-increasing-in-value dwellings remained residential.

It had been agreed that Gary and Jackson would attend the meeting, while Eleanor would wait in reception. Jackson was concerned that her continual fussing over him in the meeting would be a distraction. Gary was surprised that he got his way.

At the first chime of eleven from the Longcase clock in reception, Gary and Jackson were led to a brightly lit, and well-decorated conference room. While Gary was surprised it was in the basement, he was not surprised it smelt of sweet furniture polish. Four windows allowed in daylight and gave a view up, through railings, to the street. The opposite wall had paintings of London landmarks, Big Ben, St Paul's Cathedral, Tower

Bridge and the Tower of London. A long conference table sat at the centre of the room, its mahogany surface shining like glass. Twelve chairs, also polished mahogany, sat around it, six on either side. At the far end of the room, was yet more polished mahogany: a cabinet, on top of which sat a crystal glass jug of water and a family of tumblers. Gary thought whoever did the polishing had a full-time job just in this one room. Above the cabinet hung a large painting that Gary recognised. He assumed it was a reproduction as he'd seen and admired the original in the National Gallery. At least he'd always assumed it was the original.

Jackson had arranged the meeting with Phillip Hamilton, a family member of the original owners of the firm and a senior partner, the man who now stood facing them. His back was to the painting. Gary put the man in his mid- to late-fifties, with neatly cut salt-and-pepper hair, although tending more towards salt than pepper. He wore glasses and a dark pin-striped suit with matching waistcoat. Neatly tied with a Windsor knot, over a white shirt with detachable collar, was a blue silk tie with a crest. Gary thought it was possibly a university tie. Silver engraved cufflinks, with the letters PH, peeped out shyly from his jacket cuffs. Shaking Gary's hand, Hamilton saw Gary had observed the picture.

"You like our painting?" he asked.

"The Fighting Temeraire." Gary stared at the painting in admiration.

"Would you also know its background?"

Gary thought the question sounded condescending. "I don't pretend to be knowledgeable on paintings." Gary added a sharpness to his voice. "I do know the original was painted by

Turner." He stared at Hamilton, trying to remember what he'd read during one of his and Anne's visits to the National Gallery. "J.M.W. Turner. It shows an old warship from the Battle of Trafalgar being towed by a steam tug up the Thames, to be broken up. The blue sky behind it against the tug, and sun going down with red and darker colours there," he pointed, "symbolises changing times, sail to steam, the dawn of the new industrial age. History in a painting."

Hamilton smile broadly. "Very good." Gary thought his tone was a fraction less condescending. A small fraction, true, but noticeable. "It was a gift from a client to one of my predecessors, many years ago." Hamilton pointed towards two of the chairs. "Please make yourselves comfortable."

All three sat at the painting end of the table, Jackson and Gary on one side, Hamilton across from them. Gary looked at the vast surface of the table, wondering how often the whole thing was used. As soon as they were seated, a secretary, as if secretly awaiting her cue, brought in and served fresh coffee, before taking a seat to Hamilton's right. Hamilton exchanged pleasantries with Jackson, showing a knowledge of Jackson's work history. Gary and Jackson had agreed that only Jackson should speak about the case. Eventually, Hamilton brought them back to their reason for the visit. "Well, Mr Jackson, and Mr Stevens." The secretary made a note on a pad. "What can I do for you? I understand you are also interested in some history."

Jackson nodded and brought a file from his bag. "We're researching into a violent robbery that took place over a hundred years ago, near Aldershot. A large quantity of money has never been recovered. It's a bit of a mystery, and it may also have a bearing on a more recent death; a descendant of one of the suspected perpetrators died in circumstances that are currently being investigated by the police. I—"

Hamilton held up his hand, obviously someone who liked to get to the point as soon as possible. "It sounds fascinating, but I fail to see what it has to do with us."

"If I could just finish," Jackson replied sharply, then continued to give a brief outline of the theft and those involved, pausing only once to take a sip of the coffee.

Phillip Hamilton sat back in his chair listening and saying nothing. As directed by Jackson, Gary watched Hamilton. The solicitor's concentration on Jackson's story was clear. His arms were crossed, and he frowned. To Gary, Hamilton looked a little apprehensive.

Jackson continued. "The reason for our visit is that a firm of attorneys called Cooke Hamilton represented the mother of the main suspect. His name was Spencer Treloar. This same firm supervised annual payments to a family in Cheltenham whose ancestors were innocent victims of that robbery. Finally, this same firm represents the current owners of an inn, who are the descendants of another suspected perpetrator. The inn is near where the robbery took place."

Jackson tapped his file. "Naturally, we have evidence of these facts." He opened the file, its label identifying the solicitor's name, and removed a typed A4 sheet. Jackson slid the paper easily across the polished table to Hamilton before taking another sip of his coffee. Taking the sheet, Hamilton did what Gary always found amusing: he lifted his glasses onto his forehead to read. Jackson put his empty coffee cup down. "The name," he said, "was changed in the 1920s to Hamilton

Associates, which I believe is..." he looked around and, holding up both hands, indicated his surroundings, "...this establishment. That sheet identifies the people mentioned and their details."

Hamilton passed the A4 to his secretary. "Assuming all you say is correct Mr Jackson, you appear to have done your homework. What can we do for you?"

"We appreciate all this happened many years ago, and thought perhaps you could help spread a little light on the matter. We are looking for a name, a contact, a link between the past and the present, perhaps the name of a client." Jackson waited and Gary watched Hamilton, saw him shuffle in his chair; the solicitor was clearly uncomfortable. He took out a spotlessly clean white handkerchief from his jacket pocket and wiped his lips and hands. He then took the pad from his secretary, reading it, as if taking time to gather his thoughts. He handed it back to his secretary.

"Mr Jackson, can I start by saying I agreed to this meeting with yourself and Mr...," he glanced sideways at the pad on his secretary's knee, "Mr Stevens because of the respect I have for you and your work. I enjoyed reading your historical articles. I also read your book on the Spanish Civil War, which I found absorbing." Gary glanced at Jackson, who gave Hamilton a nod of appreciation, and made a mental note that perhaps he should read some of Jackson's work.

Hamilton leant his arms on the table, fingers entwined. "This practice was called Cooke Hamilton, before my family took a larger more active role. We have a number of clients who have used our practice for many years, but I am not at liberty to give information on any particular clients, past or present, or their circumstances, regardless of how long ago." His words were definite, firm and decisive. "Anyway, it was a long time ago, those involved would be long gone." He poured another cup of coffee, for both himself and his secretary, then offering the jug around. When he continued, he sounded careful, if not evasive. "However, you mentioned an incident, a recent death."

Jackson leaned forward, copying Hamilton's entwined-finger posture. "Tom Lewis, a descendant of Corporal Price, who we believe was one of the perpetrators, was found dead near Oak Cross, after a possible struggle. Naturally you can check with the police." He raised his eyebrows. "Perhaps a client may be able to help?"

Hamilton sat upright "I can assure you," his speedy reply indicated he was speaking without thinking, "I doubt very much if any client has knowledge of this incident, and she would certainly not be involved."

He stopped abruptly, shooting a look at them both. Gary glanced at Jackson, who did not return the look. Gary guessed Jackson had also picked up on Hamilton's loose tongue. Jackson closed his file. "I assure you, we are not implying anything, Mr Hamilton, although we do believe your firm is somehow a link between the past and the present." He placed his index finger on the table and drew a straight line towards Hamilton, demonstrating his comment about past and present.

Hamilton did not even glance at the gesture. "I am sorry Mr. Jackson I do not see how I can help with your suspicions."

Jackson glanced at Gary, then back to Hamilton. The solicitor's face was taut, his eyes narrowed. His hands were clenched together on the table, his knuckles white, and he shook his head slowly. When Jackson spoke, his voice was strong and clear, but without sounding threatening. Gary wondered if he was getting a glimpse of the old Jackson that Eleanor spoke about. "Suspicions? We seem to have a misunderstanding, Phillip. These are not suspicions. We have sufficient evidence to *know* this company can help us, if it wants to."

Hamilton opened his mouth to object but Jackson held up his hand. "We are not here to make trouble, apportion blame or find scapegoats." He smiled. "I have read, 'Integrity is telling myself the truth; honesty is telling the truth to other people'." He had Phillip Hamilton's full attention, even the secretary had stopped note taking. "This crime," Jackson continued in an even tone, "was committed by people long gone." He rubbed his palms over his files. "History tells us fortunes were not always made in as honourable a fashion as we would like to believe." He spoke as if offering a response to a defence Hamilton hadn't given. "This story may be in the spotlight for a while but," he shrugged, "people have short memories, especially after a hundred years." He stared at Hamilton. "The truth may hurt for a little while, but a lie hurts forever." Gary listened in awe. Jackson had full control of the meeting. Now he softened his tone, sounding conciliatory. "Phillip, I've chased this story half my life. With his help," he indicated Gary, "this is the closest I have ever been to the truth. I feel I am near the end of my journey, in more ways than one, so I will not shy away from the facts, and would rather work *with* someone than *against* them."

Gary looked from Jackson to Phillip Hamilton, each staring at the other. To Gary it felt as though he and the secretary were invisible. But when he looked back at Jackson, Gary realized the man suddenly looked tired, his face had become ashen. Gary thought about interrupting, but realized that would likely be futile. He heard Jackson take a deep wheezing breath.

"Gary is a descendant of one of those perpetrators, and also of Tom Lewis. I don't know who you are protecting Mr Hamilton," Jackson expelled a short bark of a laugh, "but I can make a good guess. If Gary can live with the truth, can you or your clients continue hiding behind silence? After all this time?" When Hamilton didn't answer, he added. "Silence is never empty, Phillip. It's often full of answers." He sat back in his chair, colour now completely drained from his face.

Hamilton stood, walked to the cabinet and poured himself some water. To Gary, he looked worried. Hamilton shook his head. "I wish it were as simple as that, Mr Jackson."

"It is that simple," Jackson replied, shuffling forward in his chair. "If we want it to be." His voice was weak now.

Hamilton returned to his seat, sipping the water as he did so. Gary noted he didn't offer to pour anyone else a glass. "As I said," Hamilton put the glass on the table, "I wish it was that simple. Shame, dishonour, these things are important to some people, Mr Jackson."

"Perhaps, but truth, honesty – do these not have a place? What about those people I mentioned? The farmers. They were hanged. Were they not shamed? Their family dishonoured? Your own ancestor, Simon Hamilton, thought so. He tried to represent them."

Hamilton raised his eyes, as if surprised at Jackson's knowledge. The secretary turned to Hamilton, as if unsure Jackson's comment should be noted. Silence filled the room, Hamilton, lowered his head, deep in his own thoughts. Slowly, he looked up. "There lies the problem, Mr Jackson. Maybe you're right. Perhaps I could speak to certain parties, if I had a few days."

Jackson shook his head. "I've waited too long. Look at me, I don't know how long I have."

Hamilton glanced at Gary, then to the Turner painting. Gary followed his gaze. Eventually, Hamilton's attention returned to Jackson.

"There is a small public house we use on the next corner. I will make some phone calls and perhaps we could meet there, in" he looked at his watch, "say, an hour? Please order some food as our guests." He turned to his secretary. "Reserve a booth."

"I cannot make it clearer, Phillip," Jackson said as he stood, his voice weak but clear. "We just want answers to a very old secret. No one gets comfort from hiding a lie."

They found the pub easily enough, although it was busy. They mentioned Hamilton's name and were shown to an individual booth with high-backed wooden benches laden with loose cushions. Gary was reminded of church pews. The three of them made themselves comfortable, and Gary had a lemonade, as was driving, Jackson a whiskey and water, and Eleanor a white wine. Colour had returned to Jackson's face and, despite his insistence, Eleanor fussed, handing him his tablets. They ordered two ploughman's lunches, with Jackson sharing one with Eleanor, and as they ate Gary regaled Eleanor with details of what had happened. When she enquired whether they would get some answers, no one answered.

Just under an hour after they arrived, Phillip Hamilton strode into the pub as if he owned it. He sat facing Jackson, who introduced Eleanor. "I have made my phone calls," Hamilton said. "They do not want to meet you." His tone was as blunt as his message. Jackson's mouth opened, but this time it was Hamilton who held up his hand. "I am sorry, I have my instructions. They were, however, upset about hearing of the death of Tom Lewis." He turned to Gary. "Can I ask, is he to be buried in the village?"

The question surprised Gary. "Yes. The funeral's planned for Wednesday. Why?"

"No reason." Hamilton looked at Jackson. "Perhaps you're right, Mr Jackson. I will ask again, but for the moment that is all I can say. Now I must go, please stay, have another drink." And he stood and left.

Jackson was silent, they had reached an impasse. Gary saw Jackson's disappointment clearly, the old man's shoulders were slumped, a distant look in his eyes. Gary remembered Eleanor's words: 'nothing stopped him when he thought he was right'. Jackson stared at Gary, unsmiling, unblinking. Gary nodded, acknowledging the search must continue. He knew Jackson was also wondering about Hamilton's client, whoever *she* was?

Chapter 24
Saturday

The drive home had been slow and quiet, the atmosphere melancholic. While negotiating the traffic out of London, Gary had risked a quick look in the mirror. Jackson, sitting alone in the rear of the car and staring out the window, was clearly absorbed with his own thoughts. The old man had bucked up a little upon hearing Eleanor invite Gary and Anne to lunch again on Sunday, but he'd slumped when she'd added that he must rest on Saturday. Gary had happily accepted the invitation; he knew Anne would be pleased – she enjoyed the company of his new best friends as much as he did. He also thought it the perfect opportunity to present his latest theory, with Anne as backup in case Jackson didn't take it well.

Saturday morning began overcast but with no rain predicted, so Gary returned to the garden and finished ripping out bushes and clearing vegetation. Once satisfied, he moved on to the area where the stable had once stood. This patch was to be their vegetable garden. Along one side of the marked-out area he began digging a trench, for the foundations of a proposed new greenhouse. Whilst Gary dug, Anne planted some cabbages and sprouts. She wore old jeans, a T-shirt and a jumper that was almost as tatty as Gary's gardening clothes. Their portable transistor radio sat on the kitchen step, and it was whilst Frankie Valli was singing about rag dolls that Anne suddenly stood, her head cocked. Gary realised he had missed the doorbell and he watched Anne wipe her hands on an old towel then walk around the side of the house to see who was visiting.

After a few minutes she returned followed by Kate Richie. Gary was surprised to find her just as attractive as he remembered – he'd begun to believe his memory must have been playing tricks. Her cream slacks, leather bomber jacket – light grey – and matching grey scarf, complemented her complexion and black hair. It was as if she'd been dressed to appear in a movie. Gary leant on his spade, unable to stop his mouth gaping as he stared. Anne stepped in front of him, blocking his view. "You have a visitor," she said, her face lit with a mischievous smile, "aren't you lucky."

"Hallo, Kate." Gary ignored Anne's sarcasm and gathered himself. "Surprised to see you again."

"But pleased," Anne said under her breath as she moved to Gary's side.

Gary glanced at Anne before returning his attention to Kate. "You on your own?"

"If you mean is David Reynolds here, he's not. I persuaded him to let me talk to you." She held out both hands, palms up, as if making a presentation. "He wasn't sure he would be welcome."

Gary stopped himself from making a snippy reply. No point in saying anything until he'd heard what she was here for.

"Can you stop your work for a while, Gary, so we can talk, please?" Kate looked disparagingly at where Gary was labouring. They both turned to Anne, questioning.

"I was just going to suggest we stop for a drink. Shall we all go inside?" Anne said. "I'm Anne by the way, Gary's wife." She led the way through the patio doors into the kitchen and, again, Gary ignored her sarcasm.

Once inside, Kate made a show of making herself comfortable on a kitchen chair while Gary filled the kettle and switched it on. He put instant coffee into three matching mugs. They had been wedding presents. Turning to Kate, while he waited for the kettle to boil, he asked, "How can I help you?"

"Is there anything new in your investigations?"

Gary's attention was caught by Anne taking two-finger KitKats from a tin in a cupboard and placing them in a star pattern on a plate. Looking back at Kate, he saw her beautiful smile, revealing perfect white teeth. Despite her designer clothes he found her expression to be by far the prettiest thing she wore. It made him want to smile back.

Gary collected himself, trying not to be distracted by her looks. "One or two surprising things have turned up," he said, choosing his words with care. "We haven't found the money yet, but my uncle was found dead by the canal. He was the one who gave me those photographs." Kate looked away, embarrassed at the blunt retort. Gary glanced at Anne, who frowned.

"I know," said Kate. "I read an accident report at the paper. He lived at the inn, right? David told me the police interviewed him. He was not happy about it. I don't know why they thought it necessary."

Gary refrained from giving his opinion, instead he concentrated on adding boiling water to the instant coffee in the mugs. He added sugar to his own drink, placed a mug before Kate and Anne then offered a bowl of sugar to Kate. She shook her head. Anne, who was also now sitting, unwrapped a KitKat.

Kate continued. "I am sorry, Gary." She turned to Anne. "I really mean that." She returned her attention to Gary. "So sad. A terrible accident."

Gary stirred his coffee, frowning. "Let's wait and see what the police say," he said.

Kate took one sip of her coffee and grimaced as if Gary had given her soapy water. "What else have you found?" she asked eventually.

Taking a seat opposite Kate, and lifting the mug in his two hands as if to take warmth from the hot drink, Gary laughed. "You don't really expect me to tell you."

Kate went to take another sip but stopped. "David has a proposal for you to consider."

"Why didn't he come and make it himself?"

"I told you. He wasn't sure of the welcome he'd receive," the intensity of her smile went up a notch. "David and I have become very close and I want to help him. I know, as you do, his ancestor was a Treloar." She took a sip of coffee, grimaced again, then placed the mug on the table. "Not a lover of instant coffee; bit strong for me, sorry."

Gary ignored the comment. "You were saying."

"David can't help what happened in the past any more than you, or anybody, but that's where he wants it left. He's a good man, Gary, with a sharp brain and promising business interests. He doesn't want those interests disturbed by unnecessary questions, which could happen if someone wanted to cause him embarrassment. He also has ambitions for public service. He wants to serve the community, and if I can help him I will. So, I said I would be his messenger."

"Because he wants to hide whatever we find? Perhaps also cover up the truth?"

"No." The word was almost shouted, startling both Gary and Anne. Kate steadied herself, "If you have found any evidence, it should be told, it must be told, but perhaps also controlled so that it doesn't hurt anyone living." She looked at the mug, shifted in her chair and sat upright. "I told David that, unfortunately, you'd recently been made redundant from a sales role; he thinks he could find you a permanent sales position in one of his businesses."

Gary stared, surprised, unsure how to answer. He lowered his mug to the table and stood, turned to stare at the garden, at the work he'd been doing. Finally, he turned to Anne, who raised her eyebrows. "And what," he faced Kate, "does he want in return?"

"If you were working for David, you may feel more inclined to share what you have found. We could—"

"I don't believe it," Gary felt anger begin to bubble within him. "He can't get me sacked from my job, like they did to Jackson, because I haven't got a job. So he thinks he can buy me off by offering me one." He found himself laughing at the irony.

"What are you talking about?" Kate stared; surprise clearly written on her pretty face.

"Ask your boyfriend." Gary's anger was about to hit boiling point. "Then tell him he can forget it. I've been wondering about the guilt of his ancestor, but if Reynolds is anything like Treloar, perhaps Jackson was right all along. Where were you both last Monday, Kate?" he asked suddenly.

Kate froze, her eyes wide. "Why?" She sounded angry that she was even being asked.

"You want to help David, tell me where he was." Gary spoke slowly, for clarity. "David Reynolds. Last Monday." Finally, he added with force: "The morning my uncle had his 'accident'."

Kate's face flushed and she stood. Her reply was filled with fury. "We were together. Over the weekend. And all day Monday."

Anne lifted her hand. "Gary, please, calm down."

Ignoring his wife's interruption, Gary continued shouting, his face crimson. "You come here for information, to help him cover up anything we find."

"No," she was resolute. "I told you. I don't want to cover up anything."

"Don't lie, Kate. It doesn't suit you." He thrust a finger at her. "Well, here's my answer. Drink or don't drink your coffee, then get out of my house."

Anne's jaw dropped and, embarrassed, she spoke sharply. "Gary!"

"No," he said, pointing towards the front door. "I mean it, Kate. You're not welcome here, you or him." Gary snatched up his mug, slopping his coffee, and marched towards the patio doors, trying to control the anger that shook his body. At the doors he turned to Kate, who stared at him, her face as scarlet as his. Somehow it made her look even more beautiful, Gary thought, then chided himself.

"Please, Gary," Kate said. "It's complicated, and such a long time ago."

"Not long enough, Kate, not long enough. Tell *him* that." Gary stared into the garden, he half turned hearing Anne's chair scrape on the hard kitchen floor and saw Anne standing, facing Kate. "He doesn't understand," Kate said. She turned towards Gary, who faced the garden again to avoid eye contact. He heard footsteps as both women left the room, and then the front door open and shut. He turned to face Anne as she returned. "You were a bit dramatic," she said.

"Can you believe that?" Gary felt his anger rising again. He fought to bring his trembling under control, pointing at the door through which Kate had left. "What a bloody cheek."

"Calm down, Gary." Anne raised her hand. "She's gone, and she's just a messenger, who's in love."

Gary stared, unsure what to say, feeling himself slowly calming. "What are you talking about? In love? Who with?"

"Oh, come on, Gary," Anne said, amused. "Well, it's not you. Surely you can see and hear? It was so obvious." She placed her hands on her hips and tilted her head, delighting in the game, waiting for a response as Gary gave her a confused stare. "This David Reynolds person, you idiot," she explained, grinning.

Gary shook his head. "Poor her." Anne's laugh helped cool his anger and he busied himself collecting the mugs and spoons. He deposited them in the sink, then sat and helped himself to a KitKat. He snapped apart the two chocolate fingers and contemplated Kate, and Reynolds and his job offer. Had he been too angry, he wondered, too quick to make his decision? Absently, he watched Anne turn the tap and immerse the mugs and spoons in hot water.

Gary broke one chocolate finger in half and began eating it. If he took that job, he knew he would be not only selling himself short, but also accepting it against his principles. It was his attitude to work. 'Conscientious', his annual appraisals usually said. But, he wondered, these days could he afford to be too principled? He was aware that while he was chasing Jackson's clues, the search for work was on the back burner. He nibbled the second half of the chocolate finger and watched Anne wash the mugs. He was not a single man anymore. He had responsibilities, a large mortgage to pay, a future with Anne to plan. Did he have the right to turn down a job offer? Perhaps he should have discussed it with Anne first. He watched her dry the mugs with a chequered tea towel: she was as attractive as ever, even in her gardening clothes.

In the same way that he nibbled the chocolate finger, worry gnawed at his thoughts. The investigation had come to a halt, and all the time Jackson was getting sicker and more fragile. Gary was concerned about how long Jackson could carry on. Perhaps it was time to consider throwing in the towel before being forced to.

If they did abandon their project, he knew it would mean making an embarrassing phone call, grovelling and apologising to Reynolds. True, in his old job he had made many difficult phone calls to customers, but he didn't like the idea of working for Reynolds. Not one bit.

"Do you think I should have considered Reynolds' offer?" Gary enquired of Anne's back.

Anne stopped drying, turned around. She was clearly angry. "Are you mad?" It took Gary by surprise.

"It would get me back into a job, and I do need a job."

Anne banged the mug on the metal draining board, stepped to the table between her and Gary, slammed both hands on its surface and leant forward. "You want to get back into your career, I know that, but surely not at the price where you're indebted to someone. Where's this coming from?"

Gary's brow furrowed and he looked at the table. "I'm unemployed, we have bills, can I afford to be chasing around with Jackson?" He looked up and was surprised to see Anne smiling again.

"Gary Stevens, you're worrying unnecessarily as usual. I

know and I love my daft husband. We're a team now, right?" Gary nodded. "And at the moment we are in choppy waters, but we haven't hit rocks or sunk. Together we'll get through this. You know you're good in a sales role. You *will* find another position." She nodded. "And if you took Reynolds's offer, how long would that last? How would you feel, letting Tom, Fred, Eleanor, Jackson, down? No," she said with a firmness that shocked him. "Finish your investigation, finish your KitKat, stop talking rubbish and let's get back to the garden." She turned back to finish drying the cutlery.

Gary didn't eat the last piece of KitKat. Instead, he walked to Anne, took the towel and spoons from her and laid them gently on the side before pulling her into his arms.

"What do you want?" she giggled, not resisting. Gary kissed her on the lips, and the warmth of the kiss lingered as Gary slid his hand up her back, under her jumper and T shirt. Her skin felt soft, and his fingers tingled as he caressed the silkiness of her back. Anne returned his kiss, only harder. Eventually, Gary pulled his head away while still holding her tight to him. He looked into her deep brown eyes, his expression one of pure love.

"Kate's not the only one in love. And I propose we extend our coffee break; let's take it upstairs." He flicked his head, indicating the direction they were to take.

"Do you?" she replied with tenderness. "Then I second that." She gently kissed and bit his lip.

"Going to need a shower," said Gary. "I'm feeling very dirty."

Anne laughed. "Oh, good."

Chapter 25
Sunday

Sunday lunch at the Jackson's was as traditional as one could get: roast beef, Yorkshire pudding, thick gravy and all the trimmings. Gary licked his lips as he poured the gravy, swamping his meal.

The four of them sat around a square table, which was covered in a linen tablecloth, and laughed as they ate, comfortable in each other's company. Jackson fussed – to Eleanor's amusement – around Anne like an old uncle. Eleanor raised her eyebrows at Gary as he rose once again, holding the wine bottle, to fill Anne's glass. It was the third time he had done this. Tears rolled down Eleanor's cheeks as Anne related how Gary almost burst a blood vessel ordering a beautiful woman out of their house, believing she was trying to bribe him. Jackson slapped his leg hearing the story. "Good for you, Gary," he said. Self-mockingly, Gary objected to the ridicule, but his laughter showed he was taking it in good spirits.

After they'd finished their syrup sponge and custard, and at Eleanor's bidding, Jackson, Gary and Anne, with wine glasses in hand, moved through to the lounge – a room painted predominantly beige, with windows on two sides and an open log fire on the third, which kept the place warm. Alcoves were darkened with brown flock wallpaper, and the wooden shelves that lined one wall were filled with books piled on top of each other. As far as Gary could see, there wasn't room for another book to be added. Jackson settled himself into a high-backed chair. Gary thought it looked comfortable – the dark brown leather worn shiny through use. Jackson made a loud "Ahh" as he sat, then lifted his feet onto a matching footstool. Gary and Anne settled themselves on a floral-patterned settee. Finally, Eleanor followed them into the room with a tray, on which stood a coffee percolator, cups and saucers. She placed the tray on a coffee table of dark wood and sat in a chair identical to Jackson's. Gary watched her pour the coffees and, despite the relaxed atmosphere, he finished almost a full glass of red wine in one swig. He needed some courage before he spoke.

"You may not like this, Jackson," he said, trying to sound casual. "But I have another theory on Treloar. If you're interested." He was still not sure how his ideas would be received.

"Go ahead." Jackson remained outstretched with his feet on the footstool, swirling his merlot, smelling the bouquet. He was ignoring a saucer of coloured tablets that Eleanor had placed on the chair's arm. Gary thought the wine was having a relaxing effect on the old man. "Speak your mind, son," said Jackson. "If you believe it, say it."

"Hear, hear," said Anne, giving her husband a warm smile. Her cheeks were glowing as she took a coffee cup from Eleanor.

Gary looked at Anne, whose raised eyebrows were encouraging him. Eleanor sat back in her chair, looking both perplexed and filled with anticipation.

Gary wavered, knowing his anxiety was showing. His mouth felt dry despite, or maybe because of, the red wine.

Jackson waved his hand. "Come on, son. We are all intrigued now, so you must tell us."

Gary took a deep breath and shuffled on the settee. "I

wonder," he began, "if you have not become too fixated at Treloar's guilt." He'd been wondering how to phrase the next sentence, and seeing Jackson lower his glass and more lines appear on the old man's forehead, Gary continued quickly. "Could you have misread Treloar's character? Perhaps got him wrong?" The words escaped quickly, as if a cage had been opened, releasing his thoughts. He was now unable to put them back into captivity.

Jackson swung his legs off the footstool and shook his head violently, his actions shaking the chair and causing the saucer of pills to fall from its arm. Eleanor shouted his name as she sprang to retrieve the tablets.

"Not again," Jackson's voice was loud and angry. "You have mentioned this before. Why do you persist in questioning his actions, and how on earth do you come to that conclusion?"

Gary stood his ground. "I said you may not like it. But I wonder if your opinion has been clouded by your anger at the Treloars for what they did in your past?"

Jackson started grinding his teeth, the veins in his head pulsing, his eyes wide. Gary ignored the coming reaction and continued, keeping his voice low and even. "In the same way as I felt towards Reynolds wanting to buy me off, offering me that job."

Jackson glared, mouth open.

"It's all in your evidence, Jackson. I'm not criticising," appealed Gary. "I'm just questioning, using your files and books." His mouth was still dry and he licked his lips. He saw Eleanor smile. "Perhaps Treloar had a different motive. Perhaps I have seen something different."

Gary stood, went into the hall. He returned carrying his

briefcase, some files and books, to a lounge that was silent. He placed everything on a side table by a window and remained standing as he removed notes from his case, as if he were a salesman preparing to make a presentation to a potential customer. Finally, he faced the others and held up a book. He was feeling more assured, having taken the first step and, besides, he was confident of his theory.

"Russell's journal clearly states Treloar was involved; he was a vicious villain, who perhaps with others masterminded everything."

Jackson nodded, sitting back.

"But we have other evidence of Treloar's character, and his actions after the robbery." Gary placed the book on the table and turned to his audience. "Let me ask the question I asked before: why not resign his commission so that he doesn't get sent to Africa?"

"May not have had the opportunity. And he was under suspicion, that's why," answered Jackson flatly.

Gary held both his hands wide apart. "And again, I answer why should he care? He was gentry, although it's true the family estate was in trouble. Having hidden the stolen money, why not stay and use it?"

"Events overtook him," replied Jackson, impatiently. "He got his orders before he could resign."

"I question that. Anyway, he goes to South Africa. Let's look at other evidence."

"About what?" Jackson blustered. "What else do you want to know? He was killed in battle, with sixteen-hundred others." His hand slapped the armchair. He was clearly adamant his theory was correct, that it was the only right one.

Eleanor interrupted, holding the retrieved saucer and tablets. "Let Gary speak. He obviously has another theory, which we should hear."

Jackson waved a hand in the air, reluctantly indicating for Gary to continue.

Gary lifted one of Jackson's files, "Let's start with why he was even in the battle of Isandlwana. His post was Rorke's Drift. The official records show what his responsibilities were during the campaign." He opened a file. "John Chard won the VC commanding the mission station during the battle of Rorke's Drift. His report states he and Treloar rode the 10 miles to the camp at Isandlwana on the morning of that battle. The camp was on alert, Zulus had been sighted. Chard immediately rode back to Rorke's Drift, concerned they could be heading that way. Treloar stayed. With the possibility of battle, why did he not leave with Chard and save himself?"

"That's obvious, Gary," Jackson's voice was condescending. "If the enemy were heading for the Drift, surely he was safer in a camp with over a thousand men than at a small mission station with only a hundred. The bastard's cowardly self-preservation made his decision for him."

"Jackson!" Eleanor shouted, her voice sharp, reprimanding. She turned to Anne. "I am so sorry my dear, shall we leave them?"

"No way," Anne said, a little affronted. She turned to Gary, smiling, encouraging.

"Very well," Eleanor eyeballed her husband. "Jackson, I also want to hear this. No more foul language or I will get angry."

Jackson, head bowed, feigned an apology. "Your right. Sorry, my dear. Sorry, Anne. Gary, please continue, I'll stay quiet." He pulled an imaginary zip across his mouth.

"Fat chance of that," replied Eleanor, her face resolute. "But let Gary speak."

Gary, taking another deep breath, continued. "There is other evidence." He replaced the file on the table. "Let's look at what happened once the battle had started." He picked up a hardback book, showing them the front cover, then turned it so he could read the title.

"*My Life in Command,*" he said, then looked up at his audience. "The memoirs of General Sir Robert Butler, a junior officer on the staff of Colonel Pulleine, officer in charge at the battle at Isandlwana. Butler was a survivor of Isandlwana, and later fought in Egypt, the Boar wars, becoming a commander under Sir Douglas Haig in the First World War."

Jackson's laugh filled the room. "You have been doing your homework." Eleanor shot him a glance.

Gary shrugged. "It was easy, with your files," he replied cheerfully, beginning to enjoy himself.

"I know this story," said Jackson. "He was ordered to leave the battlefield, ride to the town of Helpmekaar, beyond the Drift, to warn them. He took Treloar's horse."

"Not quite correct," Gary opened the book at a page he'd previously marked. "They exchanged horses." He began reading: "'Treloar was ordered by Pulleine to ride to Helpmekaar. The situation worsening, Treloar dismounted his fine horse to question his orders, suggesting I go in his place'." Gary looked up and said, "Pulleine agreed and that decision saved Butler's life." Returning to the book and speaking slowly, he added: "'In appreciation of Treloar's selfless act, I kept that horse as my own, until it died.'" Gary looked up again. "Now, if the battle was looking bad, why, with an opportunity to escape, would he elect to stay? His new orders meant he could bypass Rorke's Drift and go straight to safer territory. Eventually back to England, as Butler did."

Leaning forward, Jackson raised his hand like a schoolchild. "Can I answer?" Eleanor nodded. "Perhaps he was scared, not wanting to be in the open on his own. The Zulus could be anywhere. No, sorry. Nothing you have said so far changes my mind one bit."

"But he's giving it a good try don't you think." Anne said, then sipped her coffee.

Gary looked at Eleanor. She was smiling, her head tilted slightly, like an animal showing interest at something strange. Gary winked. Addressing Eleanor, he said: "Russell thought it strange."

"How do you know that?" asked Eleanor, her surprise at hearing her ancestor's name obvious.

Re-opening the book, he slid his finger down the page until he found the paragraph he wanted. "Butler, overhearing the conversation between Russell and Treloar, questioned Treloar's reasons for staying." Once again Gary looked up at the others. "He writes about his journey and South Africa, but there is this one piece." He looked down at the book. "'Treloar, whose friendship I made on our journey to South Africa, was under a cloud back home, a suspect in a serious incident. Brevet Major Russell, also at Isandlwana and his main accuser, was surprised we changed horses, questioning Lieutenant Treloar's opportunity to leave.'" Gary looked at Jackson, "Butler, later adds Treloar's actions were that of a brave officer."

Gary noted with satisfaction that his audience was

engrossed. His mouth was no longer quite so dry but he took a sip of tepid coffee anyway.

"After Butler left," he continued, "we have the evidence of the articles written by South African Natal officer, Christian Janssen, another survivor, who fought at both Isandlwana and Rorke's Drift. His articles appeared in Durban and London newspapers, and he became quite a celebrity, having survived both battles. He made personal lecture tours." Gary picked up the last of the files on the table and flicked through it. "Treloar now had Butler's horse, probably the only way to escape the battle, but he helps an injured Christian Janssen, who talks of Treloar in glowing terms." Finding the piece in the article he wanted, Gary looked at his audience, especially Jackson. He knew he was stating facts, which he thought were meat and veg to Jackson. And by the look on Jackson's face he knew the older man was absorbing the facts. "Janssen recognised the battle was lost." Gary returned to the article. "He states Treloar knew that also: it was every man for himself. Treloar had organised a defence around wagons, and gave up his own, or rather Butler's, horse. This gave Christian, like Butler, the chance to escape." Gary held the article high. "It's obvious, Treloar could have escaped. Janssen is very clear about this." Looking down, Gary quoted from the article. "'The Zulus were encircling us. I was injured, the battle lost, Treloar gave me his own horse, encouraging me to leave, which I was able to do, arriving at Rorke's Drift, to help those stationed there."

Gary looked at them all. "Why would Treloar do that? He's planned and carried out a successful, and violent, vicious robbery. He's now rich beyond anyone's wildest dreams, able to clear family debts, and rebuild his family estate." Gary took another deep breath before continuing. "But no, he allows himself to be posted abroad, finds himself in a battle, where he has three," he raised the requisite number of fingers as if to validate his suggestion, "not one, but three, chances," he raised his voice for his finale, "to get away, but he takes none of them and ends up being killed. *Why*?"

The room was silent. Gary watched Jackson moving his tablets on the saucer, making a circle, mixing the colours. Then Jackson, with a wince, pulled himself out of his chair and walked carefully to the window. He stared into his garden. Outside, the constant rain was keeping the lawn and flowers well-watered. The silence was broken only by the hiss of a lump of coal as it fell deeper into the glowing depths of the fire. Gary drank the rest of his coffee. It was now cold but he finished it in one mouthful. He felt drained; he'd been going over and over his theory for days. Anne stood, percolator in hand, and topped up his cup. Jackson turned to face the room and Gary thought the old man looked tired, his face was sunken, blotchy with liver spots on his cheeks and forehead, but he was smiling.

"The one thing I have learned when investigating, Gary, is to expect to find the unexpected." He chuckled. "And trust you to do just that." He ran his hand over his face. "Perhaps you're right. I was convinced of Treloar's guilt." Jackson shuffled back to his chair and slumped into it. "So, what conclusion do you have? Do you think Price and Ox planned it alone, and somehow involved Treloar?"

"I don't know. We do know Treloar was involved. He had to be, being at the canal that night, escaping with Ox, but his later actions..., were they also part of some greater plan?" Gary shook his head, disagreeing with his own thoughts. "But how could that be? How would he know there would be a battle, let alone being in one of our worst military defeats in history?" He paused to tidy his books and files while considering his next question. "Treloar's reputation was damaged, so did that have any impact on his decisions?"

Jackson's gaze shifted to the circle of tablets. "I must admit it's a line I never considered. And even after all this time it's hard to consider it now." He looked at Gary and smiled. "But you make some good arguments." He turned to his wife. "Don't you think, Eleanor?"

"Makes sense to me," she replied. "Something to consider."

Jackson drummed his fingers. "Let's assume what you say is true," he said. "Perhaps he only did it for his family and estate, and don't forget his sisters." He pointed his finger at Gary. "I always thought his sisters were involved. Perhaps they got the money. Reynolds is wealthy, don't forget. That makes sense, don't you think?"

"Reynolds' money was from his father's side of the family," Gary corrected. "And why the dividend to Cheltenham? Why does my family have a link with Hamiltons? Don't forget, the Treloars lost their estate. Lady Treloar, after her husband's death, lived out her life quietly in Oak Cross."

"As Eleanor said, certainly something to consider." Jackson's breathing was becoming heavy, and he was looking increasingly tired.

Eleanor came to him, knelt before him and lifted the saucer. "But not now, Douglas. I think you should take some more medicine and have a rest." Her love and concern obvious from her tone. Jackson nodded and broke the circle of tablets by taking one, then another, without argument.

"Perhaps we should be leaving," said Anne, standing up.

"Funeral's Wednesday, right?" Jackson's voice was low, croaky, his eyes cloudy. "What time?"

Gary stood. "Ten thirty at the village church." He couldn't hide his surprise.

"I think we would like to attend." Jackson said, offering a smile to a friend.

"We can talk about that later, Jackson," interjected Eleanor.

"See you Wednesday," Jackson whispered.

Gary nodded. Although knowing the old man only a short time, he felt they had a bond of friendship. He liked Jackson and Eleanor, as – he knew – did Anne. He sighed, thinking of Jackson's illness. He knew the theory he'd just presented had complicated things, and so feared that they may never solve this mystery. Their friendship may not last long, but whilst it existed he would continue searching as enthusiastically as Jackson.

Eleanor waved Gary and Anne from the room, and eventually joined them in the hall.

"I hope," said Gary, "Jackson wasn't too upset with my theory."

Eleanor shook her head. "He just told me he couldn't think of anyone he'd rather be working with. No, you keep him thinking, that's what I want to see."

"He should rest for a few days," said Anne, her medical experience taking over. "Perhaps Gary should not call him until after the funeral?"

Gary felt disappointment, but nodded.

"That won't be necessary." Eleanor folded her arms, and gave them a resigned smile. "You heard him. We will see you on Wednesday morning."

Chapter 26
Tuesday: I

Gary slowed as he approached the Oak Cross Inn. His legs felt heavy, his shoulders were hunched and his anorak collar acted as protection against the chill wind. He was contemplating the events of the past few days: the trip to London, Kate's visit, explaining his theory to Jackson, and Sunday night ending with a headache. Yesterday – Monday – he'd managed to block out all thoughts of the century-old robbery and had actually enjoyed the day. He'd spent it with Anne and, despite the ground being sodden, had finished the digging for the greenhouse foundations. Today, his back still aching from his exertions, he was taking a rest. In fact, visiting his cousin, thinking perhaps that Fred and Ethel may want help with tomorrow's funeral. He wasn't sure why, but he still felt some responsibility for Tom's death. Crossing the car park for the inn, Gary saw Detective Sergeant Wright walking to his car, a Ford Cortina. Seeing Gary, Wright stopped, car keys in hand, and waited by his car.

"Morning," Wright said. Gary replied with the same greeting, and added, "You have news?"

Wright shook his head, showing his disappointment. "Just met your cousin," he nodded at the inn. "Unfortunately, it's not good news. Other than the couple who found Tom, I'm afraid we don't have anything else so—."

"You're stopping further investigations?"

The policeman shrugged. "It's the manpower I'm afraid. Obviously, we'll keep the file open, should anything turn up.

What about you? Any further in investigating your robbery?" Gary was sure Wright was changing the subject through embarrassment that his own enquiries had come to nothing.

"Some," replied Gary, wondering if his and Jackson's own investigations were as ineffectual as those of the police. "We think there's good evidence a descendant of those involved may be alive, but no name yet."

"And those old photos," the detective sergeant raised his eyebrows, "that Jackson showed me when I interviewed him…" he turned to his car, found his key, which was attached to a chain with a St Christopher enamel fob, and inserted it into the lock. Like his question, he left it hanging as he turned back to Gary. He's eager to get away, and only partly because the weather's cold, realised Gary, just as Wright finished his query. "…have you confirmed their authenticity?"

"Difficult to confirm for certain. The clues we have found, we believe, show the man in the picture was who we thought. And he was involved in the robbery." Feeling disappointed, Gary thrust his hands into his coat pockets. "I always believed those photos were linked to both investigations. Tom's death and the canal robbery."

Wright shook his head. "You said Tom showed them to a few people."

Gary nodded. "Only when he thought Fred was not looking." He tried to smile. "He told me it annoyed Fred, showing them around." He recalled how Tom could easily wind-up Fred.

"Shame we don't have any names. It may have helped with my investigation." Wright turned back to his car, his hand on the key, he turned his head, looking back at Gary. "Perhaps it's you," he paused as if recognising someone passing, then finished with, "owning the picture."

Gary shivered, not understanding, and waited for the officer to continue. "Just a thought." Wright rubbed his chin. "But what if there is someone else who knew the original story, and saw the photos." He pointed at Gary. "And also met you. And it was *you* that gave the pictures some authenticity. Just a thought."

Gary shook his head. "Apart from Tom, the only other people, involved or aware of the original story, before the newspaper article, were Fred, Jackson and David Reynolds." Gary turned and looked at the inn, deciding he wanted to get inside to get warm but, having now mentioned Reynolds, he pushed his hands deeper into his coat pocket. He asked, "In fact, I hear you interviewed David Reynolds." Gary still felt residual anger at the man's job proposal, or attempted bribery as Gary thought of it.

"We did," the Detective Sergeant nodded, then faced his car again and turned the key. The chrome button inside the door popped up. "He was away, on his own, but has as solid an alibi as you can get." Gary thought the policeman sounded flippant. "If you can be on your own, that is, at a conference." The DS spoke patiently: "He was in a Croydon hotel, Sunday to Tuesday."

Gary stared at Wright's back and remembered what Kate had said. "You sure?"

Wright answered while opening his car door. "Absolutely. He was a speaker on Monday morning. Both the hotel and over 20 people can confirm he was there."

Gary said nothing. His eyes narrowed and his mind raced. He scratched his head, confused, unsure if he should make accusations. Perhaps he had misunderstood what Kate had said, after all he had been angry when they met. Gary took one of Tom's photographs from his inside pocket and stared at it. He had carried it since Tom gave it to him, other than when Jackson took a copy. He refused to part with it, feeling as though carrying it would eventually tell him something he didn't know.

Detective Sergeant Wright slid onto the driver's seat and pulled the door shut. Seeing Gary holding the photo, he wound down the window. "Is that the photo? Can I see it again?" He inserted the key into the dashboard and twisted it. The engine roared like a lion. Gary passed the photo through the open window, his mind full of questions about Reynolds' alibi.

Wright took the picture, studied it, giving Gary a sideways glance, as he pressed the clutch pedal, his free hand slipping the gearstick into first. He laughed. "That's amazing. When Jackson showed it to me, it didn't register at the time. The family resemblance to you. You are like a clone."

Gary blinked as if a light had gone on in his head. He stared through the car's open window. Watching Wright view the photo he remembered the word 'clone', he had heard it used before, recently. Eleanor used it regarding the newspaper article: a clone of Jackson's original, which was how she described Kate's story. He had wondered about it at the time, and how much extra work Kate Richie had contributed. She had said that, by pure coincidence, she had come across the original story from fifty years ago. She had also claimed her paper was no longer interested. Yet she obviously still was, and had been assisting Reynolds. Just when, his asked himself, had she originally been aware of the story?

Although it was cold and few cars were entering or leaving

the car park, he felt like he had fallen into a sealed chamber – his surroundings had disappeared. On Saturday, he remembered, Kate had also been vociferous, making it clear she wanted the truth. But if she'd only recently become aware of the story, what did she think was the truth? He put his hand to his forehead – his headache was returning.

DS Wright handed the picture back to Gary. "Except for that scar, you both having similar moustaches." He put his finger to his own philtrum. "You could be mistaken as twins. Except you're from different centuries."

And then it struck Gary. It felt like someone giving him a hard slap across his face, sharp, stinging. Twins from different centuries. He felt dizzy and put his hand against the top of the car, steadying himself. The photograph dropped to the ground and he left it there. His mind trying to put everything together. "No," he said. "It couldn't be."

"Pardon?" Detective Sergeant Wright released the handbrake and looked up at Gary. "Mr Stevens?" Gary barely heard him. He slumped, leaning back against the car's rear door, and he turned away, as if looking at the policeman would derail his train of thought. A photograph can tell a story. Others had seen that photograph, and probably realised the story but not acted upon it. Why? Because, he answered himself, it was not believable. It was just a fanciful story told by an old man wanting a drink. And why would anyone believe Old Tom? His eyes were wide, yet he wasn't seeing anything. His thoughts raced. But what if someone had their own reason. He leant forward, steadying himself. Perhaps someone wanting vengeance. Gary looked at the face in the photograph, on the ground, staring up at him.

"You all right?" Wright's head was half out the window. The policeman pulled the hand brake, put the vehicle into neutral, opened the car door and slid out. He stooped, retrieving the photograph, holding it out to Gary. "Perhaps you should sit down?"

Gary took the picture and stared at it. Wright was right. His ownership confirmed its authenticity, and he realised that picture was a clue.

"I'm fine, thank you. I just remembered something." Gary turned to the Detective Sergeant with a growing smile of understanding. "There's someone else you should interview for Tom's death, but I need to get my thoughts together." Like Russell, all those years before, Gary thought, he only had suspicions. "It may need some checking."

"Tell me. Checking is my job," said Wright.

Gary faced the policeman, seeing Wright's interest renewed, and – for fear that if he spoke slowly he would forget it all – quickly explained.

After listening, Sergeant Wright drove his car, at speed, through the streets, eyes focused on the traffic. Gary sat in the passenger seat, repeating his accusation, speaking slower this time, whilst Wright asked questions. Reaching their destination, Wright stopped on a double yellow line. He was still talking as they both got out. "Why didn't Fred mention the name, when interviewed?" He sounded annoyed, as if Gary had deliberately held something back.

"Because he didn't know," said Gary, identifying the detective's annoyance. He stepped to one side to let a pedestrian pass, then hurried to catch Wright. "It was Tom who told me who he'd shown the photo to, not Fred." Gary and Wright were now both hurrying, as if to catch a train. "Like everyone else he showed it to, they were not interested. I didn't connect it until now. Tom always showed the pictures discreetly. He knew it would annoy Fred if he made a fuss."

"Well, I'm going to make a fuss now," Wright replied sternly and stopped outside the offices of the *South Counties Herald* to compose himself. "Gary, this is not exactly correct procedure. You are here at my request. I will do the talking." He pushed open the door.

As long as it leads to answers, thought Gary.

Chapter 27
Tuesday: II

The bell tinkled as they entered, and Gary approached the same woman he had met before. She looked up as the detective sergeant flipped open his warrant card. "Is Kate Richie here?" He asked as if it was just a personal enquiry.

This time, unlike Gary's last visit, the woman stopped typing and stood. She stared at the warrant card. Probably, thought Gary, having never seen one before. He certainly hadn't before all this had started. "She has a visitor at the moment." The woman's nerves were clear in her voice.

"Then I need to speak to your editor, or whoever is in charge." Wright turned and pointed at the front door. "Is that the only way out?"

Frowning, the woman removed her glasses, letting them hang on a cord around her neck. She glanced at Gary and stammered her answer, clearly worried she could get someone into trouble. "No, but everybody signs in and out through me. Why?" Her curiosity – Gary thought, amused – getting the better of her.

"Just call your editor, please. Tell him to come down here. Now. And can I see that register?" Wright spoke with just the right air of authority, such that the register was quickly swivelled towards him. The receptionist turned to her phone and picked up the receiver. While she spoke, Gary walked over to the framed photographs in the cabinet. Wright joined him and Gary pointed at one. Gary was aware the woman was keeping her eyes fixed on the two of them.

It didn't take long for a man to appear. Bald and wearing a blue shirt with a top button undone and a loosened striped tie, he appeared to be in his late fifties or early sixties, and, from his complexion, on the verge of a heart attack. Gary decided being an editor was not a job he wanted. Wright showed the man his warrant card, introduced Gary and explained what they wanted. They followed the editor to the counter, where they all read the register, then followed him through the door behind the reception desk to a spiral staircase. Gary looked back and saw the receptionist lean over the counter, standing on tiptoe, watching them go.

Kate Richie and David Reynolds were at the top of the stairs, waiting. As the staircase was a tight, narrow spiral, wide enough for only one person, they did not know who was ascending until all were on the landing, Gary was the last to arrive. "Hi, Kate," he said.

It was cramped at the top of the stairs. Detective Sergeant Wright looked at Gary for confirmation, who nodded, then he turned to Kate. "Kate Richie. Could we have a few words?"

It was Reynolds who answered. "We're just leaving. And you and me, we have already spoken."

Wright gave a patient smile. "And now I wish to speak to Miss Richie." Despite the restricted space, he managed to produce his warrant card and show it to Kate. "I am Detective Sergeant Wright. This won't take long. Just a few questions." He turned to the editor. "Is there somewhere we could all talk, privately?"

The editor pointed along the corridor. "Use the small conference room." He rubbed his finger around his sweat-stained collar, as if too hot.

No one moved. "What's this about?" Reynolds was trying to take control.

"All in due course. The small conference room. Kate?" Wright held out his hand, as if courteously allowing her through a door first. Although his tone was friendly, it was clearly an order. Kate backed up then led the way. Wright didn't immediately follow though, he held back, talking to the editor. It gave Gary a moment to look around. The upstairs, he thought, didn't look in any better condition than the downstairs. Old and need of renovation. Wallpaper beginning to peel.

Kate opened a door and switched on the light in a room so small that when Gary entered, he thought a large cupboard was a better description than a conference room. Three chairs were pushed close to a small wooden table on which sat a cream Olympia typewriter, notepads and pencils. Nothing else was in the room, no pictures, no cupboards, no windows. The place was airless and lifeless. Kate, Reynolds and Gary squeezed into the room, standing around the table, and a few minutes later Detective Sergeant Wright entered. Immediately he pulled out one of the chairs and sat down. The others remained standing.

"What's he doing here?" Reynolds pointed at Gary. "I don't want him here."

"Mr Stevens is kindly helping with my investigation into the death of Tom Lewis. I believe he has information that will help my enquiries. He is therefore here at my invitation." It was clearly not a matter for discussion.

"Well,' an indignant Reynolds pointed at Gary. 'If he stays, then I'm staying too."

"I have no problem with that, if Miss Richie has no

objections. It's just a few questions. I just need some clarification." Wright smiled at Kate and pointed to a chair.

Reynolds watched Kate sit. "It's okay, David," she said,

Reynolds grabbed the other chair, as if worried someone else was going to take it first, and positioned himself next to Kate. He took her hand in his.

"Thank you," the policeman remained smiling at them both and took his pen and pad out of his inside pocket. Gary leaned his back against the wall and folded his arms. Reynolds gripped Kate's hand, but his eyes – anger burning in them – were fixed on Gary,

When he was ready, Wright spoke. "Did you know Tom Lewis? Old guy? Lived at the Oak Cross Inn?"

Kate's expression was that of an animal caught in headlights. "Maybe," she looked to Reynolds for support, "I saw him when we drank at the Oak Cross." Reynolds nodded in agreement.

Wright made a note, then continued without looking up. "Did he show you something? When you were researching the canal robbery? Photographs perhaps?"

"No." Her answer was fierce. She was flushed and a bead of sweat appeared on her brow. Gary recognised her sharp tone from Saturday.

"The same photograph that Mr Stevens," Wright glanced at Gary, "showed you when he visited you recently?"

Kate shook her head.

"Did you ever meet Tom on the canal after your meeting with Gary?"

"Why would I?"

"That's not an answer." The policeman stared at her.

"Look here," Reynolds leant forward. "Are you insinuating

something? Where is your evidence? It is very clear Kate has nothing to hide."

Wright gave the impression of a man calculating. "Kate, what made you interested in the canal robbery?"

"I was looking through some old copies of the paper. I found the story and showed it to my editor. He thought, as it was near the anniversary, it would make a good article." She was, Gary thought, shifting the decision to publish onto the editor.

Wright smiled but his tone dripped scepticism. "Now, that's interesting. Where do you find 50-year-old copies? Your editor just told me something as old as that would be in storage. If, indeed, kept at all." He leant back, his eyebrows raised. "So that's not true is it, Kate? He also told me you brought him a copy of Jackson's original story. And it was you who told him about the anniversary." He used his pen to point at her.

Kate again looked at Reynolds, who this time was staring back, questions in his eyes. He released his grip on her hand – which Gary noticed was covered in the thin sheen of sweat – took out a handkerchief and wiped his own palm.

"When someone lies to me Kate, I question everything they tell me."

Gary spoke quietly; he was unsure whether he should speak at all. "Kate, when I showed you the photograph of Corporal Price, it shook you. I think you were shaken because Tom had showed it to you before."

Wright glanced at Gary, but remained silent, before looking back at Kate Richie.

"I don't know what you mean." She looked down, her eyes unable to meet anyone's. Reynolds went to speak but Gary continued quickly. "Tom told me he had shown the photograph to an attractive dark-haired woman a few weeks before, and that this woman showed little interest, and left. That was you, Kate, wasn't it?" All three men stared at Kate. She said nothing, but wiped her trembling hands on her coat. Her eyes were wide with fear. She bit her bottom lip.

Gary offered her an understanding smile. "Kate, please. I now know this story so well from working with Jackson. You weren't researching his story. You already knew it. You cloned his story, that's why you were so annoyed when he started calling this office. I don't think you realised he was still alive, let alone lived locally. Come on, you know this story, just like Tom, like me, like Jackson." Gary pointed at Reynolds. "And like David here." Reynolds looked confused He stared at each of the others in the tiny office, as if expecting an explanation.

Reynolds spoke, although not so loud this time. "Now look Detective Sergeant, who's asking these questions?"

The police officer tried again. "Kate?" His eyes were fixed on her.

Kate sat straighter. "It's a story, and I am a journalist," she said in justification, although she didn't stop biting her lip.

The officer turned to Reynolds. "Mr Reynolds, can I ask, how did you and Miss Richie meet?"

"Katie came to interview me about my family, and the area, for an article, or perhaps it was to write a local history book. Whatever, it had to include the robbery. That part of my family history is well known to me. I have nothing to hide. It was a long time ago." His answer was business-like, devoid of emotion.

"So, you knew David was a distant relative of Spencer Treloar, the man implicated in the robbery?" Wright looked from Kate to Gary, as if wanting confirmation he had got the details right.

Reynolds looked annoyed, "Now look here, I will not—"

"Mr Reynolds." the Detective Sergeant help up his hand. "Interfere again and I will ask you to leave. Do you understand?" Reynolds nodded, Wright returned to Kate, his expression clear he was still awaiting an answer.

"Kate," Gary kept his voice low, sympathetic. "Don't you also have personal interests?" She cowed, staring at him, her face frozen; yes, his suspicions had just been confirmed. She looked like a child, her hand was once again clutching David's. His fingers were turning white as she squeezed the blood from his hand. Gary touched Wright's shoulder, who looked up at him and nodded. Gary remembered how Jackson had pushed Hamilton.

"Kate." Gary kept his voice soft. "The truth may hurt for a little while, but a lie hurts forever." Her frightened eyes flicked from side to side, like a child caught lying, found out, now terrified to admit the truth. "You told me you were with David when Tom died, but that's impossible. He was in Croydon. And the register shows you didn't sign in here, until just after midday on the Monday of Tom's death." Kate said nothing, just twiddled her long hair with the fingers of her free hand.

Gary continued. "Your interest is also personal, isn't it? You were still interested even though – what was it you said? – your paper was not." Gary took a breath. "Your own family were also involved, weren't they Kate?" She turned away sharply, still not speaking.

Unable to contain himself or hide his confusion, Reynolds spluttered: "What connection would Kate have, for God's sake? She's just a journalist."

"She's also a twin."

Kate's pale face surveyed Gary. Her hand released the tight grip on Reynolds, and he looked down at his hand as the pressure eased and the blood returned. He looked at her, seeing her tears. Gary stepped closer to Kate. Wright said nothing, he didn't need to. Gary had his evidence, and now he was ready to get his answers.

"The Wellers owned a farm. They were innocent but they still hanged the father and his *twin* sons. His wife poisoned herself. The farm was sold and the surviving two children were sent elsewhere. Everything was gone." He crouched. "Kate, you are a twin. You pointed that out to me when I first met you. The pictures downstairs of your twin sister Louise. Twin genes run in a family." He glanced at Wright. "I am sure the Detective Sergeant can check the records with Somerset House or wherever it is family records are kept."

Katie's head dropped into her hands and the sound of her sobbing was clear to all in the room. Gary stood and stared at the Detective Sergeant, who nodded a gesture of thanks. Contradictory emotions flooded through Gary: he felt proud of himself at what he had deduced, yet utterly ashamed that his deductions were making this grown woman cry.

Wright waited as Reynolds put an arm around Kate's shoulder, comforting her. "Katie," Reynolds whispered, "you never said." He took her hand and she looked at him with eyes that were red and raw.

"How could I? I wanted to hate you, your family." She pointed at Gary. "His family, for the pat. I intended to write something that would shame you. But after meeting you, I couldn't hate you. You weren't Treloar. Never could be, and as we got to know each other better," she turned her face to him, her tears leaving trails of mascara down her cheeks. "I found… I found I loved you." Gary saw it was Reynolds' turn to squeeze her hand.

Wright sat straighter, to his full height, and re-took control. His voice took on a fatherly tone. "Do you want to tell us what happened Kate? In your own words. Start at the beginning."

As she spoke, she attempted a thankful smile. Gary heard her sniff and swallow and thought she look relieved, as if a weight was lifting from her body. "I never knew my grandmother. She died the year Louise and I were born. She was the youngest of the Weller children, and must have been about six or seven when her family were destroyed. She was sent to stay with an aunt who lived in Reading, in a small, terraced house not big enough for her own family let alone another child. She idolised her older sister who must have been ten or eleven years old. She went to live in London, and had to find work. My grandmother never saw her sister again. It was my father who repeatedly told me the family story. How they lost the farm. I was always more interested in family history than Louise." Kate looked dejected, unstoppable tears rolled down her cheeks. Reynolds passed her a handkerchief, which she used. It left black mascara smudges. "Dad said that his mother could never tell the story without crying, seeing as she was just old enough to still remember her life on a farm, the freedom. It was all so cruel." Reynolds draped an arm around Kate's shoulders.

"And Tom?" the detective sergeant asked gently.

She focused, her head shaking forcefully, her long hair curing around her face and wide eyes. Her voice became steadfast. "That was an accident. I swear, Sergeant. I did use

Jackson's original article. And I visited the inn to obtain copies of those old pictures on the wall." She paused to gather her breath. She wiped her eyes again. "Tom showed me photos and he wanted to talk. I looked to humour him, then made excuses, and left." She stopped, looking up at Gary, who offered her a smile, seeing a frightened, beautiful woman who needed a friend. "When you showed me the same picture, Gary, I knew where you got it from. Then you told David and me you were working with Jackson. I thought they must be genuine and I had to speak to Tom, on my own." She hesitated. "Just a talk, surely I deserved that." She looked down, then up to David with a forced and unnatural smile.

"Now, I wish I hadn't met him, believe me, David. It was stupid, I know that now. I saw him walking up Standish Lane towards the canal, so I parked in the car park and followed." She looked pleadingly at Wright. "He was having a smoke, by the bridge, I asked about the photograph. I wanted to know more. He got abusive, just laughed and told me to clear off. I got angry, told him I knew who he was, what his ancestors had done." She looked at all of them, one by one. Gary thought she was frightened to finish her story. "He pushed me away. I slipped and fell down, but he stumbled backwards, tripping, falling against the bridge and hitting his head, and then he stumbled into the canal." Both hands covered her eyes. "I tried pulling him out, but he was so heavy. Suddenly, from nowhere a dog was by me, barking loudly. I heard people calling, so knew they were close. I panicked and ran back to my car." She look at Reynolds, pleading. "It was an accident, I swear."

She buried her head into his shoulder and sobbed, the sound muffled by his jacket. "We'll prove it, Katie," he said, kissing her hair. "I love you, and we'll prove it was an accident." He looked up at Gary, his eyes also brimming with tears. "I am so sorry, Gary."

Once the police car arrived, it didn't take long for the newspaper's employees to line the office windows and stare down at the vehicle. Gary wondered if it was really necessary for it to have its lights flashing. Across the road, shoppers had stopped to watch and pointed as the police car drove away with Kate Richie and David Reynolds inside. Standing at the newspaper's door, Detective Sergeant Wright turned to Gary. "I'm following them to the station to get statements. Can I give you a lift home?"

Gary shook his head. "It's all right, thank you. I'll make my own way. I'll also let Fred know."

Wright nodded and held out his hand. "Thank you," he said, appreciatively. "Without you knowing this story, well, I can't think who else would have made the twins connection."

"You believe her? It being an accident, I mean?" Gary asked his eyes remaining on the police car.

Wright waited, musing, watching as the police car turned a corner and disappeared from sight. "Yes, I think I do. All that history in her family confused her, made her act without thinking. It helped cause the accident. Like you, she wanted answers, I don't see the court being too harsh." Gary nodded, agreeing. He was pleased; he'd been thinking the same.

"I will need a statement from you, but that can wait until after the funeral." Wright went to turn away, then stopped. "I would like to attend, if that's okay."

Gary nodded, and told the policeman he was welcome.

"Thanks. Now, must go." Wright grinned. "My report will

make interesting reading." He added, "I hope you find your answers. Anything I can do, give me a call. I owe you." Gary turned away, his hands in his pockets as he walked to the taxi rank.

Today they had established how Tom died; tomorrow they will bury him.

Chapter 28
Wednesday

It's strange, Gary thought, staring into nothing while gusts of wind chilled his cheeks, how a mood can change over twenty-four hours. Yesterday he was elated, discovering the movements that resulted in Tom's death. Today, with Tom's funeral, melancholy weighed heavily on him. Fred and Jackson's responses to Gary's explanation of how Tom had died had been similar to each other. Fred had said little. He'd turned away, genuinely grateful to know what happened, and placed an affectionate hand on Gary's shoulder. Jackson, when Gary phoned him, had also been lost for words, stunned at hearing the connection with the Weller family.

Gary blinked and, returning to the present, looked around. He glanced at Anne, thinking again how lovely she looked, even in funereal black. He brushed fluff from his own dark overcoat. Like Anne, he had also taken time choosing appropriate clothes, ensuring he looked smart and respectful in memory of his uncle.

Beneath an overcast sky that was almost as dark as his coat, Gary and Anne walked, hand in hand, to the church. Radio 2's weather bulletin had warned of possible storms due from the West; Gary hoped it would stay clear and dry for the funeral. He and Anne stopped at the memorial lychgate that led into the church grounds. Leaning against the wall by the gate was a large blackboard whose hand-written chalk inscription advised mourners: 'The Old Oak Inn is closed to the public for the day. Those attending Tom's funeral are welcome to use the car park'.

That made sense, thought Gary, remembering Fred and Ethel had invited everybody back to the inn, after the service, to raise a glass to old Tom.

Gary and Anne passed the village hall car park, next to the church. Cars were pulling in, circling and leaving, not finding a space. Seeing a continuous stream of people crossing the village green from the inn, he guessed a number of mourners had already taken up Fred's offer.

Gary's elder brother, George, had already arrived with his wife, Sheila. Gary and Anne approached them and exchanged greetings. After a while, when the weather was being discussed, Gary looked away. Mourners were coming from every direction, all wearing dark colours, some carrying wreaths or brightly coloured sprays of flowers.

Looking back across the village green in the direction of the inn, Gary spied a man who was taller than those around him who were also making their way to the church. The man strolled casually and alone, obviously in no rush, and wore a dark overcoat and trilby. He held three identical wreaths, two over one arm and the third in his other hand. Three wreaths, Gary thought, was a bit excessive. Gary squinted and finally recognised Phillip Hamilton, who was now about 30 or so yards away and looking to his left, in the direction of the main road. Gary, hidden within his family group, guessed Hamilton was unaware of being watched. The solicitor raised the hand holding a wreath as if he were waving. Gary was sure Hamilton gave a nod of recognition before, curiously, turning and leaving the path. He walked away from the other mourners.

Gary turned to look in the direction Phillip had been facing. Many people were approaching the church. He could see

Cousin Fred talking to a couple with a black dog, Sergeant Wright, and others further away. His eyes darted from mourner to mourner, some people he didn't recognise, others he did: local residents and neighbours. There were cars dropping off passengers, along with a local taxi, whose driver was kindly assisting a small, elderly woman from the rear of his cab. Gary felt a hint of recognition and was trying to place her when, to his surprise, David Reynolds appeared beside him.

"Can I have a quiet word please, Gary?" Reynolds sounded apprehensive.

Gary stepped away from his family; Reynolds followed.

"I hope you don't mind me coming to show our condolences." Reynolds kept his voice low. "Kate wanted to be here, but she felt ashamed." He shuffled, looking around, as if frightened he might be overheard. Instinctively, Gary also glanced about. He figured Reynolds, the muscles in his face tightening, was feeling embarrassed. "I'll go," Reynolds said, "if you prefer, but I'd like to stay."

Gary stared, wondering what he did feel. He swallowed some of his own anger and frustration, guessing Reynolds was wanting to put things right. Perhaps, Gary thought, Reynolds believed it would help with Kate's appearance in court, sometime in the future. He was about to tell Reynolds exactly where he could go, then remembered Anne saying Reynolds was a man in love, and so should be shown understanding. Gary glanced at the church, a symbol of forgiveness, took a deep breath and held out his hand. "Thank you for attending, David. It is appreciated."

"Thank you," Reynolds sighed, his relief clear, and he clasped and shook Gary's hand. For a moment Reynolds looked away. "Looks like a good attendance," he said, then paused, still holding Gary's hand. Gary speculated the man wanted to add something and was trying to find the right words. Reynolds cleared his throat. "Kate and I," he said slowly, "have decided, when this terrible incident is finally behind us, that we are both putting all that other history behind us as well. We're… we're looking to a future together." He hesitated, averting Gary's eyes. "She hopes you and your family will, in time, forgive her."

Gary stared, feeling a spark of irritation. "David, I am pleased for you both." His hand still gripped David's. "And I am finding we all have family secrets. Perhaps Kate's ancestors, the Wellers, suffered more than most, but it will take a while to forgive Kate's lying, or your high-handed attitude, thinking you can buy me off with your wealth. None of that was necessary." He felt Reynolds try to pull his hand away but kept his grip and, having got that off his chest, thought reconciliation should start here. "Tom's death was a terrible accident, unnecessary but an accident." He pointed at an approaching Detective Sergeant Wright. "I'm sure even he thinks that."

Wright walked up to them. "Everything all right here, Gary," he growled, looking at Reynolds suspiciously.

Gary released Reynolds's hand. "Everything's fine, Sergeant. Right, David?"

Reynolds's face flushed, but he held out his hand to the detective. "Yes, Sergeant. I think we understand each other." They shook hands.

Over the detective sergeant's shoulder, Gary spotted Jackson's Volvo turning from the main road into the approach to the church. "Excuse me," he said, breaking away. He grabbed Anne's hand and they made their way along the road. Eleanor was driving, her head just visible above the dashboard. Seeing Gary stepping into the road, holding his hand out, she stopped by the grass shoulder. Gary stood by the driver's door, and Eleanor wound the window down. Jackson, in the passenger seat, leaned over her. "Hallo, son." Anne walked around to the passenger door.

"He insisted on coming," said Eleanor, "I hope he'll be all right, but he's still tired."

"Of course," Gary opened her door and Eleanor stepped out. Gary escorted her to the safety of the grass shoulder. Anne held the passenger door open, letting Jackson out. Gary was surprised at Jackson's appearance: the old man's shoulders were slumped, even more than before their visit to the solicitors. Gary knew the London trip had tired him, and figured the news about the Wellers hadn't helped. Both Jackson and Eleanor wore black but, while Eleanor looked elegant, Jackson was dishevelled: his white shirt appeared several sizes too large. There was a gap between his shirt collar and neck big enough to stick most of his hand down it if he'd wanted. The oversized Windsor knot of his black tie was skewed to one side. While Eleanor grabbed his overcoat from the rear seat, Jackson produced a wooden walking stick from the car. Looking at Anne, he brightened. "Still don't know what you see in him," he nodded at Gary before taking Anne's arm for support.

"I sometimes wonder," replied Anne with a smile. Jackson burst into laughter, which quickly turned into another bout of deep and harsh coughing. He took a minute or so to get himself under control. Once he had, he pointed a finger at Gary's chest while his other hand rested on the walking stick. "Gary, I've been thinking about your theory on Treloar—"

"Jackson! Really." Eleanor stepped over to her husband. "I don't think anyone wants to hear you at this time and it's certainly not the place."

Jackson glared at Eleanor, defiant. He leaned into Anne. "Next time Gary visits, you come also so we can talk more."

Anne squeezed his arm, moving closer. "I will."

Eleanor shook her head, straightened Jackson's tie and helped him into his overcoat. A car horn blared behind them, making them jump. Gary realised Jackson's car, with both doors open, was partially blocking the narrow lane. He turned to Eleanor. "You both go with Anne into the church. Give me your keys and I'll park at the inn." Taking the keys, he slid into the driver's seat, pulled the doors shut, and waved to the car behind to pass. He then had no option but to follow the Ford Escort as it drove around the full church car park, before exiting and heading out to the main road.

As they both approached the entrance to the inn's parking area, the car in front slowed and waited for a white Jaguar XJ6 to leave the car park. Ahead, Gary could see the driver of the Jaguar checking the traffic before pulling out and heading in the opposite direction. Gary felt assured the driver had not noticed him. Certainly, there was no recognition from the driver, Phillip Hamilton.

Gary parked the Volvo and made his way across the green, his mind on Hamilton. Seeing the hearse turn into the road leading to the church, he forgot the solicitor and jogged the rest of the way.

He squeezed into the space on the pew that had been reserved by Anne, just as a bell pealed and the coffin holding the body of Tom Lewis was carried slowly into the church. It was held by four pall bearers from the company who arranged the funeral. Strangers. A green wreath lay on top of the coffin.

Looking around the church, Gary remembered the last time he had visited. That had been during Reverend McDonald's charity day. He and Anne had read some of the old plaques around the walls, He also remembered reading pamphlets given out at the charity fair: the church had been rebuilt in the late 1800s. Gary thought it still looked sturdy and well-built. The pews were packed, overcrowded even, as people squeezed in together. Others stood at the back. Seeing so many attending, Gary was pleased. He recognised some as family from London, and many he saw were locals. Fred and his wife Ethel sat in the front pew with a woman he recognised from family functions – Patricia, Tom's only daughter – and her children. She had no husband or partner with her.

Looking back at the coffin being slowly carried down the nave, Gary saw David Reynolds, sitting with Detective Sergeant Wright. Continuing idly looking around, he saw a couple with a black dog. They were sat towards the back. Fred had told him he had invited the couple and the dog, Enzo, who had found Tom, and Gary assumed this was them. He recognised others from the village, or who he had seen drinking in the inn. Jenny, the girl who worked behind the bar, was there, along with the aging couple who owned the local newsagents. Gary's gaze stopped at an elderly lady dressed totally in black, partly hidden behind one of the columns. He recognised her as the lady who had been helped out of the taxi. It was Miss Turner, the previous resident of their house, and who had move into a local old people's home. He recalled Tom saying how he and Carrie Turner had played together as children. The woman glanced over her shoulder towards the vestibule, then bowed her head in prayer. Sensing movement in the vestibule Gary also turned and saw the reverend in his cassock slowly walking down the nave to the coffin. The vicar bowed when he reached it and made his way back to the pulpit before starting the service.

They sang *All Things Bright and Beautiful*, and the reverend said a few words about Tom being one of the village's oldest residents. He told brief stories of Tom's life, which Gary had no doubt been supplied by Fred. The congregation laughed in all the right places. Gary grinned to himself, thinking how Fred had omitted the fact that Tom was the son of a thief and murderer.

After the service, the coffin was carried by the pall bearers to the family plot where Tom could forever lay beside his wife. Everyone crowded around, wrapping their coats tightly about themselves as they watched the coffin being lowered into the grave.

As the funeral drew to its end, Gary took the opportunity to look at the surrounding headstones and small tombs, some many years old, covered in lichen and with inscriptions barely legible. The name on a headstone, about 15 feet away, jumped out at him. The headstone was shaped like a curved gothic window, with a recessed facia where the glass would have been.

Gary marvelled at the expertise of the workmanship and chiselling. The top of the facia had three raised crescents set into the curve. Just below these scallops a mason had chiselled the words, '*To the memory of*' above three lines of large text. The first was the name that had attracted Gary's attention:

Sir John Treloar

Died 31 October 1879

In the 51st year of his life

Then a fourth line, in a much smaller font and capitals:

MAY A LOVING GOD ACCEPT A SINNER

Three further lines had been added:

ALSO, THE DEAR
LADY FRANCES TRELOAR
DIED 15 MARCH 1906, AGED 74

And finally, in an even smaller font:

Loving Wife, Mother and Companion

This headstone, Gary had to admit, despite some age-related discolouration, was clean and in better condition than most of the surrounding gravestones. There were no weeds or ivy or other unwanted growth on the plot. Leaning against the stone was one of the wreaths Phillip Hamilton had carried.

The service finished, and everyone filed past Tom's grave, looking at the many wreaths and flowers laid neatly side by side. Considering it was autumn, the assortment of vivid colours was eye catching. Amongst the numerous tributes, Gary spotted the second of Hamilton's three wreaths. Stooping, he read the few words on the unsigned card, 'Rest in peace'. Gary guessed Hamilton must have laid the wreath, but had he placed it there for himself or on someone else's behalf?

Everyone drifted to the lychgate where Jackson leaned

against the wooden arch, allowing the congregation to pass and leave the church grounds. Gary introduced Jackson and Eleanor to his brother and his wife. When asked if they were going over to the inn, Eleanor made it clear she and Jackson were going home. Jackson said nothing, accepting defeat.

When his brother and sister-in-law had departed for the wake, Gary turned to Eleanor. "Give me your keys, I'll get your car." He jogged across the village green, zig-zagging between those walking in the direction of the inn. As most people were going to the wake, it didn't take him long to exit the car park and drive the car back to the church. He found Anne, Eleanor and Jackson standing alone.

"We should meet later," said Jackson. "We have things to discuss." Behind him, Eleanor shook her head and mouthed the words: "Needs to rest."

Gary shrugged. "I should stay here, with the family today. Perhaps we can meet tomorrow or the day after? I'll ring you in the morning." Gary was keen to talk to Jackson, who nodded but glanced at Eleanor. Gary thought he knew why.

Jackson reached out and gripped Gary's shoulder. "Okay, but with no more leads, son, perhaps re-think where we go next." His words were followed by another bout of coughing. Once he had recovered, and with his voice low and raspy, Jackson once again expressed his obstinacy. "Perhaps, with your theory, we should also re-think who could help? We certainly need someone." With difficulty, he climbed into the passenger seat.

Gary went round to the driver's side, where Eleanor was already sitting behind the wheel. Gary thought she looked like a child in the driver's seat. She wound down the window and smiled at him. "Ring tomorrow morning," she said. "We can arrange something."

Gary and Anne, hand in hand, watched Eleanor and Jackson drive away, then they strolled to the Old Oak Inn to raise a glass to the youngest of Corporal Price's children.

Chapter 29
Wednesday

Arriving at the Old Oak, Gary, with Anne, George and Sheila in tow, found mourners squeezed into the bar area as well as a side room that was used for private functions. It was standing room only and everyone accepted that. As people shuffled around, allowing others to pass, Gary felt as if he was negotiating the London Underground during rush hour. Unlike the Underground however, no one seemed to care. Raucous laughter, loud voices and a barely audible music system made the atmosphere even more numbing. Looking around, Gary was surprised but pleased at the number attending. Tom had obviously been held in high regard.

Mourners swapped stories of old Tom, family members reminisced about Tom's antics at Christmas parties, and locals joined in, adding their own stories. One of the older village residents made his audience laugh with a story about Bonfire Night on the green; everyone would watch out, for Tom had no compunctions about throwing a lighted banger or jumping cracker at their feet.

A light buffet appeared: ham sandwiches, cheese sandwiches, ham and cheese sandwiches were piled on large platters that were placed along the bar. Neatly aligned high towers of paper plates flanked them. Fred and Ethel, with Jane's help, were busily working behind the bar, serving the first drink to each mourner for free.

After a short while, Fred left the bar, pushed his way to the fireplace, stood on a chair and gave a short speech about Tom. He joked about the number of free drinks Tom had got out of him over the years and, with Tom's sad demise, hoped he'd make a bigger profit – that's why he was buying everyone a drink today. His audience applauded.

Gary and Anne stood with George and Sheila. The bothers weren't close, but they tolerated each other. Despite the talk and laughter, Gary's mind was elsewhere. As he nibbled at a sandwich, he thought about Jackson's comment: who else could help? There must be someone, he thought. The hubbub continued unabated and may even have got louder as the early lunch came and went. The food disappeared and people began buying their own drinks. Earlier, a glass of cold lager had been thrust into Gary's hands, and he slowly sipped it, ignoring those around him. With nobody making any effort to leave, Tom's party had truly started.

Feeling a sharp punch to his shoulder, Gary roused himself from his deliberations. His brother, George, leaned into him. "Did you hear me?" He shouted above the rumpus, sounding annoyed.

"Sorry, George, no. Just thinking. What did you say?"

"You were miles away. I asked if you wanted another drink."

"No fine, George. Thanks." He held up his pint glass, still half full.

Anne leaned towards Gary as George turned away. "Are you okay?"

"Yes fine," he nodded. "Just need to think. Do you mind if I go for a walk?"

"Do you want me to come?" Her gentle voice, Gary thought, was filled with concern. He put his arm around her shoulder, his mouth close to her ear. "No, thank you. Just need to think."

Anne shifted position, putting her mouth close to his ear. "I'll come with you if you want."

He shook his head. It was too loud, too crowded here.

"Then go," she said. She took his glass and kissed his lips.

Under the overcast afternoon sky, Gary returned to the cemetery and stood by Tom's grave. The headstone had been removed for Tom's name to be added beside his wife's, so a simple wooden cross marked their resting place. Gary walked to Treloar's headstone and stared at it, hoping some answers would appear. With his hands crossed in front of him, he thought again how clean and well-maintained the grave looked.

His thoughts went to Hamilton, guessing he had placed the two wreaths, Tom's and this one, which was leaning against the face of the headstone, obscuring the inscription. Hang on, had someone had moved it? When he had first seen the wreath he was positive it had been leaning against the side of the headstone. Hamilton could not have moved it, he'd departed. Lines grooved Gary's forehead as he remembered seeing Hamilton drive away. Before the funeral.

Then he remembered: Hamilton had held three wreaths. Gary had accounted for two; so where was the third? He looked around but couldn't see it. He began striding along the gravel path, looking side to side for the third wreath.

He stopped. There it was. On the other side of the graveyard. He stood and stared, his eyes drawn by the shape and colour of the headstone. It looked almost identical to the Treloar's and just as well maintained.

He walked closer. The third wreath was identical to the other two and also placed to be leaning against the headstone, obscuring some of the lower inscription. Once close enough, he read:

Margery Piggott-Turner
Precious Daughter & Mother. Died 1919, aged 41

His eyes widened when he saw the next three lines.

Mary Anne (M.A.) Turner
Mother, Widow, Friend to Lady Treloar
Born 1858–Died 1930

He reached out and rubbed his fingertips along the chiselled letters. Mystified, he muttered: 'Friend to Lady Treloar'. He moved the wreath, seeing smaller text partially hidden below the date. *"I wish I could lose this feeling as fast as I lost you"*. Shaking his head, bewildered, he wondered at its meaning.

He vaguely remembered Tom or Fred had spoken of a Ma Turner, and he also had memories of the fete, of being shown an old sepia photograph. Staring at the headstone, Gary shivered. Reading it again, he realised the initial letters of her Christian names made the name 'Ma'. The stallholder at the fete had said Ma Turner, who once lived at their cottage, was also a friend of Reverend McDonald.

Did finding either of these headstones help? Wondering this, Gary left the churchyard, walked slowly with his hands buried deep in his pockets. A tuneless version of 'The Lambeth Walk' drifted across the green from Tom's wake and broke Gary's concentration. He guessed it must be getting hot inside the inn as, despite the cold, a few mourners had ventured outside to drink. Still not comfortable returning, and with his thoughts still revolving around the gravestones, he changed direction, crossing the main road between the light traffic, and headed up Standish Lane to the canal.

Reaching the bridge, he made his way down the slope to the towpath and walked a short way beside the canal. The bridge reminded him of Tom, and the cold air brought tears to his eyes. The silence was broken only by the sound of birds from the nearby trees taking to the sky as his presence disturbed them, their wings fluttering loudly. He could feel the wind that was making leaves and branches sway; the quiet seemed to make the cold more pronounced. Buttoning up his warm Crombie coat, he leant against a tree and recalled Russell's journal. It must have been around here that Russell relaxed, smoking his pipe and pondered what to do, before confronting Treloar.

He looked up at the bridge, imagining Treloar and the mysterious woman riding past. Then he stared at the old bridge itself, his eyes blinking like the shutter of a camera, wishing the stones of bridge could talk, could reveal what they knew. He looked along the canal in both directions and, with canals having no current, nothing stirred. The water stretched out, its surface like a dusty mirror reflecting the trees and greenery along its edge. Occasional gentle ripples were caused by the wind, and by five ducks in a line paddling by. Each looked in his direction but, seeing as he made no move to feed them, continued on their way. After a while the water settled again, taut.

Russell had chosen a good place to deliberate, Gary thought, then his own mind returned to the two graves he had just discovered. Why, he wondered, had Hamilton – having placed three wreaths – leave without attending the funeral? Had he placed them for someone else? And then left trying to hide his own attendance. No point asking him, Gary thought. Hamilton wouldn't tell him. His thoughts moved on to question of who Hamilton had acknowledged when crossing the green.

Feeling cold from keeping still, and beginning to lose feeling in his feet, he began walking. He looked into the trees, not seeing the tangled branches, while he tried to sort out his jumbled thoughts. Remembering when Hamilton had waved, he'd looked to see if anyone responded, seeing Fred and David Reynolds, but there were also so many others. Feeling more bewildered, he stooped, plucked a pebble from the path and threw it into the canal, watching the ripples spread outwards from the tiny splash, eventually affecting the whole surface of the canal.

He turned back towards the bridge, trying to concentrate, focusing on the graves: M.A. Turner and a Piggott-Turner, her daughter. His thoughts suddenly circled closer to home. He and Anne had brought their house from a Miss Turner. Could she originally have been a Piggott-Turner? If so, she may have known Ma Turner. Was it possible both lived in the same cottage?

His imagination jumped and landed unexpectedly on another possibility: Ma Turner was identified as a friend of Lady Treloar; could she also have known Lady Treloar's daughters? He desperately tried to remember ages, and guessed Mary Anne Turner and the daughters could have been similar ages. His stride increased as he felt the beginnings of elation. Miss Piggott-Turner, was she now perhaps just Miss Turner? Could she be another living person they could question? His fingers clenched, making fists, and he punched an imaginary hole in the air. He felt pleased and proud at having worked this out without Jackson's help. Now, though, he wanted to share it all with Jackson.

Having reached the bridge, he climbed back up the slope to the road and tried jogging back down Standish Lane. His long coat restricted him from going too fast. As he approached the inn, he could hear the cacophony emanating from it. It sounded as if the whole village was singing, 'She loves you'. More mourners, chatting and laughing, glasses in hand, had spilled onto the green itself. Tom was, Gary thought, certainly getting the party he wanted.

He burst inside, found Anne, tried to drag her outside, gave up and so, gripping her arm, he excitedly explained about the old lady he had seen today, the one who had also sold them their house. It was a long shot, he reasoned, but she was related to a friend of Lady Treloar and may be able to help. Perhaps he should telephone Jackson?

"You will not," commanded Anne, her face rigid. "He's ill, Gary. You promised Eleanor; you just can't."

Gary couldn't hide how downhearted he felt. Anne looked at him then glanced at her watch. Her face softened. "But," she said, "it's only mid-afternoon now. You could still visit Miss Turner to see if it's worth pursuing. Then you'll have something to tell Jackson tomorrow." Anne was now beaming at Gary. "Miss Turner knows you from the funeral today, and from the house sale." Anne stopped, her smile vanishing. She took Gary's hand. "But what home is she in?"

"Damn," Gary said, not having thought of that. "It can't be too far away, though." He turned away, scratching his head.

Anne's smile returned. "Fred may know."

Fred and Ethel, along with Gary's brother and his wife, standing by the fire giving a bad impression of the Fab 4, were still singing 'She loves you' at the tops of their voices. All the villagers who knew the words were accompanying, which was just about everyone. Gary shouted Fred's name a couple of times, over the partying, without success. On his third attempt, he screamed Fred's name and heads turned towards Gary. He rubbed his throat and coughed, wondering if he had strained anything. Fred stared quizzically at Gary, who waved frantically for Fred to join him. Fred left his group, a near empty glass of beer in his hand.

"Fred, I need to ask you. Miss Turner, the woman who lived in our house."

Fred smiled, still watching Ethel, and leaned into Gary to listen. "She was related to Ma Turner."

Fred shouted his reply. "Yes, yes. That was her grandmother, they lived together. But Ma Turner died when I was very young."

Gary persisted. "Do you know what old persons' home Miss Turner went to live in?"

Fred shrugged, laughed loudly and pointed at Ethel. "Look at her."

Gary stamped his foot. "Fred, listen." He shouted above the cheering, as the now Fab 3 started singing 'Help'.

Fred finally dragged his attention back to Gary. He finished his drink as he thought. "Probably, the Oak Manor." Gary knew it: he'd seen the sign along the main road. "Anyway," Fred said, already turning away. "That's all history now, Gary. Forget it." Laughing and slapping villagers on their backs, Fred went back to join his wife and the others, waving his arms to encourage even more to join in the singing.

Gary turned to Anne, who put her finger gently to his lips. "I will see you later," she said. "Back home."

Taking her face in his hands he kissed her then stepped back, his eyes bright, a devoted expression of love on his face.

He left the inn feeling light-headed. His smile remained as he hurried home in order to collect his car. His pulse raced as if he were sprinting and he found he was enthused at his intentions. Laughing openly to himself, he was confident Jackson would be pleased he was about to investigate his newfound clue.

Chapter 30
Late Wednesday

Oak Manor Residential Home was a two-storey Georgian mansion that stood almost a mile south of Oak Cross village, at the top of a drive so long the building was invisible from the main road. Its exterior gave the impression it had recently received several new coats of white paint. Gary drove between pillars at the entrance and squinted. With a summer sun on the building, he thought, the reflection would be blinding. He followed the quarter-mile gravel drive to the car park. The darkening grey of the sky against the bright, bold white of the house gave the place an eerie, out-of-kilter, feel.

He stared at the home and its features, admiring the square-cut decorative stone cladding, the large windows comprising small glass panes, the steep, red-tiled roof. White pilasters could be seen above the windows, and there was a pedimented single entrance. Windows in the roof showed that rooms were also to be found in the loft space. Gary nodded in approval at the well-maintained mansion. It wasn't a stately home, but was still impressive.

Gravel crunched underfoot as Gary crossed the car park to the main entrance. Down the side of the mansion he could see movement through the floor-to-ceiling windows of a brightly lit modern extension. Feeling the wind increasing as the clouds chased each other across the sky, Gary looked up. In the distance darker clouds were gathering from the west. There will be a storm later, he thought.

A white-coated attendant answered the doorbell and listened politely to Gary's request: having seen Miss Turner that morning at the funeral, could Gary speak to her? The attendant gave a pleasant smile and, not seeing any issue, led him through to a large room. Radio 4 was blaring from a far corner. Feeling uncomfortably hot, Gary removed his Crombie. The heating was turned up high. Typical for residential homes, he figured, where warmth must be vital.

As well as being large and airy, the room to which he'd been led was very light. He guessed this was the extension he'd seen. Half a dozen residents were passing their time in plush chairs. The attendant pointed out Miss Turner – a small woman, thin, and still dressed in black. She was sitting quietly in an armchair, pen in hand, concentrating on a crossword. He recognised her, both from when he and Anne had brought her house and from earlier that day, at the church. Beside her was a Georgian marble fireplace that had carved corner blocks and whose grate was boarded up. No fire would ever be lit there. But there again, with the central heating cranked up, it was not necessary. Over the fireplace hung a painting, which Gary vaguely recognised. He read its title from a plaque built into the frame: "Scarlet Sunset". He thought it apt for a picture in what many would call an old people's home.

Gary thanked the attendant, who nodded, stepped away but didn't leave the room. It was as if he wanted to be sure his charge was okay with this new, unknown, caller. Miss Turner's watery eyes widened with surprise at seeing her visitor, then her expression contracted into a frown. She removed her glasses, laying them, with her crossword and pen, on her lap, and smiled. It was a guarded smile, wanting to be pleasant but unsure whether this visitor should be fully welcomed. Gary remembered that she'd proudly informed them, when he and Anne had brought her house last year, that she was in her late seventies. Gary had thought then she looked younger; she still did. Her hair was short and wiry and the colour of a milky hot chocolate. There was little grey in it. A gold chain hung loosely around her neck, from which was attached an old-fashioned watch. It lay on her chest and moved as she breathed. It reminded Gary of the watches nurses wear.

Gary returned her smile and apologised for disturbing her. He pulled up a footstool and sat down, so that they faced each other at the same height. "Miss Turner," he began slowly, "do you remember me? My wife and I brought your house last year. And I saw you at my Uncle Tom Lewis's, funeral this morning. I was hoping, as you've lived in Oak Cross for a good few years, you could answer a few questions."

She stiffened, sat forward and her smile suddenly looked false. A trembling hand pushed an invisible strand of hair behind her ear. She began fidgeting, attempting to pick up her glasses, crossword and pen, which escaped her clutches and she had to grab again, before trying to place them all onto a small round table to her side. She ended up clumsily dropping them, as if her fingers didn't have any strength. Gary picked them up and deposited them on the side table. Finally, she stared at Gary. "Yes. Yes, I do remember you." She sat back in her chair, beginning to relax. "So, Tom was your uncle? It was lovely funeral. I knew him for many years. Many. But my memory is not so good now. What do you want to ask Mr…, I am sorry," she shook her head and offered him a sad smile. "See, I can't even remember your name. Sorry. Is there something,

something wrong with the house?"

Gary grinned but perspiration began to drip down his back, it also slicked his palms. He resisted the urge to find a chair with a back he could wriggle against. It was so hot in here. "It's Gary Stevens and the house is lovely. We love living there. It's Oak Cross village I am interested in, and its inhabitants. You lived there all your life. I think you knew a Piggott-Turner?"

She sat upright, and glanced stiffly around the room. Two women hobbled past, entering the room, one using a walking stick, the other her friend, for support. "Hallo, Carrie," they both said, but were looking at her visitor. Gary nodded politely, waiting for Carrie Turner to answer. Her fingers were entwined, thumbs twisting over each other. "Piggott-Turner was my mother's married name. My father's surname was Piggott. He was an officer who died fighting in the Boar war." She looked about once again, as if expecting someone else to answer "I dropped the hyphenated name, it sounded a little pretentious. My mother died of Spanish Flu."

"And her mother would be Mary Anne Turner?" Gary tried to conceal his eagerness. He wiped sweat from his forehead, unsure whether it was due to excitement or the central heating. He pulled from his pocket the scrap of paper on which was the note he'd made at the cemetery. Now he was sure his excitement showed. "So, you changed your name, and lived with her until she died." He looked at the note. "In 1930."

"Ma Turner was what the locals called her. After father died, we lived with Gran in the cottage you bought. Why? What is this about Mr Stevens? It's all a bit personal. I thought you wanted to ask about Oak Cross."

Enthusiastically he held up the note. "I am sorry, please bear with me. She's buried in the village cemetery, and so is a Lady Treloar. Her headstone is almost identical to that of Ma Turner's." He leant forward. "Did your grandmother know Lady Treloar well? Or perhaps she knew Lady Treloar's two daughters?"

Carrie Turner glared at Gary, her mouth opening and closing, and a blush rose from her wrinkled neck. She tried clearing her throat. Finally, she twisted the watch that hung from her necklace, ostentatiously looking at the time. "I'm sorry,' she said, her voice croaky. 'It will be time for dinner soon. I don't think I can help you anymore. Would you please leave?" She glanced at the other residents in the room, as if expecting help. Gary leant back, surprised at her reaction. He realised he may have been a little blunt in his questioning. He'd been hoping for a different response and had assumed she would at least have been inquisitive.

He leaned forward again and spoke, not much above a whisper. "Miss Turner, I don't mean to press you, but a hundred years ago in Oak Cross – Old Oak Crossroads, as it was then – there was a robbery. Have you heard this story?"

She looked at him with wide eyes. "Please leave me alone. I cannot help you." Her fingers twisted the chain that held her watch. Hating himself, Gary persisted. "Miss Turner, please. I don't want to badger you, but your grandmother's headstone says she was a friend of Lady Treloar. Also, have you ever heard of a company called Hamilton Associates?"

She gave a small, unexpected scream, making Gary jump, then half raised herself from the chair, her voice surprisingly loud. It echoed around the room. "Mrs Greenwalk. Mrs G."

Others in the room looked towards them; Gary sat

speechless, mouth open, bewildered.

Miss Turner turned away to face others in the room, all of whom were staring at Gary. Seemingly from nowhere a tall woman in a brown cardigan and long tartan skirt appeared. Gary assumed it was Mrs G striding towards them. A white-coated attendant followed her, trying to keep up. "I am the owner here. Why are you upsetting my guests?"

Gary stood looking from Mrs G to Miss Turner and back again, embarrassment burning his face.

He heard Miss Turner sigh as she relaxed back into her chair. He assumed her confidence was returning; she looked at her support group and spoke in a loud voice so all could hear. "Please make him leave." She fixed her gaze firmly on Gary, her face crimson, her voice angry. "I can't help you; I don't know anything about any robbery, I don't know any Lady Treloar and have never ever met anybody from Hamilton Associates." The words flowed.

The look of surprise shown by Mrs G and her sudden glance towards Miss Turner was spotted by Gary. "Do you know Phillip Hamilton, Mrs G?" Gary asked her quickly.

"No, she does not." Carrie Turner's reply was just as quick, but louder. "Please go. *Now.*"

Gary looked about, trying to figure out what was going on, whether there was any help he could call upon. There didn't appear to be just the other residents closing in and the 'Scarlet Sunset' painting beside him.

"You must leave." Mrs G commanded. Gary ignored her and looked closer at the painting, its colours burning into his thoughts, forming a connection. He'd definitely seen the painting before, or one very like it. The hand that held his note started shaking, the paper making a soft rustle as it fluttered.

He pointed to the painting as memories coalesced, recollections of seeing the original in the Tate Gallery: vivid colours, a river, a bridge, a shadow in the background. Inset into the frame was the plaque with the title that he'd first viewed on his arrival. Below the title, screwed to the wall, was a separate panel he'd not spotted before. In smaller print is stated: 'By J.M.W. Turner. Gifted by a resident.' He felt his skin tingling, this revelation tightening his stomach. He turned to face Carrie, who sat rigid, watching him, apparently too scared to move. He felt like he had found a long-lost and forgotten photograph and was discovering its details and meaning all over again.

"You know it all don't you." It wasn't a question. His eyes fixed on the elderly lady, and he tilted his head. "You, or your family, gave the Turner painting to Hamilton's."

Mrs G sounded louder and even more adamant. "I have asked you politely to leave."

Carrie Turner's mouth was open, yet she was speechless. Her wide eyes darted to the painting and back to Gary. Her expression, Gary understood, told him everything.

Oblivious to all those around him, Gary wiped a handkerchief over his sweating brow and continued. "Phillip Hamilton telephoned you last week, didn't he? When I met him, with my friend Jackson."

Mrs G turned to the attendant. "Get Dougie, quick."

Gary was aware of the whole room watching, some occupants standing for a better view. The portable radio in the far corner, on full volume and blaring out Radio 4 news, had lost its interest, neighbouring rooms had emptied to see the excitement.

"It was Phillip who told you the arrangements for Tom's funeral, after our visit, wasn't it? And the three wreaths were from you?" Carrie Turner blinked and looked away, confirming his suspicions.

The nurse sent to fetch Dougie reappeared, pushing through those watching. Gary, waiting for a reply, continued staring at Carrie Turner, who tried to maintain her own tearful stare at him. Her hands were clenched together so tight her knuckles appeared bone-white. Gary swallowed, tasting guilt at upsetting an old woman and tried to think of something to say. He wondered how Anne would have handled the situation better. Not like this, he suspected.

A tight grip encircled Gary's upper arm and he turned. Dougie was about 30 years older than Gary, although shorter, and Gary assumed from his clothes that Dougie was the handyman or gardener. Whatever he was, his grip was firm. Gary made no movement to remove the grip. "Don't worry," he said loudly. "I'm going." He looked back at Miss Turner. "You're Phillip's client and you have the answers don't you, Miss Turner." Another thought struck him. "Turner. Is that also a lie?"

She glanced up at him, her tears now flowing, and ran a hand through her hair. "I am sorry." Distress filled her voice. "I cannot help you. Please go."

Gary nodded and turned to leave, but another idea struck him. He saw the pen Miss Turner had been using for her crossword. Despite Dougie's firm grip, Gary grabbed the pen, scrawled his phone number on his scrap of paper, and dropped it into the elderly woman's lap. "Please," he said, "if you should change your mind..."

Miss Turner glanced at it before looking up at him. He offered her the warmest, friendliest smile he could manage while being manhandled. Another, stronger, tug on his arm told him he was leaving.

Dougie maintained a tight hold of his arm and, with Mrs G one step behind, Gary was accompanied from the room. At the main entrance, Dougie released his grip. "Don't try to go back or—"

Mrs G interrupted by thrusting her face so close to Gary's that he feared she may kiss him. Her cheeks were crimson with anger. "How dare you upset my guest. If you ever come here again, I will call the police. Is that understood? Now, leave."

"I'm sorry. I didn't mean to upset Miss Turner," Gary pleaded.

Ignoring him, her voice furious, she almost spat out her words. "I don't care. I'm not interested. I want you off these premises." She pointed down the drive. "Dougie, see he leaves."

The two men crunched the gravel in unison as they walked to Gary's car. Dougie stood guard as Gary started the car and took one last look at the house in the hope that Miss Turner would appear. Glancing at the extension, he caught movement by the window. A small and frail woman – he assumed Miss Turner – stood at the window looking at him.

Skeletons that had been packed away in this woman's life were returning, he thought. He felt sure this old lady could bring the past alive, that she knew the story. Now, he thought – angry at himself for what he'd done – how the hell do he and Jackson get her to tell what she knows? He chided himself for being so stupid, for getting overexcited. He should have waited and spoken to Jackson, and agreed what questions to ask, before approaching her.

He would talk to Jackson tomorrow, get him to contact Miss Turner, perhaps speak to Hamilton again, and hopefully arrange another meeting with Miss Turner. Perhaps Jackson could retrieve something from his mistake. He drove away, down the quarter-mile drive, stopping at the entrance and looking in the rear-view mirror. Dougie was standing in front of the house, ensuring the unwelcome visitor did actually leave the premises.

The sky to the west had changed and was now as black as Gary's mood. He heard thunder, soon followed by another flash of lightening. Counting, he reached six before hearing a rumble. Six miles away he thought. He remembered reading somewhere that lightening was once thought to be a manifestation of the gods. He wondered whether he'd disturbed the peace of some gods, and, if so, whether they were in heaven or hell.

Chapter 31
Thursday

The night following the funeral, a storm raged with such violence that sleep, for Gary, was impossible. He lay staring at the ceiling, frustrated and angry with himself. It felt as if the gods he'd disturbed were directly overhead and annoyed. He winced as thunder boomed and rolled; blinking as lightening illuminated the bedroom. It seemed to be going on forever, the storm having decided to torment him and him alone. He glanced at the bedside clock: 5:40. Despite his twisting and turning and what could have been a full battle raging outside, Anne had somehow slept soundly. How she could sleep through the end of the world, he didn't know. He moved slowly, sliding himself smoothly out of the bed. He didn't bother keeping quiet because the thunder was loud enough to cover a Deep Purple concert. Even so, Anne turned over, as if aware more of his absence than the gods throwing a tantrum. Quickly, he collected clothes, went downstairs, dressed and clicked on the kettle.

Just after half seven, Anne appeared at the kitchen door, snuggled in a thick fluffy dressing gown and wiping sleep from her eyes. The storm had finally blown itself out about ten minutes before. "Couldn't sleep?" she asked, lifting and shaking the now-empty kettle before filling it and switching it on. She found a mug, added instant coffee, and only then kissed him good morning. He understood her priorities.

"My mind's all over the place," he said, holding out his own mug for a refill. "I charged in yesterday like a bloody idiot." He clenched his fist in anger. "I found another connection, someone with answers and what did I do? I blew it."

"Stop beating yourself up." Anne said sympathetically as she leaned against the worktop. "You've found a good link." She yawned, poured boiling water into her mug and did the same to his. Coffee for two. Sitting down at the table, she placed her legs up onto his knees. He liked that she always did this. He found it reassuring. She continued: "You just have to find a way to talk to her again." She wrapped both hands around her hot mug and offered a mischievous grin. "Which, having been thrown out of an old person residential home – impressive, my darling – may be a problem." She blew on her coffee before taking a tentative sip.

"I was not thrown out;" he replied, indignant. "Just asked to leave."

Anne looked furtively at Gary over her mug as she sipped her coffee. "Still, a bit embarrassing. I never thought I'd marry a man who could get himself ejected from a home for the elderly."

"I was not ejected." Gary laughed. "Or thrown out." He began tickling his wife's legs. Anne twisted trying to escape, almost spilling her coffee, shrieking for him to stop. It was the ringing of the telephone that interrupted their play. Gary went to the hall to answer the phone while Anne, still giggling, adjusted her dressing gown.

Returning ten minutes later, he stopped at the doorway, eyes wide, his mind still deciphering the call. Anne looked up expectantly while spreading butter on hot toast. His lips curved into a satisfied grin. "That was Mrs Greenwalk, from the home. My god she was angry," he chuckled. "She disagreed with everything before I knew what everything was. Then she put Carrie Turner on."

Anne stopped spreading, her complete attention on Gary, whose grin turned into the sort of broad happy smile he would use in a chance meeting with an old friend. "Carrie Turner wants to talk," he said, unable to hide his curiosity. "It seems she thought about it overnight. Evidently, she didn't sleep either." He stepped into the kitchen. "This morning she insisted Mrs Greenwalk telephone me. She wants another meeting." He tapped his head. "Boy, am I glad I left my number." He wrapped his arms around Anne, feeling her warmth through the dressing gown. Anne dropped the butter-covered knife and returned the hug. "She even apologised, hoping she didn't wake me."

"I told you it would work out."

"She said it was hearing my determination, and speaking to Phillip Hamilton last week." He hugged Anne tighter, kissed her neck. "And that's not all…" Anne looked up at him, waiting. "I asked if I could bring Jackson. She said of course, I could bring anyone I wanted."

Anne took a step back, holding Gary at arm's length, "What did you say?" Her eyes were wide.

"That we'll be there," Gary said, puzzled.

"When is this meeting?" She couldn't keep the excitement from her voice.

He frowned, tilting his head. "Today, this morning, ten thirty, at the home."

Anne glanced at the clock on the wall. "It's nearly eight," she muttered to herself, then said to Gary: "Right, you ring Jackson and arrange to pick them both up. I'll shower."

"Both?" he said, confused, still holding Anne at arm's length.

"Because, my dear, Eleanor and I are also coming."

He pulled her back, close to him, and kissed her lips. Anne put her hands on his chest and pushed herself away. "Time for that later. Now, make the call." She disappeared up the stairs before he could say anything else.

* * *

The rain was finally stopping; shallow puddles in the gravel car park rippled from the last few drops wrung from the dirty grey sponge of a sky. The four of them – Gary, Anne, Jackson and Eleanor – stood together, admiring the white Georgian mansion. Gary thought Jackson looked in better health than the last few times they had been together. It was true, he thought, how good news can buck up one's spirit. Jackson planted his cane into the gravel to steady himself, one hand on top of the other. "You do know where we are?" Jackson stared at the house, a knowing look lighting his face.

"Oak Manor Residential Home." Gary was bemused, unsure of Jackson's question.

Jackson looked at Gary, his smirk increasing. "That," he raised his cane, pointed with it, "was the Treloar family home."

Anne gasped and Gary stared, as if seeing the building for the first time, putting it into its original context and surroundings.

Two people appeared at the main door and stood like sentries, as Gary and the others approached. "That," he whispered, "is Mrs Greenwalk. She runs the place. And that," he nodded, "is Dougie."

Once close enough, Gary offered his friendliest smile and

held out his hand. "Hello again, Mrs Greenwalk." The gesture was ignored.

"Let me make it very clear," her words were harsh and aggressive, as if she were spoiling for a fight. "I objected very strongly to calling you, but Miss Turner insisted."

Gary's smile disappeared and he straightened his back.

"So, I warn you, Mr Stevens," she pointed at his chest, "any repeat of yesterday and I will terminate this meeting. Is that clear?"

"Absolutely," Gary answered with exaggerated courteousness. "I promise that won't happen." He had to stop himself from bowing.

"What happened yesterday?" Eleanor looking with concern at Gary. Beside her, Anne started to snigger, putting her hand to her mouth to smother her laughter.

Gary shot a look at Anne, his lips tight, eyes half closed in embarrassment. "Just a misunderstanding," he said. "Afraid I got a little over enthusiastic." Mrs Greenwalk turned to Dougie. "Dougie, you carry on with your work. I can handle this." Dougie looked disappointed, took one step back and stared at Gary. While he wasn't actually snarling and showing his teeth, Gary thought he had the appearance of an enthusiastic guard dog being told to sit. The group followed Mrs Greenwalk into the house, where she cultivated a smile and nodded to residents. They arrived at a room whose sign identified it as the 'Recreation Room'. "I have closed off this room for a couple of hours." She spoke as if it was Gary's fault and he should be ashamed at the difficulties he'd caused. She knocked on the door then opened it before there was a reply.

The room was large enough to have two table tennis tables

in the middle, and three card tables against one wall. Bookcases whose shelves were filled with books and magazines ran at half height along another wall. Two fluorescent tubes on the ceiling gave excellent lighting. At the far end Carrie Turner, holding a glass of water, sat in an armchair. Phillip Hamilton stood beside her, his back to a window that overlooked the garden.

"We have your guests, Miss Turner. And…" Mrs Greenwalk glowered at Gary. "…there won't be a repeat of yesterday, will there?"

He shook his head.

"Now, do I stay, or shall I leave you all alone? I think it would be better if I stayed, don't you?" Her gaze never left Gary.

"Please, Mrs G." Miss Turner looked up from her glass. "I think you should hear this as well."

"If you really think so." Mrs Greenwalk nodded, sounding magnanimous.

Gary grinned to himself, doubting if Mrs G. ever had any intention of leaving. He introduced Anne, Jackson and Eleanor to Miss Turner and to Hamilton, who smiled at Jackson. "We meet again."

Everyone, except Hamilton, pulled chairs from various parts of the room, making a semi-circle around Miss Turner. Hamilton, standing at Miss Turner's side, straightened his tie before speaking.

"Miss Turner advised me, and I agreed, to answer your questions, as long as they are not too personal." He ran a hand through his salt-and-pepper hair. "I have one condition. Before you take any further action, such as publishing, you tell me your plans first."

Jackson shifted in his chair. "We can agree to that. However," he said, pointing at Gary. "We have reached this point because Gary found Miss Turner. I have therefore decided that, this time, it's for him to lead the questioning."

Gary gaped at Jackson's grin, then glanced at Anne and Eleanor, both of whom were nodding. Jackson was actually handing over the reins.

"Thank you, Jackson," Gary replied awkwardly and looked back at Miss Turner. She moved her hands and revealed a box on her lap. It was square, the type of tin brought at Christmas and which held a biscuit selection. It also looked old and, although the picture on the dented lid was severely faded, Gary could just about see a painting, a scene of children wrapped in scarves and woolly hats pulling a sleigh across snow. Christmas bells filled one corner, and a not very lifelike running dog completed the tableau. Gary wondered what was inside the tin and figured they would find out eventually.

"Then I suggest we start, if you are ready Carrie?" Hamilton touched Miss Turner's shoulder, while still looking at Gary. "Gary, when you're ready." Hamilton leaned back against the window frame.

Gary smiled and tried to sound apologetic. "First, I am sorry for yesterday. Excitement got the better of me."

Miss Turner chuckled, shamefaced. "I was partly to blame," she said. "You took me by surprise. And," she said, turning to Hamilton. "I spoke to Phillip last night."

Gary ignored Hamilton and spoke to Miss Turner. "Did you know Tom's father was Corporal Henry Price?"

She nodded. "We were children from same village, although Tom was slightly older, so yes, of course we all knew each other. Gran befriended Tom's family." Her voice wavered slightly.

"Tom boasted about his father's activities, even though his father planned to desert the family. Gran gradually persuaded Tom to stop his boasting; it made him look silly." She offered a sad smile, exposing her dentures. "Obviously he changed his mind."

"He told me the story after the recent local newspaper article," Gary said.

"I saw that story. I have copies of that and your original, Mr Jackson." She glanced at Jackson, then opened her tin. Letters and photos were inside. She leafed through everything, eventually holding up copies of the two newspaper articles. She then replaced them. "I wondered at the time if it would cause trouble. I couldn't understand anyone writing about something so very old and forgotten."

"Old, perhaps, but not forgotten," Gary replied. "It's a long story, but what you may not know is that the writer of the latest article was involved with Tom's death. Also, she has personal connections with the story." Carrie exhaled, more of a wheeze, and looked at Hamilton. She shook her head as if it were too heavy. "It never goes away." She looked at Gary. "What happened? No. Tell me later. I'm not sure I…" She stared at the tin.

Gary coughed and produced a photograph from his wallet and held it out. "Miss Turner, we are pretty sure this is a photo of Corporal Henry Price."

She ignored the picture, her voice was suddenly clear and unrepentant. "He was an evil man, Mr Stevens. He should have died with the others in the battle. I, for one, wish he had."

"Please, call me Gary." He waited a moment, smiling while he got his thoughts together; he did not want to mess it up this time. She eventually nodded.

"Your grandmother, Mary Anne or Ma Turner, was also part of the Treloar family."

She shook her head. "No, I am afraid that is not correct."

"Are you sure?" Jackson leant forward on his cane. Gary grinned to himself; he'd known Jackson wouldn't have been able to stop himself from getting involved. "I thought," Jackson said, "she may have been a relative, maybe one of the Treloar sisters."

Gary leaned back upon seeing Carrie Turner's look of amazement. She shook her head vigorously and pulled herself upright. She turned to Hamilton. "Good grief. Now where did they get that idea from?"

Gary was not sure where to go next. He had been convinced – as was Jackson – the link was Treloar's sisters. He glanced at Jackson, who clutched his cane with both hands, his head forced down with the weight of realisation that Miss Turner was telling the truth. They had got it wrong.

Finally, Jackson raised his head. "Was her real name Turner?"

"No," Hamilton interjected. He stood straighter, no longer leaning against the window, and unfolded his arms. "No," he repeated in a stronger voice. "My ancestor, Simon Hamilton, assisted Mary Anne in making a new life, with a new surname." Either he couldn't prevent his pride from showing or he didn't try. "Simon had a great love of Joseph Turner's paintings."

Gary leaned forward, eyes on Hamilton. "Can you tell us her real name?"

Carrie Turner held up her bony hand, stopping Hamilton from answering. "Married or maiden?" Everyone's eyes turned back to elderly woman.

His mouth dry, and thinking before replying, Gary said, "Married."

Carrie hesitated, before answering. "Farrant." She spat out the name as if swearing.

"Farrant?" Jackson's cane slipped from his fingers to the floor. "Farrant as in Captain Farrant? Farrant as in the man in charge of protecting Colonel Standish and his treasure? No." Jackson shook his head, either in denial or wonderment. "Like Lieutenant Norton, he disappeared the night of the robbery. Unlike Norton his body was never found. I always assumed it would turn up at some point."

"Captain Farrant's wife?" muttered Gary as he leant down to pick up Jackson's cane. He passed it back, still blinking.

"Yes, she was married off to Farrant when she was only just seventeen. Her father arranged it. He had four sons and one daughter. He didn't want a girl." Loathing dripped from her voice.

Gary scrutinised Miss Turner, unsure what to ask next. He swallowed hard; questioning was more difficult when your theory was busted. Gary felt Jackson's eyes on him and, when he looked, Jackson nodded, telling him to continue. Gary took a deep breath. "So," he said, while considering this new information. "You are the granddaughter of Captain Farrant?"

Once again, she shook her head. "No, I am not." Firm and decisive.

Gary wished he had a drink, water or something stronger; his brain was overheating. Around him were confused faces. "If you're not Farrant's granddaughter, then who are you?" His voice sounded high, even to himself.

"I," she said, loud and proud, "am the granddaughter of Spencer Treloar."

"Treloar? No," cried Gary.

"Never." Eleanor spoke for the first time.

"Impossible," shouted Jackson before his outburst turned into a coughing fit.

Ignoring the coughing, Miss Turner replied, a little angry: "I assure you I am. I have the proof right here." Her fingers tapped her box and she looked at everyone in turn and everyone stared back.

Phillip Hamilton stepped forward and, placing one hand on top of Carrie's chair back, looked at her as she took a deep breath. "Carrie, can I suggest we stop the questioning and you tell the full story, as told to you by your grandmother, and what we've deduced about Spencer." Hamilton moved his gaze across the group as if looking for approval. Everyone turned to Gary who, dumbfounded, nodded.

Carrie exhaled a large pent-up breath. She took a sip of water. There was a slight wheeze in her breathing.

Gary sighed, relieved the questioning had stopped. He glanced at the door, hearing muffled talking in the corridor. Another world, he thought, away from Treloar, Price, Farrant, Russell and the others. He turned back to Carrie as she began her story.

"My grandfather, Spencer Treloar, and grandmother, Mary Anne Farrant, loved each other very much, but it would have been seen as a terrible scandal – a junior officer having a very secret affair with a senior officer's wife." Her face showed a weary sadness, and she shook her head. "They had such little time together. Whenever speaking of him, she quoted those words on her headstone. It was their love that pulled them into a web of secrecy and deceit." She looked up at Hamilton who, for once, offered a generous smile.

She spoke clearly, telling the story of her family as it was told to her, and what she and Hamilton had surmised, every so often pulling evidence from the tin box: a letter, a document, a photograph, passing it around for all to see and always waiting until everyone present had understood its significance before returning it to her box and continuing her tale.

Carrie Turner held their attention and they were taken back to 1877.

Part 3

1877

Chapter 32
March–August 1877

He listened to the clip-clop of hooves on rough, hard ground. Knowing he and his mount would be out most of the day, and not wanting to tire his horse, he forced himself to keep to a leisurely pace. Looking up, there wasn't a cloud to be seen. It was as if a paintbrush, drenched with bright azure dye, had been drawn across a clean canvas. He sighed; the day was bright, unlike his mood.

While, this August morning, he had no duties, he did have worries. More than he wanted. He felt as though he had a persistent head cold. He shook his head, slowly, as though the movement hurt, and recalled comforting his mother that morning. Her silk handkerchief had been wet from repeatedly dabbing at the tears that flowed from her puffy eyes. Falteringly, she had told him of his father's latest botched dealings and more losses, and of how his father had yelled and slammed his hand on the breakfast table, insisting she make even more domestic savings. His family was in trouble, the estate was in trouble, and the poor workers were living in conditions that made him feel ashamed.

He slumped in his saddle as he approached the village. His despondency increasing as he saw new ruts in the road and cottages in a dilapidated condition. He knew he was powerless to change things and it made him feel physically sick.

As the great oak came into view his spirits lifted slightly. He remembered the special relevance of this place. It was here, only six months earlier, he first met Mary Anne. It had been March, spring had arrived early, and he had thought it a good day for a ride. There had been almost no wind and so the light clouds had taken their own, unhurried, time passing in front of the sun.

She had been under the branches of the great oak, looking troubled and had asked for his help. With her head held demurely low she explained that her horse was skittish and that her saddle needed adjusting. Spencer Treloar was unable to resist. She remained astride her horse whilst he adjusted her stirrup leather and girth, occasionally looking up to admire such a pretty heart-shaped face beneath her hat and veil. A blue-eyed beauty.

That afternoon they rode together over the heath.

After that first meeting Spencer couldn't think clearly. His thoughts each day were of Mary Anne – her bright smile, those beautiful, beautiful eyes, how easily he talked to her, and her to him. Of course, as well as the dizziness of that first meeting, he also felt some guilt. She was, after all, the wife of Captain Farrant. However, her presence intoxicated him, and like all intoxications made the normally rational act like fools. Hearing she often rode in this area he waited under the oak tree a few days later hoping to meet her again. Upon seeing her approach he found himself waving like an excited child. Then through spring into summer, when time allowed, they rode together, taking the same route over and over again. The scenery became part of them.

She listened to his worries, and he to hers. With a lump in her throat she told him of her loveless marriage to Alfred Farrant, and he heard how unkindly Farrant treated her. As the year progressed and the weather grew warmer, so did their love. Spencer even hinted at a possible future together. Mary Anne, he realised, was more of a realist, and refused to discuss a future unless things changed. Spencer prayed things would change. He didn't know it, but this August morning, with its cloudless azure sky and leisurely clip-clop of hooves accompanying his approach to the old oak, today his prayers were about to be answered.

He sat upright in his saddle the moment he saw her. He shivered with excited anticipation, knowing he and Mary Anne would end the afternoon, as in many previous outings, making love. They even had their favourite spot, hidden under a shelter of thick bracken. He twisted in his saddle and patted the green blanket they used, confirming it was still tied across his horse's loins.

When he looked back, he saw her under the long branches of the great oak, sitting astride her piebald horse, waiting for him. Spencer's heart beat faster and his mood lifted. His worries, perhaps not entirely forgotten, were definitely set aside. Mary Anne had become his life, their meetings loving and sensual. He twisted his heels into his horse's rump, the rhythm of his mount's hooves speeding as if attempting to equal his heartbeat. His whole body desperately ached to hold Mary Anne tight.

They'd worked it out: to avoid unnecessary attention their encounters followed a carefully arranged routine. The first to arrive would wait until they saw the other and then ride ahead, up the track towards the canal, where they would meet on the heath and ride together.

As he watched, Mary Anne started riding up the track, but suddenly she halted and leaned forward, her hand stroking her horse's soft mane. She appeared to be waiting, as if seeing someone coming from the direction of the canal. As Spencer approached, he recognised her husband, his superior, Captain Alfred Farrant. He was riding a small black cob, swaying, with one hand gripping the pommel of his saddle. Farrant looked decidedly unsteady on his mount.

Trembling, Spencer rode passed Mary Anne. He glanced at her, their eyes locking in a shared understanding. Her face was pale and she was biting her lip. He overtook her, trying to act as if she were a stranger, and as his superior officer approached Spencer saluted. Instead of returning the gesture, Captain Farrant just held up his hand to halt Spencer's progress.

Farrant showed no signs of surprise at seeing his lieutenant. In fact, he appeared to be enjoying the situation. A broad triumphant smile split his features. He smoothed his bushy moustache, pointed at the Old Oak Inn, and barked orders for them both to follow him.

The inn was empty except for a farm labourer slouching at the bar, his head bowed almost low enough to be in his tankard. Farrant found a table by the window, through which they could see both church and oak tree. After ordering, Mary Anne and Spencer sat one side, Farrant the other. Spencer unconsciously drummed his fingers on the table. The landlord brought their drinks. Farrant paid and waited for the landlord to return to his post behind the bar, he then took his time lighting a cigarette, eventually blowing foul-smelling smoke across the table.

"You are having a secret liaison with my wife, lieutenant." He sat back, relaxed, in control.

"We are in love, Captain." Spencer felt his cheeks burn as he blushed.

"And, I am sure, enjoying her delights. Which should be for

her husband only."

"You were never a true husband, Alfred." Mary Anne spat the words out.

Spencer turned and saw her crimson countenance. He realised she had a stronger side he'd not seen.

Farrant leaned across the table, his breath stinking of alcohol. He pointed nicotine-stained fingers, which still held his cigarette, at Mary Anne.

"You are still my wife," he reprimanded, his eyes narrowing.

"I haven't been your wife," she emphasised the marital title, "for months. You seek your pleasures elsewhere. You don't even like me. You'd rather be rid of me." It was her turn to point. "You married me for my father's money. We're husband and wife in name only." Spencer took her hand, trying to ease her anger.

Farrant sat back, taking a draw on his cigarette, grinning, wiping his moustache and nodding. "True, very true. I had debts you see, Spencer. I needed her dowry." His words were slurred, and Spencer understood the captain had not only been drinking, but drinking a lot. "Always seem to have debts. Have debts now." Farrant threw his arms wide. "But her money has gone." He slapped the table. "I need more."

"How did you know about us?" Mary Anne turned her head away and clenched her hands together, her knuckles whitening.

He grinned, flicking his cigarette. "You changed. You suddenly became almost pleasant." He turned his finger on himself. "Regardless of how I treated you." He snorted a humourless laugh. "A groom at the stable. You told him you usually rode this way, so I started to watch, and it was just a matter of time before I saw the reason you came here." He nodded at Spencer.

The edge in Mary Anne's voice was unlike anything Spencer had heard from her before. "So what are you going to do?"

Farrant sat forward and, in no hurry, took another cigarette from his case and used the first to light the second. He stubbed the dying cigarette into a terracotta dish, then placed his arms and elbows on the table, hands together.

"Treloar here..." His cold gaze shifted to Spencer. "…is going to help me get some money."

"I have a little money left, not much, after spending it on some property." Spencer whispered, rubbing the inside of his collar.

Sitting back, Farrant let out a scornful laugh. The labourer at the bar glanced over at the noise. "I don't need *a little* money," Farrant said, suddenly leaning forwards, sneering. "I need a lot." His voice dropped to a whisper. "And I know just where to find it." His eyes widened. "It's my income you see, Treloar. It does not don't cover my lifestyle." He tipped his cigarette at Mary Anne. "And a wife like this does not help." Mary Anne looked at the floor. "I borrowed money from a senior officer, a Colonel Standish, who lends money, oh yes, but at such interest… You know Standish, Treloar? Your father does."

Spencer gritted his teeth and looked away, unable to make eye contact. Every nerve in his body telling him to strike the man. Farrant raised his tankard, swallowed a large mouthful of ale, and wiped his mouth with the back of his hand. Froth was still smeared over his moustache.

"I am sure you have heard the stories about Colonel Standish. What you may not know is that he plans to retire soon and move to his new estate. Well, I, along with few others, intend to relieve him of some, if not all, of his wealth. And you, Spencer." He leaned further forward. "You are going to help us." His cold unblinking eyes stared at Treloar.

Spencer went to stand but Farrant's hand shot across the table and grabbed his sleeve. "Who said you could leave?"

"I will not be party to any of this." Frowning, Spencer glanced at Mary Anne. She stared up at him, her mouth open, fear filling her eyes.

Farrant gripped his sleeve tighter, pulling downwards. "Sit down, Lieutenant. If you leave." He nodded towards Mary Anne. "She will be dumped at your parents' house this very day, in what she's wearing now. You will be the talk of every company mess by this time tomorrow. You won't be able to show your face at the camp. I will bring shame and disgrace on you and your family name."

Spencer lowered himself back into the chair and Farrant released his grip. Turning to Mary Anne, Spencer saw her tears. He put an arm around her shoulders. This was also a devastating shock to her, he realised.

"That's being sensible, Lieutenant." Farrant emptied his tankard in one gulp, then stood and stubbed out his second cigarette, his grin wide and evil. "Now, I will take your leave so you can both talk and, who knows, enjoy what's left of your day." His expression was that of the victorious. "Treloar, we will talk again soon. And privately. I will tell you what I expect you to do." He went to leave then stopped, as if re-thinking things. He turned back, put both hands on the table and leaned forward until his face was inches from Spencer's. His grin had become a scowl. "Don't think of reporting this. You have no evidence. I have all the cards, Lieutenant Treloar." He shook his head.

"And, believe me, my associates wouldn't like it."

"One thing, Captain." Spencer kept his eyes fixed on Farrant, unblinking, while he attempted to keep the pleading from his voice. "Nobody gets hurt." He took a deep breath. "Not Standish, not anyone else."

Farrant sneered. "If you do as you're told…" he held his hands up, as if in surrender, "… then why would anybody get hurt? It's just about the money. Then I disappear." His sneer twisted into a humourless grin. "With me gone, you can console my wife. I think you may both like that, making a life together."

Spencer felt his hands clench into fists, but he dropped his head. Farrant turned to Mary Anne. "No need to rush home, my dear," he said, before leaving the inn. They heard him whistling as he went.

Feeling as though he might throw up, Spencer covered his mouth. Mary Anne, her cheeks soaked with tears, took his other hand and squeezed it hard. Being blackmailed had now been added to Spencer Treloar's worries, along with the likelihood of dishonour. But maybe, he thought, maybe if Farrant got what he wanted, then things would change, Mary Anne would be rid of her husband, and would be free.

Like a fish on a line, Spencer Treloar had been hooked.

Chapter 33
Return to October 1877

The canal barge pushed its way through the water, the surface of which was a blanket of fallen leaves. Rain began to patter, causing ripples. The darkness of night closed in on the men on board. Those awake were aware that the barge's progress was little more than walking pace. Spencer Treloar, his cape wrapped around him, was definitely awake, alert and trying to keep as dry as possible. His stomach churned after seeing knives discretely passed to two soldiers by Ox – a giant of a man, easily over six foot tall and with a broken nose. Knives? Why? He was told nobody would get hurt. He stared into the night, feeling a soft bump as the barge brushed against the bank. He saw movement: the son of the bargee jumped to the canal path, rope in hand ready to tie up. Treloar heard a sudden shout from Farrant: "Now!"

He froze as the two soldiers, each with a single thrust, killed the soldier beside him then moved on to the next victim. As he stared, Ox killed another, then stood, smirking, his wide forearm tight around the neck and mouth of Lieutenant Norton. The night's darkness exaggerated Treloar's terror, and he heard his own teeth chattering. He blinked his wide, shocked eyes, not believing the carnage before him. Cold sweat suddenly soaked his body. Shivering, he wiped his face with his sleeve, unsure whether he was wiping sweat or rain, feeling demons were all around.

In the well deck, Captain Alfred Farrant, having used his

hunter's knife to kill Standish and the bargee, lifted a dirty rag off the wet deck and passed it one of his men to clean away the blood. Trembling, Treloar gripped the side of the barge and, unable to control himself, leaned over the side and vomited into the canal.

From somewhere he heard someone cry: "Throw knives over the side." He looked up, wiping his mouth with the back of his sleeve. A bearded soldier, unknown to Treloar, but about his age and height, stood on the bank, hands on his hips and looking into the barge. A mariner's cap sat on his head while an open coat revealed an army uniform. Treloar's muscles tensed when he saw, laying on the path, the lifeless body of the bargee's son. Unable to control his shaking, he touched his own revolver and knife, needing their reassurance. One of the two soldiers stopped his investigations of the dead, wiped his knife on the cloth he held and looked at the new arrival. "Hallo, Price," he called. "Wondered when you would show up."

Corporal Price stepped towards them, menacing. "I said, throw your knives over the side. You know my orders. No evidence." The soldiers leaned over the side and Treloar heard soft, almost delicate, splashes. Price rubbed his nose and exchanged a grin with Ox, who still had his arm around the lieutenant's neck. "Well, what have we here?" Price stared closely at Norton, who was making useless attempts at grappling at the thick branch that was Ox's arm. The bag man easily lifted Lieutenant Norton and swung him round, laughing as if showing a trophy.

"Passenger, Pricey." Ox's words had a twang as if he was speaking through his nose. Footsteps on the wooden deck made Treloar turn. Farrant approached. "Fool hitched a ride." He brushed his moustache. "But then I thought, adding another passenger would confuse things even more, when people look into this." Treloar thought Farrant sounded pleased with his actions.

"Good thinking, Captain Farrant." Price looked at the young, terrified officer, whose bloodshot eyes flicked from side to side, desperate to find help. His legs shook and he gasped for breath. Price turned to Treloar, grinning. "Finish him, Ox."

Second Lieutenant Norton's arms flopped loose against his body as Ox casually broke his neck. The sound made Treloar fight against more rising vomit. He wasn't squeamish; he'd been in battles, seen men maimed and die fighting for their country, but nothing like this.

"Get rid of your knife, Ox," a soldier shouted and Treloar thought he sounded anxious. Ox crossed his arms and stared back at both soldiers, defiant.

"Come on, Ox," said Price, "You know my orders."

Still smirking, Ox walked to the far side of the barge and leant over the gunwale such that his actions were masked from the two soldiers. But not from Treloar. Ox dropped something into the water, which made a soft splash, but it wasn't his knife. This, he slid back inside his tunic.

Incensed, Treloar turned to Farrant. "This is not what was planned." Both his voice and body trembled with anger. His Adam's apple bobbed like a drowning man in a heavy sea.

Farrant raised his eyebrows in mock surprise. "Plans change."

Treloar pointed at the lifeless body of Norton, slumped and askew on the wet deck. "You said…" he fought for his words. "You assured me no one would be hurt." His voice grew louder.

He was almost shouting. "That was murder." He shook his head. "I will not be part of this. Just Standish's money, that's what you said." His swung his arm impotently from side to side. "Not this. You said nothing about killing." He pointed at Price, "And who is he?"

Farrant stepped towards Treloar, lines of irritation taut on his forehead. "Now listen Treloar." He flashed a sideways glance at Price. "Corporal Price here is working for me. I told you I had associates. And, let us be honest, you are already a part of this. You can't deny that. And if we are caught, we will all say it was your plan. After all, as far as everyone else is concerned, you're the only one who knew what Standish was doing today. The fewer that know a secret, the better, right?" His eyebrows rose above eyes that appeared to be too wide. "I'm sure you know what I mean."

Treloar wiped his clammy hands on his trousers, and looked at the cold contempt on Price's face. Farrant turned away and removed a cigarette from his silver case. He watched, as did Price, as Ox and the two soldiers on the canal path knelt over a large oak chest encircled with beaten iron straps.

This chest stood over two feet high and three feet wide, with inset handles large enough for even Ox's hands. Its lid had been opened and some of its contents removed to make it lighter and easier to move. Despite the scattered coins and jewellery glittering on the towpath, Treloar thought the chest and its contents still looked almost unmanageable. He stared, feeling there were now two worlds: theirs – organised, calculated, murderous and ruthless – and his own – confused, threatened and scared. He shook his head and the thought hit him that, to survive, he had to understand their world. And quickly.

He watched Price and Farrant walk away together.

"That Standish?" Price pointed.

Farrant nodded. "Insisted on joining us."

Price chuckled. "Bet he regrets it now." He turned serious. "The wagon is there, Alfred." He pointed towards the nearby bridge with his unlit cigarette. "And we have a hole dug further up the canal." He turned and indicated the opposite direction. "To bury the bodies." He nodded towards Norton. "And include that officer." Farrant looked in both directions and also nodded.

Treloar studied the two men, their movements lit by the light of a lantern in the well deck.

Farrant stepped confidently off the barge and a flare from a match briefly illuminated his impassive features before he lit his cigarette. He watched the first chest being dragged towards the wagon. "Excellent. Carry on, Price."

He sounded arrogant, Treloar thought. Behind Farrant, and unseen by him, Price curled his lips into a thin sneer and made an obscene gesture with his hand. He mouthed something abusive, before turning and meeting Treloar's gaze. Neither moved, each weighing up the other. Eventually, Price sniggered, stepped off the barge and passed Farrant. Questions began to form in Treloar's mind as to who – despite the impression Farrant wanted to give – might actually be in charge.

Treloar pulled his cape tighter and looked at Farrant on the towpath. He was idly smoking his cigarette, as if out for stroll and had only stopped to watch some men work. This man, Mary Anne had told him, was a selfish fool, simply out for what he could get. Talk around the camp about his character had confirmed that. When something needed doing, Farrant would leave it until tomorrow or the next day, or even better still get someone else to do it. Treloar remembered hearing a senior officer ask, "Why on earth did Standish choose Farrant to head his escort? Good God, the man might be shrewd in business, but he has no idea how to select men. Farrant is the last person I would choose even for the simplest of jobs. The man's a buffoon."

Spencer Treloar had felt ashamed, unable to say he was the one who proposed Farrant for the escort. That had been the first of Farrant's many demands.

Treloar slumped against the barge rail. Farrant had made the last few months difficult, to say the least, especially with their shared secret regarding Mary Anne. And Treloar now fully understood the meaning of the word 'powerless'. He felt sickened, angry and empty. When Farrant had made his second demand, he had sounded like an officious schoolmaster. "You know the area, Treloar. Find somewhere close to the canal to conceal the chests, to be left for about a month or two, nice and secure and easy to get to and from. We need them safe until any investigation is declared over."

Well, he had found such a place and, shortly before the robbery, had told Farrant of its general location. He had, however, kept back the actual hiding place, waiting for Farrant to ask. Which he never had; his lazy attitude obvious in his response: "Good man." A callous smile had cut across Farrant's face. "I knew I could rely on you." He grinned, victorious. "But then again, I have the upper hand. Don't I, Lieutenant Treloar?" Farrant had turned away, adding: "I must go. Card game scheduled." Treloar had realised then that Farrant, with his total belief in his own control, trusted him. Farrant simply could not believe that Spencer Treloar would fail to follow an order.

Treloar watched Ox ready himself like a weightlifter, then grab the chest and heave it onto the wagon where it was quickly refilled. Rubbing his tired eyes, Treloar began to wonder about trust. Yes, Farrant currently had the upper hand and control, but who did Farrant actually trust? Watching him smoking alone, Treloar assumed that others, such as Price, knew of their shared secret. Then he began to wonder: did Price know? Really? Was there distrust between Price and Farrant? If so, Price may know nothing of Mary Anne.

The final drops of rain splashed to the ground as fear burned in Treloar's body. It felt as if he were sitting too close to an open fire. Could he retrieve some control? It could save his life. Perhaps he could exploit any distrust between these villains? Using his cap, he wiped his sweaty face, his mind racing until his eyes focused on the money chests.

They were, he knew, simply too large and heavy to be taken far before the alarm was raised. Leaning over the side, he scooped a couple of handfuls of canal water to cool his face. He wiped the residue with his cap, realising that these villains needed him or, rather, they needed his hiding place. It also became clear that, once the spot was known and they were satisfied with its security, he would no longer be needed. Could more treachery be planned? He repeated Farrant's earlier words quietly to himself. "The fewer that know a secret, the better." The hiding place, he wondered, could he use that to survive tonight?

Ox, with a loud grunt and with muscles and veins bulging, heaved second chest onto the wagon, placing beside the first. Treloar watched Price pick up some the scattered coins and jewellery from the towpath, pocket some and put the rest in a bag, which he placed on the wagon. Soldiers picked up the rest and refilled the second chest, before moving on to the third.

Hearing Farrant call his name, Treloar stood, flipped his cap of excess water and replaced it on his head. He watched Farrant drop and stamp out his cigarette before stepping back onto the barge.

"Now, Spencer, let's hide these chests."

Price followed on to the barge. "I will sort things here, Captain Farrant. You take Ox to help move the chests." He looked at the towpath as if this conversation had no importance.

"Good idea, Henry," said Farrant eagerly. His words were quick, thought Treloar. A little too quick. It was as if the question and answer were from the script of a well-rehearsed play. He guessed Ox had been given other orders.

"No." Treloar spoke, loud and decisive. "Just you and me, Captain Farrant."

"What?" Farrant's eyes narrowed. He pointed. "We can't move those heavy chests on our own. We must take Ox." Price moved closer, listening to the conversation.

"Just us two, Farrant."

Price suddenly pushed past Farrant, forcing him to stumble backwards. Anger boiled in his voice. "You will do as you are told, Treloar. Or end up like the rest."

With a deep intake of breath, and using every ounce of his willpower, Treloar held his ground while trying to hide his shaking. He knew he couldn't afford to show fear. Price thrust his head so close Treloar could smell the man's breath. It stank of something rotten.

"Corporal," said Treloar, surprised at how steady his voice

sounded. "You need me. I am the only one who knows the actual hiding place." He pointed at Farrant. "Even he doesn't know yet, just its general location." He sedately shook his head, as if explaining something obvious to a dull child. "And I don't trust you. So it's Captain Farrant and me, only." He spoke slowly, wanting no misunderstanding. "Or you have to find another hiding place. And now. Before dawn."

Price shot a glance at Farrant, who – red-faced – averted his eyes, confirming Treloar's suspicions. They stood looking at each other, their exhaled breaths floated in the darkness. Price was the first to move: swift as a magician his right hand slid up his left sleeve and reappeared holding a knife – a thin, horn-handled weapon with a seven inch blade. Its point pricked Treloar's throat, but it was Price was called out. "Ox," he yelled.

Hearing his name, Ox lumbered along the path and jumped aboard the barge.

Farrant straightened himself, blinking in surprise. He held out his hand, stopping Ox, then stepped beside Price. "Wait, wait." His sounded nervous, but Treloar stood firm. He was sure Farrant was wavering, seeing the money slipping away. "Henry, please. We can sort this out like gentlemen." Both his hands were raised in as if he himself were being attacked.

"That's not how it was planned," Price shrieked, his dark eyes glowing, his red anger aimed at Treloar.

Farrant didn't drop his hands. "I know, I know. But you can leave this to me."

"No," shouted Price. "If Ox doesn't go, then I do., I must know where it's hidden."

"You're not listening, Corporal." Treloar felt a brief wash of confidence, and prayed it was not misplaced. He knew he wasn't supposed to get out of this alive. Yet there was division between these men. "My decision is final." He nodded at Farrant. "The captain can tell you its location."

Price grabbed Treloar's throat, his grip so tight Treloar could feel the man's callouses. The knife no longer pricked his skin, but he knew it couldn't be far away. Spittle flew as Price spoke. "Don't tell me what to do. Think you're so superior. This will be done my way." He squeezed.

Treloar didn't even bother to pull at Price's wrist. He knew it would do no good. "You need me, corporal," he croaked. "And we both know it."

Farrant placed one hand on Price's shoulder, the other on the large hand gripping Treloar's throat. "Henry, please. He has as much to lose as us. Believe me, I know."

"But I don't." Price's glare switched to Farrant as Treloar's eyes closed. Despite the pressure on his neck, inwardly he sighed. Price knew nothing of his involvement with Mary Anne.

Eventually Price released his grip and took a small step back. Not far, but something. Treloar rubbed his neck.

When he was sure he could speak clearly, he did. "Captain Farrant and I hide it. He returns and tells you where. I return to the camp and report we were attacked, as per Farrant's instructions. Ox and the others make their own way back. I don't trust any of you not to come back here." His confidence was strengthening. "And Corporal, don't ever put your hands on me again. Understand?"

The scraping of the final chest along the path was the only noise. It sounded loud in the dark.

Price glared at Farrant, his fury sending plumes of hot breath into cold air. The soldiers who had done the killing appeared, looking into the barge. "Hey," said one. "We need help here. Over here."

Farrant, now with a frightened look on his face, pleaded. "We're running out of time, Henry. Leave this to me. I know what needs to be done. Trust me."

Price turned to Treloar and raised his knife, waving it before Treloar's eyes. "You mess this up and you will answer to me."

"Corporal Price," Farrant's voice was now loud, "enough." The knife disappeared back where it had come from – the leather sheath on the Corporal's left forearm. "Make it work, Captain." Price stepped off the barge and began walking along the canal path. He didn't look back.

"Price, wait. I said wait," Farrant called after hum. "I give the orders here." Price ignored him, and, after Ox and the other two had put the final crate on the wagon they fell into step behind Price as if he were some kind of pied piper. An embarrassed grin appeared Farrant's flushed face. Treloar smiled upon hearing Farrant mutter: "Damn that Price, who does he think he is?"

Treloar leapt off the barge and walked to the wagon, checking the chests were secured. He climbed into the seat, picked up the reins and waited for the Farrant to join him. When he did, neither man spoke.

A flick of the reins and the black mare strained in its bridle against the weight of the wagon, then began to move slowly down the track.

Treloar risked a looked back. He could see Price, hands on his hips watching. Looking ahead, Spencer Treloar chewed his lip, wondering whether he could save himself and his beloved Mary Anne.

Chapter 34
Alfred Farrant

"That's the last bag." Farrant pressed both hands against his lower back, and stretched upright, then wiped the sweat from his brow. Not only did his back ache, but his biceps were still screaming. For almost an hour he and Treloar had heaved partially filled chests off the wagon onto the road, and then into Treloar's hiding place. Finally, they had them refilled. The hardest and most strenuous job had been carefully lowering each chest, with rope looped through its handles, inch by inch down the side rails of the ladder. After which, it was back up to gather the contents that had been removed to enable them to move the damn thing, and then on to the next chest. A pair of hanging lanterns supplied just enough light.

Their clothes and hair were soaked, their sweat not allowing the earlier rain to dry. Despite the cold, both men had put their uniforms, capes, revolvers and holster into the wagon, working in collarless flannel shirts, their trousers held up by braces. Following Farrant's lead, Treloar wiped his own forehead, only he used an empty hessian sack he'd taken from a nearby pile. His stomach churned as if he'd eaten something rotten. He was conscious of Farrant watching him.

Farrant brushed the end of his moustache; a drop of sweat fell on to his saturated shirt. "There's a fortune here. I must congratulate you, Treloar. No one will think of looking in this place." Farrant rubbed his hands together, whether it was for warmth or pleasure Treloar couldn't tell. He looked from the hatch to the ladder they'd just withdrawn. "Remote, perfect to retrieve later." Farrant nodded as if considering. "It could stay here for months. No one would suspect." He took a drink from a canvas water bag, then lit a new cigarette. "And you say no one else knows this place?"

"No one except me. And now you," Treloar said with regret. His eyes narrowed and he stared into the night. A thin vein of purple light edged the eastern horizon. "Dawn's breaking soon."

Farrant looked anxiously to the east and flicked his fresh cigarette to the ground. His eyes flashed from side to side. "I must get the wagon back for Price." His words tumbled out as if frightened of themselves. "I will check the wagon. You stay here and finish up. Then come back when you're ready." Without waiting for an acknowledgement, Farrant took one of the lanterns and hurried away. Treloar watched him head down the track towards the wagon. He was almost running and looked small on a track wide enough for a two-wheeler gig.

Contemplating his next move, Treloar closed the hatch and stood the ladder against a rough wall, glancing often down the track. There was now no sign of Farrant or his lantern, just the silhouette of the wagon against the lightening sky. He shivered, unsure whether it was the night air that had chilled his perspiration, or it was simple fear. He shook his head, turned to the pile of hessian sacks and, from under it, retrieved his own hunting knife. Seeing Ox conceal his knife earlier had given him the idea to hide his own, but close by, where he could get it. Cradling his knife in his cold, clammy hand, his stomach tight, the anticipation of what he was about to do made him shiver again. He swigged from the same canvas bag Farrant had used, his hands trembling and he stared again towards the wagon when he heard Farrant call for him to hurry.

Turning away and keeping low, he moved fast, staying as close to the nearest building as possible, moving away from Farrant and the wagon. He didn't stop at corner of the wall, but turned on to a path, which was at least five feet wide and ran along the back of the building. At the next corner he followed the wall around the third side of the building. He stopped at the final corner and peered around the brickwork. In the pink early morning light, he could see the wagon, its lantern swinging and unlit. He could also see the flickering candle of the lamp taken by Farrant. It was sitting on the ground.

All was quiet now, but shortly, he thought, labourers from the farms and estate would arrive in the surrounding fields. He swallowed. It had to be now. Movement by the far corner of the building, where he had been moments earlier, caught his eye. He squinted, concentrating, trying to make out shapes from the shadows thrown by the lantern. Yes. Yes. There he was. Farrant, crouching, his black leather cape almost camouflaging him. He had his back to Treloar and was clearly staring in the direction of where they had just hidden the chests.

Slowly and quietly, Treloar edged along the wall, passing windows, inching closer to Farrant's back. With each step the grip on his knife increased. Farrant's head moved as he leant forward to look further around the corner. Treloar heard him call out: "Hurry up. Damn you, man."

"I'm already here," Treloar said, loud and clear. Farrant gasped, jumped and spun, his eyes wide. The knife in his hand pointed forward. Treloar hid his own behind his back and pointed with his other hand at Farrant's knife. "Expecting me to come that way?"

Farrant raised the knife, his fingers opening and closing around its grip as if it was hot. He glanced to each side. Probably looking for way to escape, thought Treloar.

A grin spread across Farrant's face, one that was clearly false. "Just a precaution, Spencer. You understand."

"I understand, Farrant. What was it you said, 'The fewer that know a secret the better'?"

Farrant's grin froze, his teeth bared, and he lowered his hand. He began edging towards the horse and wagon. Treloar took two steps forward and blocked his retreat, all the time keeping far enough away. "You are a treacherous bastard, Farrant. You're not going anywhere." He showed his own knife. Farrant's eyes widened, the flame of the lantern reflecting in them. He wiped his mouth, although his facial muscles remained rigid, then with a yell that alarmed the horse he leapt forward, viciously slashing with his hunter's knife.

* * *

With its wagon lightened of its previous cargo, the horse trotted happily up the lane onto the bridge. The lantern, still unlit, swung with the motion of the carriage. Seeing Price and Ox waiting, Treloar passed them before pulling on the reins. Once the wagon was stationary, the wooden brake was applied. Treloar kept his cap pulled down, his cape collar turned up, and his face looking forward. Behind him he heard the metal fasteners that held the rear flap of the wagon being removed. "It took you too long, Captain." Price sounded angry.

Treloar let his hand drift to his pistol as Price continued. "Got to get the wagon back." There was the rustle of a sheet being pulled off the dead body. "Quick, Ox. Get Treloar's body onto the barge with the others." Treloar could imagine Ox recognising the dead face, blinking and stepping back, mouth agape.

"It's Farrant," Ox yelled.

Treloar yanked down his collar, and kept his face blank as he returned the stares.

"You killed Captain Farrant." Price, his jaw clenched in shock, managed to swear under his breath.

"It's exactly what you planned for me." Treloar replied, adjusting his position on the wagon's seat. He pointed his Beaumont-Adams revolver so the two men could clearly see it. Ox took a step forward and Treloar aimed the weapon at his face. "Move again and I will fire."

Price remained by the rear corner of the wagon. "Where have you hidden the money?" His teeth were bared; voice harsh.

Treloar turned the gun to him and cocked the hammer, keeping a gentle pressure on the trigger. "It's safe. If that had been me…" he nodded towards Farrant; the revolver never wavered, "…what was the rest of the plan?"

"Where is the money?" Price asked again. His voice dripping with malice; his eyes slits.

Treloar let his impatience show. "I asked you, what was the rest of your plan?"

Price gripped the wagon's rear wheel trim so tight the metal banding cut into his hand. His fingers turned red, and a crazed look filled his eyes. Shallow breaths made his chest rise and fall too fast. Finally, he spoke. "Farrant raises the alarm. Later, he resigns blaming himself for what happened here. After that he planned to leave the country."

"Where are the other two soldiers?" Treloar's lips tightened. "Although I can guess." Ox turned his head. Treloar followed his stare, seeing the two new bodies on the path. Looking back, he saw Ox's hunting knife tucked back into his belt. His nostrils flared as he asked: "What of Ox and you, Corporal Price?"

Price scowled. "Ox also escapes, confirming the story. Me? I was never here." He glanced at the body on the wagon. "Captain Farrant gave me permission to be away from the camp. I have a good alibi. Later we disappear."

Treloar nodded. "Adding desertion to your crimes." His words were cold and sarcastic, and he felt nothing but distain.

Price rubbed his cut hand, smearing his seeping blood. He raised his head slightly and glared at Treloar. "That plan is ruined now. So, we must take what we can carry and run. So, where is it hidden?"

"I told you. It's safe." Treloar felt his distain twisting into taut anger. His finger tightened on the trigger of the revolver. "And it's going to stay safe." He had control; now he had to set the direction he wanted. He glanced at the barge before returning to Price. The man was now white-faced through suppressing his fury. It made him look like a ghost. "Farrant," said Treloar, "instructed me. And now I am telling you. The plan has changed."

Ox bared his teeth and stepped forward with his hand on the hilt of his knife. "I'll get him to tell us where the money is." Price gripped his arm, stopping further movement. He shook his head as Ox stared at him, confused.

Treloar's pulse raced. "Another move and I swear will shoot you both. Trust me, I really don't care what happens next. I've killed once tonight."

Ox, thought Treloar, looked like a child, uncertain what to do. Price broke the silence.

"So, what is this new plan?" As an afterthought, he added, "Lieutenant Treloar." His cold gaze was fixed on Treloar.

Treloar quivered, felt his finger twitch on the trigger. He wanted provocation, a reason to pull it. He fought to control his hatred of these two men. "This is what is going to happen," he said, surprised at how calm he sounded. "Instead of Farrant, I will raise the alarm." He kept the revolver pointing at Price and watched for the two villains' reactions. "And the chests will stay hidden. For at least a year."

"A year?" roared Price, He gripped the wheel again while shaking his head as if trying to control the pain of his cut hand. "But—"

"After a year, you both get your share. I take Farrant's and we all go our separate ways." Treloar kept his voice loud to be convincing, still amazed at how confident he sounded.

"Why wait a year?" Price's eyes were blazing. "Why so long?"

"Because that's how I want it."

"But—"

"We need time for everything to calm down." Treloar didn't know it was possible for his muscles to tense even more.

"How... how do I know you won't resign your commission? Take the money and run?"

"Run? Run to where?" Inside, Treloar was screaming in torment. "After what has happened here tonight, my life has changed forever. I'm as guilty as you. The difference is," he spat out the next words, "I feel that guilt." He touched his chest with his free hand. "I no longer have control of my actions; they control me," he scowled with regret. "You two will have to learn to wait." Knowing it had to be convincing, he concentrated on sounding resolute. His ideas were still fresh in his mind and required organising. Needing time. And for that had to convince these two men.

"What if you die, or get ill or something before the year's out?" Price's words were cold as he contemplated possibilities. Treloar found himself grinning; it was amusing coming from Price who had planned his death. "You'd better make sure I stay in good health then, or no one gets anything. So, what's the answer?" He looked up; pink-edged dark clouds were becoming visible. "It will be full daylight soon."

"I don't like it, Pricey." Ox tensed, ready to attack if so ordered. Price stared into Treloar's eyes. Eventually he turned to Ox. "It's trust him or nothing. We kill him now we get nothing. We have to wait. Trust he'll keep his word." His shoulders slumped in resignation. "Put Farrant with Standish." He pointed at the barge.

Ox lifted the body from the wagon and moved away. When Treloar judged Ox was far enough away he jumped down from the wagon, revolver still pointed, rock steady, at Price. "Is there anything else?"

Price glared, red blotches of fury appearing on his otherwise bone-white face. "We buried the bodies of the bargee, his son and the other officer." He pointed along the path. "They won't be found. It will be assumed they were either taken prisoner or involved. I have to return the wagon to the Weller's farm." His nostrils flared. "One last thing, Treloar. Farrant was supposed to implicate the Wellers. You will have to do it."

Treloar tilted his head, confused. "How was he going to do that? And it's Lieutenant Treloar."

Price spat to one side. From the rear of the wagon he produced a bag of coins. "Weller has twin sons. I leave this in the wagon and you say there were twins in the gang that attacked you. And you identify them later."

"Why is that necessary?" Treloar had not believed things could get worse.

Price shrugged. "Someone has to be blamed. They won't find anybody else." Price raised his eyebrows. "Will they, Lieutenant Treloar." When he received no answer, he continued. "It puts everyone on the wrong trail. Also, the farmer knows me, I hired his wagon. He will try to implicate me, and I will, of course, deny it. I have my alibi. And who are they going to believe?" He smirked. "Oh yes. It's all been planned very carefully."

"No." Treloar shook his head, "I know that family. Enough people have been hurt." Price shrugged, but said nothing. Lines appeared on Treloar's forehead in response to Price's lack of argument. He watched Ox easily move Farrant's body, and almost missed Price's next question.

"I think you know a publican called Parr?"

Treloar looked at him, puzzled. He lowered his gun.

"Owns two inns. The Waterloo and the Three Feathers in Battersea, by the river." Treloar remembered visiting the inn and the foul smells of the river in London.

Price grinned. "Thought you did. It was Parr who told us about Standish's wealth. And it was Parr who suggested you to Standish, for the escort." Price wiped his nose with his cuff.

"This Parr, is he also in on this?" Treloar inwardly groaned. What else there was to find out?

"He was." Price's smile had all the charm of a snake dripping venom. "With Farrant and me. That was until he thought he deserved a bigger share, just for knowing about Standish."

Despite his racing pulse, Treloar returned a level gaze. He didn't want to ask but knew had to know. "Where is he now?" Price's rotten teeth were now on full view. "On a cloud somewhere, playing a harp." He played an imaginary harp, in case Treloar was confused.

"Is that a threat, Corporal?" Treloar gripped his revolver to his side. Price faced him, his eyes as hard as flint. "You have changed arrangements twice. Try to change them a third time and you will suffer." Price paused, ensuring his meaning was understood. "We," he continued, "are similar ages, Lieutenant. And perhaps we think alike. Maybe it should have been you with us, instead of that idiot Farrant." His smile was icy and humourless. "He really underestimated you. Lieutenant Treloar."

"We are nothing alike, Corporal." Utter certainty filled Treloar's voice. "The only thing we have in common, Price, is our distain for Farrant."

Price glared at Treloar. "Don't look down on me. You toffs are no better, always looking out for yourselves. Farrant was no angel. And Standish was one of you and certainly no saint. Parr told me the stories about him." He tapped his chest. "All I am doing is looking after Henry Price." His breathing became heavy. "With the money, I can buy passage on steamship to America. At least there I can buy some respect." Treloar shook his head and held his reply upon seeing Ox reappear. He stepped back, raising his revolver, ensuring a safe distance. Caution still simmered inside him.

His hands on his hips, Price leered. "What did Farrant have on you?" Treloar imagined he could see cogs turning in Price's head as he spoke: "Farrant may have underestimated you, but I won't. He believed he had you under his control." Price scratched his head. "He would never tell me what he had on you."

Price spat, a long string of phlegm hit the ground. "That was my big mistake, not getting Farrant to tell me. He just wouldn't." Price spat again, as if using the first splat as a target, then rubbed his mouth. "But I wonder. I wonder. Perhaps you have debts like Farrant? Theft perhaps? Have a secret in the camp?" This time his smile held humour, although with more than a hint of malevolence. "Did Farrant help conceal it from your fellow officers?"

Treloar turned away from the goading. "Perhaps got a tart in trouble?" Price laughed and looked at Ox to share the joke. "Perhaps more than one? Or…" he grinned at Ox before turning back, "…are you into boys, Lieutenant?"

Treloar spun around, red faced, burning, as his anger boiled over. He stretched out a shaking arm, pointing his revolver at Price's forehead and cocked the hammer. Every sinew in his body wanting the trigger to be pulled.

Time seemed to stretch. Early morning light misted with damp air allowed Treloar to see his surroundings better. The barge, the bridge, the faces of Price and Ox. And the dead bodies. A new day had dawned but the old one still plagued his mind.

Price nodded as if he had just won some small triumph. "Whatever it is, Lieutenant Treloar, whatever your secret, I will find it. No matter how long it takes." His eyes were dark and narrow. "I will find it. Then we will see." Price turned and sauntered away.

Chapter 35
Simon Hamilton, December 1877

His slow pace enabled him to scrutinise those around him. Spencer Treloar had dressed in what he thought of as civilian clothing, so he could blend in with other London pedestrians. He glanced behind him often, always wondering whether he was being watched. Was he being followed? Did they know where he was? What he was doing? He rode horse-drawn trams, sometimes unnecessarily changing lines, always checking. Finally, for the last part of his journey, he walked – stopping occasionally to use the reflections in shop windows to check behind him – from Trafalgar Square to number 20 Leicester Square, the Hotel Cavour, for his meeting.

The hotel was busy, the reception filled with milling people, but the restaurant was quiet – which suited Treloar. Sitting at a table, with his tired red eyes focused on nothing, he was soon lost in his thoughts while he waited for Simon. He'd known Simon Hamilton since boarding school and thought of him as a close friend. Simon had been a clever and industrious student, and was now apprenticed to his uncle in the London offices of Cooke Hamilton solicitors. Treloar and Simon had kept in touch and Treloar was pleased that, over the last ten years, Simon had progressed well.

Despite – or maybe because of – all his precautions, Treloar had arrived early for this, their third, and final, meeting. As with the previous two, it had been discreetly arranged. Their friendship made Simon the perfect choice as an ally and confident. Of that, Treloar was convinced. He brushed a clammy palm over his leather satchel, needing the reassurance of the bag's presence. It held letters, deeds and his final instructions. He patted the worn leather before taking a sip of red wine. It tasted crisp and very dry, and he winced as the alcohol hit the back of his throat. It should at least help his low mood.

His mind once again returned to the continuous and painful thoughts that accompanied his life these days: the robbery and its repercussions. He shuddered: the thought of Price always put the fear of God into him. Treloar was still amazed how the aftermath of the violent crime had gone exactly as Price anticipated. First, uproar on discovery, men chasing around aimlessly trying to find a non-existent gang – the three missing from the escort – and of course the chests of money and gold. After a couple of weeks, with no answers, the investigations had slowed. He had been ordered back to his duties as remonstrations and criticisms began after finding no perpetrators, no answers, no leads, just more questions. Finally, there had been Captain Russell's re-investigation, as those more senior looked to blame an escort that had failed so badly.

He, Ox and Price had all been questioned and a farming family had been detained upon discovery of bag of coins and a knife under the seat of their wagon. Treloar shook his head. Price's work was so obviously planted evidence, but it was believed. Treloar had never been a religious man. To him, Sundays were a duty, when family followed single-file behind the father to church, like soldiers marching to war. And all to hear Reverend McDonald preach goodness. One Sunday, he had found himself, head bowed lower than usual, praying for the Wellers and asking for forgiveness. Knowing he could do nothing without incriminating himself. Price, he knew, was cunning and ruthless and experienced no such doubt, or regret or compassion. The realisation increased his desire to foil the villain.

Treloar turned, staring sightlessly at the hotel restaurant, slowly shaking his head. He had a constant headache these days. He took another drink, but it didn't help his despondency. His home life was also getting worse. He hadn't thought it possible, but his father's drinking was increasing. These days his father was always enraged, so much so that the family, and the few servants still employed, kept their distance. At every opportunity he blamed Spencer for Standish's death. Treloar believed it was not in sympathy for Standish, but the terrible knowledge of losing possible income.

It came to a head one evening after another meagre dinner. Father was drunk and screaming abuse, accusing Treloar of cowardice, of running away. His sisters were openly sobbing, and mother, poor mother, was doing what she could to intervene. And then Sir John Treloar raised his riding crop intending to hit his son, only as he tried to stand – drink clouding his mind, slowing his clumsy movements – his arms windmilled. Hearing the swish, Treloar stepped aside. Sir John staggered, off balance, and the crop came down on a side table, destroying it and sending a treasured vase crashing to the hard wooden floor, where it exploded, as if detonated. Spencer Treloar, swamped in a thick mixture of sadness and anger, simply walked out. His two sisters, close as twins, were in tears, with the elder screaming how his notoriety would affect her forthcoming marriage, and the younger – hugging her sister in support – remonstrating how she hated her brother.

After that, Treloar realised he was on his own, and was still desperate to get a message to Mary Anne. He needed allies, and the only person offering any consideration was his mother.

Later, when he managed to get Lady Treloar away from calming his father, she listened to his story. Their foreheads touched and they held hands as if she were hearing him confess to some terrible family misdemeanour. She became the first of his allies. That same afternoon she visited the widow of Alfred Farrant to offer her sympathy. She arrived in her tired landau, its paint flaking like dead skin, a blanket hiding threadbare upholstery. The two women spoke privately and a friendship started behind closed doors, with Lady Treloar eventually becoming a courier between Mary Anne and Spencer. Those outside, hearing the wailing, assumed a sad widow was crying for her dead husband, not her lover.

Movement at the restaurant door brought Treloar back from his thoughts. A man had arrived and was looking around. While he was of similar age to Treloar, he was a good six inches shorter and well-rounded. Treloar thought Simon Hamilton looked as if he needed to cut down on his diet and do some exercise. With his blond hair and clean-shaven pale skin his face lacked colour. His clothing though was immaculate; he was someone who took his time choosing what to wear and, once he'd chosen, was fastidious in dressing. His overcoat, silk top hat, and silver-headed cane disappeared with the maître de, but he retained his leather attaché case and was escorted to Treloar's table. A large grin added colour to his pale face when he saw his friend. Treloar returned the smile and stretched out a hand to greet the second of his allies.

"Spencer, lovely to see you again." He shook Treloar's hand

with a surprisingly strong grip, and looked closely at his old friend. "You do look tired." His voice was high but clear, concerned.

Treloar gestured to the spare seat. Simon sat and studied the menu. "I am starving. Beef, I think," he proclaimed.

Treloar smiled and nodded at his friend's rounded belly. "Yes, you look as if you're starving."

Simon returned the nod. "And you look as if you haven't a care in the world."

"Where does your uncle think you are, Simon?"

Simon placed the menu flat on the table, his smile now that of a mischievous boy. "Where I usually go on Thursday afternoons. The National Gallery. My uncles have shown me the wonders of art and paintings." Without asking, he filled his glass from Spencer's carafe and took a mouthful. He held his glass up, as if inspecting it for flaws. "You know, Spencer, those wonderful paintings, it's a whole new world of beauty and," he reached forward and topped up his glass, "I'm developing a growing fascination for Joseph Turner's paintings." Once again, he held his glass at eye level and stared into its depths. "His collection, so dramatic, such bright vibrant colours." His intake of breath seemed to catch in his throat. "He creates a story with his brush, Spencer. We really should go together."

Treloar spoke softly, not wanting to spoil his friend's enthusiasm. "Perhaps another time, Simon. I think we have other things to discuss."

"Of course. Of course." A blush bloomed on Simon's cheeks. "Sorry, Spencer. I get carried away."

A waiter approached, pencil and pad already in his hands, and took their order. Once the waiter had left, Spencer leaned forward, "Have you have met Mary?"

Simon nodded. "Everything is ready." With painfully slow deliberation, Simon once again held his glass up, as if its contents were more fascinating than his friend's problems.

"Then, for God's sake, Simon," Treloar scowled with frustration, "tell me the details. Please."

"It's all arranged. Just as you asked." His tone had become brusque, as if his professionalism was being questioned.

"Please, Simon. Humour me." Treloar fixed his pleading eyes on his friend. "You know my problem. You agreed to help. But I must be sure Mary Anne will be safe. I'm not doubting your ability." He put his hand on the table, as close as he could to his friend's. "I saw Price kill a boy, a child for Heaven's sake, to get what he wants." He bit his lip. "I must be assured of all the details."

Hamilton nodded but said nothing as he picked up his attaché case and from it removed narrow-rimmed spectacles and a file filled with loose pages. He looked around before opening the file and pulled out a page. He kept his voice low.

"Yes, Mary Anne and I have met," he smiled again. "A lovely girl. As we agreed, she is to travel to London in the new year on the pretext of returning north to her family. She will stay one night at a hotel before travelling by train, not north, but to Dorking, about 50 miles away. I have rented a small house for her there." He looked around again, to confirm he wasn't being overheard. "She is aware I will be following her, to ensure no one else is."

As if to stifle a cough, Treloar raised a finger to his lips as their waiter approached. The man made a performance of placing their napkins, serving their lunches and refilling their glasses before nodding and leaving.

Only when he was certain the waiter was out of earshot did Simon continue. "I will get her settled, arranging a live-in housekeeper. Mary Anne will also have a new surname." He removed his spectacles and began chewing the temple tip, "As for her new name," he raised his eyebrows, "I do have an idea for that." He folded his glasses, placed them on the table and the two men both glanced around again before eating. No one seemed to be taking an interest in them.

"Also," Simon said around a piece of beef, "I've also been to your hiding place, and seen it all." He stopped chewing and his eyes widened, the skin around them crinkling. "It is amazing. I have never seen so much. A fortune. A true fortune." He shook his head and recommenced his chewing. Eventually he nodded. "And you, Spencer. How is this whole thing for you?"

Treloar, having eaten little, lowered his knife and fork. They rattled on the table owing to his trembling hands. He ran a hand through his hair, but his hunched shoulders seemed stiff and unwilling to move. "It is ripping me apart."

Simon stopped, his own knife and fork in mid-air. He could hear the pain in Treloar's voice.

"Except for my mother, my family have all turned against me. As have many fellow officers." Treloar wiped his glistening eyes. "Price wants me dead. But while I hold the money, I am safe." He shook his head. "Believe it or not, things have got worse. I would not have thought that was possible, but…" He gazed out of the window, his red eyes blinking. Eventually, when he had control, he returned his attention to Simon: "A Captain Russell is re-investigating. And he is very good, *very good*, like a hound who has got the scent of a fox. I'm certain he suspects us all."

He grabbed his glass and emptied the contents in one mouthful. "I am at the end of my tether, Simon. I hardly sleep. I love Mary. She has become my life and it breaks me up what I am putting her through." Simon saw Treloar's knuckles whiten and he feared both for his friend and the glass. "Putting *them* through. Mary and our unborn child."

With a crack, like a gunshot, the stem of the glass snapped clean away from the bowl. Heads turned at the noise and their waiter hurried over to replace his glass and confirm no one was injured.

With care so as not to make any more noise, Simon placed his cutlery on his plate. "Spencer," he whispered through a broad smile. "A child. That's wonderful." His expression of delight faded. "Isn't it?"

Spencer laughed, but it sounded sharp and devoid of humour. "Yes. Or it would be." He scratched the side of his head. "But Price knew Captain Farrant well, and is clever enough to guess the child's is not Farrant's. And he's sharp enough to make the link to me. Which is why we must get Mary away." He steadied his breathing, trying to control his panic. "I think it is only the army that can control Price, and I have an idea to use them to do that. I have already started the wheels turning." He took a deep breath. "I have suggested reassignments to my senior officers. Transfers abroad for everyone involved. To try to bring this incident to some conclusion."

"Will it work?"

Treloar kept his face blank but he thought he could hear the scepticism in his friend's voice. "I don't know. This whole business has become embarrassing to many. My proposal is a solution which would also keep Mary safe. At least for a while. It will get Price and Ox away. Perhaps I can arrange neither return."

Simon's eyes widened and his hand covered his open mouth. Then he nodded and went about finishing his meal in silence. Treloar's appetite had deserted him, so he pushed his food around. He refilled the glasses from the carafe as the waiter cleared the plates.

Simon asked for, and the waiter returned with, a pen, blotter and ink. "I have questions Spencer, for clarification." He retrieved a single sheet from his attaché case, and placed it flat on the table in front of him.

Wiping his mouth with his napkin, Treloar nodded. He raised the empty carafe, a signal to the waiter. Another carafe appeared as Simon fitted his spectacles and then flattened the sheet.

"The money will remain where it is." Simon looked up. "And you're sure it will be safe?"

Treloar stared at his friend and their eyes locked in shared understanding. "It will be safe for as long as necessary." He stroked his chin. "I want you to start transferring it to a bank in Mary Anne's name, as discussed. But only when you think safe to do so. Then start investing it."

Simon's face lit up and his shoulders went back and his chest was thrust out. He sat upright, reminding Spencer of a proud peacock. "That," Simon said, "I am good at. And with such a large amount…, well, even my uncle compliments my way with figures and on recognising investment opportunities."

Treloar laughed. "One of the many reasons I chose you, dear

friend. If my plan is to work, I will need it invested well."

Simon looked again at his list and his pen nib started scratching, making another note. "You have cottages for Mary Anne on her return?"

Treloar nodded enthusiastically, and took documents – tied with red silk ribbons – from his satchel, and placed them on the table. He took another drink and licked his lips.

"These are the deeds to the two cottages. My grandfather left me one plot of land at the edge of the village." He held up the documents. "I have been repairing the cottages, making them habitable. Discreetly though, with our land agent's help. I told my father it was to show what can be done with little expense." He slid the paperwork across the table, relinquishing any ownership. "They are now transferred to you. And you, dear chap, will transfer them to Mary Anne on her return." He closed his satchel. "Mary only will be your client. Invent her a new background story. Remember, she will have a child. Any association with the robbery will mean prison for her. And now possibly for you."

Feeling vexed, Simon removed his spectacles. "That has occurred to me, Spencer. I am also associated with this dreadful business."

Treloar's chest heaved, and he mouthed an apology. Simon's pen scratched again. Without looking up, Simon spoke. "It occurred to me your family could use some help. I mean with your father's troubles."

"No." Treloar's voice was firm and he slapped the table; condiments and cutlery rattled. "He receives not one farthing."

Simon sat back, eyes full of surprise.

"People know my father's situation. Any fresh money that

appeared would generate suspicion." He looked up at the ornate wooden ceiling, his Adam's apple rising and falling as he swallowed hard. "I believe our estate is lost. A year, maybe two. It's just a matter of time." Treloar held up his hand, stopping Simon's interruption. "We have serious debts. Father re-mortgaged the estate. He also owes money everywhere. He drinks and gambles away what money we do have. I have tried to help through our estate manager, a good man who does his best. But father refuses to listen. He borrows money from anyone. Including Standish, believe it or not." Treloar shook his head. "Even as we speak his creditors are circling." He rubbed his aching forehead. "The estate was from Mother's family. And Father has ruined it."

"What about his friends? Surely they will help." Simon sounded conciliatory.

"Friends? Once Father loses the estate, Mother will lose her place in society, and Father will still drink." Treloar grimaced. "Remember, Simon, their son is a suspected thief and murderer."

Simon dropped his gaze to his questions, and cleared his throat. "Now we come to the last question, possibly the most important." He pulled his eyes from his paper and stared at Treloar. "Can you re-confirm your plans for the money, assuming you can keep it away from Price?"

Treloar pondered, wringing his hands. When he spoke, it was in a croaked whisper. "I helped steal money from a selfish individual, and am determined to keep it away from Price, Ox and whoever else is involved, I have lied, deceived and murdered. None of which I can change, much as I desire it." His voice grew in strength. "But I remember, as Farrant and I passed through the village to hide it, imagining how that money could have benefited that village and that whole area, and helped those poor folk living there – and those who will live there." He blinked. "And the more I thought, the more an idea and the possibilities grew. Perhaps something good could come from this tragedy." He placed his hands firmly on the table, as if steadying himself. "Farrant is out the picture, and with some luck I think I can keep Price away." Excited, he sat upright pulling his hands across the tablecloth. "If Mary returned as a rich benefactor, and perhaps with the help of other good people, the Reverend McDonald, say, and the inn keeper, our land agent, then…" he raised his hands and shrugged, "maybe all could – unknowingly – help make good use of that money." He offered a sad, regretful smile. "It may go towards some restitution."

"Is that also the reason you want me to organise payments to the bargee's family." Simon looked at his list. "And Second Lieutenant Norton's family?"

Spencer nodded. "All innocent victims, Simon." His hands clasped together as if he were praying. "Also, I want to try to do something for the Weller family." He shook his head, as if it had gained extra pounds. "But there must be no association with me." He sounded despondent.

Simon nodded and spoke with tenderness. "And when you return from wherever you're transferred, you can marry into wealth and carry on your work." He let out a rueful sigh. "Such a shame you will not see your child born, Spencer." Treloar tried to swallow but there was a lump in his throat. His headache had been dulled a little by the drink, and as he listened to the genuine sympathy in Simon's voice, he felt stinging in his eyes.

He knew his was not worthy of such allies, but was appreciative and confident in them. He raised his glass. "That will be my punishment." His voice was no more than a croak.

"Spencer," Simon Hamilton removed his spectacles, a warmth in his eyes, optimism in his tone. "Time passes quickly," he said, "and I will take care of your family. That I promise, until you are all reunited." His facial muscles tensed. "And I will make you another promise, Lieutenant Spencer Treloar. Your wishes for the money will be carried out."

Treloar exhaled before emptying his glass. His vision clouded as he stared into the distance.

Chapter 36
January 1878

In silence, they rode along a narrow path lined with chestnut trees. In summer there would have been a canopy of leaves. Now there were only branches like skeletal fingers silhouetted against a grey sky. The heath was quiet and cold, most of the creatures that lived there were huddled for safety and warmth.

Spencer Treloar forced a smile and turned to Mary. He knew neither of them wanted to talk, and could guess her thoughts were similar to his own. She returned his smile but he could see the sadness behind it. He wondered whether his own sorrow was as clear.

Much had happened in the past few weeks. Since Christmas, all correspondence and communication had been through Lady Treloar. Spencer and Mary had met only once since the robbery and that in the company of Spencer's mother. However, they had both been so desperate to see each other, and alone, before their forced separation, they were prepared to risk today's meeting.

"You are well?" Spencer asked, his voice cracking. "Your condition I mean. With our child."

Mary nodded. "I am well. I could not feel better. I think it will be a boy, Spencer. A son."

Spencer could not smile, and she saw his expression. "I am sorry."

He looked into her eyes, doing his best to disguise his sadness. "Don't be, I am as happy as you. And when this is all over, then we'll be together." He took a deep breath as if preparing himself for his next question. "When do you leave?"

Mary looked away, as if there was something interesting on the damp heath. "It's arranged for tomorrow. I take the train to London, a cab from the station to the hotel. Your friend, Simon Hamilton, will be waiting for me at the station in another cab and will follow me to make sure no one else is pursuing me." She turned back to him. "That is what you wanted, is it not?" she asked, clearly desiring confirmation she was doing everything as he wished.

He nodded, unsure what to say to make things better. Mary knew he also would be leaving in two days to go to London, and then Chatham, to travel overseas where he would take up his new posting.

"You really think all this secrecy is necessary, Spencer? Surely nobody knows about us. So how can they harm us?"

"Necessary? Yes, I'm sorry, but I'm afraid it is. I am more convinced than ever we need to maintain this secrecy. You must do everything we arranged. Everything until I have gone with Price and the others. I worry about your safety, my dear." He shook his head, trying to dislodge thoughts of what could happen. "Price is desperate to find the money. We do not know if anybody else is involved. Trust me, they will use you – and anyone else who they think may know – to get what they want. And then we have to think about Russell. He's no fool". He chewed his lip. "He thinks he's worked it out, and he's nearly right. I'm sure he will still be snooping around. There must be no established connection between you and me. None. I don't want them coming after you."

"I met him," Mary said, quietly. "Russell. He came to see me after the robbery. He was very sympathetic. He asked a few questions about my husband said he was doing everything he could find those responsible."

They rode further, each wrapped in their own thoughts against the day's chill. The year of 1878 had started bitterly cold and was showing no signs of improving. No one else was around, which is what they wanted.

"Your safety Mary is my prime concern. I must know you are safe before I leave. What about your possessions? And what have you told your friends?"

"I have few possessions, Spencer, and even fewer friends. Alfred was not at all generous. And neither was he keen for me to socialise much. I can get everything into two cases, which I will take with me. For those few friends who have been considerate and thoughtful, I have told them I am going back up north, to my family. They will soon forget me."

"Simon will travel north with you?"

She nodded. "We met last week in Guildford, as you arranged. He is a good friend, Spencer. We could not have done this without him." She sniffed, wiped her eyes. She knew that Spencer would not be with her for long, and yearned for him to stay. "I wish it could be different." She said the words they were both thinking.

Spencer leaned over and gently took the reins of her horse from her hands, and brought both their steeds to a halt. He dismounted and then helped her from her saddle, holding her longer than necessary. Neither wanted to break the moment. Eventually, they secured the horses, allowing them to graze on the meagre winter grass, and began following a path.

"I am leaving you in the best of hands," Spencer said. "Simon is a good friend." He leaned forward and cupped her chin. "You must trust him in all things whilst I am away. He will help and support you. If I can communicate, it will be through Simon and only Simon. I cannot write to you and you must never write to me. You know that, don't you?"

"I know, Spencer. But it is so unfair."

"We are still alive, remember that. We're the ones who are alive."

They walked again, hand in gloved hand. "Did you tell anyone where you were going today?" he asked, casually.

"No. I just said I wanted a ride alone across the heath one last time, for the memory. Do not worry, we are safe." She found a smile. "Do you remember our first meeting?"

"How can I forget?" Spencer's features softened as he looked into the distance. "I can hardly believe it was last spring. It feels only a month or so since we met. I can't look at that great oak without thinking of you."

"I said my saddle was loose and you stopped to ask if I needed assistance."

"I thought it was a little brazen."

The sound of Mary's laugh warmed Spencer's soul. She said, "I had seen you before, around the camp. I found out who you were and where you lived. I always rode out this way when I had the chance which, thanks to my husband, was not as often as I would have liked." Her smile was as warm and intimate as her laugh. "I could not believe my luck when I saw you; I was not going to miss my chance."

It was his turn to laugh. "You are brazen. God, I love you." He recalled that first meeting, the promise it held in the windless warmth of that spring day, the way the clouds barely moved across the clear sky, and how he and Mary had ridden through these same woods, just talking and talking and oblivious of time. When they arranged other meetings he was aware they were both pretending it was just for social rides. He knew, however, something else was happening, something they were powerless to stop.

For days after their meetings, all Spencer could think about was Mary Anne Farrant. Yes, there was guilt; she was a senior officer's wife. Although he did not like Farrant, he was still a fellow soldier and, more than that, a senior officer. Every time, Spencer tried to convince himself he would find a reason not to be at the old oak the following week. There would be something more important, some duty, some military task he would be ordered to do, anything. But he knew, deep down, he would go and she would be there waiting for him. They were both aware what was happening.

Eventually, his guilt began to subside as Mary told him more about Farrant and how she had come to be married to him.

Being the only girl among five children, with a father – a provisions merchant – who made it clear he preferred his children to be boys, she had not had a happy childhood. Her mother spent most of her time in bed with some illness or other. Mary was now convinced her mother's sicknesses were simply make believe. 'She's a delicate woman', her husband would advise anyone who asked. When Mary was introduced by one of her brothers to Alfred Farrant, her father took the opportunity to get rid of her, passing her on to someone else. Farrant agreed to the marriage so he could use her dowry to pay his debts. Soon after their wedding – which she admitted she had half wanted so she could escape her parents – Farrant was posted to

Aldershot. She had heard nothing from her family since.

Although she was pretty, Farrant soon tired of her. His preference was to spend time with drunken comrades in rowdy inns. After a while a wife became a burden to him and so the beatings began. It took time, but as she and Spencer Treloar continued to meet, and secretly became lovers, she slowly revealed to him what she had to endure.

Treloar began to contemplate what he could do to free her from Farrant, so they could be together. It was whilst he was considering options that Farrant had discovered their meetings and begun his blackmail.

Still holding hands, Spencer and Mary strolled a little way further along the footpath then, as if there was a sign, both stepped off it. They kept their horses within sight but were soon well into the woods, away from prying eyes. Although Treloar never spoke of it, Mary knew he had killed her husband on the night of the robbery. She felt no sorrow for Alfred Farrant, only sadness that Treloar had had to do it, and that he had to live with his actions and consequent nightmares. Alfred was no longer part of her life, of that she was pleased.

Finally, Treloar turned towards her, took hold of her shoulders and kissed her. She responded with equal passion he encircled her in his arms. When they finally broke he remained close, feeling the warmth of her deep breaths on his lips.

"I fear we need to go," he said, hating himself for the suggestion.

Mary fought back the tears she wanted to shed and nodded. Seeing the hurt in her eyes, he took her in his arms again.

"It won't be for long," he whispered, if I can regain the men's respect and confidence, prove to be honourable, then all that has happened will be forgotten. We will be safe and I will come home to you. Two, at worst three, years."

"And if something happens to you?"

He held her at arm's length. "Like what? No, it will work the way we have planned. I will keep those murderers away from you until everything has been arranged. Just as we planned. You know what I want to do with the money."

She nodded. "We will do it together when you return."

"It must happen, Mary. Simon will help with the bequests. That is all arranged, but the other things…" he gripped her arms tighter. "We can make a difference with that money. And we will, you and me."

She nodded again, attempted a smile and pulled herself into him, holding him close, not wanting to part, wishing the moment could go on forever.

"There is something else," he said, and pulled himself away. Reaching inside his tunic, he withdrew a number of sheets of crisp writing paper, neatly folded and tied together. He held them out to her.

"This is in case Russell or anybody gets too close, or the truth comes out and you have to return the money. I have written a comprehensive account of everything, including my involvement. If it comes to it, you must use it, Mary. It exonerates you from everything. You must be kept safe." He looked deep into her eyes. "You must think of yourself and our child. Promise me. I could not bear to leave without your assurance you will do everything to protect yourself and our child."

She stared back at him. "I can't, Spencer. How could I—"

His voice was firm. "You must, everything I have planned

relies on your safety, and the safety of our child. I did what I did. I am not proud of it. But you must be kept apart from it all. Promise me."

"But you were tricked. You wanted no part of any deaths."

"But I agreed to the robbery. Everything that happened after that was a result of the robbery. I am responsible. I have to accept that. But you are innocent, this document proves that. You must use it if it becomes necessary." He paused, and added, as if an afterthought, "Simon also has a copy. He *will* use it as I have instructed him, to keep you safe."

Knowing she could not win, she took the papers from him. "I will do everything you want. Just come back to me."

Treloar was silent for a moment then spoke in a whisper. "If anything should happen, show this document to our child when they are older. It will explain everything. But..." he added quickly, "nothing will happen."

She nodded in understanding. "You will come back to me. And this will never be shown to anyone."

They embraced once more before returning to the horses.

"Are you scared, Spencer?" she asked when she reached for her reins. "I mean in danger. Not of being found out, but in danger now."

"Why do you ask?"

"Why do you carry a gun?" She pointed to the holster on his horse.

"Those men on the robbery are dangerous. Especially Price, which is why I have made these plans. You must trust me, Mary, and ask no more questions. Everything will be all right."

They mounted their horses and rode back in silence. Each of them scared for the other's safety, but both knew she would say no more and would do as he asked.

They gave the Weller's farm a wide berth, both in case they were seen and because Spencer still tormented himself with guilt at being unable to help the family. He was sure the farmer and his sons would be found guilty and imprisoned and, despite his desire to help, he could do nothing for the Wellers other than secure them good representation.

They joined the track just short of the bridge that crossed the canal, it was only a few hundred yards to the oak tree and they wanted to stay together as long as possible. As they rode onto the bridge, Mary heard a horse neigh, to which their own horses responded. She looked in the direction of the sound and saw a soldier in uniform just below them, sitting by the canal, smoking his pipe. She recognised him immediately.

"It's Russell. Was he following us?"

Treloar looked. Russell had turned from his reverie to look at the two riders, and sprung to his feet. "No. He must also just be out riding. Quick, we must get to the crossroads."

Both horses leapt forward and they galloped down the track. Pulling to a halt at the bottom, and looking back, Treloar could see Russell had pulled his own horse up to the bridge, and was mounting it to follow. He would be with them in seconds.

"Quick, Mary. You must go. He must not find us together."

"But, Spencer."

"No. Go. I will hold him." He hit the rump of her horse, her steed flicked his tail and broke into a gallop, taking its rider on the track through the village. "And I love you," he said softly, as he watched her disappear. He turned back towards Russell and, seeing how close he was, moved his horse to intercept. Instinctively, he drew his gun and, in an action he knew was foolish, pointed it at Russell. He needed to protect Mary's identity, even though he knew he could never fire. Russell simply ignored the threat, passing him, and galloped through the village. Spencer didn't follow, instead he cantered back to the bridge. He needed to collect his thoughts, prepare himself.

Dismounting once on the bridge, he looked down into the dark waters of the canal, feeling abandoned, lost in despair. Eventually, he realised he could hear Russell shouting, the captain having returned to the bridge, obviously angry. Treloar heard the yells but was oblivious to the words, only understanding the end of the diatribe, that Captain Russell would pursue him forever. Misery filled him. He felt wretched, as low as it was possible to be. Everything he had planned was nearly lost, and pulling a gun on the captain had made it worse.

For a brief moment he even wanted to tell Russell the truth, to rid himself of this pain, but he knew he could not. He could feel tears welling in his eyes and he blinked but they would not stop. He could think of nothing other than Mary and what could happen. His mind was made up, he knew what action he was taking and knew it was necessary. He was guilty, and hearing Russell's shouts made everything clear: if he had been undecided before, he was certain now. He would go to South Africa, try to make some amends for what had happened. He would not return without having done some good, made some restitution for his part in this mess. Thinking of where he was going, what might happen there, and what he may miss back here, made his misery worse. Tears continued rolling down his cheeks as if his despair had filled him to overflowing.

In frustration, Russell rode away.

Spencer Treloar did not see Russell looking back at him, and he would never know that, for a moment, Captain Russell had even felt a little sorry for him.

Chapter 37
Death of Price

By July 1893, Mary Anne Turner had been living in the village just over 12 years. With a new name, new background, shorter hair in a new style, she had created a whole new life. She had moved into the cottage that adjoined to Lady Treloar's and become her companion. In addition, though, they had a joint love – a young child.

Reverend McDonald ascribed to the influence of Ma Turner, as she was now known, the fact that Lady Treloar was coming out of the isolation she had imposed on herself. Everyone knew it was due to shame, but similarly everyone was pleased she was now being seen out and about. In fact, Lady Treloar, along with Mary Anne, Simon Hamilton and Reverend McDonald were finding salvation and happiness in their relentless work to improve the village and its surroundings.

One bright mid-July afternoon, with the heat of the sun warming the newly designed flower beds on the green, Mary Anne Turner strolled through the village after another meeting with the Reverend McDonald. These days they always seem to be always discussing improvements. There was so much to be done, and so much they could do.

To protect her head from the sun, she wore a green bonnet, tied in a bow under her neck. Its colour matched her dress, which had low square neckline and long sleeves. As she crossed the green, she glanced across the great oak, marvelling yet again at its size, and letting out a sigh as she remembered happier times and meetings. A man and a small girl were walking towards her. The man wore loose trousers, a jacket and waistcoat, but the jacket was frayed around the edges, its colour fading from wear. It could have been chestnut brown once. A sweat-stained flat cap covered his head. The little girl wore a black dress with ruffled shoulders. It had also clearly seen better days. On her feet were black clogs. She looked about three or four and was hopping whilst holding the man's hand. The two of them were still ten feet away but the man was staring directly at Mary Anne. She smiled, thinking he must be someone from the village, but she couldn't place him.

The man looked about, and immediately gripped the girl's hand harder. She stopped skipping. He took off his cap in case anyone was watching, a gesture as if introducing himself.

Once he was close enough to be certain Mary Anne could hear, he spoke. "Hallo, Mrs Farrant."

Mary Anne halted, her smile freezing, her small bag dropping from her grasp. Her mind raced in shock, she had not heard that name for over a decade. She still didn't recognise the man. He was about six foot tall and had a seriously deep scar on the left side of his face.

It was the combination of his cold eyes and snarl, reminding her of a predator seeing new prey, which brought – with a shiver – recognition. She remembered him with short black hair, much bulkier, without the horrible scar.

She tried to bring her surprise under control, although she thought her shallow voice gave a good indication of her concern. "Corporal Price, I thought you were dead, had been killed."

"You wish. Bloody close, too bloody close. I was lucky. Except for this." He touched his scar. "And all your lover's fault." His eyes were as black, hard and unforgiving as coal. The little girl pulled his hand, wanting to carry on skipping. He yanked her back. "I've been watching you for a while," he said. "I was surprised to see you here. And you have a kid, born after we left for Africa." He stroked his chin and nodded. "Then I started to put it together. That fool of a husband wanted rid of you. And yet here I find you living next door to that rich snob, Lady Treloar. But she's not rich any more, oh no." He grinned, but there was no humour there. "Then it dawned on me, what that idiot of a husband had over Spencer Treloar. Well, I am back, to get what's mine." He ignored the little girl as she pulled his hand, kept his eyes on Mary Anne, contempt dripping from him like venom. His small girl started crying, and Price hit her head. "Shut up."

"Don't," yelped Mary Anne, holding up her hand. "Don't hurt her."

He looked around, still no one in sight. His lips curled as he scowled. "Tomorrow, same time, up by the bridge over the canal." He turned away, back towards the inn, yanking the little girl violently, letting her howl. Mary Anne watched, shivering even though the sun shone. She felt as though she had seen a ghost, one who could ruin all those plans of Spencer's.

The following night, after the meeting with Price by the bridge, Mary Anne sobbed to Lady Treloar. "He wants it all," she said, "and he means to get it."

They were sitting in Lady Treloar's front room, which was crowded with furniture and ornaments. Lady Treloar may no longer live in a large Georgian house, but that didn't stop her from trying to fit as many items from that house into her new home. Taking a leaf from Queen Victoria's book, she still wore black all the time, even though her husband had been dead these last four years.

Mary Anne took a shaky sip of Madeira from a crystal glass handed to her by Lady Treloar. "I tried to reason with him." Mary Anne continued, watching her own her hand tremble, "but he is unreasonable. He threatens anonymous letters to the authorities. He is a despicable man. I wonder if the fighting affected him."

"That would not surprise me." Lady Treloar, having also poured herself a drink, took a seat. "If he fought at Rorke's Drift… he was lucky, unlike my son. But we have to decide what to do."

"Shall I telegraph Simon?"

"No, Mary. He advises on business matters only. We have to sort this. When is Price coming back?"

"Tomorrow night, at eleven. Said he is planning to leave the village and wants his due." She stood, began pacing the room, unable to relax. "It is such a shame, Frances. I took the time today to check on him and briefly met his wife. I wondered if she knew about me, but don't think so. She's a nice woman. Pregnant again. She works for Longhurst at the inn, and wants to make a home for her and family in the village. I'm not even sure she knows he intends leaving."

"We can't have Henry Price staying in the village. If he does it'll never be over. Even if he doesn't, I'm not convinced he'll leave us in peace. We must work something out. We must." Lady Treloar slapped her hand on the lace doily on the table.

Henry Price arrived the following evening, at quarter past eleven. A small holdall, clearly empty, dangled from one hand. Mary Anne was waiting, wondering if his tardiness was deliberate. She held a lamp with a single candle; it offered meagre light. Price nodded and then without either of them speaking he followed her down a path, passing a gig.

It was a bright night, with thousands of stars flickering in the cloudless sky. The moon and lamp together gave just enough light to see.

"Where you taking me?" Price asked, cautious.

Mary Anne stopped in front of a stable door. "The horse," she said, "is in the field at the moment."

"So?"

"You wanted to know where it was hidden," said Mary Anne, unlocking the door. "Well, here we are."

Price looked at the door and pushed it open with his foot. "In here?" He sounded amazed.

Mary Anne stepped inside. Without any suspicion from Price she deliberately kept the lamp low, lighting the floor only. Price followed. Mary Anne placed the lamp on the floor away from Price and quickly moved loose hay across the floor, revealing a trap door in the floorboards. She lifted the recessed handle. The wooden door was heavy and she had to use both hands to pull it upright. Price didn't offer to help. She strained and eventually the door fell open with a *thunk*. Perspiring now, Mary Anne lifted the lamp and revealed a hole about seven feet deep, ten feet long and six feet wide. Price stared into the pit and saw three wooden chests sitting side by side. His lips curled into a grin. The last time he saw those chests was sixteen years ago. "Assume," he muttered, "you have a ladder so I can check the contents."

"You think the money's still there? You fool," Mary Anne muttered.

Price was fast, suddenly in front of her, one hand tightly around her neck. "Don't ever call me a fool, bitch." Saliva sprayed from his lips; fury filled his eyes. "People like you make me sick. So upright, so noble. You're no different, just like your husband." His grip tightened as Mary Anne flailed, trying to pull his hand away. "Your idiot officer husband got himself killed by Treloar, you know that? And then that bastard wrecked everything for me." Mary Anne shook with fear, terrified, desperate to breathe, seeing the madness in his him, his hand squeezing tighter, as she tried to plead about having a child. Henry Price ignored her struggles, put his face close to hers, his eyes burning holes into her. Spittle hit her as he spoke. "Spencer Treloar tried to beat me. He failed, got himself killed, but I survived. Henry Price always survives, even fighting them Zulus, I killed dozens, even at night, when we couldn't see 'em as they came out of the dark, see 'em only in the light of the burning hospital, I fought 'em, scarred me for life, I am not a fool, I win, that money is mine, all of it, now where is it?" His hand released her throat as fast as it had grabbed her. He stepped backward, away from the pit.

Mary Anne's hand went to her throat, and she wheezed loudly, trying to get air back into her painful lungs. It took her a couple of long, rasping, red raw minutes, before she could speak much beyond a croak. "Have you any idea how much there was down there?" Her voice didn't sound like her own. "As well as thousands in cash, there was jewellery and investment certificates and bonds, personal loan guarantees, it was fortune. Like a treasure trove."

Price licked his lips. "Now it's mine. How do I get it?"

"Corporal Price, Henry, please, can't we talk?" She turned to get a leather bag off a small bench, under a cobwebbed window.

Price stepped back, his right hand went to his left arm. "Careful, bitch. What you doing?"

"Just getting a bag." She took the leather bag from the bench. "I have three-hundred pounds. It's yours if you would just go, leave us alone."

Henry Price laughed, the tension in his body fading as he relaxed. He could see no danger now. "Are you mad? Listen, bitch. This is what is going to happen. I will take that three hundred and as much as I can carry now, then I will write to you, every month, telling you where you can send me more." His eyes fixed menacingly on Mary Anne, as if he were about to pounce. His gaze moving up and down her body.

Mary Anne's voice, still rough, cracked some more. "Please, be reasonable."

"It's my money and I want it." He moved closer to Mary Anne, forcing her to take a step back against the bench, her free hand sliding along its jagged surface feeling for a weapon, finding a club hammer. "What about your family?" She tried to hold his attention.

Price saw the movement and stopped. "Family, hah. My ticket to travel around is as Henry Lewis, unmarried. Not Henry Price. So that lot of dead weight are no longer my responsibility. I talked about the money, but that was years ago. Now she wants to settle down, but that's not me. I don't. And finally I've found what's mine." His voice was cold, resolute. His expression turned to one of self-satisfaction. "I planned it. All of it. Me, a humble soldier. All right, a man called Parr told me of Standish's wealth, but it was me. I put the plan together, got your husband involved because he was greedy. And he failed me. Now I'm going to get me what's owed." Once again, he looked into the hole, before raising his blazing eyes back to Mary Anne. She nodded, terrified, unable to move, her whole body shaking as if the temperature had dropped below freezing. She had never felt so scared in her life. This man was evil, insane. He had to be stopped.

He saw the terror in her face and a vile smile appeared as new ideas occurred to him. He moved forward, and began licking his lips again, coating them, making them shine like fresh meat. "And now bitch, I think I'll get some interest off you, personally."

Mary Anne moved further along the bench away from him, raising the small club hammer so he could see it.

"Oh, I've faced worse. No, your husband failed me, your lover deceived me and so you are going to recompense me." He stepped forward and laughed. "I've seduced in dirtier places."

Shaking, Mary Anne stared, his insanity clear to her. The moment she saw movement over Price's shoulder, behind him in the shadows, she gripped the hammer tighter. Price saw her eyes flick to something behind him. He had always lived on his instincts, he knew when something was wrong. With exceptional speed, his right hand moved to his jacket sleeve. He pulled out the ten-inch hunting knife from the leather sheath strapped to his left arm. Feeling a presence behind him, he swung around just as a figure emerged from the darkness, running at him, a weapon, like a spear, pointing at him. He froze in terror. This was his nightmare; even now, years later it woke him, terrified, in the night, sweat soaking his body and nightwear, his heart pounding as if to attempting to escape, his mind back in another time, thousands of miles away. He screamed, "Zulus!"

His hesitation was his downfall as the figure thrust the tines of the pitchfork into his stomach. Price howled like a wounded animal, dropping his knife, trying with both hands to grab the pitchfork. Lady Treloar pulled sharply and the prongs exited with a sucking sound. Knowing he was wounded, but not fatally, Henry Price grinned as the reality of the attack rescued him from his nightmare. He could take these women, he thought, both of 'em, just before the club hammer landed on his head, splitting the back of his skull as if it were no more than a melon. Price's eyes opened wide in disbelief before he toppled sideways into the pit. There was a thump as his body hit the chests before it rolled off into the dirt. Lady Treloar, still dressed totally in black, stared into the pit. Slowly, she lifted the black lace veil, exposing her ageing lined face. She had not worn the veil since her husband's funeral. The long black gown and black sleeves hung loosely on her frail body.

As arranged, for protection, Lady Treloar had concealed herself in the corner of the stable. Her initial confidence, standing totally covered in black, had receded as she waited, pitchfork in hand. Hearing Mary Anne and Price, she had frozen as the door was unlocked. She dreaded Price turning and seeing her, but Mary Anne, she realised, had been thinking ahead and so held the lamp low, ensuring as little light as possible lit the stable. And Mary Anne had quickly opened the door to the pit, so Price's attention went straight there, with no thought of his surroundings. She had listened to his black-hearted talk, her resolve growing to get this loathsome reptile out of their lives forever. Once Price's intentions were clear she had taken action. Now, with Mary Anne, she stared into the pit. "What did he scream?"

Mary Anne, still shaking with shock, took her companion's cold hand. "Something about Zulus."

"How strange." Baffled, Lady Treloar looked at Mary Anne, who had tears running down her cheeks. "Don't cry, my dear. His actions took Spencer from us, you heard him. He planned it all. No, I won't shed any tears for *that*." Her voice was a strange mixture of hatred, spite and sorrow. She dropped the pitchfork onto the body, Price's holdall landed after it. Finally, Mary Anne released the club hammer so it followed. "It's done, Mary. We had to sort it, and we have. Now we can carry on with Spencer's, your love's, wishes. Without any threat of *that* hanging over us."

Mary Anne's shaking began to subside, like the ebbing of a once-strong wave. She nodded towards the pit. "And him?" she asked.

Lady Treloar squeezed Mary Anne's hand hard. "We fill in this pit forever."

Chapter 38
Return to 1977

Silence filled the room. Even the sounds of breathing, including Carrie Turner's previous slight wheezing, seemed to have been sucked away. Even Jackson wasn't coughing. It was as if, thought Gary, the room was waiting.

It was Jackson who spoke first. "But its hiding place, where exactly was it?"

Carrie smiled at him, exhausted, but also relieved. She turned to Gary, and raised her eyebrows.

"Oh," he said, finally understanding. "Of course."

"Well?" Eleanor was on the edge of her seat. If she shifted any further, thought Gary, she'd fall. He smiled, not at the thought of Eleanor hitting the floor, but at the beauty of his realisation.

He stood, a couple of steps and he was the centre of them all. He glanced at Anne and he thought he could see, from her expression, she was only a minute or so behind him in figuring it out.

He cleared his throat, then began. "If you remember, Spencer Treloar had the deeds to two cottages, and was repairing the dwellings. It was to prove to his father that it didn't need to be expensive. Captain Russell rode past them." He looked from Jackson to Eleanor to Anne, and on to Phillip Hamilton.

"Well, Treloar had a pit dug under the small stables, where the horses were kept, at the rear of the house. The boxes were stored there. When Treloar didn't return from South Africa, the money was gradually moved and banked by Mary Anne when she returned and by Hamilton." He paused, taking his time to think. "Correct me if I'm wrong, Miss Turner, but I believe the solicitors took ownership of the cottages. We know that shortly after Spencer Treloar's death, Sir John died and Simon Hamilton helped Lady Treloar sell the estate. She must have had huge debts, but probably by selling the estate they were cleared. Simon Hamilton would have ensured there was some money, even if only a small amount, left, for her and her daughters to live on. She moved her into one of the cottages. I believe that's when they started to move the money and gold, depositing it into the banks for Mary Anne. She returned to the village a couple of years later, with Treloar's daughter. They lived in the other cottage." He couldn't prevent a smile when he looked again at the faces round him, all totally enthralled. "From what Carrie has told us and from what I've gathered, Mary Anne's daughter married a soldier called Piggott, who died, coincidently, in South Africa. But a different war. They had a child, who is Miss Piggott-Turner, Carrie's mother. Treloar's daughter died in the Spanish Flu epidemic just after the First World War. After Lady Treloar died, Mary Anne Turner dropped the Piggott from her Granddaughter's name, had the two cottages converted into one and carried on living there, with her Granddaughter as her own daughter.

"And this house, you know where it is?" Eleanor asked Gary.

It was Anne who answered. "We brought it from Miss Turner, six months ago. In fact," she smiled at her husband, a wouldn't-you-know-it smile, "Gary was clearing out the garden, and the area where the stables were, before he got distracted by, well, all this."

Simon Hamilton leaned forward. "You own the house where it was hidden?"

Gary and Anne nodded in unison.

"And the money?" Jackson was grinning like a schoolboy. Gary didn't think he seen the old man look so energised. "What happened to it?"

Carrie Turner shifted in her seat and took over. "Mary Anne carried out Spencer Treloar's wishes. She used it for the benefit of others, including the village and its surroundings. Some of it went into looking after Lady Treloar and her family, although one of her daughters married into money and never needed any. The other was given a small income and lived in Sussex. Other amounts went to the victims secretly, one-off gifts and annual gifts, like the family in Cheltenham, as restitution for what they had lost."

She paused, allowing them to absorb what she was saying. "Spencer knew what he had done and knew he could never put it right, so he decided that some good must be made with the money. He even tried to help the Weller's at their trial, but their fate was sealed even though they were not involved. When Mary Anne came to help them after the hangings it was too late, the family had broken up and the wife had killed herself, but everyone else who was a victim was compensated secretly, in some way, including the boatman's family. Even the relations of the soldiers who were in the escort. The rest went into the village. Mary Anne became its benefactor, helping those who needed help, and supporting various projects, such as getting the school started. She contributed to the church, helped bring shops to the village and help the poorest workers, and from what I understand, they needed it."

Gary spoke. "She even helped my family to buy the pub, even though we were related to Price."

"Why?" Eleanor furrowed her brow as she tried to understand.

Carrie Turner spoke as Gary shrugged. "When Price came back, years later, he recognised Ma Turner as she had become known. He must have realised the hold Farrant had on Treloar and he tried to blackmail her, but he wasn't prepared for the strength of two women. I believe they killed him, then buried his body in the pit where the money had been hidden. Over next few months, they simply filled in the pit."

There was silence, until Anne spoke. "You think he's still there, under our garden?"

It was Jackson who answered. "We'll get the police to dig out the pit. They should find him and anything else that's down there. He won't be there for long."

Anne nodded, uncertain, while Carrie continued. "After his death, everyone believed he'd run off, just disappeared, making his," she nodded at Gary, "your family, almost destitute. So Ma Turner helped them stay in the village. They carried on working at the inn and when the opportunity came to buy the pub, Ma Turner helped again."

She glanced again around the room, her gaze lingering in Simon Hamilton, who gave the briefest of nods. "Eventually, once the money is almost all gone, what little is left, I – as Ma Turner's granddaughter – use it to live here, at the Manor residential home. It seemed appropriate as it was once was the Treloar's home. And that's the full story." She sat back in her chair, exhausted.

Gary looked at the other occupants in the room, seeing the

huge grin lighting Jackson' face. Gary didn't know how long the man had left but, at that moment, his friend looked totally alive, healthy and enjoying life. It was something else had, unwittingly, achieved and for which Gary was grateful.

As far as Gary was concerned, Spencer Treloar had atoned for his sins and made sure ill-gotten money helped those who needed it.

It was a fortune.

Epilogue

No article telling the truth about the robbery was ever written, and no charges were brought against Kate Richie, which pleased everyone. She received a caution for not reporting an accident and death. That caution received no publicity, which also pleased everyone.

Fifteen months later, Kate married David Reynolds. Gary, Anne, and Eleanor were all invited and attended the wedding. Sadly, Jackson died of heart problems nine months after the mystery was solved; he remained close to Gary until his death.

The story of canal robbery was again forgotten, another tale lost – like a single drop of water in an ocean – amongst the infinite stories of history. No one talked about Henry Price or tried to find his body, and Oak Cross remained a village where one would want to live. Fred and Ethel Lewis ran the Old Oak Inn until their deaths, when a large brewery group made an offer for the inn – a bid which their family could not refuse.

At the start of 1978, having finished clearing the garden and started on decorating the house, Gary had an interview with a large and established American company. He was offered a good sales position. The company recognised his talents as the London papers had recognised Jackson's, and over the years he gained further promotions. At the same time as Gary was offered his new job, Anne found she was pregnant with their first child. Three years later she had their second.

In 1999, on a business trip to South Africa, Gary visited Isandlwana, where there are a number of mass graves situated on the battlefield. These graves are identified by white painted boulders. He stood for a moment in respect of those buried there.

Eleanor became like an aunt to the family, spending much time and every Christmas with Gary and Anne, until she died in 1985. In her will she left them a small A5 journal written by Brevet Major Iain Russell, a St Christopher pendant given to Russell by Maggie from the Three Feathers. Eleanor had worn it all her life. She also bequeathed them a large house just outside Farnham, which Gary's mother would have called "posh detached double fronted". Gary and Anne are still there today.

Historical Details

Corruption has always existed, in all classes, and has contributed to much wealth. I have used a little imaginary licence to establish how Standish built his fortune to establish the origins of his wealth, and used the same licence to place him, during his military career, in Woolwich.

Part of my reason for this was to use the Basingstoke canal as the backdrop to the robbery. The canal was built in 1797 but never made money for its investors. Its high points were during the wars with Napoleon and supplying materiel when the army camp at Aldershot was first established. At the time of this story, a service still existed between Woolwich and Aldershot, and beyond to Basing.

As for placing those involved in South Africa, the history books tell us that the *Himalaya* sailed to South Africa with the 2nd battalion of the 24th Regiment in February 1878.

G Company of the 2nd Battalion, the company to which Ox and the other villains were assigned, was the only company of the 2nd Battalion left at Isandlwana on the morning of 22 January 1879 under the command of Lieutenant Pope.

Lord Chelmsford had left with the other six companies of the 2nd Battalion earlier that morning, heading towards the Zulu capital of Ulundi to find the Zulu Impi, or army, thus splitting his force in enemy territory.

The other Imperial companies remaining at Isandlwana were five companies of the 1st Battalion, commanded by Colonel Pulleine, to whom I assigned Major Russell as member of his staff. Colonel Pulleine, his battalion, Lieutenant Pope and G

Company – and, of course, Russell and others – were all killed during the battle.

I also based Lieutenant Butler on a real-life character who was one of the few survivors of the battle and became a senior officer in both the Boar and First World Wars.

B company of the 2nd Battalion, in which I assigned Price, was the company who fought and held the mission station, come hospital, at Rorke's Drift. It was in this battle that a number of its defendants, the highest number in a single action, won the Victoria Cross.

It is also fact that John Chard, played by Stanley Baker in the film *Zulu*, an office of Engineers stationed at Rorke's Drift rode up to the main camp at Isandlwana on the morning of the 22 January for breakfast, thus enabling me to place Spencer Treloar at the battle.

John Chard returned to Rorke's Drift soon after arriving at the main camp, thus avoiding the slaughter and certain death, and so rode into history as the officer commanding the mission station at Rorke's Drift. He also won a Victoria Cross.

The history books also tell us that many man were slaughtered trying to escape down Fugitives' Drift, as it later became known, and that none of the survivors from the battle of Isandlwana were wearing Red army uniforms. Cetewayo, the Zulu chief, had ordered his men to kill all those wearing red coats, so those wearing army dress uniforms (blue) or other colours, such as the men forming part of the Natal colonial army, stood more chance of survival, which was fortunate for Christian Janssen.

Dennis Jones

* 9 7 8 1 8 0 4 6 7 8 1 2 1 *
WS - #0102 - 091123 - C0 - 198/129/24 - PB - 9781804678121 - Matt Lamination